I0600325

Fates Intertwyned

Whispered Prayers Series
Emily Jean

Copyright © 2025 by Emily Jean Decker. All rights reserved.

Cover design © 2024 by Nigel Andreola with Starry Night Media, LLC

No part of this book may be reproduced in any form or by electrical or mechanical means including information storage and retrieval systems, without permission in writing from the author. The only exception is by a reviewer, who may quote short excerpts in a review.

This manuscript shall not be utilized in order to train Artificial Intelligence systems. Any use of this publication to "train" generative artificial intelligence (AI) technologies to generate text or audiobook is expressly prohibited. The author reserves all rights to license use of this work for generative AI training and development of machine learning language models.

This book is a work of fiction. Names, characters, places, and incidents either are products of the author's imagination or are used fictitiously. Any resemblance to actual persons, living or dead, events, or locales is entirely coincidental.

EMILY JEAN

Visit my website/blog at emilyjean.org
Visit my Instagram @emilyjean.author
Printed in the United States of America.
First Edition: 2025

ISBN: 979-8-9929228-0-6 (softcover)
979-8-9929228-1-3 (hardcover)
979-8-9929228-2-0 (e-book)

Cover formatting: Hannah Pennington
Interior Art of LA Skyline: Seaborn Studios
Interior Art of NYC Skyline: StamGoods
Editor: Tracey Williamson
Proofreader: Michaela Bush
Formatter: Michaela Bush

Contents

I dedicate this book to my Grandma, Alice Ellera.
Thank you for always believing in my talents and encouraging me no matter what.

Prologue

"IT'S NOT HAPPENING, LUCY. I'm not planning on going," he said into his phone to his manager as he paced around his patio.

"Sirius, you really should reconsider," she replied.

He could hear the frustration in her voice, and she was starting to drive him crazy. "Luce, I have a new script to read, and I'm making plans to go visit my family for a while. I don't need to fly all the way to New York City for this movie premiere that I had nothing to do with."

"Please, it will be good for you. Think of the publicity," Lucy urged him.

"Do you even know who you're talking to," he scoffed, shaking his head.

"Of course, I do, but still, it would be a good opportunity. Owen is going to be there, and we all know he is looking for someone to be in his next movie," Lucy explained.

"I was just there not too long ago, and you know I don't care about publicity or the big movie roles. They are fun, but I don't need to do them all of the time, especially since I just finished a big movie," he explained as he rubbed his temples, trying anything to relieve his pounding headache.

"I'm surprised you're even looking at another script right now," she laughed.

"Honestly, I am too, but a friend asked me to be in his movie forever ago. I told him I would whenever he got his plan and script together," Sirius replied. "So again, not the best time to go to New York."

"I understand." Lucy sighed. "Just—if you change your mind, let me know."

"Thank you, I'll do that."

"Have a good week, Sirius."

"Same to you, *ciao*." He hung up the phone, and he immediately went to his kitchen coffee bar to make himself an espresso. He never drank coffee for the caffeine until recently, but he hoped it would relieve his headache. His manager had been bugging him about this movie premiere for days now, and ironically, that's how long he'd had this killer headache. It was getting worse by the day, and nothing would help it—not medicine, not home remedies, and not his usual meditation. He felt like it was going to be the death of him. "What is going on?" he asked himself, as he stood alone in his lavish kitchen. He was even starting to feel anxious, and that's something he hadn't felt since he was in his first blockbuster movie. *Is this the universe telling me something?* He groaned loudly, as he picked up his phone and sent the three-word message to his manager—"I'll be there." He quickly put his phone on the kitchen table, and for some reason, he immediately felt some relief from his ailments—no headache and no anxiety; they just disappeared. "Wow, this must be fate," he said out loud as he continued to go about his day, making his travel plans for New York City.

Chapter 1

Monday, February 25th

"Ugh! Why?" Aurora mumbled as she walked down the hall of Sawmill Middle School. It was 7:20 a.m., and school was not the place she wanted to be at that moment.

"What was that, Aurora?" her friend Hunter asked. She figured he could easily tell from the grimace on her face that she was in a very bad mood. He always knew. That's probably why they were best friends, with their friend Ethan being a close second.

"Nothing, it's just—I really don't want to be here right now," Aurora grumbled.

"Do we ever want to be here?"

"Guess not, but definitely not at 7:30 in the morning! It's inhumane and stupid. Our brains aren't even functioning properly yet." She quickly walked up to her locker and twisted the door open.

"Can't argue with that," Hunter agreed.

Aurora struggled to grab all her needed books out of her locker for the day, as she tried to ignore his gaze. She peeked over at him and looked into his blue eyes, but quickly turned away.

"What happened last night?" she heard him ask.

"Why are you asking such a dumb question?" Aurora wondered sarcastically. She stacked her books into one arm, but the weight of it was too much for her. She cursed loudly, and ungracefully dropped her stuff on the grimy floor. "Ugh! Come on!" she slammed her locker door with a thud.

"Chill out, will ya?"

"I can't!" Aurora argued as she bent down to grab her books.

"Did something happen last night after we did our homework and I left?" Hunter questioned. She looked up at him and knew he was concerned about her.

"Yep," she growled out, not wanting to have that conversation.

"What?"

"Don't worry about it." Aurora sighed loudly. She struggled to keep hold of her textbooks as she stood back up. Walking next to Hunter, maybe she would make it to her first class without dropping anything else. Before they even made it to the classroom door, someone hit Aurora's shoulder with their own. Aurora clutched her right shoulder in pain, and in the process, dropped her stuff once again.

"Ouch," Aurora muttered.

"Hey! Watch it, foster rats!" she heard a voice shriek.

"Get lost, witch!" Aurora snapped at the girl to which the grating voice belonged. She looked back and sighed, knowing Jane was walking up behind her, smirking.

"Ummm, excuse me, little rat?!"

"Get lost, Jane. I'm not in the mood," Aurora declared. She gulped as she turned around and came face to face with the witch of Sawmill Middle School. She was waiting for Jane to spew out more insults, probably about the way she looked or dressed. She always did, and there was nothing Aurora could do about it, without teachers nearby to stop the bullying. Aurora's foster parents didn't care about her or what she wore. She always had to go to a church closet for clothes or anywhere else she could get free items, because no one else looked after her but herself.

"What happened to you?" Jane questioned, looking Aurora up and down with a wicked grin. "Sleep on the streets again, or maybe in a rat-infested motel?" Aurora forced herself to look up at Jane instead of at the floor, and regretted that decision the moment she saw the evil grin glaring at her. It sent chills down her spine.

"None of your business!" Aurora seethed, turning around and attempting to walk away with her head held high. Her loyal friend close at her side gave her an encouraging but warning look, which she agreed with completely. She was really hoping to avoid a fight. Thankfully, Jane didn't come after her—Aurora was in too much pain to be pushed into a locker that day.

"Hey! I was talking to you, ally rat!" she heard Jane yell, making one last attempt to get under her skin.

"Go bug someone else, Jane, if you know what's good for you!" Hunter yelled back at the fuming queen bee.

Aurora glanced over her shoulder and saw her nemesis walking away, probably to her own locker to check her already perfect makeup.

"Thanks," Aurora squeaked out, trying to hold back tears. She let out a sigh of relief as she grabbed her forgotten books from her faithful bodyguard.

"So...what actually happened to you?" Hunter asked, as they stopped in front of the classroom.

"I don't know what you mean."

"Yes, you do. You are obviously in pain. What happened?" he asked. He pushed a strand of her unwashed dirty-blonde hair out of her face and behind her ear. He stared into her bright green eyes, concerned, waiting for her to answer him.

"My foster dad happened."

"What did he do now?" he wondered.

"He beat me up pretty good last night," Aurora confessed. "But not before yanking my arm out of my socket."

"Oh my gosh, Aurora, I'm so sorry. Did you go to a doctor?"

"Why do that when your evil foster mother is a registered nurse and can check it herself? Not to mention, that would show my foster parents as the abusers that they actually are, which would only make things worse," Aurora mumbled.

"I'm sorry."

"You say that a lot, and there's no reason for you to be sorry. It's not your fault," Aurora stated.

"I know, but..." he started to say, but Aurora cut him off.

"Hunter, just drop it. Please. See you and Ethan later at lunch."

Before he could respond, Aurora walked into English class just in time, and sat down at her assigned desk in the back of the room. She hoped the unfamiliar substitute teacher wouldn't call on her, and everyone would just mind their own business. She didn't want to be there, but she also dreaded having to go home to her foster parents' house later; she hated it there. They were terrible to her and were just playing the foster care system for money. She just wanted to escape the abuse, and that's exactly what she was planning to do. As soon as she had enough money and food, she would run away and never look back. She along with her friends Hunter and Ethan have been working on this plan for months now. What could go wrong?

Chapter 2

Friday, March 1st

"'Ora! 'Ora! Hurry up! We need to go!" Aurora heard Hunter yell from outside.

"I'm coming! I'm coming!" Aurora yelled from her open bedroom window, as she waved at Hunter looking up at her nervously from the sidewalk below. She glanced at the sunset just before she ran from her bedroom and made a dash down the dimly-lit flight of stairs.

"Aurora Bennett! Aurora! Get in here! Now, you brat!" her foster mother screamed after her. She ignored the yelling along with the other voices inside the house. All she could think about was getting outside into the fresh air, running through the front door as fast as she could.

"I'm here!" she said loudly, announcing herself. She jumped off the front porch and landed shakily on her feet.

"Finally! Let's go," Hunter said as they walked briskly down the dirty, suburb sidewalk, trying to get Aurora as far away from the house as quickly as possible.

"Crud!" she exclaimed, as she almost had to sprint to catch up to him.

"Hey, what's wrong with you?" Hunter questioned, eyeing her suspiciously. "Why are you limping like that?"

"Don't worry about it," Aurora stated.

"Don't tell me not to worry, Aurora. As your best friend, that's my job. What happened?"

"My foster mom happened this time," Aurora admitted, trying to avoid his glare.

"What did she do now?"

"Nothing out of the ordinary—she's still using me as a punching bag. Same old, same old."

"Is that all?" Hunter probed. "I mean, it can't be worse than normal, right?"

"Not really, she just pushed me down the stairs last night," Aurora admitted.

"What!? From the top?" Hunter questioned.

"No, not from the top, it was just the last few steps, but I tripped over myself and landed weird. Now my ankle hurts," Aurora whined. "As I said, same old, same old."

"Alright, let's just get out of here."

"And what's your hurry?" Aurora wondered.

"Um, is that a trick question?" Hunter asked sarcastically. "Maybe to get away from your evil foster parents before they come out here and drag you back inside."

"True, but it's the same threats they always use. I'm not scared of them. It's not as bad as some of the other homes I've been in," Aurora stated. "I can just run again."

"You should be scared," Hunter said.

"Okay, I get it; you want to get away from the house, but we don't have to rush. It's not like we have somewhere we need to be," Aurora explained.

"Ummm...yeah, we do! What about at the library doing school work?"

"School? Really? That's funny," Aurora laughed. "They haven't cared if I have done my homework or shown up for classes the last few weeks. Why would someone start to care now?" she asked.

"That's true. At this rate, we're probably gonna graduate high school when we're thirty," Hunter teased.

"Graduate? Seriously!? That's what you're thinking about—when will we ever get to do that?" Aurora quickened her hobble to match Hunter's longer stride.

"Maybe someday—by some miracle."

"Hunter, we aren't even in high school yet! And at this rate, I will be in seventh grade for the rest of my life."

"Speak for yourself. I'll be starting high school next year, and you should be in high school next year too. Maybe you would be if you didn't cut classes *all* the time."

"Ok, Hunter, so what are you now, my mom?" Aurora teased. "School is pointless. No one cares about us. Even the teachers only care about their stupid paychecks; and everyone passing the standardized tests, so they can keep their stupid jobs."

"You're not wrong, but didn't you love school before? Remember that? Or was that a dream?"

"I used to. That was before Ms. Davis had me sent to Sawmill. The teachers are creepy, and the students are horrid, including the one who shall be nameless, who still bullies me every waking hour. I swear the teachers are failing me on purpose." Aurora sighed.

"I know what you mean."

"It's not fair," Aurora whined loudly. She looked behind her and suddenly felt nervous, as if her foster parents were going to come running up behind them. "You know, you're right Hunter, we gotta hurry. We have to be at Ziegfield Theater before it gets too busy. We need to get going to the bus stop, so we can get to that one subway station; you know, the one near Times Square."

"Yeah, yeah, I got it."

"Good, that movie premiere is tonight, and we need to be ready," Aurora explained.

"'Ora, we need to be careful, like really careful. If we get caught, we are going to be in so much trouble—like possible jail time trouble, and you're hurt."

"Hunter, don't worry. I'll be fine. This is nothing as bad as what I've dealt with before. Remember when my foster dad broke my hand? That was worse and hurt so bad! This is like the hundredth time we have done this. We've gotten away with it before, and we can do it again," Aurora explained. "You really need to stop worrying all the time."

"I know." Hunter sighed. "You may have nothing to lose; but if I get caught, I'm dead. My grandparents are going to throw me back into the system. They threatened me before, and I don't wanna give them a reason to actually do it," Hunter stated.

"Don't worry."

"Why? Did you say a prayer or something?" Hunter asked.

"Don't even start with that."

"You did, didn't you?" Hunter pushed her arm teasingly.

"Hey, watch it, and yes, I did. I always do."

"It's not going to change anything. You have been moved around from one bad home to the next. It changes nothing," Hunter pointed out.

"That's not true. The other homes were worse—so much worse; this is better."

"If you say so."

"Whatever. Just remember, please, if something happens, run. Run as fast as you can. It will be dark, so it will be hard for the cops or anyone else to catch us. Also, they don't know our hiding spots. And if worse comes to worst, we'll just throw Ethan under the bus," Aurora teased, changing the subject.

"He would deserve it. Ethan is just sometimes—you know..."

"A major jerk?"

"That's a kind phrase for it. I was thinking of a different one." Hunter laughed. "Also, it was his fault we almost got caught last time. So, remind me again, why are we letting him tag along?"

"Because he's still my second-best friend, and he's in a bad foster home too," Aurora explained. "Anyway, stop worrying. We'll be fine. You trust me, right?"

"Yeah, yeah, you know I trust you," Hunter admitted. "But 'Ora, if anything happens, we bail—right away. Promise me."

"I promise."

"Are you going to be able to make a break for it?" he asked, pointing to her leg.

"Uh, yeah. I already told you, I'm fine. Don't worry, and if everything goes according to plan, we will be super rich!" she teased.

"Rich as kings and queens," Hunter said in a phony British accent.

"Ummm, yeah," Aurora laughed, smiling and looking over her shoulder. She took a deep breath, and started to feel a little nervous, but wasn't sure why. "You know what, Hunter, you're right. What are we waiting for?"

"That's what I've been saying. Let's get going! We need to meet Ethan and get our game plan going," Hunter declared as they sprinted the rest of the way to the bus stop to meet their friend.

As they got to the graffiti-covered bus stop, Aurora quickly checked her pockets, and Hunter wandered to the far end to meet Ethan. She had brought just enough cash for the trip to the theater, the trip back to the subway, and a taxi just in case they needed a quick getaway.

If we have a good night, we will be living large. If not, our lives will continue to be horrendous. I just don't know if our lives can get any worse, Aurora thought to herself. She boarded the bus with Hunter, who had a pouting Ethan in tow, and quickly sat down to give her injured leg a rest, saying a quick internal prayer. *Please God, let everything be alright.*

Aurora sat with the boys, fidgeting nervously on top of a fire escape. They were waiting at a darkened apartment down a nearby alley from the Ziegfeld Theater, but from where they sat, they had a clear view of the front entrance. It was a late, bustling evening in NYC, and from where they sat, they could see glimpses of celebrities exiting their fancy cars and making their way onto the red carpet to the famous theater. They could hear all of the cheering from the fans and see the flashing lights from the paparazzi's cameras. From where they sat, it was mesmerizing and nerve-wracking, knowing they were about to pickpocket some of the most famous American celebrities at a public movie debut.

"Why are we waiting?" Ethan complained, interrupting the relative peace and quiet of the fire escape. "Let's go now!"

"No, we have to wait," Aurora said.

"You have got to be kidding me," Ethan whined.

"Knock it off, Ethan. You know a wild animal doesn't just pounce on its prey, but stalks it and waits for the best opportunity," Aurora explained.

"I know it's gonna seem like forever up here, Ethan, but Aurora's right," Hunter said. "It's a movie premiere and after-party. Security is really tight right now. Do you see those two armed bodyguards with that lady in the red dress walking down the carpet now? Well, as the night goes on, security will be more lax. Also, the stars will be drinking and partying all night."

"Yeah, at the end of the night, they won't be sober enough to understand what's happening, or even walk straight." Aurora chuckled.

"Are you two serious? It looks so crazy over there with all those fans screaming and the paparazzi flashing their cameras, I don't think those hotshots are gonna know the difference between bumping into someone and getting pickpocketed right now," Ethan said, starting to stand up on the fire escape platform.

"Ethan, don't be an idiot!" Hunter hissed, grabbing Ethan's arm and pulling him back down.

"I'm not an idiot," Ethan mumbled under his breath as he pulled his arm free from Hunter's grip.

"Ethan, I won't have you ruining our whole plan just because of your impatience. We can't be reckless," Aurora said.

"I got it. I'm not stupid!" Ethan seethed.

"Well, we need to be smart. Also, we shouldn't be seen together when we go over there. It will look too suspicious. And don't pickpocket a bunch of people at once," Aurora added. "We aren't professionals, guys. We're just trying to survive, so we need to be careful."

"We know, we know," Hunter groaned.

"I was talking to Ethan." Aurora rolled her eyes at Hunter this time.

"But that doesn't make sense, 'Ora!" Ethan whined. "It's better if we work together. We usually make more money that way."

"No, Ethan. That only works when we are in a very busy area," Aurora explained. "We have a plan. We need to stick to it, or you'll get us caught again."

"It is busy down there! Just look at how many people are packed along the red carpet on the sidewalk and the street," Ethan said.

"It ain't busy enough, Ethan. We would need the place to be jam-packed, like during the summer when we worked Grand Central Station or Times Square," Hunter said.

"Those places were insanely busy, flocked with families and their kids. Remember how you couldn't move without bumping into someone? Here, it's not that busy, and there are no other kids. We'll be out of place. We need to be smart," Aurora pointed out.

"You guys are no fun," Ethan complained.

"This is not supposed to be fun. It's survival," Aurora said irritably.

"But can't it also be kinda fun?" Ethan teased, trying to relieve the tension he felt from Aurora and Hunter.

"It might give us a rush in the moment, but Aurora is right. For you two, this is actually a matter of survival," Hunter said. "Take from the rich and give to the poor."

"Ummm...Hunter, we keep the cash for ourselves. We aren't exactly Robin Hood." Aurora laughed at his analogy.

"Hey, so what are we if we ain't poor? We aren't exactly living in luxury," Ethan said, laughing.

"That's true," Aurora agreed. "But we only take what we need—not what we want." She looked away from the boys and murmured under her breath, "Oh God, I hate being a thief."

"So can we start yet?" Ethan asked again.

"Are you serious, Ethan!?" Aurora questioned. "Where have you been this entire time? Have you not heard a thing we said?"

"Well, I'm bored. Let's at least get something to eat," Ethan suggested.

"No way. We are not wasting our cash for food," Hunter scolded.

"Why not? We brought extra cash," Ethan said.

"That money is for emergencies only. That's why," Hunter argued back.

"Come on! No fair! I'm hungry now," Ethan complained.

"Then you should have thought of that earlier, and brought something to eat. We already agreed that the money reserved for emergencies is to be used for emergencies only," Aurora explained.

"We can get food later, after we are done working. The money we make tonight needs to last us for a couple of months at least," Hunter added.

"That's true. I guess I can go without food for now," Ethan agreed.

"It shouldn't be too much longer. We've been here for a few hours now. Hopefully, they'll all be drunk. If they can't walk straight, then there's no way for them to catch us," Hunter laughed.

"That would be great and would make our lives so much easier—for once," Aurora added. "Hopefully, this money will help us turn our lives around."

"Do you think we will be able to make enough for train tickets?" Ethan asked.

"We have to, because I can't stay at my current placement much longer," Aurora said, tearing up just thinking about how terrible her foster parents are to her. Unfortunately, Ethan knew just how she felt, as he also had terrible foster parents who abused him. "Hunter, if Ethan and I stay much longer at our placements, we'll either starve or be beaten to death."

"Don't you guys trust Ms. Davis to help? I'm sure she would help if you went to her and asked," Hunter suggested. "She is your social worker."

"There's no chance of that. She just wants us out of her hair," Ethan said.

"Yeah, and I'm sure she's the cause of all of our problems. All she cares about is the money she gets from the government. No one cares about us," Aurora declared. "Hunter, we are just a burden. Why else would they just cast us out like trash whenever they feel like it? I would have loved to stay with the Bakers, but they had a baby and needed more room. That's what I was told, anyway."

"That's how it goes. When a family starts to have their own children, they throw us out. Why would they want other people's unwanted children when they can have their own?" Ethan asked. "Unless it's a baby, and then they'll want to keep it."

"You can say that again!" Aurora agreed with Ethan. "Nobody wants a good-for-nothing teenager."

"I guess," Hunter mumbled.

"You should count yourself lucky, Hunter," Aurora said. "You get to live with your grandparents instead of strangers, and they aren't that bad."

"Yeah, it's cool. I feel bad you two aren't living with family," Hunter said.

"I'm fine with that; it could be worse than our foster homes." Aurora sighed, looking away from the boys.

"Aurora's right. If we were with family, how do we know they wouldn't be as creepy and terrible as our foster families?" Ethan questioned.

"Okay, okay, but what if you had the chance to be adopted out of the system? Would you take it?" Hunter asked.

"I don't know," Ethan said. "Same question as before—how do we know they wouldn't be as creepy and terrible as what we gotta deal with now?"

"But...what if they were great—if the placement was with a loving, caring family?" Hunter questioned.

"I guess I would wonder what the catch was," Aurora answered.

"Same here," Ethan agreed. "Everyone we know has an agenda. They are only nice, because they want something."

"Alright, but what if there was no catch?" Hunter asked.

"If there was no catch, I would go for it," Aurora confirmed. "It would be nice not having to constantly watch my back."

"I still don't know. I'm not sure if I could trust anyone that much," Ethan admitted.

"That's something we would need to work on, I guess," Aurora said. Aurora tuned the boys out as they continued their discussion. Foster care was scary. She never knew what each day had in store for her. Would she get kicked out of her foster home? If so, where would she be placed next? She hated having to constantly worry for her safety. Maybe one day, she wouldn't have to worry anymore.

Chapter 3

Friday, March 1st

IT WAS DARK, A little before midnight, and the only light came from the lights of the city. It was the perfect time to get to work. Aurora looked around nervously. Her heart was racing, and she had butterflies in her stomach; but that was normal right before they did something like this. However, this time, something didn't feel right. Aurora didn't know what, but something felt off.

"So, guys, I think it's time for us to get to work. What do you say, 'Ora?" Hunter asked, interrupting her thoughts.

"What?" Aurora wondered, looking to where Hunter sat crouched in the shadows.

"He said, are ya ready?" Ethan clarified. "Didn't ya hear him?"

"Umm, no, I was just thinking," Aurora answered.

"Well, think later. It's time for us to get to work, right, 'Ora?" Ethan coughed dramatically, getting her attention.

"Absolutely!" Aurora declared, trying to psych herself up to a level she wasn't feeling. "Now, let's get ourselves some money!"

"And remember guys, we can't be seen together over there. We don't wanna bring too much attention to ourselves," Hunter explained.

"We know, we know," Ethan said as he started climbing cautiously down the rusty fire escape steps.

"Also, at the first sign of trouble, you better run," Hunter said just loud enough for Aurora and Ethen to hear, as he quickly followed Ethan down the escape.

"Yeah, run like your life depends on it, because it really does," Aurora added, following after Hunter. "You get all that, Ethan?"

"Yeah, yeah, I got it," Ethan grumbled, almost inaudibly, as he dropped down onto the pitch-black alley pavement. His skinny frame cast a ghoulish shadow on the brick wall of the apartment building opposite the fire escape.

"Are you sure you've actually paid attention to all the rules, Ethan? 'Cause the last time we pickpocketed, we almost got caught, because *you* were being too loud and not quick enough," Aurora said.

"Yeah, I got it! Sheesh, guys. I won't do anything stupid this time," Ethan promised.

"Good, then let's do this," Aurora said, as she fist-bumped both of the boys as they approached the street. Hunter and Ethan seemed to be in good moods, so why couldn't she shake off the uneasy feeling that something was going to go horribly wrong? Aurora tried to redirect her wandering and panicking mind. *Get your head in the game, girl, or else you're gonna end up in an even worse place than with an evil foster family. This is your only escape to freedom.*

As soon as they reached the street, they walked cautiously but casually down to the brightly lit Ziegfeld Theater, where the movie premiere and after-party were being held. It was late in the night, and the party was ending. The paparazzi were long gone by now, and the movie stars would be heading home. It was the perfect time for them to pickpocket the unsuspecting actors and actresses. Hunter and Ethan gave Aurora their agreed-upon hand signal to let her know they were both going to walk to the left of the main entrance to avoid security's attention, which meant she had no option but to turn right—alone.

Aurora walked with fake bravado to the right side of the theater, losing sight of her friends. She hoped she would go unseen until she made her move. Standing with her back against the old stone wall covered in peeling movie posters, she waited. She peeked around the corner and spotted the few armed security guards who were keeping watch outside. Avoiding them was usually easy. They would be looking for bigger trouble, not knowing a few random teens would be running around pickpocketing. Thieving was a game of cat and mouse, and it was a game Aurora and her friends had gotten better at over the last few years. Most times when someone was pickpocketed, the person being robbed didn't realize it until a few moments after when they checked their pockets.

As a pickpocketer at an event like this with armed guards, she knew she either needed to get away fast or risk getting caught. She was taking a big risk as an amateur and injured thief at this location. *God, please don't let me get caught,* Aurora silently prayed, *I really, really need everything to go perfect tonight. If it does, I promise this is the last time I will ever steal from anyone.*

Looking around the corner, she saw a few celebrities walk out of the entrance. One was an older man in a disheveled tuxedo. He stumbled while he walked—a good sign he had drank way too many cocktails. The perfect target. As he walked closer, she could see his wallet in his left front pants pocket. It was sticking out so much that it could have fallen out while he was walking. *Such an easy target,* she thought.

Aurora started to walk towards him just before he could round the corner where she was hiding. She slightly bumped into him as she grabbed his wallet and didn't dare to look back at him; she didn't want to look suspicious or feel guiltier than she already did. Half-hobbling, half-running, she made her way across the street and ducked into a semi-dark alley. She cautiously looked behind to see if her robbery victim suspected anything, but he just kept walking, singing an off-key Frank Sinatra tune. Since she obviously wasn't followed by her victim or a security guard, she opened the wallet to see how much cash she had scored. She counted three hundred dollars, mentally did a little happy dance, and shoved the wallet into her bag. Aurora was proud of how well she had done already. A few more scores like that, and she would be living better than she had in a long time. *Maybe God is answering my prayer after all! I shouldn't be so nervous,* she told herself.

After several minutes, she started to walk out of the alley shadows to the theater entrance. Out of the corner of her eye, she saw a younger man exit the theater. The man seemed tall and was dressed in a dark purple suit. Even though it was dark, she could tell he had dark, tousled hair and piercing brown eyes. She watched him as he went to the right side of the theater with long strides, heading towards the sidewalk.

Aurora wasn't sure if she should target him or not. He was walking normally; he didn't act as if he had been drinking and partying all night. With a sigh, she turned around, intending to go back to her hiding spot in the alley, but she glanced back at him. She saw him stumble, barely catching himself on the corner of the building. She wondered if perhaps he was dizzy from all the alcohol he drank. *Another perfect opportunity*, she thought with a smirk. Her cockiness was now evident as she forgot about hiding at the right side of the theater before making her move.

The man had already walked a few steps away from the theater, and she approached him slowly from behind. That's when she saw his leather wallet sticking slightly out of his back pocket. *So easy*, she thought to herself. *Maybe too easy...* Aurora started to back away before he realized she was only a few steps behind him, but stopped herself. She mentally slapped herself. *I've done this a hundred times. This is gonna be a piece of cake. I can do this; there is nothing to worry about.* Why was she still feeling so anxious, as if something terrible would happen if she reached for this particular wallet?

All she had to do was quickly reach her hand toward his back suit pants pocket, grab the wallet, and run back across the street into the dark alley, hopefully without being noticed. She inched closer, until she was right behind him—close enough to touch. Taking a deep breath to calm herself, she reached into the celebrity's pocket and snatched the wallet. Aurora turned on her heels to make a quick getaway. So far, it was all going according to her plan.

"*Ehi!*" a loud male voice yelled.

She wanted to run, but a large hand grabbed her arm, while another hand was quickly placed over her mouth. Frantically trying to take in her surroundings, she could tell she was being pulled past the right-side corner of the theater, deeper into the darkness of the night. Aurora thrashed and struggled, but he held onto her tightly, giving her no chance for an escape. She took a deep breath and stopped struggling, taking a moment to think and lessen her rising panic. *There has to be a way to get out of this predicament! Come on 'Ora, think,*

think, think! But there was no escape. Whoever held her captive was too strong.

Whoever it was, let her go just long enough to push her back into the theater wall. Terrified, she started to fight against him again, but he held onto her arms, keeping them by her sides. "What do you think you are doing?" he asked.

"Let me go!" she yelled. "Let me go!" She struggled to get free. Aurora had mostly grown up on the streets, and she knew how to fight, even when injured. She kicked at his legs, trying to get him to free her completely, but he was too strong. The man continued to hold her arms tightly, so she couldn't escape.

"Hey! Stop it!" the man yelled at her. Aurora tried tuning him out and frantically continued to thrash against him. "*Oh mio Dio,* girl, will you please calm down!? Listen, I'll let go of your arms, but you need to promise me you won't run away," the man said loudly. She stopped struggling and took some deep breaths, trying hard not to panic or attract attention from the nearby security guards.

"Please, let me go," she whimpered.

"I just want to talk. Alright?" he asked.

Aurora nodded her head up and down to signal a yes.

"That's not good enough." He sighed, frustrated. "I need to hear you say it."

Aurora looked defiantly at the ground; her fists clenched. *Who did this guy think he was? He was the one who just assaulted her!*

"Well?" She heard the man ask impatiently.

"I won't run away. I promise," Aurora said quietly, but still fuming inside.

Finally, the man slowly let go of her arms, and took a step back to give her some space.

"Good. Now, what I want to know, young lady, is what made you think it was such a good idea to pickpocket me at a movie premiere?" he questioned her.

"I don't know what you're talking about," she said as she looked down at the ground, wishing she could disappear.

"You don't? Huh... well, I could have sworn I caught you trying to *steal my* wallet. Did you think I was so drunk that I wouldn't notice?" he questioned.

She shrugged her shoulders.

"Okay, I see. So, you aren't bothered that you just tried to steal from me. Well, I am bothered by this. Now, let me ask you another question: what do you think I should do about this predicament?"

Intimidated by his closeness, she leaned away from him, trying to put some distance between them. She could feel him staring intensely at her, as she looked up at him and shrugged.

"I see," he said almost to himself. She watched him closely as he reached into his pocket and pulled out his phone.

"What are you doing?" she questioned him quietly. When he didn't answer her, she noticed he was dialing 911. "Wait!" she yelled, as she grasped his arm, trying to grab his phone. "Please don't," she begged.

"Excuse me?" he asked as he pulled his arm out of her grip.

"Please. Please don't call the cops!" she cried. He sighed as he pushed the end call button and put his phone back in his pocket.

"How old are you?"

"I'm sixteen," she said, her voice shaky. She quickly looked back down, trying to avoid his gaze.

"You're sixteen? Are you sure?" he questioned.

"I...I'm sure," she stammered, trying to stop herself from fidgeting.

"Really? Cause you don't sound too sure of yourself." He hooked a finger under her chin and gently pushed her chin up, so she would have to look at him. "Look at me." She immediately looked him in the eyes after hearing the authoritative tone in his voice; she knew she had no choice but to comply. At this point, she was in too much trouble not to. The man's voice called her back to reality. "Alright, let's try this again, and I would think twice before lying to me again. How old are you?"

"I'm sixteen." She tried to look away, but she found herself looking into his dark brown eyes. Sighing, she admitted the truth. "I'm thirteen."

"Okay, so I'll make you a deal. I won't call the *polizia* if you return the property you stole," he explained. "Fair?"

"Yes, sir," she replied.

"Good. Then may I have my wallet back, please?" he asked, holding out his hand. She reluctantly handed him his wallet. "*Grazie.* Now did you steal from anyone else? I expect you to tell me the truth." She nodded, as she pulled out the wallet and cash she had stolen earlier. "Show me who it belongs to." He gripped her arm and led her to the front of the theater. "Well?" he asked.

She looked around, trying to find the man she stole from earlier. She silently hoped he would be long gone by now. "He's over there," she told the man, spotting him near the entrance of the theater, surrounded by a few of the security guards.

"Alright, this is what you are going to do. You are going to give back what you stole, and you are going to apologize. Agreed?"

"Yes, sir," Aurora grumbled, rolling her eyes. Still gripping her arm, he pulled her towards the entrance.

"Hey, Owen," he said, as they approached the man.

"Oh, hey, Sirius. I thought you left," the man he called Owen said, walking away from the security guards to where Aurora stood with the mysterious celebrity.

"I was heading out, but something came up," Sirius stated, looking down at Aurora.

"Is everything alright, Sirius?" Owen asked.

"Yes, everything is fine. However, this young lady has something she needs to do. Isn't that right, girl?" He looked down at Aurora.

"Is that so?" Owen questioned, looking straight at Aurora.

"Don't you have something you wanted to say?" Sirius asked her. He gently pushed her forward.

"I think this is yours," Aurora said quietly. She handed Owen his wallet.

"Where did you find this!? I've been searching everywhere for it!" Owen exclaimed.

"I found it," Aurora lied, looking down at her feet. She thought she wouldn't feel so guilty if she wasn't looking at the two men while lying to them.

"Found it? Are you sure that's the story you want to go with?" Sirius questioned her, nudging her in the back. "Well?"

"No, sir," Aurora sighed, looking back up at Owen. "I stole it."

"Wasn't there something else you wanted to say?" Sirius asked.

"I'm sorry, sir," she apologized to Owen. She looked down at her feet again, feeling so ashamed, and hearing their disapproving tones didn't make her feel any better.

"I see," Owen said. "Well Sirius, I'm guessing you caught her trying to steal from you?"

"Yeah, I did. She tried taking my wallet too, but she did do the right thing and returned our property," Sirius explained.

"Did you steal from anyone else, little miss?" Owen asked her.

"No, sir," she answered quietly.

"Well, what do you want to do about this, Sirius?" Owen questioned. "She has returned what she had stolen, so I see no reason to hand her over to the security guards or get the authorities involved, especially this late at night."

"I agree with you, my friend. Well, have a great rest of your night, Owen."

"Thank you, and same to you." He shook Sirius' hand and looked down at Aurora. "And as for you, keep your nose out of trouble. Next time someone may not be kind enough to show you compassion," Owen said. "Now, go home; it's late."

"Yes sir, and thank you," she answered as Owen turned to leave and walked away.

"Alright, I believe he's right; it's time for you to go home. It's past midnight, and the streets are no place for a child," Sirius stated.

"Yes sir," Aurora answered. "And thank you for not calling the cops."

"You're welcome. Can I give you a ride home?"

"Um, no thanks. I can make it on my own," she said, looking up at the man. She looked at him intently, taking in his features. He had brown hair that was tied back, and he had a bit of facial hair. She thought he looked familiar, but she wasn't sure where she had seen him before.

"Are you sure you can get home safely by yourself?" he questioned, interrupting her thoughts.

"Yeah, I'll be fine. I can take care of myself," Aurora said, exasperated that the man was still persisting in talking to her.

"Very well. Just be careful, and go straight home. Understand?"

"Yeah, okay, whatever," she remarked, hobbling away.

"Remember, straight home," he called out to her, but she didn't stick around to hear him say anything else.

She ran as fast as her ankle would let her. After being a good distance down the road, she slowed down to a walk. She looked down the narrow alley and shivered. She didn't want to walk through the dark, creepy alley at this time of night, so she decided it would be a better idea to walk down the brightly-lit 6th Ave. She headed to the entrance of the subway station at the end of the road. Looking around, she searched for her friends who were supposed to be waiting for her. "Rats," she said out loud when she realized she couldn't find them. She figured they were still pickpocketing or left without her. Then again, she didn't see them earlier either. She wondered if something terrible had happened. *Did they get caught? Or did they see me get caught and bail on me?* she thought frantically.

She waited around the subway station entrance for a few more minutes before she decided to just go a few blocks over to where she would feel safe crashing for the night. Since it was way past 7 p.m., she knew couldn't go home. The doors would be locked. Her foster parents would refuse to let her in if she got home past her curfew. There were times she was able to get in, but her foster parents would hear her, kick her outside, and lock her out once again. She would have to sleep in the backyard, which wasn't much better than if she

30

was sleeping on the front steps, especially since they lived in a crumby neighborhood. Also, if she stuck around the house till morning, she would have to deal with the wrath of her foster parents for disobeying the house rules. It was better for her to break into a church or hide away in a school playground for the night. It was much safer, and she almost never got caught. If she did, most times whoever found her would tell her to be on her way, or just left her alone and minded their own business.

Aurora came up to the gate of the school playground. She quickly and effortlessly climbed over the gate. Quietly, she walked over to one of the benches and crawled underneath. She took a breath of relief as she laid down. She was so incredibly thankful that the men at the event showed her the compassion they did. If not, they could have handed her over to the security guards or the cops. Then they would have contacted her social worker, Ms. Davis. Aurora shivered at the thought. Facing the wrath of Ms. Davis was so much worse than her foster parents. She tried not to think of what could happen to her. The best-case scenario was another home or a group home, but the worst case was juvie. She dreaded even the thought of it.

She closed her eyes and tried to fall asleep. Aurora might not have a family, but she did have her two friends, Hunter and Ethan, who hopefully were safe. They were probably going crazy wondering what had happened to her. She also was thankful for those two celebrities whom had showed her compassion. *Stuff like this never happens to me. Maybe my life might just be taking a turn for the better.*

Chapter 4

Saturday, March 2nd

As Sirius drove back to his hotel, he decided that he needed to make sure this girl was safe. It was late, and she was so young to be out on her own in the big city. So, he decided to quick turn around and check on her. Thankfully, he was able to find her; and he ended up following her, driving some distance away so she wouldn't notice his Ferrari. She was noticeably nursing an injured leg, and he only wanted to make sure she got home safely, even though he didn't entirely believe that's where she would be heading. He watched her as she stopped in front of a locked gate and parked his car across the street from where she was. That way he could keep track of her but also remain out of sight. From his tinted car window, he watched her as she quickly and effortlessly climbed over the gate. Seeing how easy that was for her, Sirius assumed she had done this more often than she should.

Wanting to get a better look, he quietly stepped out of his car and walked across the street. He read the sign on the building next to the gate: P.S. 111. Looking through the gate, he saw her limping through the school playground. She stopped at one of the wooden playground benches and crawled underneath it. He had watched her for a couple more minutes. During those minutes, she hadn't moved and he figured she had fallen asleep. Sirius walked back to his car and watched the area surrounding the public-school playground as she slept. He wanted to make sure she stayed safe. He thought sadly, *No child should have to sleep on the streets*. That's all he remembered before he had fallen asleep as well, tired from the long day.

Sirius had awakened to the sound of a police car siren. He glanced briefly at his wrist watch. It was five o'clock in the morning. Bleary-eyed, Sirius rolled down the window of his Ferrari to see a NYPD patrol car parked on the other side of the road. A female police officer walked with the girl, who was now in handcuffs. He quickly got out of his car and ran across the street.

"Officer! May I have a word?" Sirius asked her.

"What can I do for you, sir?" the officer asked as she put the girl in the back of the patrol car. The girl cast a shocked look his way, obviously surprised that someone she had tried to pickpocket the night before was standing right in front of her. She looked like she wanted to say something but was unsure what to think about the situation.

"The girl—where are you taking her?" Sirius questioned.

"The police station. You know her?" the officer wondered, eyeing Sirius suspiciously.

"Yes, I actually do, and I'm quite concerned for her welfare, officer," Sirius assertively responded. "Is there someone I would be able to talk to about her situation?"

"I suppose. If you come down to the Midtown North Precinct, I'm sure someone would be happy to answer any questions you may have," the officer explained curtly.

"Thank you," Sirius responded. He watched the patrol car drive off with the frightened girl staring at him from the back window. Slowly, he walked back to his car and headed to the Midtown North Precinct.

As he walked into the precinct, he looked around the bustling room for the girl. He was surprised the station was so busy, as it was only six o'clock in the morning. Finally, he spotted her sitting in the back of the room next to one of the offices. She was talking to someone whom he had assumed was a detective. Sirius had figured it out from the detective's apparel—a dark blue dress shirt and black jeans rather than a standard police uniform. He inched closer to them to try to hear their discussion.

"Aurora, what were you thinking?" Sirius heard the detective ask her.

"I don't know," she answered, rolling her eyes as she crossed her arms over her chest.

"Wandering around in the dead of night, and trespassing on school property—does any of that sound like a wise decision to you?" the detective questioned, his voice rising with every word. "What if something happened?!"

"It was late, and I was tired. I needed somewhere to sleep," she retorted.

"Excuse me," Sirius interrupted, taking in the shocked look on Aurora's face. "Would it be possible to have a word with you, Detective?"

"It's Detective Stone," the tall, copper-toned detective responded. "And of course. And you would be...?"

"Thank you, and it's Sirius—Sirius Marino."

"You know, I thought you looked familiar! You starred in that hit movie *King Without Faith*." Detective Stone smiled politely as he led

Sirius into his office. Before he closed the door, he leaned out the doorway. "Aurora, stay put. Ms. Davis is on her way and will be here soon," he said just before closing the door.

"What's going to happen to her?" Sirius asked.

"You mean Aurora? Well, her social worker Ms. Davis is going to pick her up shortly," Detective Stone said.

"Social worker? She's in the foster care system?" Sirius questioned.

"Yes, she is," Detective Stone said matter-of-factly, not entirely trusting the actor standing in front of him, despite his obvious stardom.

"What's going to happen to Aurora? Is she going to be charged for breaking and entering?" Sirius asked.

"I'm not entirely sure. That's up to her social worker," Detective Stone continued, eyeballing Sirius suspiciously.

"What about the family she is living with? Couldn't she go back there?" Sirius asked.

"I don't know the details, but I personally don't think that will be a possibility," Detective Stone responded.

"May I ask why not?"

"To be frank with you, Mr. Marino, I'm not at liberty to discuss that information. That is something you would need to discuss with her social worker directly."

"Excuse me, Detective Stone," a lanky, and shorter officer interrupted, barging into Detective Stone's office and slamming the door shut behind him with a thud.

"Officer Logan, have you heard of knocking?" Detective Stone asked sarcastically.

"Yeah, sorry. But Ms. Davis is here, and she's in one of her moods. She has demanded to speak with you immediately," Officer Logan answered, slightly out of breath still from hustling into the office. "Oh, yeah, and she made sure to mention she wants a *private* meeting with you."

"Alright." Detective Stone sighed. "If you would excuse me, Mr. Marino?"

"Of course," Sirius said.

"I should have taken a picture with you to show my daughter, she's a huge fan! Oh well, no time for that now with Ms. Davis waiting. But please, if you ever need anything when you're in the Big Apple, Mr. Marino, please don't hesitate to give me a call," Detective Stone said as he handed Sirius his card and led him out of his office, closing the door behind him.

"Thank you," Sirius answered. Sirius watched the Detective as he walked over to a tall woman with platinum blonde hair. Sirius could hear him mumbling under his breath, probably dreading whatever conversation he was going to have with this Ms. Davis.

"Ms. Davis, you wanted to speak with me?" Detective Stone questioned.

"Yes, I would, and in private, please!" Ms. Davis answered, obviously irritated.

"Sure, that would be fine. Please, step inside my office. I'll be right with you," Detective Stone said to her. "Mr. Marino, it was nice to meet you."

"Likewise," Sirius answered.

"And as for you," Detective Stone said, as he turned to Aurora. "Stay put, and please be considerate," he whispered.

"Yes, sir," Aurora responded, just before Detective Stone closed his office door. "What are you doing here?" Aurora asked Sirius, as she gave him an uncertain glare. "Are you here to make sure they arrest me for trying to pickpocket you?"

"Not at all—I was concerned about you," Sirius answered.

"Why?" she questioned as she fiddled with her sweatshirt.

"Why not?"

"Well, then you would be the first," Aurora answered.

"I'm sure that's not true. What about your foster family? I would hope that they care for your well-being," Sirius stated.

"The Millers? Care about me?" she scoffed. "That's a joke!"

"Why do you say that?"

"Because they don't care about anyone but themselves," Aurora explained. "All they care about is the check they collect every month from the government."

"Don't they treat you well?" he asked.

"What do you think?" she snapped. "It's none of your business! Just go away!"

Sirius raised his eyebrows at her as he studied her appearance. Aurora looked skinny, like she hadn't eaten in days. Her pants were full of holes and covered in dirt, and the dark sweatshirt she wore was baggy and grungy from spending the night sleeping on the ground. "Why did you spend the night on the playground?" he questioned.

"Um, I was tired, and I didn't feel like taking the subway home."

"Really?" Sirius asked. He couldn't believe what he was hearing; he couldn't understand why she was sleeping under a bench instead of at home in her own bed. Didn't she realize how dangerous the streets could be for a child?

"Yeah," she stated quietly, as she nervously wrung her hands together.

"Well, I recall offering you a ride, so you wouldn't have to do that. Also, I could have sworn I heard Detective Stone mention this was not the first time you slept on the streets. It seems as though it happens more than it should." He crouched down in front of her, so they were at eye level. "How about you tell me the truth?" he asked, looking into her bright green eyes.

"I slept on the street, because they wouldn't have let me in," she answered. She looked down at her hands, not wanting to make eye contact with him.

"What do you mean?" he asked.

"They have a curfew for the foster kids. Their rule is be at home by 7 p.m. or be locked out."

"They lock you out?" he questioned, shocked by what he was hearing.

"It's either sleep on the streets or sleep in the yard," Aurora explained.

"So why don't you just sleep in the yard? It would be much safer."

"You don't know anything," she argued.

"Well, then how about you tell me?"

"The foster home is in a bad neighborhood," she explained. "That's why I sleep in the school playground. It's locked up, and the police patrol that area. It's a lot safer."

"That's not right. Why don't you tell your social worker?"

"She wouldn't believe me. She never has. She would just say that I'm lying and that I'm just a—"

"Aurora," Detective Stone cut into the conversation before Sirius found out how Aurora would describe Ms. Davis. "Ms. Davis wants to speak with you."

"Do I have a choice?" Aurora asked sarcastically.

"No," Detective Stone said. "Sorry, Aurora."

"Fine, let's just get this over with," she mumbled.

"And Aurora, please try to tolerate her; be nice," Detective Stone suggested.

"I'll try," she answered. She quickly walked into the office and slammed the door shut.

"Hello, Miss Bennett," Ms. Davis greeted her coldly.

"Hi, Ms. Davis," Aurora responded quietly, as she saw Ms. Davis sitting at Detective Stone's desk.

"Have a seat, Aurora," Ms. Davis stated.

"I'd rather stand. Thanks anyway," Aurora said.

"Aurora, what on earth am I going to do with you?" Ms. Davis questioned.

"You could send me back to the Millers," Aurora remarked.

"That's not going to happen. The Millers want nothing to do with you. You steal, run away any chance you get, and show them absolutely no respect. Why would they want a brat like you back? If only I could send you to the moon," she taunted.

"Ms. Davis, I never stole from them," Aurora stated.

"Well, that's not what they told me."

"I swear I never stole from them. They're lying."

"Aurora Bennett, be considerate for once in your life. They took you in out of the kindness of their heart, so show them some respect."

"That's a joke," Aurora said under her breath.

"Aurora!" Ms. Davis snapped.

"Maybe if you placed me in a better home with a decent family, things would be different."

"I find that very doubtful, Miss Bennett. However, if you really want to prove yourself, then you will mind your manners, especially where you'll be going." Ms. Davis stood from her seat and walked over to the office door. Opening the door, she called out to Detective Stone, "Detective, will you please have one of your officers transport her to the Juvenile Detention Center?"

"You're sending me there?" Aurora yelled.

"Aurora, hush!" Ms. Davis scolded from outside the office.

"Are you sure you want to put her there?" Detective Stone questioned. He was about to continue, but quickly decided it would be better not to question her further because of the glare she was giving him. "Whatever you say, Ms. Davis. I'll get Officer Logan to do it."

"Very good," she stated. She turned to Aurora. "You stay put till Officer Logan comes to fetch you. Understand?"

"Yes, Ms. Davis."

"Good. And don't you dare give anyone trouble while you are there, or I'll make sure you stay there till you're eighteen. Understand?"

"Fine." Aurora crossed her arms and glared at Ms. Davis, obviously angry and afraid.

"Aurora, be respectful!"

"Whatever," Aurora responded, rolling her eyes. She went to the door and slammed it shut. She wished she could lock the door, so Ms. Davis couldn't come back in. But then she would be in even more trouble, and that's something she couldn't afford. She sat in front of the door and put her ear to the door, hoping to hear what they were saying.

"I'm guessing she didn't like the idea that she's going to the center?" Detective Stone asked Ms. Davis.

"No, she apparently did not. I may just transfer her case to another social worker. If I keep having to deal with her, I swear that child is going to be the death of me," Ms. Davis complained.

"Excuse me, Ms. Davis. You're sending her to jail?" Sirius questioned as he approached her.

"I'm sorry. Who might you be?" she asked, looking Sirius up and down and scrutinizing him closely. Ms. Davis quickly took notice of the designer suit he was wearing, as well as the Italian shoes which must have cost a fortune.

"I'm Sirius. Sirius Marino," he declared.

Ms. Davis studied him for a moment. "You're Sirius Marino? The actor?" she asked curiously.

"Yes, that's me," he answered confidently.

"Well, it's very nice to meet you, Mr. Marino. I have to say I'm a huge fan. I loved the movie you were in—*Destiny: Can't Escape Fate*," she complimented.

"Thank you," he said politely but cautiously, not surprised that her whole demeanor had changed when finding out exactly who he was.

"What's the new movie you are starring in? The one that was just released?" she asked.

"Umm, *King Without Faith*," he answered.

"Oh yes, that's the one!" she declared. "So, what are you doing here in New York?"

"I had an event last night at the Ziegfeld Theater."

"For the movie, I presume?"

"Sure," he answered, quickly. "Now, back to Aurora."

"Very well, and you know Aurora—how?" she questioned, her tone immediately changing after mentioning Aurora's name.

"Well, we just happened to run into each other. I asked her if she needed a ride home, and she politely declined. I was concerned about her well-being, so I followed her. I didn't think it was okay for a young teenage girl to be wandering the streets in the dead of night," Sirius explained.

"You happened to run into her? Don't you mean you caught her stealing from you?" she asked. "I wouldn't be surprised if she did. That girl is a menace."

"Why would you assume that?" Sirius questioned.

"Mr. Marino, she has quite a reputation for causing trouble. That child has been in multiple foster homes, and each time she has been kicked out for her unacceptable behavior," Ms. Davis explained.

"I see. However, is it wise to send her to jail at her young age? Couldn't you place her with another family?"

"First of all, she's not going to jail. It's the Juvenile Detention Center. Second, putting her with another family is not a good idea. I don't feel it would give her what she needs."

"And you think jail will." Sirius paused. "*Scusi*, I mean the Juvenile Detention Center?"

"Yes, it will give her a stable environment until she can be moved to a suitable group home."

"Ms. Davis, I agree she needs a stable environment, but she also needs positive attention. The only kind of attention she gets is negative. Have you thought maybe she acts out on purpose? That way she can receive the attention she craves—even if it is negative."

"Well, I'm sure she will get that positive attention you say she craves at the center and at the group home, as well as the professional help she needs," Ms. Davis explained.

"What kind of professional help?" Sirius asked.

"I'm sorry, but that information is confidential and can only be given to those who are serious about adoption or fostering. Unless you wish to do so, I cannot give out that information," Ms. Davis said in an icy tone. "And I'm sure someone like you would never want to adopt a misfit like Aurora."

"Excuse me, Ms. Davis, but why would you assume that?" Sirius asked.

"Well, Mr. Marino, if you must know, it's because it would be bad for your reputation. You are a very distinguished young man, and you wouldn't want to do anything to tarnish your good name—like associate yourself with riffraff like Aurora."

"I'm sorry, did you just refer to that young girl as trash?" Sirius questioned.

"Of course not, I'm just saying someone like her will never amount to anything. She will always be looked down upon. I'd be surprised if she completes her schooling and doesn't end up in federal prison or dead in a gutter somewhere. She's one of those types of girls," Ms. Davis explained. "Now, if you'll excuse me, I have somewhere to be."

"Ms. Davis, I must say, you really don't know what's best for that girl, especially if that's what you think of her," Sirius stated.

"Of course I do. Why do you think I'm having her transferred to the Juvenile Detention Center? It's for her own good," Ms. Davis said.

"That girl needs a home—a loving home with a supportive family," Sirius declared.

"Well, I have tried that, but Aurora just causes problems and runs away," Ms. Davis stated. "I don't know where I would find her a home. Who would want her?" Ms. Davis turned away from Sirius and headed to the door.

"I would," Sirius asserted, knowing at that moment his life would change forever as soon as the words left his mouth. "Now, I would appreciate it, Ms. Davis, if you could explain how I would go about becoming a foster parent for Aurora."

"You are not serious, Mr. Marino?" Ms. Davis seemed to be choking on her words.

"I actually am, Ms. Davis," Sirius said. "Now, what do I have to do?"

"Well, with your schedule, I don't see how you would be approved as a foster parent. You would have to adopt her. It's quite a long, involved process."

"Ms. Davis, I can either get the information from you, or I could go talk to whoever is in charge. Perhaps I should talk to my lawyer."

"Oh, no, no, you don't need to do that," Ms. Davis quickly countered, laughing nervously.

"I'm very glad to hear that," Sirius declared, watching her intently. He thought he saw her scowl at him, but if she did, she quickly regained her composure.

"Yes, well." Ms. Davis cleared her throat, as she reached into her bag and pulled out a stack of papers. "This is the application for fostering and adoption, as well as other forms including child abuse clearances. Also, here's my card. Fill all this out and have it faxed to me." She handed him the papers. Sirius was surprised she didn't throw them at him.

"Thank you, and I'll have my lawyer be in touch as well."

"Fine," she scoffed. "Now, if you'll excuse me, I have somewhere else I needed to be fifteen minutes ago, as I'm sure you do as well."

"That I do. Have a great day, Ms. Davis," Sirius said kindly.

"Yeah, same to you," Ms. Davis muttered, glaring at him and walking quickly out of the precinct.

"I'm surprised you're still here, Mr. Marino," Officer Logan stated, hooking his fingers into his belt as he walked up to Sirius.

"Yeah, me too. Now that I have the information I need, I can head out. I have a flight to catch." Sirius sighed.

"Back to Hollywood?" Officer Logan asked.

"Yes, I need to get back there and deal with all of this." Sirius chuckled, waving the stack of papers in the air.

"Well, I'm glad to see you survived your first encounter with the wrathful Ms. Davis," Officer Logan teased.

"That I did. Do you know her well?" Sirius asked.

"I know her well enough. Every time Aurora is brought in, Ms. Davis pays us a visit. I have to say this is one of the more pleasant encounters we've had with her," Officer Logan explained.

"Why do you say that?" Sirius questioned.

"Ms. Davis is...Hmm...What's a kind way to put it? Not a people person. Also, I don't think she likes kids very much," Officer Logan explained.

"But isn't her job supposed to help children and families? How can she not like children or be a people person?" Sirius wondered.

"Though, after that conversation I just had with her, I think she should find a new career path."

"I agree, but I'll tell you one thing—I feel bad for Aurora. She has been through so much, and that woman hasn't helped her situation one bit. I really hoped the last family she was with would be good for her."

"Do you think they treated her well?"

"Not really. They seemed nice enough whenever I had to drop her off, but she ran away every chance she got. I figured if they were good to her, she would have a reason to stay; however, it didn't happen that way," Officer Logan explained. "You know what I mean?"

"Yeah, I do," Sirius answered.

"I'm sure my two cents isn't worth much, but I think it would be really good for her to be placed with someone who would really care about her, like you. You seem like a genuine person, and someone who cares," Officer Logan said.

"Thanks, Officer. That's good to know, and your opinion is worth a whole lot."

"Thanks, Mr. Marino. Anyway, I need to get her to the center, or Ms. Davis is going to throw a fit." Officer Logan sighed. He walked over and knocked on the office door. "Hey, Kiddo! It's time to go," Officer Logan said to her through the door. Slowly, the door opened, and Officer Logan could see Aurora peeking through.

"Do I have to go, Officer Logan?" Aurora questioned.

"I'm afraid so. How about you go outside? I'll be right there," Officer Logan answered. "Oh, and Aurora," he whispered to her. "Just thought I'd let you know—my wife packed some of her famous sugar cookies in my lunch bag. And they are just waiting for a healthy appetite in the front seat of my patrol car."

"Really?" she whispered back, smiling up at him.

"Yeah, go to the car and help yourself. I don't need them as much as you, and I have a feeling you won't be getting treats like that for a while," Logan responded, patting her head and making Aurora chuckle. "Go on."

"Okay, thanks, Officer Logan," she said quietly, as she turned and stumbled through the crowded entry room towards the entrance. Officer Logan and Sirius watched her as she quickly swung her bag over her shoulder, walked to the front, and then to the patrol car parked right next to the precinct entrance.

"Hey, Mr. Marino, hope you have a good flight, and again, it really would be great if you could do something about Aurora's situation," Officer Logan said, looking hopefully at Sirius.

"Thanks, I'll see what I can do," Sirius said as he walked outside to the parking lot with Officer Logan.

"Excuse me, Mr. Marino?" Sirius saw Aurora walk up to him from the patrol car as she put her bag on the ground.

"Yes, Aurora?" he answered.

"I just wanted to say thank you. You know, for not ratting me out."

"No problem, and I really hope all goes well for you."

"Thanks," she responded, picking her bag up from where she dropped it. As she reached down, her long dirty-blonde hair fell over her shoulder and bared the side of her neck and back. Her shirt was so big that he was able to see the back of her neck and her upper back. Hidden under her hair and shirt were bruises on her neck, and he was pretty sure he saw scars, running as far as he could see down her back.

He hadn't seen them at the theater because it was too dark, but now in the daylight, he could clearly see them. The more he stared, the more he was concerned. *She was not safe at that home, and Ms. Davis probably allowed it to happen,* Sirius thought to himself.

He continued to watch as she put her bag over her bony shoulder and limped tiredly back to Officer Logan's patrol car. He slowly walked to his rented Ferrari. He watched Officer Logan hand Aurora the brown bag with the cookies. The patrol car pulled out of the parking lot and drove off, as Aurora desperately looked out the window straight into his eyes, looking like a trapped animal. Her eyes said it all. She needed someone to rescue her, or it would be too late.

"I have to do something," he thought out loud, "Or Ms. Davis may be right—Aurora could end up in jail, or worse, dead in a gutter somewhere."

A car honking behind Sirius pulled him back into the reality of NYC traffic. As he was driving to the airport, he mused. *So many things have changed in my life just in the last twenty-four hours. Let's hope that I can somehow get Aurora the help that she needs.*

Chapter 5

Monday, March 4th

Aurora woke up to the lights turning on throughout the hall and the piercing sound of the PA system. She looked around frantically, as she momentarily forgot where she was. Then it all came back to her—getting caught by that actor while attempting to pickpocket him, getting arrested for trespassing on the school playground, being brought to the precinct, having to face that same actor as well as her terrible social worker, and being brought to juvie. She rubbed her hands over her face, trying to take deep breaths. The harsh light in the cell did nothing to calm her anxiety; internally, she couldn't help but panic. She was trapped, and there was no escape.

This was only her second day waking up as an inmate at the Juvenile Detention Center. Ms. Davis had told her she would only be there for a day or two, but Aurora didn't believe her. She was nervous she would be there longer. She knew Ms. Davis would forget about her and let her rot in there if she could.

She sat up in her bed. There were a few cells in this unit that had two beds for the girls going through intake or for the girls who would only be there for a couple days. This is where she was placed. She looked around her small cell of hard concrete floors and a heavy steel door that locked her in. There were no windows in these cells, and Aurora hoped she would be moved to a cell with a window if she did have had to stay longer.

Aurora had already observed that life in the center was incredibly boring and predictable. Yesterday, they were woken up at 6 a.m. sharp, then escorted to the intake unit common room at 7 a.m. for breakfast. From 8 a.m. onwards, she and the other girls had spent the day doing schoolwork, eating lunch, and other mundane activities until they were escorted back to their cells at 5 p.m. They spent the rest of the day in their cells until lights out at 8 p.m. Depressingly, the only visitors they received during free time were the guards who brought in dinner, the counselors who came to talk to them, and the warden. After running through the events of the last day in her mind, she laid back on the bed and closed her eyes, trying to think of a way to convince Ms. Davis to send her to another family instead of to the group foster home.

"Hey, Bennett!" her cellmate, Sandra Ward, yelled from across the room; she had the loudest voice Aurora had ever heard.

"What do you want, Sandra? You're going to get us in trouble if you don't keep your voice down." Aurora sighed.

"Just making sure you are up. You know from yesterday how those guards get when we ain't awake when they come in to check on us," Sandra said, running her fingers as a comb through her curly brown hair.

"That's true, and thanks."

"No problem. Hopefully, they will be getting us for breakfast soon. I'm hungry," Sandra said.

"Yippee, another dull start to another boring day," Aurora whined sarcastically, trying to ignore the gurgle her stomach made, alerting her to how hungry she really was. "And thanks for bringing up food," Aurora grumbled at her cellmate.

"You're welcome, and this has to be better than being stuck in a bad foster home," Sandra retorted.

"Not really, this is worse—for me, at least."

"You serious? You like being used as a punching bag?" Sandra asked, raising an eyebrow.

"No, of course not, but I don't want to be here either. I hate feeling trapped."

"From what you told me last night, didn't you feel trapped in your last home?" Sandra questioned.

"No, they couldn't have cared less about me. As long as I stayed out of their way, they left me alone. I was able to go and do wherever I wanted whenever I wanted," Aurora stated.

"It wasn't terrible?"

"It definitely was bad. That's why I didn't hang around the house. If I did, my foster parents would find any excuse to beat me up," Aurora explained.

"I know how that is," Sandra said sympathetically. "Did you ever have any really bad ones?"

"Yeah, I had one home that was an absolute nightmare. Some nights I was so afraid that I hid a pocket knife under my pillow when I slept, but one of the foster parents took it away from me. She probably threw it away, since I couldn't find it after that."

"Being locked in here bring back any bad memories?"

"Not really," Aurora responded, half lying. She remembered one of the homes where her foster parents never allowed her to play outside. When she had tried to escape through a window, her foster parents caught her and started beating her. She tried to get away, but they called the cops, and the cops called Ms. Davis. "So far, juvie is better than most of my foster homes, but I still hate the feeling of being trapped."

"I get that," Sandra commented.

"I just hope the group home isn't too bad." Aurora jumped up from her bed and walked over to the locked door, staring out the small window. "I hear group homes are the worst."

"I heard the same. Something about how it's the end of the line till you age outta the system," Sandra mentioned.

"That's just great." Aurora sighed.

"So girl...would you rather have a foster family who is kind or who lets you do whatever you want?" Sandra asked, changing the subject.

"That's easy—kind. If they are kind, then they will let me do stuff. They would at least give me what I need, so I wouldn't have to steal."

"Why don't you just beg? You can make a lot of cash," Sandra suggested.

"Beg? I don't—" Aurora started but was interrupted by the PA system. "Ugh, that's the breakfast announcement."

"Time to line up, then," Sandra commented, bouncing off her bed.

"Yippee," Aurora uttered sarcastically.

"You sound super excited," Sandra teased.

"Nope," Aurora snapped, just as the buzzer went off and the cell doors in the hall opened.

"Let's go, girls!" a female guard yelled. Aurora glanced at her uniform name badge—Walters, as she walked by them. "We don't have all day, girls!" Officer Walters barked out in a raspy, impatient voice.

Aurora and Sandra quickly got in line with the other girls and walked down to the common room. As soon as they arrived, they were instructed to sit at the tables in the galley area.

"This food stinks," Aurora heard one of the girls at her table say, as she shoved her tray of food away.

"I agree with that," Sandra declared. "What do you think, Aurora?"

"The food's not bad."

"You being serious?" Sandra asked.

"Yeah, I've had a lot worse. This is at least edible," Aurora said.

"So, what are you here for?" a dark-haired girl with dark brown eyes seated across from Aurora asked.

"Just being held here till they find me a placement in a group home," Aurora responded.

"That's not too bad. I'm Lexi—Lexi Anderson—by the way," Lexi introduced herself as she fiddled with her long black hair.

"Nice to meet you, Lexi. I'm Aurora—Aurora Bennett," she introduced herself. "So why are you here?"

"My dad called the cops on me and is pressing charges," Lexi explained.

"Your dad? Why?" Sandra asked. "What did you do?"

"Well, he's my step-dad, but I've known him basically my whole life. Anyway, I stole his motorcycle, and I may or may not have totaled it," Lexi stated. "It wasn't exactly the first time I did something stupid. I guess he had enough and wasn't joking when he said that he would call the cops next time."

"Why did you do that?" Aurora questioned, horrified. "I mean, you have a real dad, and aren't stuck with terrible foster families like Sandra and me!"

"I dunno. I guess 'cause I was bored? I wanted to have some fun," Lexi said, smirking.

"You're officially crazy," Aurora declared, teasingly.

"Bennett! Get up," Officer Walters instructed, walking up to their table, and apparently still in a grumpy mood from the morning wake-up call.

"Yes, ma'am," Aurora replied, as she quickly did as she was told.

"Seems you're done with your breakfast. Let's go. Your social worker is here," Officer Walters said, hands on her hips.

"Girl, looks like you getting out of *here*!" Sandra said, loudly enough for the girls at the other end of the room to hear.

"Ward, lower your voice," Officer Walters instructed, obviously annoyed. "Bennett, let's go." She led Aurora out of the common room, and down a hallway she hadn't walked through before.

"Does this mean I'm leaving?" Aurora asked.

"I don't know. Your social worker has the details," Officer Walters answered curtly but not unkindly. Aurora continued to follow her down the hall until they walked up to one of the offices in the next unit. Another guard opened the door and escorted her into the room. Aurora immediately saw Ms. Davis sitting at the large table.

"Hello, Miss Bennett," Ms. Davis said as Aurora walked in.

"Hi," Aurora responded quietly. She didn't want to cause a fight and give Ms. Davis a reason to make her life even harder.

"Sit down, Aurora," Ms. Davis said with her usual annoyed and impatient tone.

"Do I get to leave here soon?" Aurora asked, sitting down. She nervously bit her lower lip, waiting for her response.

"That's what I need to talk to you about, along with a few other topics," Ms. Davis responded, sighing and looking even more annoyed.

"Like about the group home?" Aurora questioned.

"Yes, among other things."

"Like what?" Aurora asked. She fidgeted in her seat, tapping her right foot on the ground.

"Well, first of all, I got a call from your school principal."

"You did? Why?" Aurora held her breath, worrying what on earth the principal wanted.

"He said you hadn't been in classes for weeks, but that is a discussion for another time. The thing is, he searched your locker."

"So?" Aurora questioned.

"Well, after I called him to notify him you won't be returning, he had your locker cleaned out. Do you know what they found?"

"Nothing."

"Are you sure that's the answer you want to give?" Ms. Davis questioned. Aurora nodded her response, scared to see where this conversation was going. "Well, what they found were a bunch of empty wallets, so I'm assuming you took what you wanted and then stashed the wallets there till you were able to dispose of them."

"Ms. Davis, that's impossible, because I didn't do it!" Aurora said angrily in protest. She clenched her hands at her sides.

"Then how do you explain the wallets?"

"I don't know, but they aren't mine! If I did pickpocket someone, I'm smart enough to get rid of the evidence and not leave it where it could easily be found. I'm not stupid!"

"Well, since there is no evidence to say otherwise, Judge Herold, Detective Stone, and I had a conference. We discussed the situation at hand along with your constant lack of respect, and we decided it would be best for you to stay here for the time being."

"What? Why!?" Aurora questioned, jumping up from her seat. "Because some random wallets mysteriously turned up in my locker?! What happened to being innocent until proven guilty? And why wasn't I there at this conference *discussing my* life?!"

"Aurora! Sit down and shut up, or I'll have you thrown in solitary," Ms. Davis scolded her. Aurora quickly did as she was told and tried as hard as she could to keep her mouth shut, knowing Ms. Davis would love nothing better than to make her punishment worse. "Now, Aurora, you are guilty, so just tell the truth for once in your life. Also, you didn't need to be there; we have your best interests in mind."

"I am telling the truth!" Aurora shouted, furious and frustrated. She banged her fists on the table. "I swear I'm *not* lying!"

"Well, lying or not, you have been sentenced for sixty days by Judge Herold with intent to reform your behavior, unless you do something that gets you even more time." Ms. Davis stated harshly.

"That's not fair!" Aurora yelled.

"Aurora Bennett, you need to keep your voice down! You have been in and out of foster homes. You run away any chance you get, and now you have resorted to stealing. The plus to this is it keeps you out of my hair," Ms. Davis said, much too cheerfully. "Anything you want to say?"

Aurora didn't say a word. She glared at Ms. Davis and crossed her arms. There was no point in defending herself any further, since Ms. Davis was going to believe whatever she wanted to and would kick her to the curb in the process. *Ms. Davis will never side with me*, Aurora reminded herself. *Stay on the defensive and don't ever trust her.*

"Well, there's another topic we need to discuss."

"What else did I do?" Aurora questioned sarcastically.

"Nothing more that I know of now," Ms. Davis said, and then unexpectedly added, "Do you remember Mr. Marino?"

"Mr. Marino?"

"Yes, that would be the man from the precinct two days ago," Ms. Davis answered, obviously annoyed by her question.

"What about him?" Aurora questioned.

"I was contacted by his lawyer."

"You were? What did he want?" Aurora asked nervously, afraid he had ratted her out, and all his promises had been empty ones like every other adult she had ever met since she entered foster care.

"Well, believe it or not, he sent over an application for your adoption." Ms. Davis answered in an extremely aggravated tone of voice, like it almost killed her to say it.

"Adoption? He wants to adopt me?!"

"Yes, he first wanted to apply to be your foster parent; however, I told him it wouldn't work with his lifestyle. So now he is working on the process to legally adopt you," Ms. Davis explained.

"Are you serious?" Aurora questioned, hope rising in her chest like she hadn't felt since before she was thrown into the foster system. *God, could Mr. Marino be the answer to my prayer for escape? Please let this be real, please, please, please...*

"Yes, I am serious," Ms. Davis answered, her right eyebrow twitching oddly. "However, I would not get my hopes up if I were you. Your sentence may just change his mind. I actually hope after hearing about all those stolen wallets in your locker, he will come to his senses."

"What do you mean?" Aurora asked, fear striking her mind again.

"Do you really think he wants to be a guardian to a teenage delinquent? He has his reputation to consider." Aurora didn't know how to respond, so she just sat there quietly. "I'll take that as a no?" Ms. Davis asked, commenting on Aurora's silence.

"What if he still does want to adopt me?"

"After you complete your time here, then he will be your legal guardian. Well, until he throws you back into the system, especially with your history of corrupt behavior. From what I've been told, you will be placed in unit two or general population. I'm sure you will be in good company." Ms. Davis quickly stood up and walked to the door. Opening the door, she turned to Officer Walters. "Officer Walters, you can take her to see the warden now. He mentioned wanting to speak with Miss Bennett, before she gets settled into her unit."

"Let's go, Bennett," Officer Walters instructed, apparently in an improved mood. *Maybe she just isn't an early morning person. I'll have to remember to not to ever aggravate guard Officer Walters before 9 a.m.*, Aurora thought.

"Yes, ma'am," Aurora responded, as she got up from her seat and followed Officer Walters' short strides down the hall. She walked in silence as she followed the guard to the warden's office.

"Mr. Sanchez," Officer Walters stated, opening the door to the office. "Miss Bennett is here to see you."

"Come in, Miss Bennett," Warden Sanchez said.

Aurora slowly walked into the room and saw the warden standing near the large desk in the center of the room. "Good morning, Warden Sanchez," Aurora greeted the warden.

"Please have a seat," Mr. Sanchez pointed out the chair on the other side of his desk. Aurora watched him carefully as he sat down across from her. "Aurora, I know I spoke to you a little bit during intake, but since you will be moving into unit two, I need to talk to you about some other topics."

"Yes, Warden Sanchez," she responded, sitting down and leaning back into the chair.

"Good, first, I have papers I need you to read and sign, confirming you understand this facility's rules and procedures," he explained, handing Aurora the papers. Aurora took the papers from him and started to skim the words, instead of actually reading it. It was a long list of rules; to sum it up, it was basically the same rules she had to follow at school—no fighting, no bullying, etc. The only difference was that she had to sleep here overnight and had a schedule to follow throughout the day. *This is going to be the most boring sixty days of my entire life,* Aurora thought, grimacing. Once she finished reading, she signed her name and handed the papers back to the warden, who asked her kindly, "Alright, any questions or concerns about the rules or procedures?"

"No, Mr. Sanchez," Aurora mumbled.

"Alright, next thing I want to discuss with you is your release date. Judge Herold gave you sixty days, so you have a predetermined release date for May 2nd. This means you won't get any extensions. However, I think you should complete a program here."

"What kind of program?" Aurora asked.

"Well, I think the 'Rewind, Press Play' program would be really good for you," Warden Sanchez suggested.

"What is that?"

"It's a program designed to help the students here overcome personal challenges, achieve their goals, practice important life skills, and assist them in making plans for the future. I think doing this program would really benefit you, so if you agree, I will be talking to your social worker and the judge about enrolling you into it. Does that sound good to you?"

"Why are you asking me? Especially if you're going to make decisions about my life whether I like it or not," Aurora questioned.

"I just want to make sure you understand what's happening. I'm telling you all this to give you a heads-up. You may not have much control over certain decisions we are making, but I want you to know what's going to happen. We want to help you work through your challenges along with dealing with the emotions that you're feeling in your situation. Does that make sense?" he asked.

"Yes, sir," Aurora answered, examining her dirty fingernails and not wanting to reveal to Mr. Sanchez that she was extremely upset and wanted to cry out of frustration.

Mr. Sanchez's deep baritone voice jerked Aurora back to the conversation. "Good, one more thing I want to talk to you about is your placement."

"My placement?" Aurora panicked for a moment.

"Yes, I'm sure Ms. Davis talked to you about Mr. Marino," Warden Sanchez said, looking concerned at Aurora's panic-stricken expression. "What did she tell you?"

"She said that he put in an application for my adoption—for him to be my legal g-guardian." Aurora stumbled on the last word. She could hardly believe it was true, hoping it wasn't another one of Ms. Davis's cruel mind games.

"That's correct. I received some more information. He called me himself this morning to give me an update," he explained. "Ms. Davis apparently called him and told him Judge Herold's verdict on your case. She also gave him my number just in case he wanted to talk to me, and he phoned me to talk about your case. He is very serious about adopting you, Aurora," Warden Sanchez said, allowing a sympathetic smile to cross his face. He knew how lucky foster teens like Aurora were to be considered for adoption into a good home; sadly, too many of them never get the chance.

"What did he say?" Aurora questioned, eagerly as well as a little nervous. She scooted forward in her chair, not wanting to miss a word.

"A couple of things. First, he wanted to let me know that he submitted all the paperwork he was required to submit—his clearances, his home study, and the family detail applications he was given. Second, he wanted to see if he could come visit with you here in person."

"He did?!" Aurora nearly fell out of her chair in shock.

"Yes, he did," Mr. Sanchez said, smiling at Aurora's obvious excitement. "Most times we don't allow our inmate students to have visitors unless they're family. However, since Mr. Marino is petitioning to become your legal guardian, I think it would be a good idea for the two of you to get to know each other a little better. So, I'm going make an exception and allow it. However, you can't let the other girls know that I'm bending the rules. Does that sound fair to you?"

"That sounds great!" Aurora declared, beside herself with rising excitement. "But...what happens if he changes his mind?"

"Why do you think he would do that?" Mr. Sanchez asked, looking at her curiously.

"Well, Ms. Davis said not to get my hopes up, because he could change his mind. She said he might decide he doesn't wanna be a guardian to a delinquent like me," Aurora explained.

"She said that to you?" Mr. Sanchez asked, raising both eyebrows in surprise.

"Yes. Is that true?"

"No, it's not true. From my knowledge, he is not going to back out because of your prison sentence. If anything, I think it's making him even more determined. He doesn't think the sentence you were given is fair, and it seems he really wants to ensure that you will have a good future."

"Really?" Aurora asked, hopeful again. *Maybe God is really answering my prayers*, Aurora silently thought to herself, her eyes lighting up with a spark of life that had been missing for a long time.

"Yes, Aurora. Really," Mr. Sanchez confirmed, laughing good-naturedly; he was happy that this kid had gotten a really lucky break, as it didn't happen too often. "Aurora, before you get settled back into your unit, I want to do something for you—just to get rid of any doubts you may have." Mr. Sanchez picked up the phone in his office and pushed the hold button. "Hi, Mr. Marino, I'm back, and I have Aurora here with me. I'm going to hand the phone to her now, alright?"

"Sounds good," Aurora heard the crackling voice of Mr. Marino over the phone from where she sat. Her heart skipped a beat. *Is this really happening to me?!*

"Aurora, here you go," Mr. Sanchez said, grinning from ear to ear while handing the phone to her.

"Thanks." She slowly took the phone from him. "Hello?" she said into the phone hesitantly.

"Hi, Aurora, this is Sirius Marino," he said. She recognized the accent again when he spoke.

"Um, hi, Mr. Marino," she answered nervously.

"How are you doing? How is life in the center?" Sirius questioned.

"I'm fine, and it's kind of boring. There's not much to do here," Aurora said.

"Are they treating you well? Have any of the guards or other inmates mistreated you?"

"I'm okay. They treat me fine; I haven't had any issues with anyone."

"Alright, that's good," Sirius answered, sounding relieved. "Has Warden Sanchez kept you updated on all the details on your case?"

"Yeah, he has. He told me that you—um—you submitted papers for my adoption. Did you really do that?" she questioned, not sure if she should sound excited about it or not over the phone.

"Yes, Aurora, I really did," Sirius confirmed.

"Why would you do that?" Aurora asked, feeling ashamed that she tried to steal from such a kind-hearted man.

"To provide you with a safe and loving home. After meeting and talking with you, I feel it's something you've lacked for quite a while, and I think it's time for a change," Sirius explained.

"That doesn't make sense," Aurora said coldly, fighting the tears that wanted to come to the surface. "Why would you even give me a second thought, after what happened?" She took a deep breath. She didn't want to say anything in front of Warden Sanchez about how they met; she was terrified that it would get her in more trouble. "What's the catch?"

"There is no catch, Aurora," Sirius answered. "And believe it or not, how we met is one of the reasons why I'm doing this."

"You're a movie star and probably a millionaire. You rich folks usually have an ulterior motive. So, what's in it for you?" Aurora questioned, still trying to get a feel for whether or not Sirius Marino was the real deal; she needed to know if she could trust this man to be genuine. "Is this some kind of publicity stunt?"

"Of course not, Aurora! Despite what you may think, there are people in this world who will show kindness without expecting any-thing in return. Unfortunately, not everyone is like that. Also, this is not a publicity stunt. In fact, I'm trying to keep this matter private, so it would be helpful if you didn't talk about it to anyone other than Warden Sanchez and the counselors at the center."

"Why?" Aurora asked, curious to why he would want that.

"Because we don't want the paparazzi swarming around the deten-tion center." Sirius laughed.

"Would they really do that?" Aurora asked.

"They might. They wouldn't be able to get past the gates though, since they don't give passes to anyone except family members. They can be a real nuisance, so do your best not to tell anyone, at least for now."

"If you say so." Aurora sighed.

"I do, Aurora. Now, I suggest you do your best to stay out of trouble. I don't think you want to stay there any longer than you have to, and I think you may want to be careful with Ms. Davis. She seems to have it out for you." The warning tone in Sirius' voice about Ms. Davis confirmed to Aurora that he definitely had her best interests at heart. If he could see through Ms. Davis already, then there's hope that everything was going to be fine.

"Yeah, she hates me. She would leave me here to rot if she could," Aurora said.

"I don't think she could actually do that, but I wouldn't put it past her to try something. So please be careful," Sirius requested.

"I will," Aurora answered.

"Aurora, I don't know if Mr. Sanchez mentioned this, but I am going to try to visit you there," Sirius said, changing the topic to something happier. He could sense Aurora felt very uncomfortable talking about Ms. Davis.

"He did, but how is that going to work?" Aurora asked skeptically.

"What do you mean?" Sirius wondered.

"You said that you didn't want anyone to know about the adoption. If you come to visit me, you will be recognized; then someone will eventually figure it out. That seems kind of stupid to me."

"Don't worry about it, Aurora. Just leave it to me and Mr. Sanchez." Sirius' voice sounded confident and reassuring.

"Umm, okay," she responded.

"Well, you need to get settled, but I will keep in touch with you as much as possible, alright?"

"Yeah, alright." Aurora sighed, not wanting this amazing conversation to end.

"Good—now, be smart," Sirius said mindfully. "Talk to you soon. *Ciao.*"

"Okay, bye," Aurora answered, hanging up the phone.

Mr. Sanchez, who had turned his back to Aurora to give her some privacy during the conversation, turned around and spoke. "Now that we have that all settled, Officer Walters is going to take you to Unit Two, Aurora."

"Okay, thanks," Aurora commented.

"You are very welcome, Aurora. That's is my job—to make sure every girl who passes through here gets the help she needs," Mr. Sanchez answered. He picked up the radio that was on his desk. "Officer Walters, my office please. Transit Bennett to Unit Two."

"10-4," Officer Walters confirmed. A few seconds later she opened the door and escorted Aurora to Unit Two via a series of hallways covered with inspirational quotes. The one that caught Aurora's eye was the one that read, "Find the courage in yourself to change." They continued down the hall until they stood outside a cell. Opening the locked cell door, Officer Walters said, "Here is your home away from home, Bennett. I suggest you make the best of it."

Taking a deep breath, Aurora hobbled slowly into the cell. She jumped as she heard the metal door close and lock behind her. She felt like she couldn't breathe. It was like all the air had been pulled out of the room, and for a moment, she thought the walls would close in on her. She looked around the small cell as she tried to pull herself together. There was a bed with a thin mattress on one side, and a tan plastic desk with a neon orange plastic chair on the other; and there was a metal toilet and sink in the back corner of her room.

"Bennett!" someone yelled behind her. Aurora quickly turned around and saw a guard standing at the cell door. She was surprised to see a male guard on duty. Maybe they needed someone who was stronger for the really bad offenders in this unit. Is that why Ms. Davis had placed her here? *Of course she would*, Aurora thought bitterly.

The tall, muscle-bound guard opened the cell door and walked in, introducing himself in a surprisingly soft, but deep voice. "I'm Officer Edwards. Here are the linens for the bed." He handed her a sheet, pillow, and blanket. "If there is any kind of emergency, you can call me or any other guard on duty by ringing the alarm button in your cell." Officer Edwards pointed to a red button near the door. "We have twelve-hour shifts, and switch off at 6 a.m. with the wake-up call. I'll be leaving now to give you some privacy to settle in."

"Thank you, sir," Aurora answered quietly, taking the bedding from him and trying to keep her hands from shaking. She watched as Officer Edwards walked out of the cell, closing the door behind him.

She dropped her stuff on the desk and sat on the bed. "Oh God, please help me," she said aloud in a whisper, and took a deep breath. "I don't know what to do." She laid down on the bed and closed her eyes, holding back the tears and trying not to cry. "Please help me, God."

Chapter 6
Friday, March 8th

"Ms. Davis, I understand your concern, but my answer is still no." Sirius spoke into his phone, pacing around the island in his large, Tuscany-style kitchen.

"With all due respect, Mr. Marino, I don't think you fully understand my concerns," Ms. Davis said in a condescending tone. "Aurora has been nothing but trouble for every foster family who has tried to start the adoption process. Your notion to adopt her is admirable. It really is; but mark my words—you will throw her back into the system in less than a month, which might do more damage to her than if you didn't go through with the adoption at all. That child is uncontrollable!"

"That is your opinion, Ms. Davis," Sirius replied, gritting his teeth to stop himself from saying what he really thought of her professional opinion.

"I just wish you would listen to reason. She is only going to hold you back!"

"*Ne dubito.* I doubt that," Sirius answered.

"Who do you think would hire you in Hollywood when you have to drag around an uncontrollable teenage misfit?"

"And what do you mean by that?" Sirius questioned.

"That girl is going to need constant supervision. As her legal guardian—trust me when I say this—you can't just be going off to make your movies and leaving her at home by herself. If you don't keep a close eye on her, she is going to do nothing but cause problems!" Ms. Davis explained.

"Again, that is your opinion. I don't believe that she will cause any problem for me. If anything, she will make my life better," Sirius said. He heard a loud bang on the other end of the call, which nearly made him drop his own phone.

"You are making a huge mistake!"

"*Non credo*. I don't believe I am, Ms. Davis. I have listened to what you have to say because you are her social worker," Sirius answered. "I assure you that I will *not* be backing out, and there is absolutely nothing you can say to change my mind."

"You are as insufferable as that brat is," Ms. Davis grumbled under her breath.

"*Cosa*? What was that?" Sirius asked sternly.

"Mr. Marino," Ms. Davis said, with a change in tone, and completely ignoring his question. "I really don't understand why you are even considering adopting her. I honestly don't."

"Really?" Sirius questioned. "I'm surprised to hear that. Here I thought I mentioned it many times." He shook his head.

"Sirius, may I call you Sirius?" Ms. Davis asked.

"You already do on occasion." Sirius sighed.

"Well, Sirius, the thing is—you are well-liked within Hollywood as well as in the European film industry," Ms. Davis explained. "I did some background research on you this past week, and I found you to be admired by fans all over the world, as well as recognized for your work with many humanitarian organizations. You are a young actor with such a promising future. You could be one of Hollywood's most established performers."

"Could you please get to the point?"

"Of course. With that being said, there is no reason for you to adopt Aurora—especially for publicity."

"You really think that I'm doing this as a publicity stunt?" Sirius questioned, his hands whirling in the air with frustration.

"What other reason could there be?" Ms. Davis scoffed.

"Ms. Davis, could it possibly be because I actually care for Aurora's well-being?"

"Her well-being is fine, now that she is at the juvenile detention center!" Ms. Davis said snappily. "The only concern you should have is her destructive behavior patterns."

"Perhaps, her behavior will change when she is in a better environment."

"Well, I see I'm not going to change your mind any time soon," Ms. Davis grumbled.

"That is correct," Sirius confirmed. *Why can't this woman just believe that I don't have an ulterior motive?*

"Sirius, you are quite young to become a father to a teenager," Ms. Davis continued like a broken record but changed her tune to a more disdainful tone.

"So?"

"Perhaps you're not fit to be a parent," Ms. Davis said coldly.

"Is that a threat!?" Sirius questioned angrily, with his hand gestures punctuating every word.

"Not at all. However, if I can't convince you not to make such a detrimental mistake, by adopting an unruly child such as Aurora, then maybe I have to take some drastic action."

"Then it is a threat," Sirius stated, trying to calm himself. *I will not let you get a rise out of me, Ms. Davis.*

"Oh, it's not a threat at all, Sirius—just an observation," Ms. Davis answered smugly. "Well then, that's all I have to say. I'll let you know if I need anything else from you."

"I don't think you will," Sirius answered, fuming and furious that Ms. Davis showed Aurora, and now him, so little respect. "Ms. Davis, in the future, if you want to relay information to me, I think it would be better for you to go through my lawyer. I will send his information to you directly." There was a pause on the other end.

"Of course," he heard her say curtly.

"Have a nice day then, Ms. Davis." Ms. Davis disconnected the call before Sirius could say anything else. "It was nice talking to you too," Sirius said sarcastically, to no one in particular. "Oh, *è una cosa incredibile.*" Sirius sighed, running his hands through his shoulder-length hair.

"Were you talking to me, Sirius?" Sirius turned to face his aunt, who had just entered the kitchen to refill her empty morning-cup with espresso.

"No, Aunt Liv. I was only thinking out loud."

"Is everything alright?" she asked.

"Yes, everything is fine. Why?" He followed his aunt from the kitchen to the family room room, knowing she wouldn't be satisfied with the short answer, and would want a longer conversation to satisfy her concerns.

"You just seem to be distracted the past few days," Aunt Liv pointed out, sitting on one of his plush, black leather couches.

"I guess I have been distracted lately. This whole situation with Ms. Davis has been *pazzo*," Sirius admitted, starting to pace around the family room.

"*Pazzo*, huh?" Aunt Liz raised an eyebrow at her nephew's use of the Italian word meaning 'crazy.'

"Oh yes, very, very *pazzo*. If she keeps it up, she is going to drive me mad." Sirius sighed as he rubbed the back of his neck.

"I'm sure you will be able to handle whatever this woman throws your way," Aunt Liv said, picking up a stack of papers from the coffee table. "Sirius...you know you barely looked at the movie script your manager sent this past week." She tapped the stack of papers.

"I've been *molto* busy," Sirius answered.

"Oh darling, I know it was a role you so desperately wanted. Are you sure you want to turn it down?"

"Yes," Sirius answered, as he continued to pace around his family room. "This is more important. There will be other roles in the future."

"What did your manager Lucy say?" Liv asked.

"She wasn't thrilled about my decision, but she'll get over it," Sirius stated.

"Are you sure about that?"

"Yes, especially after I mentioned how easily I can find another manager."

"Oh, Sirius," she murmured. "Are you absolutely positive about all this?"

"*Sì*, I am, Auntie," Sirius said.

"As long as you've thought this out."

"And here I thought, you didn't like me working in Hollywood. Something about taking me away from the peace of our home and Italian paradise?" Sirius teased.

"You know I'm just looking out for you," Aunt Liv lectured, gesturing at him with her pointer finger.

"I believe what I'm doing is right, *zia*," Sirius stated. "As I said, there will be other roles."

"I understand, dear."

"What's frustrating me is something isn't right about the whole adoption process. I just have this bad feeling about it."

"That Ms. Davis isn't going to make it easy for you," Aunt Liv commented, as she was always extremely perceptive about personalities.

"No, she's not," Sirius agreed, sitting down on the black leather couch opposite to his aunt. *I wish I could let zia Liv meet Ms. Davis. That would be an interesting conversation,* he laughed to himself.

"What did she say when you were talking to her just now?"

"Nothing out of the ordinary—just how I'm a young actor with a bright future. She's implying that adopting Aurora is going to ruin my future with Hollywood."

"Well, you are young, considering you just turned thirty-four this past February, and you do have a promising future." Aunt Liv looked at him lovingly as well as concernedly. "Have you really thought this out?"

"Yes, Auntie, I have. You know that," Sirius stated. "I wouldn't have made it this far in life if it wasn't for you and Uncle Dario. You took a chance on me, and I feel like I am passing on the gift you gave me by taking a chance on Aurora."

"Very true, but I just hope you know what you are doing; teenage girls can be very difficult. Anyway, has Ms. Davis caused you any grief other than the pestering phone calls?"

"Nothing too bad. However, she did just say something about me not being a fit parent."

"No, she didn't?" Aunt Liv questioned.

"Yeah, if I wasn't worried before, I'm certainly worried now," Sirius thought out loud. "Now, the latest complication is that Aurora has to stay at the detention center longer than necessary."

"What changed?"

"Apparently, Aurora hid a bunch of wallets she stole in her locker at school. The janitor found them when he was cleaning it out, so now the juvenile court judge has sentenced her to stay at the center for sixty days before she's allowed to be adopted," Sirius stated.

"Sirius, she tried stealing from you before. Aren't you worried she's going to try to steal from you again and then take off?" Aunt Liv questioned, looking at him tenderly.

"No, I don't believe she did it," Sirius justified.

"But didn't they find the wallets in her locker?"

"They did, but she seems like a smart girl. She wouldn't have hidden them there if she stole them."

"But she did steal from you before," Aunt Liv said hesitantly. She didn't want to hurt her nephew's feelings, but she wanted to make sure he was looking at the reality of the whole situation.

"She did, but she returned it," Sirius answered, still adamant about defending his future daughter's character. *Maybe I will make a good father, despite what Ms. Davis thinks. I am already starting to think of Aurora as my future daughter.*

"Perhaps Aurora only returned your wallet because you threatened to call the police," Aunt Liv suggested.

"Perhaps, but Ms. Davis doesn't actually know how Aurora and I met," Sirius admitted.

"She doesn't?"

"No, Auntie, I may have failed to mention it to Ms. Davis on purpose."

"Why?"

"Because at the time, Aurora seemed to be in enough trouble."

"Okay, looking into the future, what if she does this again?"

"The last time I was a bystander; if it happens again, I will be her legal guardian," Sirius answered. "I'll make sure it doesn't happen again."

"Alright, I would just hope that Ms. Davis doesn't find out; she already has it out for Aurora."

"I can't argue with that. For some reason, Ms. Davis doesn't like her and is doing everything in her power to make her life absolutely miserable." Sirius sighed. "One thing Ms. Davis said was that Aurora would need professional help; she mentioned this the first time I spoke to her about Aurora. She didn't clarify it at the time. However, I received some of Aurora's information from her case file; Warden Mr. Sanchez was kind enough to send it to me, and there is nothing stated in there about needing professional help."

"Do you really think she would feed you lies to deter you from adopting Aurora?"

"It seems that's the case, and now she's threatening me. This is going to be *assurdo*," Sirius grumbled.

"What else is bothering you?"

"I don't think it's wise for her to be placed in the juvenile detention center; however, ever since I've talked to Warden Sanchez, I'm feeling much better about it. He explained a program that she can participate in, and I think it would be good for her," Sirius explained.

"Well, I'm glad you feel that way," Aunt Liv said as she stood up from the couch, and started walking back into the adjacent kitchen. "Tell me again, how long has Aurora been there?"

"It's been about a week since she got moved to the new unit," Sirius answered, his voice raised so his aunt could hear him from the kitchen.

"Okay. One week down, about seven more to go—if all things go according to plan," she said, walking back into the family room with a stack of books in her arms.

"So *zia*, are you really going to leave me without giving me more of your expert advice?" Sirius teased, seeing the stack of books in his aunt's arms.

"As a matter of fact, yes, I am. I think I've given you enough of an earful for today. However, I did get you these." She placed the books in his lap.

"Parenting help books?" He laughed as he read the covers.

"Yes, I thought it would be wise for you to research what you are getting yourself into," Aunt Liv explained, patting her nephew reassuringly on his shoulder.

"Thanks, *zia*," Sirius chuckled. "I know I can always count on your genius for everything." He held his aunt's hand and gave it a squeeze.

She really will be the best nonna ever for Aurora, Sirius thought to himself. *I can't wait until the two of them meet!*

"I'm your aunt, sweetheart. It's my job to give you advice." Aunt Liv briskly walked back into the kitchen and picked up her purse from the center island. "And another one of my jobs is to make sure your Uncle Dario doesn't burn down my kitchen. I've been away from home long enough."

"Yeah, that would be important, especially since I'm the one who did the majority of the work on the remodel. Don't let *zio* destroy it." Sirius laughed. He knew the real reason Aunt Liv was in a hurry to get back to his Uncle Dario—the two of them were still in love, even after so many years of marriage. *Maybe someday I will have a marriage like they do...and it would be a great for Aurora to have a mom.* Sirius shook himself back to the reality of Aunt Liv saying goodbye to him and leaving for the airport to catch her flight.

"Don't worry, I won't let your uncle burn down my beautiful kitchen," Aunt Liv responded playfully, laughing. She walked through the grandiose front door, as Sirius followed behind and collected her red Italian leather suitcases. She turned around and looked up at him. "And Sirius, please at least look through those parenting books."

"I will. *Promesso*," Sirius said, placing his right hand over his heart.

"Thank you." Aunt Liv walked to her car with Sirius right behind her. "Love you, dear," she said, watching Sirius load her suitcase into the trunk of her rental car.

"Love you too, *zietta*. Have a good flight," he said, giving her a hug and opening the car door for her. He then waved to her as she pulled out of the driveway. "This adoption is going to be an interesting process," he thought out loud, before walking back inside his California mansion.

(Friday, March 8th)

"Mrs. Hansen, Aurora Bennett is here to see you. Are you ready for her?" Officer Walters asked, escorting Aurora into the counselor's office.

"Yes, I am. Thank you, Officer Walters," Mrs. Hansen, a petite woman with auburn hair and a bright smile, replied. "Welcome to my office, Miss Bennett. Take a seat," she said, watching Aurora's movements closely while taking out a notepad and pen from her desk drawer. Aurora slowly sat down in the chair across from where she sat. "So, how was your first week here?"

"It was fine," Aurora answered, wary of Mrs. Hansen taking notes about her.

"Well, what made it fine? Did you make any friends?" Mrs. Hansen asked in a kind tone.

"You've got to be kidding…" Aurora scoffed under her breath. *How does she expect me to have friends in one week of juvenile detention?*

"As a matter of fact, I'm not," Mrs. Hansen replied.

"Does it matter if I made friends or not?"

"Well, Miss Bennett, making friends can have a positive impact on your life. Didn't you have friends at school?"

"Nope," she lied.

"I'm just curious; what was your relationship with the other students at Sawmill Middle School like?" Mrs. Hansen questioned.

"It was normal. I guess."

"Why would you describe it as normal?" Mrs. Hansen asked, writing Aurora's response on her notepad. She put her pen down, looked up, and waited patiently for Aurora's response.

"Um, I don't know," Aurora answered. "I passed kids in the halls, and I saw them in class. That's pretty much it—tried my best not to get shoved into a locker or thrown into a trash can."

"So you didn't have any friends, at all?" she questioned.

"No, I didn't," she lied again. She didn't want to mention Hunter, Ethan, or anything else about her life outside of the detention center. It was none of Mrs. Hansen's business.

"Well, it's always nice when you have friends you can count on; it can make life easier when you are going through hard times," Mrs. Hansen replied. "Let's talk about another topic: how would you describe your relationship with your previous foster parents?"

"Nothing worth mentioning," Aurora answered, nervous about the change in conversation.

"Why do you say that?" Mrs. Hansen asked, looking at Aurora somewhat concerned.

"They treated me like trash, and they didn't treat any of their other foster kids any better."

"Alright, how did that make you feel?"

"Are you seriously asking me that?" Aurora questioned, rolling her eyes. "How do you think it made me feel?"

"I don't know, Miss Bennett. I haven't been in your situation. Only you can tell me how you feel," Mrs. Hansen explained.

"I felt—well—like trash. They didn't care about me. All they cared about was the check they got from the government." She crossed her arms as she leaned back into the chair.

"I'm sorry about that, I truly am. I'm sure it didn't make life any easier." Mrs. Hansen jotted down another note on her paper. "Next topic: what do you want to share about your relationship with Ms. Davis? Is it any better than what you had with your foster parents?"

"Not really. She hates my guts," Aurora said quietly.

"Why do you say that? Has she ever given you reason to think she doesn't like you?"

"That's funny." Aurora snickered.

"Why?"

"Because all she does is treat me like trash," Aurora answered. "She has never said one nice word to me."

"Well, do you have any ideas of why she's so mean to you?" Mrs. Hansen asked.

"I don't know, and I don't care why," Aurora quickly looked down. *I don't want the counselor to know that I lied. I know exactly why Ms. Davis was mean to me. It was because I wouldn't be an obedient puppet.* "No one should be treated like that. It's wrong." Aurora tried desperately to hold back tears.

"I agree. I feel the same way," Mrs. Hansen replied. "So going back to the question I asked at the beginning of our conversation, how do you think your first week progressed?"

"And I already told you: it was fine."

"What about other than fine? Maybe use a more descriptive adjective," Mrs. Hansen suggested.

"Um, it was," Aurora paused, thinking of a good word to use, "irritating."

"Alright, that's different than your previous answer. Why would you describe it as irritating?" she questioned as she brushed a loose strand of hair into her tight bun.

"Those girls are so annoying," Aurora complained, rubbing her forehead with her hands, trying to soothe an oncoming headache. "They are constantly fighting and swearing at each other. No one can get any peace and quiet. I thought my foster families were bad; this is worse. There's way too much drama going on here."

"Didn't you have drama at home?"

"Probably, I just avoided it. And it wasn't my home."

"Then how would you describe it?" Mrs. Hansen asked.

"Not as a home, that's for sure; maybe a house of terrors," Aurora answered.

"Alright, is there anything you would like to talk about? A topic you want to discuss?"

"Nope," Aurora stated, standing up from her seat. "Can I go now?"

"Yes, you may," Mrs. Hansen replied.

"Thanks." Aurora turned to the door.

"Miss Bennett, I just want you to know my door is always open, so if you want or need to talk about anything, just let me know," Mrs. Hansen explained kindly.

"Why do you care?" Aurora asked, turning again to face Mrs. Hansen.

"Well, it's my job to care," Mrs. Hansen started explaining.

"So, you really don't care; it's just your stupid job!" Aurora stated loudly.

"That's not what I meant, Miss Bennett."

Aurora curled her hands into fists. "My name is Aurora, and that is exactly what you said. You get paid to sit in your office and listen to our drama. When it comes down to it, all you care about is your paycheck."

"Is that what you really think?" Mrs. Hansen asked, leaning back in her chair.

"Of course," Aurora declared. "Because that's all you people care about. It's always all about money."

"Miss Bennett, I'm sorry—I mean, Aurora, I'm sure you met a lot of people who do have that mindset. But let me tell you a secret," she whispered, only loud enough for Aurora to hear. "It's not money that makes the world go round. It's passion."

"So?" Aurora asked as she sat back down, now really curious to hear what she had to say.

"People do things according to their passion. For example, if someone has a passion for making money or obtaining power, they will do whatever it takes to get it. They won't care who it hurts or who they have to walk over to get it; they overlook compassion and humility," Mrs. Hansen explained.

"You pretty much described everyone I know," Aurora stated.

"Really? What about Mr. Marino?" Mrs. Hansen questioned.

"What about him?" Aurora asked cautiously, not knowing where the conversation was going. She put her elbows on the desk as she leaned forward.

"Well, he didn't seem to be like that type of person. From what I've heard about him, he seems to care very much about people. That's the other category of people—those whose passion is to put the needs of others before their own. They put all their energy in what is best for others, and some people are lucky enough to get paid for it. In other words, I care very much about you and all the girls here. My paycheck is just a bonus. Do you understand?"

"Sure," Aurora answered. "Mrs. Hansen, do you really think Mr. Marino cares about me?"

"Absolutely! Why would you think otherwise?"

"Ms. Davis said he doesn't really care about me, and the only reason he's considering adopting me is for publicity, but when I talked to him, he said he was concerned about me. He is trying to keep the adoption private."

"Ms. Davis said that to you?" Mrs. Hansen questioned, raising her pen to take notes again.

"Yeah," Aurora answered.

"I see. Well, from my knowledge, what Ms. Davis said is not true, and what Mr. Marino said is. In fact, there is no mention of his plans in the media. I do believe he is trying to keep the entire matter private," Mrs. Hansen explained.

"Really?" Aurora asked, her bright green eyes widening in shock.

"Yes, Aurora, really," Mrs. Hansen reassured her. "Now, are you sure there's nothing else you want to talk about today?"

"Maybe next time. Thank you, Mrs. Hansen," Aurora answered, as she got up from her seat.

"You are welcome, Aurora. Now go make good choices and maybe make some new friends."

"Whatever," Aurora said, walking out the door and closing it behind her. She walked down the hall, leading to the common room, as she thought about her conversation with the counselor.

"Hey, Aurora!" Sandra yelled from across the room, waving her arms to get Aurora's attention.

"Hi Sandra!" Aurora yelled back, waving as she quickly walked over to the couches, where Lexi and Sandra were sitting, gossiping away.

"How was your talk with the shrink?" Sandra asked.

"It was good. I guess," Aurora answered. She fell back on one of the couches.

"What did you two talk about?" Sandra asked.

"Sandra, their conversation is supposed to be confidential," Lexi said.

"True, but only if Aurora doesn't want to share. So what happened?" Sandra asked again.

"Nothing interesting," Aurora replied. "She just asked me stuff about my ex-foster parents and my social worker."

"What did you say?" Sandra asked.

"I told her the truth; my relationship with them was terrible, if you even want to call it a relationship. Didn't go into too much detail though," Aurora explained.

"Why not?" Lexi asked.

"Because it's not any of her business, that's why," Sandra declared loudly.

"You said it," Aurora agreed. "But it would be nice to tell someone—someone I can trust."

"That won't happen, like ever," Sandra stated. "You can't trust nobody."

"That's true. Well, that's why we have journals," Lexi said as she doodled in her notebook.

"I don't know. I don't feel comfortable doing that either. Journals can be stolen, and then nothing stays private," Aurora responded.

"That's also true," Sandra said, biting her left pinky nail nervously. "Anyway, you hear anything about your placement, Aurora?"

"Um, no, but it sounds like I might be placed with another family, or sent back to the Millers," Aurora distorted the truth, remembering what Mr. Marino had said about keeping the adoption to herself.

"Sorry about that. That really stinks," Lexi remarked.

"Hopefully, you'll get a good placement," Sandra said, her dark brown eyes showing genuine hopefulness.

"Yeah, that would be nice," Aurora answered.

"Serious question: if you could have *anyone* foster you, who would you want it to be?" Lexi asked, smiling widely.

"Umm, I don't know," Aurora responded. "I never really thought about it."

"I know who I'd want—maybe the President of the United States or the King of England," Sandra stated, using a British accent on the last few words.

"Why them?" Aurora asked.

"Because you would be rich and powerful. No one would mess with you if they were your guardians," Sandra explained. "It would be awesome!"

"I totally agree. It would be so awesome," Lexi said.

"Is that all you care about, being rich and powerful?" Aurora asked.

"No," Lexi stated. "I would also like to be popular."

"But would you be happy?" Aurora questioned.

"Who cares? I'd be rich," Sandra stated.

"What are you girls talking about?" Aurora, Sandra, and Lexi looked up to see a red-haired girl approaching the couches.

"Oh hi, Carmen, nothing interesting," Aurora answered, making space for Carmen to sit next to her.

"We were asking—if you could have anyone foster you, who would you want it to be?" Lexi commented.

"That's easy," Carmen expressed, grinning.

"Please don't say the President of the USA," Aurora responded, groaning playfully.

"No, I think it would be so cool to be fostered by a movie star," Carmen said.

"Like who?" Sandra asked.

"Mmm, like Felix Clarke or James Demm," Carmen answered.

"Why them?" Sandra asked.

"'Cause they're hot." Carmen laughed.

"Ohh, what about Sirius Marino? He is gorgeous!" Lexi swooned, fake-fainting on the couch.

"O-M-G, yes! Did you girls see him in that new movie?" Sandra squealed.

"Is that the only trait you guys can come up with? What about their other qualities?" Aurora interrupted, feeling uncomfortable about how they were talking about Mr. Marino. She didn't disagree that he was good-looking, but he might end up being her father. *This is so bizarre that he is the topic of our conversation, and he might be my future dad!*

"Who cares!" Carmen exclaimed. "We'd be rich, popular, and have incredibly hot fathers."

"That's not disturbing at all," Aurora teased. "I wouldn't care who I was placed with, just as long they were nice and actually cared about me."

"Aurora, you are nuts," Carmen said.

"Whatever, I'm going to go journal or something, so I'll talk to you girls later," Aurora announced.

"Okay, TTYL," Lexi and Sandra answered in unison.

"So what did you girls think of the movie?" Carmen asked. That was all Aurora heard before she was out of hearing distance. Aurora looked back at the girls before she disappeared down the hall, walking to her cell. "You girls are ridiculous," she mumbled to herself. She thought those girls were really annoying. *All they care about is being placed with someone who is rich, famous, good-looking, and powerful. They have no idea what they want,* Aurora thought. She wished she could tell them about Mr. Marino and how there seemed to be more to him than being rich and famous, but he had asked her to keep quiet about it. She knew she would have to respect his wishes. She was afraid he might change his mind just like Ms. Davis said he would. *This is a once in a lifetime opportunity for me to have a good life, and there is no way I am going to do anything to mess it up.*

Chapter 7
Monday, March 11th

"Good morning, Mr. Sanchez," Mrs. Hansen said as she opened the door to Warden Sanchez's office and poked her head inside.

"Mrs. Hansen, what can I do for you?" Mr. Sanchez asked, as he flipped through a stack of papers on his messy but somewhat organized desk.

"I need a couple of minutes to talk to you in person about a sensitive matter," Mrs. Hansen said, stepping into his office and closing the door behind her. "It's about Ms. Davis, the social worker who is assigned to Aurora Bennett's adoption case. Is now a good time?"

"Of course, what is on your mind?" Mr. Sanchez picked up his favorite NY Yankees mug containing his coffee and took a sip, looking attentively at Mrs. Hansen.

"I met with Aurora Bennett a few days ago for our first counseling session. She mentioned some problems connected with Ms. Davis, and I am really concerned," Mrs. Hansen explained, sitting down quickly in an arm chair opposite the desk.

"What did Aurora share with you?" Mr. Sanchez furrowed his thick eyebrows in concern.

"From what I could gather from our conversation, she doesn't get along with Ms. Davis and definitely doesn't trust her. Especially after Ms. Davis lied to her about the likelihood of Sirius Marino wanting to adopt her. Frankly, from the few times I have interacted with her, I've found her to be underhanded and abrupt. I feel that she acts one way toward the adolescents she works with and another toward the adults."

"To be honest, I feel the same way. Every time I have a conversation with that woman, something always seems off," Mr. Sanchez agreed. "I have dealt with many social workers over the last twenty years who are very professional and love the kids they are trying to help, but when it comes to Ms. Davis, I don't feel the same way."

"Perhaps it's your dad senses kicking in," Mrs. Hansen teased.

"Probably," he laughed. "Do you have any ideas on how to handle this situation?"

"I'm not quite sure. It would be so much easier if Aurora would open up to me. Then I would know how to handle the situation better. Right now, we just need to assure Aurora that she can trust us, and that she is in a safe place so she will feel comfortable enough to tell us whatever we need to know about Ms. Davis," Mrs. Hansen explained. "Until then, you may want to touch base with Mr. Marino and make sure you are both on the same page. It would be good to hear what he has to say about his own experiences with Ms. Davis. We wouldn't want him to be given false information that would deter him from continuing with the adoption."

"Do you think Ms. Davis would actually go that far?" Mr. Sanchez raised his eyebrows and took another sip of his black coffee.

"I really hope not; however, when I think about it, my experience tells me to say yes. I honestly think she might. She seems to be feeding Aurora lies, as well as playing mind games. It's as if she has some sort of ulterior motive against Aurora's adoption going through," Mrs. Hansen said, frowning.

"I agree with you there. Has Aurora questioned the adoption at all?"

"She has," Mrs. Hansen replied. "She mentioned Ms. Davis's name many times during that conversation."

"Alright then, I'll give Mr. Marino a call and see what he has to say. He is adamant about going through with the adoption process, and I doubt he will be deterred by any of Ms. Davis's dishonest comments."

"I agree, and he seems to be rising to the challenge of becoming an adoptive father to Aurora," Mrs. Hansen added.

"Good, he'll need that outlook. Especially after everything is finalized, he will probably get a lot of attitude from the press and crazy fans, as well as Aurora herself. She is certainly her own person and refuses to let anyone get in her way." Mr. Sanchez chuckled.

"That's an accurate way to describe her." Mrs. Hansen smiled.

"Agreed," Mr. Sanchez said. "Anyway, let me know if you have any more concerns. In the meantime, I'm going to give Mr. Marino a call."

"Now?" Mrs. Hansen asked, looking at her watch. "It's only 6:30 a.m. in California right now. Do you think he is even awake at this hour?"

"Well, there's no time like the present to discover the answer to that question." Mr. Sanchez laughed, picking up the phone and dialing the number.

"That's true, and good luck," Mrs. Hansen said, as she walked to the door.

"Thanks, I'll probably need it," he responded, glancing at Mrs. Hansen briefly before she closed his office door. "Hello, Mr. Marino," he said into his office phone. "This is Warden Sanchez from the Turning Point Juvenile Detention Center."

"Yes, hello, Mr. Sanchez. I'm almost afraid to ask—is everything alright?" Mr. Sirius Marino asked, sounding like he had just woken up. "Has something happened?"

"No, everything is fine; there is no need to worry."

"Good, I was worried that Aurora may have gotten herself into trouble, or Ms. Davis was causing some more issues," Sirius stated.

"Nothing like that. Behavior wise, Aurora has been doing fine, and as for Ms. Davis, there's nothing out of the ordinary."

"That's good to hear. I was somewhat concerned when I got your call this early in the morning, especially since you mentioned I probably wouldn't be hearing from you unless there was a problem," Sirius explained, stifling a yawn.

"Well, I hope you have some peace of mind now," Mr. Sanchez said.

"I do, but I have a feeling this was not the reason for your call."

"It wasn't. I did want to talk to you about Ms. Davis."

"Oh no, what about her?" Sirius asked.

"Has Ms. Davis said anything concerning to you?"

"You mean about Aurora?" Sirius questioned.

"Yes," he responded.

"Not a lot. In the beginning of the adoption process, she told me about Aurora's bad track record with behavior. I honestly think she was trying to discourage me from adopting Aurora, but I wasn't going to let that bother me," Sirius explained.

"Well, I've had some concerns about Ms. Davis, and now I know what I suspected was true."

"Well, I'm glad I was able to give you some clarity," Sirius replied. "Since I have you on the phone, I have some concerns of my own I wanted to speak with you about. Ms. Davis did not seem to be the right person to ask about this topic. Did Aurora say anything about her previous foster parents?"

"No, not that I am aware of. Why?"

"When I talked to her at the precinct, she mentioned some negative things about how she was being treated, and it was disturbing. To be honest, that's one of the reasons why I decided to adopt her. No child should have to go through any kind of abuse."

"I see. From my knowledge, she has said some things to one of our counselors here, but she was light on the details. However, it has brought up some concerns about whether or not Ms. Davis has been placing children in good homes," Mr. Sanchez explained. "Anyway, I'm glad you stepped in on this particular case when you did—the change from foster care to adoption will be good for Aurora, no matter what previous trauma she's experienced."

"I am glad I made this choice too. As I said earlier, no child should have to go through such things. I do have to ask one more question concerning Aurora's well-being. When Aurora was brought in, did she have a physical at all?"

"Yes, she did. We make sure all of the girls have an intake physical at this facility. Why do you ask?"

"The last time I saw her, I caught a glimpse of some bruises on her neck and upper back," Sirius explained.

"Did you?" Warden Sanchez asked, concernedly. "I wasn't aware of that."

"You weren't?"

"No, I wasn't. I'm surprised that I wasn't notified. I'll have to take a look at her records to confirm," Mr. Sanchez said.

"I'm surprised too that you didn't get some kind of note from the doctor about Aurora's bruises. They were very visible when her hair was not hiding them."

"It is standard procedure to be informed, especially as the warden; it's actually mandated by the State of New York child protection laws. Someone either failed to notify me, or there has been some sort of mix up with her records. I will look into this today," Mr. Sanchez stated. "Thank you again for letting me know about this, Mr. Marino. I appreciate you saying something."

"No problem. Is there anything else we need to discuss, then?"

"No, that is all. Thanks for your help."

"You are welcome. Just please continue to keep me updated, especially when you find out about this incident or anything else regarding Ms. Davis. Also, please let me know when would be a good time for me to visit Aurora. I know you said you were going to figure out a way to keep us out of sight."

"I will keep you updated, and I do have an idea of how to arrange a private visit soon," Mr. Sanchez replied cordially. "I will just have to talk to some of our best guards that I know I can trust to keep the meeting confidential. I'll let you know what day the visit can occur once I've spoken with them."

"Alright, sounds good. I just hope I'm not followed at all," Sirius chuckled.

"Do you think the paparazzi would really try that?" Mr. Sanchez questioned.

"Absolutely! They follow us everywhere, trying to get whatever photos or information they can. Some of the fans are just as bad, and I swear social media is making it worse. People are informed of where celebrities are in just one click of a button."

"That's unbelievable," Sanchez replied.

"That it is!" Sirius laughed.

"How do you think Aurora will feel about the paparazzi?" Mr. Sanchez asked, drinking the last sip of his morning coffee.

"I don't know. Honestly, I haven't thought about that too much. I guess we will find out soon enough whenever we have our first encounter with them," Sirius answered.

"I suppose you're right. Well, next on my agenda is a chat with the nurse, so I am going to let you go. Have a great day, Sirius."

"Thanks, I've gotta run too. *Ciao!*" Sirius replied.

"Bye," Warden Sanchez said, hanging up the phone. He quickly stood up from his desk and exited his office, closing the door behind himself. Sanchez strode briskly down the hall until he made it to the doctor's office. "Dr. Deleon!" he declared.

"Mr. Sanchez, what can I do for you?" Dr. Deleon jumped as the Warden barged into the room without knocking.

"I need to look at Miss Aurora Bennett's chart, immediately," Mr. Sanchez answered, looking intensely at Dr. Deleon. She wore her usual white coat and stethoscope around her neck.

"Of course, is there a problem?" Dr. Deleon questioned, thinking it was rare to see Mr. Sanchez this upset over an inmate's intake chart.

"Yes, there seems to be an inconsistency in her records."

"Oh, I see. Well, let me look for the digital copy," she answered in a reassuring tone. With a few clicks of her keyboard, she brought up the chart, and turned around her computer screen so that Mr. Sanchez could view it.

"Dr. Deleon, I see there is no record of any bruises or scars," Mr. Sanchez remarked, sounding even more alarmed.

She turned the computer around, so that she could see the records for herself. Looking at him strangely, she responded, "Yes, that's correct. It seems that Aurora was overall considered healthy, except for a slight limp when she was taken into custody."

"Are you positive that *all* of the data was entered correctly?" Mr. Sanchez questioned, looking at Dr. Deleon intensely.

"From my knowledge, yes," Dr. Deleon answered. Her dark brown eyes confirmed the honesty of her answer.

"Okay, one more question then. Were you the one who did the entry exam?"

"No, it was actually Dr. Morton. I had that day off."

"Are you positive?" Mr. Sanchez asked harshly, his eyes narrowing.

"Absolutely positive. That was the day I went to my sister's baby shower. I left that Friday and didn't come back into the office until Wednesday," she explained. "Why do you ask?"

"Dr. Deleon, your name is on the chart as the confirming doctor to do the intake exam," Mr. Sanchez answered, and pointed at the part of the screen showing her printed name.

"What?!" she exclaimed in disbelief, looking at the records. "How did I miss that?"

"Can you explain?"

"Mr. Sanchez, that's not right. There is no reason my name should be on the chart." She looked over the chart again. "Well, that's odd."

"What is?"

"If anyone else is present for the examination, a social worker prints and signs her name, so we know that she was there. However, the comment section is empty."

Now Mr. Sanchez knew something wasn't right. "Was Ms. Davis present?"

"I don't know. Her name is not written down, but that doesn't mean she wasn't there." Dr. Deleon looked up at Mr. Sanchez, still in disbelief about Aurora's intake exam form.

"Do you know when Dr. Morton will be in again?"

"I'm not sure. She asked Dr. Ashton to come in for her the last few days. She said she had a family emergency."

"Alright, then, can you please call her and let her know that when she comes in next, I want to see her in my office ASAP," Mr. Sanchez said.

"Of course! This is a very unusual situation; I also want to know what is going on with this exam." Dr. Deleon gestured towards the exam, still pulled up on her computer screen.

"One more thing, Dr. Deleon—I am going to have Miss Bennett come by today for another physical examination."

"Okay...may I ask why, since this would be her second exam within a few weeks?"

"I was recently notified that Aurora had some bruises and scars on her neck and back when she came in, but those details were not put in her case file or on the medical intake form. I want to be sure everything is documented correctly," he explained.

"Alright, I will make a note of that then. Should I contact Ms. Davis as her case worker?"

"No, I think it would be a good idea to keep her out of the loop for now. Sirius Marino will eventually be her guardian, and he is the only one I want notified of any findings or updates about Aurora."

"I understand completely," she said.

"Thank you, Dr. Deleon. I appreciate it," Mr. Sanchez said as he left the doctor's office.

"Warden Sanchez," Officer Walters' voice crackled through his radio.

"Yes, what is it?" Mr. Sanchez knew that tone in Officer Walters' voice. This didn't sound good.

"You need to come to the rec yard, ASAP!"

"Alright, I'm on my way. What's the problem?" Mr. Sanchez questioned as he walked swiftly to get to the recreation yard.

"It would be better if I told you the details when you get here. Let's just say some of our girls have made some *poor* choices just now," Officer Walters' tone was borderline sarcastic, and Mr. Sanchez could tell she was about to lose her cool.

"Be there in a minute! Over," Mr. Sanchez pressed the release button on his radio. As he jogged outside a minute later, he saw Aurora Bennett, Lexi Anderson, and Carmen Shaw sitting on the grass with two of the male guards keeping them separated, and Officer Walters standing with her hands on her hips and scowling at all three of them. She did not look happy at all.

"What happened, Officer Walters?" Mr. Sanchez asked. He inwardly groaned, dreading the thought of having to call Mr. Marino back the same day to notify him of Aurora's possible misbehavior.

"We're trying to figure that out now, Warden. We already brought Amy Corina and Myra Alit to solitary confinement for fighting. These three girls stopped immediately; we had them stay here so they could explain exactly what happened," Officer Walters explained in an irritated tone. Hopefully, he could get to the bottom of this quickly, to see who started the fight.

"Alright," Mr. Sanchez said, using his best disciplinarian tone, and turning to face the girls. "What happened, girls? This is your one and *only* chance to tell me the truth before I go look at the cameras. And the cameras don't lie. Understand?"

"Yes, Warden Sanchez," the three said in unison, sounding nervous. It seemed that none of them had been in any serious trouble at the center before today, so they didn't know what to expect as punishment for being in a fight.

"It was Amy who started it!" Lexi stated loudly.

"Okay, so Amy started the fight. What was this fight about?" Mr. Sanchez questioned, taking out his pocket-sized notepad and pen. He scratched Amy's name on the paper and wrote 'instigator' next to it, as he listened to Lexi continue to explain.

"So Amy went off on Myra 'cause Amy was telling us that she suspected Myra of stealing her letters that she got from her family. Amy overheard her and started cussing her out! When Amy tried to walk away, Myra grabbed her from behind and started hitting her in the face!" Lexi explained.

"Okay, but how did you, Aurora, and Carmen become involved?" Mr. Sanchez asked pointing at the three girls in turn. "Uh...ladies? Anyone care to tell me before I go have a look at the cameras?" he asked, when no one spoke up.

Finally, Carmen started talking in a raspy and strained voice, "Well...Lexi and I were trying to pull Myra off of Amy who was screaming for help. Then Aurora was trying to help Amy get away to save her face, which was getting beat on pretty bad, since the guards didn't see what was goin' on right away. We were only trying to help!"

"That's when the guards ran out and separated us," Aurora helpfully added, biting her short pinky fingernail nervously. Mr. Sanchez noted that her green eyes held no trace of a lie in them. *This might be a record for three girls in a unit all giving the same story*, Mr. Sanchez thought to himself.

"So, you are telling me that you three were only being good Samaritans?" Mr. Sanchez asked, looking at each of them in turn.

"Yes, Mr. Sanchez," Aurora replied. "We were only trying to help Amy from getting beaten up until the guards got here."

"Alright," Mr. Sanchez answered, putting his notepad back into his pocket. "Officer Walters, would you please take Carmen and Lexi to solitary confinement, while I go look at the cameras to corroborate their story and make sure everything lines up?"

"Yes, sir," Officer Walters replied, as she walked over to the two girls. "Let's go, girls!"

"Solitary confinement?" Carmen questioned nervously, sounding close to tears. "But we didn't do anything wrong, Warden Sanchez! We were only trying to help."

"And what about Aurora? Why isn't she going to solitary confinement?" Lexi asked, slightly whining, and looking over at Aurora enviously.

"She has a meeting to attend. When she is done, she will also be taken to solitary confinement," Mr. Sanchez answered, as he watched Officer Walters march the two girls inside toward solitary confinement.

"Aurora, come with me please," Mr. Sanchez said to Aurora.

"Yes, Warden Sanchez," Aurora responded, getting up shakily from the ground and following him into the center. She looked around trying to figure out where he was taking her. She fidgeted with her hands. "Um, Mr. Sanchez, where are we going?" she asked softly.

"Right here," Mr. Sanchez said, stopping in front of the doctor's office. He knocked on the door before entering this time. "Dr. Deleon, Aurora is here to see you," he announced.

"Oh, so soon?" she asked, looking surprised, but smiling reassuringly in Aurora's direction.

"Yes," Mr. Sanchez answered, gesturing for Aurora to enter the office and have a seat on the examining table behind the half-closed, dark blue curtain.

Dr. Deleon rose slowly from her swivel chair and offered a hand shake to Aurora who awkwardly squeezed the doctor's soft hand. "Hello, Miss Bennett, I'm Dr. Deleon. It's a pleasure to finally meet you."

"Hello, Dr. Deleon," Aurora said to her. "Uh, Warden Sanchez, why am I here?" Aurora asked. She hugged herself trying to prevent herself from fidgeting.

"Well, there were some errors in your chart, so I thought we should correct them," Warden Sanchez said to Aurora.

"Is Ms. Davis coming?" Aurora questioned.

"No, she is not," Mr. Sanchez answered.

"Aurora, was Ms. Davis present at your intake physical?" Dr. Deleon asked kindly.

"Yes, ma'am," Aurora responded, sounding anxious.

"Did she say anything to the doctor during your physical?" Mr. Sanchez asked.

"Uh, I'm not sure. I mean," Aurora paused, taking a deep breath. "I don't remember."

"Very well. Then I leave you in Dr. Deleon's capable hands. Doctor, when you are done, call Officer Walters to come get her please."

"Okay, will do," Dr. Deleon answered, adjusting her stethoscope to prepare for the exam.

"Aurora, please be cooperative for Dr. Deleon," Mr. Sanchez said.

"Yes, sir," Aurora replied, watching him as he left her alone with the doctor, yet another person she did not trust.

"Alright, Aurora, let's get you checked out. First, I need you to step on the scale," Dr. Deleon said, pointing to the scale in the corner of her office.

"Yes, ma'am," Aurora responded, hopping off of the table and stepping on the scale. She glanced at Dr. Deleon as she recorded her weight and measured her height.

"Okay, you weigh 89 pounds and 14 ounces, and you are 4 feet, 10 inches tall."

"Is that normal?" Aurora asked.

"Actually, there is no normal, since everyone grows at their own speed," Dr. Deleon responded, as she typed the information in her computer.

"Oh," Aurora stated. She continued to watch Dr. Deleon carefully as she recorded her blood pressure and heart rate; listened to her breathing; took her temperature; and checked her reflexes.

"Aurora, I need you to lift your shirt, so I can check your back," Dr. Deleon unexpectedly said.

"Why?" Aurora questioned, backing up slightly. *Please don't have a panic attack in front of this woman*, Aurora told herself.

"It is because there were some inconsistencies in your records, and we just need to redo your physical to make the correct changes in your chart," Dr. Deleon explained gently.

"But why do you need to see my back? Nothing is wrong with it," Aurora answered. "The doctor didn't check it before."

"That is why we need to take a look at it this time. I will just lift your shirt and take a quick look at your back and then you can pull your shirt right back down." Dr. Deleon looked reassuringly at Aurora with her dark, empathetic eyes.

"Whatever you say," Aurora muttered, slowly pulling up her shirt. She heard Dr. Deleon gasp.

"Aurora, what happened?" Dr. Deleon asked, as she looked over Aurora's back quickly. Faint white-lined scars crisscrossed down her back with newer red-lined scars overlapping them. "How did you get these?" Dr. Deleon placed a hand on Aurora's shoulder, lightly tracing her fingers over some of the newer looking scars, making Aurora shudder.

"Please don't ask me that!" Aurora choked back a sob.

"Aurora, you can lower your shirt now. I've seen what I need to see. However, I can't help you unless you talk to me," Dr. Deleon said, walking around the examining table to face Aurora. "Please, tell me who did this to you. How did you get these scars?"

"I-I can't say," Aurora responded, trying not to cry, but she couldn't stop a tear from running down her face. She wanted to be strong, but she was exhausted from the lies and the abuse itself. She was tired of the walls she had to keep up, the walls that protected her from getting hurt. *But I can't tell Dr. Deleon the truth! If Ms. Davis finds out that I talked about the abusive foster homes she had placed me in, I'm dead.*

"Was it your foster parents?" Dr. Deleon watched Aurora as she wiped a tear from her pale face with the back of her hand. She offered Aurora a tissue from her desk.

"Are we done?" Aurora questioned, quickly blowing her nose and composing herself—not feeling ready to trust someone she had just met.

"Yes, we can be," Dr. Deleon answered solemnly. She picked up her radio from its charger. "Officer Walters, can you come and get Aurora please?" she asked.

"Coming right now," Officer Walters responded.

"She should be here soon," Dr. Deleon said to Aurora. "Are you sure that there is nothing you would like to talk about."

"Yes, ma'am," Aurora answered abruptly.

"Alright, I respect your decision, but if you ever want to talk about anything—anything at all—my door is always open for you." Dr. Deleon's voice sounded genuine and sympathetic.

"Thanks," Aurora said, glancing up at Dr. Deleon briefly.

"You are welcome," Dr. Deleon responded as she heard a knock on her door. "Come in!" she called out.

"Hi Doc, you all done in here?" Officer Walters questioned, walking into the doctor's office.

"Yes, we are," Dr. Deleon said, pulling the examining curtain back.

"Let's go, Aurora," Officer Walters said to her, nodding towards the door.

"Yes, ma'am." Aurora sighed as she followed Officer Walters out of the office and down the hall. They walked in silence as Aurora was led to the solitary confinement cells. As they approached an empty cell, Officer Walters unlocked the cell door, and Aurora walked in.

"Don't worry, Aurora. If you girls were telling the truth earlier, everything will be fine," Officer Walters said, looking at Aurora and smiling reassuringly. *She actually looks pretty when she smiles,* Aurora thought.

Aurora nodded her head in response, still not trusting her voice to break after the emotional exam. She shuddered at the sound of the cell door closing shut and locking as Officer Walters left her alone. Aurora sat on the cot in the far corner of the cell with tears streaming down her face. "God, please don't let me be alone longer than a day. I can't wait to get out of here," Aurora prayed out loud. She lay down on the cot and curled herself into a ball, hoping that the time spent here in this horrible place would go quickly.

Chapter 8

Tuesday, March 12th

"Mr. Sanchez!" Dr. Deleon called out as she knocked on the office door.

"Come in," he answered. He watched Dr. Deleon open the door and walk into his office with a handful of papers in her grasp. "How did everything go the other day?"

"As well as expected," she responded, placing the papers on his desk.

"What's this?"

"Well, first things first, I redid Aurora's physical and updated her chart," she replied, pointing to the stack of papers. She started to pace around the office. "It's a good thing I did."

"Did you find any scars or bruises like Mr. Marino mentioned?"

"I didn't find any bruises. If she did have any, they must have faded during her time here. She did have scars though; a lot of them running all along her back. Some of them are old, but many are newer. I would guess she received those scars right before she was arrested," she explained. "Also, Aurora's height and weight were wrong. On the chart, it showed what they should be according to standard Body Mass Index for her age, but she is actually underweight. I believe it's from malnutrition. Also, Mr. Sanchez, there are many physical and emotional signs of severe abuse and neglect."

"She does seem small for her age. Hopefully, now that she is in a better environment, she will improve."

"Her physical health will definitely improve; I just hope her mental health and her attitude will as well. Someone with a past like hers will have more than just physical scars; she will have mental ones as well. Those won't heal easily." Dr. Deleon sighed sadly.

"What did Aurora have to say about the scars?" Mr. Sanchez asked, taking notes as Dr. Deleon continued.

"Nothing. She refused to talk about it. I personally think she is afraid to talk about the abuse. I don't know if it's because of Ms. Davis or someone else, but she is afraid of something or someone." Dr. Deleon lowered herself wearily into a chair across from Mr. Sanchez.

"Alright, I'm going to have Mrs. Hansen talk to her, just to check up on her. Perhaps Aurora will feel more comfortable talking to her counselor, since she's had a few sessions with her already."

"I hope so. If she was abused in any of the foster homes she was placed in, that would need to be reported."

"I agree. Those families should not be fostering children if that is the case," Mr. Sanchez answered adamantly.

"Also, this whole ordeal shows that Ms. Davis may have had something to do with Aurora's physical chart being altered," Dr. Deleon said.

"It does look that way. The question is—why?" Mr. Sanchez added, as he dropped the papers back on his desk. "Why would she do something that could jeopardize her career as well as having the possibility of being prosecuted, and potentially even imprisoned for hiding abuse or neglect cases?"

"I can't even imagine why someone would do something so horrible, especially since she is trusted to have the child's best interest in mind." Dr. Deleon furrowed her eyebrows concernedly. "Do you really think Aurora will talk to Mrs. Hansen?"

"I can't say. Let's hope she will," Mr. Sanchez answered, picking up his desk phone and dialing an extension to the counselor's office. "Hello, Mrs. Hansen? Can you please come to my office as soon as possible?"

"Umm, sure, I'll be down there in a bit. I just need to finish up some paperwork," Mrs. Hansen's voice crackled over the speaker.

"Mrs. Hansen, it's about Aurora, and it's important," Mr. Sanchez said, watching Dr. Deleon as she pushed herself up from the office chair.

"In that case, I'm coming right now, Mr. Sanchez. Be there momentarily."

Mr. Sanchez hung up the phone. "Doctor, could you please stay?"

"Sure, but why?" Dr. Deleon asked, turning around from the exit she was making out of his office.

"Well, I think it would be good to have you both here for this discussion. This way we will all be informed as to what is going on, and it will give us the opportunity to put our heads together and make a plan for Aurora's advancement," Mr. Sanchez explained.

"That makes sense," Dr. Deleon said, seating herself again and adjusting her crisp white doctor's coat. "But have you thought about if Aurora doesn't talk to her either? She became pretty clammed up in my office after the physical exam."

"If she doesn't feel comfortable talking to anyone here at the center, I'm hoping Aurora will talk to Mr. Marino."

"Do you really think she will talk to him if she refuses to talk to everyone else?" Dr. Deleon glanced at her supervisor skeptically.

"I hope so, especially since he is going to be her father, but only time will tell." Mr. Sanchez sighed as he tapped his fingers against his desk.

"What's wrong? I haven't seen you this upset in a long time," Dr. Deleon asked, leaning forward in the chair opposite him.

"It's just this Ms. Davis."

"Her name does seem to come up a lot in discussions."

"Yes, a little too much and for the wrong reasons."

"What are you thinking?"

"It's just that Ms. Davis has been trying to deter Mr. Marino from adopting Aurora, and that doesn't make sense to me. According to Sirius, she is apparently trying to tarnish his name. I heard from him today, and he said he received a demand letter from Ms. Davis last week, saying that he is unfit as a parent and should drop the adoption." Mr. Sanchez shook his head in disgust.

"Are you serious? What happened?"

"He doesn't know, but he had his lawyer reply. I have a feeling Ms. Davis is not going to like it."

"What do you think she'll do?" Dr. Delean asked.

"Well, in the letter, Ms. Davis said that she would take him to court if he didn't comply."

"Oh my, Mr. Marino is trying to do such a good deed by adopting Aurora, and now he has to deal with going to court because Ms. Davis is stirring up trouble." Dr. Deleon sighed. "She is taking some odd risks. If Mr. Marino was approved as a legal guardian, why wouldn't

Ms. Davis just let it go? After approval, he could take Aurora home as soon as her sentence is up, which is in a few weeks."

"You're right about that. I just don't understand why Ms. Davis is going to all these lengths," Mr. Sanchez declared, shaking his head.

"Mr. Sanchez," Mrs. Hansen said, opening the office door and poking her head inside, glancing at Dr. Deleon.

"Welcome to our crisis conference, Mrs. Hansen." Mr. Sanchez motioned for Mrs. Hansen to enter his office.

"What's so important that I needed to come here right away?" Mrs. Hansen questioned, closing the door behind her discreetly. "Is Aurora alright?"

"Yes, she is for now; but to be completely honest, I really don't know how to answer that," Mr. Sanchez answered, looking over at Dr. Deleon meaningfully.

"Well, I'm going to need more information than that," Mrs. Hansen said, taking a seat in an empty chair next to Dr. Deleon, and pulling out her notepad and pen to take notes. "What's going on?" she asked, glancing over her reading glasses from Mr. Sanchez to Dr. Deleon.

"Mrs. Hansen, Mr. Sanchez asked me to reevaluate Aurora's physical, because we found some inconsistencies in her original medical chart," Dr. Deleon began.

"What kind of inconsistencies?" Mrs. Hansen asked, glancing up at Dr. Deleon briefly.

"When I did her physical, I discovered that her weight and height were recorded incorrectly. I also found some nasty scars on her back that were not recorded at all."

"That's terrible." Mrs. Hansen paused uncomfortably. "However, I'm curious to know why you needed to redo Aurora's physical exam? Why weren't they noted in the original exam, and what brought it to your attention?"

"It was actually Mr. Marino who tipped us off," Mr. Sanchez interjected.

"Oh wow, how was he aware of it?" Mrs. Hansen questioned.

"Apparently, when he and Aurora first met, he noticed bruises and scars on her upper back," Mr. Sanchez responded.

"Good thing he notified you," Mrs. Hansen answered. "But what I still don't understand is why her chart was wrong in the first place. Who did the initial exam?"

"We are not positive, but we believe Ms. Davis had Dr. Morton put down false information on the initial intake exam," Dr. Deleon said.

"Why would Ms. Davis or Dr. Morton do something like that?" Mrs. Hansen questioned, looking shocked. "Something like that could ruin their careers."

"That's been the recurring question," Mr. Sanchez replied.

"Mrs. Hansen, before I talk to Dr. Morton, would you be able to talk to Aurora?" Mr. Sanchez asked. "She refused to talk about the abuse with Dr. Deleon. If she was hurt in any of the foster homes she lived in, we need to know as soon as possible. Maybe she will open up to you."

"I'll try my best, but Aurora isn't the greatest when it comes to opening up. She keeps herself very guarded," Mrs. Hansen said, closing her notebook.

"Also, I don't want Aurora to know that I asked you to talk to her," Mr. Sanchez added.

"Oh, of course," Mrs. Hansen answered, removing her reading glasses.

"And Mrs. Hansen—please try to talk to her as soon as you can," Mr. Sanchez said.

"No problem. In fact, I have time now, so I think I'll go see how Aurora is doing," Mrs. Hansen replied.

"Sounds like a plan," Dr. Deleon said, rising and exiting the office to return to her own office.

"I'll be waiting to hear what happens," Mr. Sanchez called out as both women walked down the hall.

Mrs. Hansen walked slowly down the hall; glancing at her watch, she saw it was ten o' clock in the morning. "Hmm...Aurora is probably in the common room for break," Mrs. Hansen thought out loud to herself. She spotted Aurora sitting on the floor with her back against the wall, writing in her journal. "Hello Aurora," Mrs. Hansen said loudly, making Aurora jump in surprise. "Oh my goodness, I am sorry—did I scare you?"

"Umm, no," Aurora replied as Mrs. Hansen walked toward her.

"I see you are writing in your journal. Writing anything interesting?"

"Nope," Aurora snapped. "What do you want?" Glaring at Mrs. Hansen, she slammed her journal shut.

"Nothing in particular—just wanted to see how you are doing," Mrs. Hansen said, smiling kindly.

"I'm fine," Aurora answered.

"Okay, how about an answer that has more syllables?"

"I'm as good as I can be considering the circumstances. That good enough?" Aurora asked, as she opened up her journal and started to write again.

"Okay then," Mrs. Hansen said.

"If that's all you wanted, then I'll just get back to my journaling now."

"Aurora, that attitude of yours is going to get you into trouble someday—in here and out there," Mrs. Hansen gently scolded her.

"Why are you really here?" Aurora questioned, looking up at Mrs. Hansen again. "If Mr. Sanchez sent you, I really don't want to hear it."

"What do you mean?" Mrs. Hansen asked, seating herself on a couch opposite of the wall where Aurora sat with her knees tightly pressed against her chest.

"You don't usually come to the common room, unless Mr. Sanchez or Dr. Deleon sends you to talk to someone. It's not a coincidence that you are here to talk to me."

"Well, then what happened to make you think that?"

"I know you didn't come down here, 'cause you have nothing else to do," Aurora pointed out. "You are too busy, and my life is not that interesting."

"Alright, you got me on one account," Mrs. Hansen confessed, chuckling and putting her hands up in mock surrender. "Mr. Sanchez and Dr. Deleon did tell me about your physical exam yesterday, but it was my choice to come down here right now and see how you are doing. Are you okay?"

"I'm fine," Aurora replied quickly, hugging her knees even tighter.

"Do you want to tell me what happened?" Mrs. Hansen questioned, looking directly into Aurora's green eyes.

"Not really," Aurora responded.

"Are you sure, Aurora?" Mrs. Hansen compassionately put a reassuring hand on Aurora's shoulder.

"Don't you already know what happened?" Aurora mumbled.

"Well, I would rather hear it from you and get your perspective."

"I don't want to talk about it." Aurora shrugged Mrs. Hansen's hand off her shoulder.

"Aurora, please—" Mrs. Hansen started.

"There's nothing to talk about!" Aurora snapped as she grabbed her journal and got up quickly. "Just leave me alone!"

Aurora ran away from Mrs. Hansen and the common room into one of the adjacent classrooms. Sitting at one of the tables, she opened her journal and continued to write. "Why won't everyone just mind their own business?" Aurora asked out loud to no one in particular.

"Because I think they enjoy driving us nuts," Aurora heard Lexi call out.

"Hey, Lexi, what's up?" Aurora said, turning to face her friend.

"Annoyed, like you," Lexi answered, seating herself backwards in the chair across from Aurora.

"Good to know. Should I even ask why?" Aurora questioned.

"Sure, you can; I just won't tell you," Lexi responded, her eyes twinkling mischievously.

"Okay," Aurora shrugged, picking up her pen again to write in her journal.

"*But*—I'll only tell if *you* do," Lexi said, getting Aurora's attention back.

"That's fair." Aurora laughed. "But you have to go first."

"Okay, fine." Lexi leaned in closer and looked around conspicuously before whispering, "Mr. Sanchez wanted to talk to me about my placement for after I get out of here."

"What's so annoying about that?" Aurora whispered back.

"My father doesn't want me back home. Something about refusing to let me in the house. From what it sounds like, I'm going to be sent to live with my mother."

"Is that a bad thing?" Aurora asked, bewildered.

"Umm, yeah, it's a terrible thing. My mother is a crack-head. I'm surprised she isn't living on the streets by now," Lexi answered, sounding riled.

"Sorry about that," Aurora replied with a compassionate look.

"It's whatever." Lexi sighed, taking a deep breath. "My mother got hooked on it when I was a baby. My father tried to help her, but she ended up leaving us. The last time I saw her was when she packed her bags and walked out, all the while screaming at my dad saying how terrible he was."

"Wasn't he trying to help her though?" Aurora asked.

"He was, but she didn't see it that way."

"That really stinks that it didn't work out between your parents. I'm really sorry, Lexi," Aurora said. "But if your mom is still doing drugs, why would you be placed with her?"

"I don't know. Why do they do what they do? Just like placing you in terrible homes where they used you as a punching bag," Lexi declared sarcastically, tossing her black hair over her shoulder.

"I know—it's the whole stupid system. Maybe your dad will let you come back," Aurora suggested hopefully.

"I doubt it," Lexi griped.

"What if you ask Warden Sanchez for help? Maybe he can convince your dad to take you back, especially if he knows where you'll be sent if he doesn't," Aurora suggested.

"It's worth a shot," Lexi agreed.

"It can't make things any worse."

"True. So why are *you* annoyed? Now that I just spilled, like, my entire life story to you, you have to tell me every single detail," Lexi said, changing the subject.

"Alright, alright, a deal's a deal." Aurora smiled faintly. "Mrs. Hansen and Mr. Sanchez are just bugging me for details about my previous homes."

"Why are they doing that?" Lexi scoffed.

"They want me to talk about the abuse. I don't really understand why—it's not gonna change what already happened." Aurora sighed, drawing circles on her journal cover with her finger.

"As I said, it's what they do—stir up trouble, and of course, we are the ones who end up suffering," Lexi said, shifting her position to sit cross-legged on the chair.

"That's true. And if any of the families found out I ratted on them, they would make my life even more miserable," Aurora remarked, shivering at the thought. "Who knows what they would say just to get back at me?"

"Okay, change of topic needed, you're sounding way too spooked right now. What have you heard about your placement? Are you getting sent to a group home?" Lexi asked, starting to braid her long hair.

"I'm—umm—not sure," Aurora said, knowing that she couldn't say anything about being adopted by Mr. Marino. "They didn't say."

"That's weird. They usually would have your placement figured out by now, unless that witch Ms. Davis is going to let you rot in here."

"That's what I'm afraid of," Aurora replied. *This is getting really hard to keep quiet about the adoption. I wish I could tell one person, but I promised Mr. Marino I wouldn't. I can't break his trust.*

"Anyway, I'm gonna find Sandra, see if she wants to play a board game or something," Lexi said, breaking into Aurora's internal conversation. "You coming or what?"

"Umm, sure! Sounds like fun," Aurora answered, standing up and following Lexi back into the common room. *God, please let me get out of here soon,* Aurora prayed desperately. She didn't know how much more teen prison she could take.

(Thursday, March 14ᵗʰ)

"Hey, Sirius." Sirius heard someone call out to him at the Expresso Café. He looked around, curious who was calling out his name for the whole café to hear, when a hand roughly clasped his shoulder. Sirius quickly turned around to see who was invading his personal space, and chuckled. "Thought that was you, Felix." He stood up and shook his best friend's hand before sitting back down at his table.

"Wow, I've only been your best friend for the last ten years, and that's the greeting I get," Felix joked, punching his best friend playfully on the shoulder and laughing out loud.

"Man, it's good to see you! How are you doing?"

"I'm doing well. Getting ready for an audition for the show *Thieves of the West*," Felix answered. "So, what are you doing in the Big Apple again? I thought that movie premiere was a few weeks ago."

"Yeah, uh—the movie premiere went well. You might even say it was life-changing in some ways. Anyway, I flew back to my home in Cali for a couple of days to meet with my manager and see Aunt Liv, who came to visit. I had to fly back yesterday evening, since I have some personal business to take care of," Sirius answered, a little hesitantly. *Eventually, I will share the news with Felix about Aurora's adoption. I wouldn't want him to hear about this from the tabloids, but also, I don't want to get into it in such a public place.*

"Gotcha. So, you waiting for someone?" Felix asked, grabbing a nearby chair and carrying it effortlessly to Sirius' corner table. Felix thought that it was a little odd that Sirius was immaculately dressed in a full suit today; since he knew what Sirius did in crowded cafes to avoid being recognized. He would get a corner table, wear a baseball cap and sunglasses, and try not attract too much attention; so, he assumed that maybe Sirius had an important business meeting.

"*No, no*, not meeting anyone. Just thought I'd get out of the hotel room, grab a decent cup of espresso, and try to clear my head," Sirius answered, as Felix sat down across from him. "Why do you ask?" *Hopefully Felix doesn't ask too many questions, not today.*

"Well, you don't usually dress so formal unless you have a reason. Dude, what's up with the tie?" Felix teased, pointing out Sirius' navy suit and silver tie.

"Nothing, just trying to blend into the whole NYC businessman look instead of my usual disguise. So, change of topic—what are you doing here today?" Sirius asked, hoping Felix would drop the subject.

"Waiting on my fiancée," Felix responded, grinning and taking the last sip of Sirius' espresso without permission.

"Aha, I see," Sirius answered, laughing at his friend's antics. "*Ciao,* Bridgette!" Sirius called out, seeing Felix's long-time girlfriend and now fiancée walk up to the table behind Felix. She was indeed gorgeous; and with her height, she could easily have chosen modeling as a career. Sirius always poked fun that Felix had to find a girl who was taller than him to lower his huge ego.

"Hi Sirius! Long time, no see," Bridgette said cheerfully, as she approached them in her designer dress and matching shoes. "There you are, honey; I thought I lost you!" Bridgette placed her coffee and croissants on the table.

"Nope, right here, and enjoying every minute more now that you are here, Java Love," Felix answered.

"Oh, stop it!" Bridgette laughed, as Felix pulled up an empty chair for her. She looked over the table at her fiancé's best friend whom she hadn't seen in months. "How are you, Sirius?"

"I'm well, how are you, *bella*?" Sirius grinned at the cute couple across from him. *I am so happy that Felix found the love of his life. Bridgette is definitely the right choice to keep my crazy best friend out of trouble.*

Bridgette's soprano voice pulled him back to the conversation. "I'm well—just trying to get this guy to actually help me with the planning of our wedding. It's right around the corner, and I want everything to be perfect," Bridgette said as she bit into her chocolate croissant.

"Well, that's easier said than done," Sirius laughed. "Sorry, Felix."

"Hey, can't argue with that." Felix chuckled.

"Do you have somewhere you need to be, or do you have time to catch up?" Bridgette asked, glancing curiously at Sirius' suit and tie.

"Sure, I have some time."

"What's been going on with you, Sirius? We haven't heard from you since we went to that party a few months ago."

"Has it been that long?" Sirius asked, shocked at himself for letting so much time go by without checking in on them.

"Yeah, and you know you don't call or text. I thought we were buds," Felix teased, with a fake hurt expression on his face.

"We are, *amico mio*," Sirius laughed. "I've just been dealing with a lot."

"Like what?" Bridgette asked.

"Oh, is it because of that girl?" Felix questioned, grinning slyly.

"Girl?" Sirius questioned, attempting to keep himself composed. He leaned back in his chair, concerned that Felix may have heard something about Aurora.

"You know? Sierra? That influencer girl you were seeing," Bridgette prompted his memory.

"Right, umm...no, it's not about Sierra. I actually haven't seen her since I took her to that new restaurant, Otium."

"And?" Felix added, stealing a bite of Bridgette's pastry.

"It was really good. I think it will be a very popular restaurant," Sirius replied, remembering the great European appetizers and main courses.

"Well...I wasn't talking about the restaurant," Felix laughed deviously. "I was referring to Sierra."

"Felix, really?" Bridgette asked, slapping Felix's arm gently. "Sirius, you don't need to answer that." She looked apologetically at Sirius.

"It's all good," Sirius responded, chuckling. "As for the date, it was okay, and Sierra was a great dinner partner. I mean, she's outgoing, beautiful, and smart—nothing not to like."

"So why haven't you asked her out again?" Felix asked.

"I've just had a lot on my mind," Sirius stated.

"Oh yeah, like what? What has got you so stressed out that you are not even calling your girlfriend?" Bridgette probed.

"I'm not stressed," Sirius declared, "and she's not my girlfriend!"

"Dude, you are definitely stressed out. You look like you haven't slept well in days," Felix said, sitting back in his chair and going for another bite of Bridgette's croissant.

"I'm not stressed! I just recently made a big life decision," Sirius explained. "I'm dealing with everything that comes with it."

"A big life decision, huh?" Bridgette asked, narrowing her eyes.

"Oh boy, what is it?" Felix questioned. "Are you trading in your Streetfighter for a more practical vehicle? Please just tell me you aren't getting a minivan!"

"No way would I ever get rid of my Streetfighter," Sirius laughed. "That's my baby—one of them, anyway."

"Good, I was worried for a second there," Felix said.

"Yeah, there's no need to worry about that." Sirius chuckled.

"So...spill, Sirius. What's this big life decision?" Bridgette questioned.

"It's better that I don't say," Sirius explained, looking directly at Felix and silently pleading for his friend to rescue him.

"Don't tell us you have a secret engagement," Bridgette teased.

"No, not at all, who would I even be engaged to?" Sirius laughed.

"I don't know. Maybe some mystery woman whose name is actually Sierra," Felix joked, not being helpful at all.

"No, there is no secret engagement!" Sirius answered, glaring at Felix.

"When did your life become so boring?"

"I assure you, Felix, my life has been anything but boring lately," Sirius answered, trying not to reveal anything about the adoption, but also trying to appease Felix and Bridgette's curiosity. *I can't wait until I'm able to fill them in on all the excitement. They are not going to believe it.*

"So, you're not getting a new vehicle, and there's no girlfriend," Felix stated matter-of-factly. He curiously raised his eyebrows, as he watched Sirius intently.

"Seems like you've covered all of the bases," Sirius answered, looking away from Felix briefly. He took his phone out of his pocket and started to reply to a text.

"Who's Mildred Davis?" Bridgette asked, peering over the table and seeing the name on the phone.

"Nosey much, sweetheart," Felix teased.

"I was just curious," Bridgette responded defensively. "Come on! Who is she, Sirius?"

"No one," Sirius answered dismissively.

"I take it back," Felix stated.

"Take what back?" Sirius asked, putting his phone back in his pocket.

"There is a girl." Felix smirked.

"No." Sirius cleared his throat, knowing he was losing the battle for secrecy with these two sleuths. "There's no girl that I'm interested in dating at this direct moment in my life."

"Then why you're dressed so nicely?" Bridgette asked.

"I have a business meeting," Sirius answered.

"Makes sense," Felix stated. "You heard him, Bridgette."

"Hold on, you can bug him but I can't?" Bridgette complained.

"Um, yeah, I'm his best bud; you're just my fiancée," Felix teased.

"Felix, be nice to her. As you said, she's your fiancée and soon to be wife; you know what will happen if you upset her," Sirius said teasingly, trying to redirect the focus of their conversation.

"On a serious note, is everything alright, Sirius?" Bridgette asked. "I mean is this personal, life-changing decision something we should be worried about?"

"Everything is fine, and there is nothing to worry about," Sirius confirmed.

"You don't have a serious health condition, right?" Bridgette questioned, concernedly.

"No, not at all, everything is good. It's a good life change," Sirius said.

"That's good to hear. Well, Bridgette, we should get going. I need to meet with my manager before my audition this weekend."

"Well, good luck, *amico mio*," Sirius replied.

"Hey, Sirius, we should get together when we are all back in L.A., maybe on Sunday," Bridgette suggested.

"Sounds like a plan," Sirius answered. He watched his friends stand up and leave the café. He wished he could tell them what is going on, but he had to think about Aurora. Aurora had been through so much, and he didn't want to cause her any more stress or anxiety. He decided it would be better to wait until Aurora was placed with him, so the process could proceed without any issues.

He looked out the front glass window as Felix and Bridgette headed down the road in the direction of the courthouse but walked right past it. Sirius continued to watch them as he followed behind, but stopped outside the courthouse. As he approached the entrance, he saw his lawyer standing outside waiting for him. "Jameson!" he called out. "It's good to see you, but I wish it was under better circumstances."

"Sirius, it's good to see you too, and if we always met under better circumstances, I would be out of a job," Jameson laughed.

"This is true," Sirius agreed.

"Should we go in and deal with this circus?" Jameson asked, gesturing Sirius to walk ahead.

"Yeah, ugh, hopefully, this will go well." Sirius groaned loudly as they walked into the courthouse.

"What are you so worried about, Mr. Marino?"

"Oh, Jameson, you really have no clue what Ms. Davis is like," Sirius stated as he fiddled with his tie.

"I think I have a pretty good idea. You did tell me all of the details, so this hearing should be easy," Jameson explained.

"That's what you think. There isn't supposed to be any hearings until the adoption finalization hearing—maybe conferences, but not hearings. Yet here we are," Sirius complained.

"Well, Ms. Davis did send you that demand letter, and considering this hearing, she did not like the reply you had me send. I don't doubt she's trying to put a stop to the adoption."

"I'm sure she is, since she's trying to paint me as unfit." Sirius sighed. "I'm about to hire a private detective; something isn't right here. I mean, why would she want to stop someone from adopting a child?"

"There's probably more to it than that."

"I'm sure there is, but none of this makes any sense. Jameson, any idea what information she has?"

"No, I don't, so we'll just have to be ready for anything."

"Oh, I am," Sirius declared.

"At least, they can't blame Aurora for anything, especially since they dropped the theft charges."

"That's only because the person who actually did it—the one who set Aurora up—came forward. He said something along the lines of being paid to do it, and the only way he's going to give names is if he gets a deal," Sirius explained. "I'm glad you had that checked out."

"Me too," Jameson agreed. "Perhaps he has a big rap sheet, or maybe he knows something about Ms. Davis and wants protection."

"That's a possibility. That woman is *una piantagrane*," Sirius said.

"Well, Mr. Marino, didn't your mother teach you not to call people crude names? It's not polite," Sirius heard a female voice behind him.

"Ms. Davis, *che piacere vederti*. How lovely to see you again," Sirius smirked, turning to face her. "And from my knowledge, neither is eavesdropping."

"Oh, I doubt that, Sirius, and it's not eavesdropping if you're discussing private matters in public," Ms. Davis sneered.

"No, I suppose not," Jameson said.

"Well, I'll see you two inside. I assume you don't want to keep the judge waiting, especially since you want this to go in your favor," Ms. Davis said, striding away from them to their assigned courtroom.

"Ms. Davis," Sirius called out. "What's it going to take for you to see that I'm doing this for Aurora's best interest?"

"Oh, I highly doubt that. The way I see it—here I have an irresponsible celebrity trying to adopt a child, for what? For some good publicity and to tug on some heartstrings," Ms. Davis stated. "It's my duty as a social worker to protect the kids in my care, especially Aurora. She's been through so much, and I don't think you adopting her will be good for her."

"Is that so?" Jameson questioned.

"Yes, of course. Your client is just unfit to be a parent, and I'm just doing my job. Isn't that right, Sirius?"

"It's Mr. Marino, Ms. Davis," Sirius said sternly. "What you're doing isn't protecting children. You're messing with their lives. From my knowledge, it's your job to make sure these kids are put in suitable homes and adopted by good families."

"I'll see you in front of the judge, gentlemen," Ms. Davis said quickly. Not wanting to draw any more attention to their soon-to-be heated conversation, she swiftly turned on her heels and walked away.

"Well, you were right," Jameson said.

"About what?" Sirius asked.

"That woman is *una piantagrane,*" Jameson said, shaking his head.

"She is a trouble-maker for sure," Sirius answered, before following his lawyer into the courtroom. Ms. Davis was starting to stir up trouble for no good reason, and it was starting to make Sirius angry. How could Ms. Davis stop someone from adopting one of the kids and rescuing them from the foster care system? It didn't make any sense to him. Hopefully, this would be the first step in putting a stop to her antics.

Chapter 9
Saturday, March 16th

THE SUN SHONE BRIGHTLY as Sirius walked over the warm sand, making his way to the water. Watching the choppy turquoise waves, he gripped his surfboard in his one hand and his towel and phone in the other. "*Ciao,* Felix!" he called out, as he saw his friend walking towards him at one of their favorite meet-up place: a quiet, California beach.

"Hey man, how's it going?" Felix asked, giving Sirius a high-five.

"Good—all is good. Great day to go surfing, *si è vero*?" Sirius grinned.

"Isn't that why you called me up this morning? To see who can catch a better wave?"

"Nah, we already know that," Sirius teased. "Bridgette is better than both of us combined!"

"Can't argue with that," Felix laughed. "So... tell me, bro—what's going on? You told me you would fill me in on why you've been so mysterious lately?" Felix and Sirius walked side by side towards the ocean, with the roar of the waves creating calming background noise to their conversation.

"I did, and I will. It's just—it's a private matter." Sirius looked over at his best friend with a serious expression. *I hope Felix and his loud mouth will really keep what I'm about to share confidential,* Sirius thought to himself.

"Since when have you not been an open book? Come on, Sirius, spill it." Felix elbowed Sirius hard in the side, almost knocking him over.

"Alright, alright!" Sirius answered, throwing his stuff down on the sand and sitting next to it. "Felix, you can't tell anyone."

"Sure, no problem."

"Felix, I'm serious. Until further notice, this stays between us. *Mi raccomando.*"

"Dude, you're starting to scare me. What's going on? Are you a witness to a crime or something?" Felix asked as he sat on his neon orange beach towel next to Sirius.

"No, nothing like that. As I said before, it's a personal matter, which doesn't just involve me. It's a sensitive situation."

"Okay, don't worry; I won't tell a soul. You know you can trust me, Sirius," Felix answered.

"Well, here's the thing," Sirius started, clasping his hands behind his head as he considered what to say for a long, quiet moment.

"So?" Felix asked, breaking the silence.

"Fine. I'm in the process of adopting a child from the foster care system in New York City," Sirius admitted.

"You? Adopting a kid!?" Felix questioned, his jaw dropping.

"*Sì,*" Sirius answered.

"Yeah right," Felix laughed. "That's a good one. Come on, Sirius, what's really happening?"

"I'm serious."

"No, you're not. Tell me you're joking. You are joking, right?"

"No, Felix, I'm not joking. I'm being 100% serious. I'm adopting a child—a young girl, actually."

"What? Why would you do that?" Felix questioned.

"I have my reasons."

"Such as?"

"Seriously, Felix? You know my past," Sirius stated.

"I do. If it wasn't for your aunt and uncle, who knows what would have happened to you? Especially after all that drama with your grandparents."

"Exactly, and this girl, Aurora, has nobody. Well, she has nobody who cares about her, except for me."

"Oh wow," Felix commented. "So, how did you even meet her? Is this something you planned?"

"No, it just happened; I met Aurora by chance. You could say it was an unlikely meeting." Sirius chuckled. "Actually, I met her after I confronted her."

"Hold on, you confronted her? Why did you have to do that?"

"Because she attempted to pickpocket me," Sirius mumbled under his breath.

"Say what?" Felix raised an eyebrow and leaned back on his beach towel.

"Aurora attempted to pickpocket me." Sirius leaned back and let the sunshine on his face for a moment before sitting upright again.

"Let me get this straight—this young girl pickpockets you; then you decide out of the blue to adopt her?"

"Not exactly, I caught her trying to pickpocket me, and I confronted her. I told her I wouldn't call the police if she returned my property, and she did. I honestly was curious to know why a thirteen-year-old was lurking around the streets of Manhattan after midnight," Sirius explained. "I was worried something might happen to her, so I followed her."

"You followed her home?"

"I would have if that's where she was going; but as I followed her down the street, I watched her climb over a fence into a public school's playground," Sirius paused, taking a deep breath. "I found out later that's where she was planning on crashing for the night. I was concerned for her safety, so I stuck around and watched until I must have fallen asleep. I woke up to a siren, and then saw an officer putting her into the back of her car. I ran over to find out what I could, and the officer told me to go to the precinct if I wanted more information."

"So, you just went to the precinct?" Felix looked at Sirius in disbelief.

"Yeah, when I got there, I asked some questions. I found out Aurora was a foster kid, and she was in a really bad situation. I talked with a detective, another officer, her social worker, and Aurora herself. From the sound of it, her foster parents were abusive, and her social worker isn't much better. That woman is—I don't know what to make of her. She hates her job and hates kids."

"Wow—dude, that's unreal," Felix cleared his throat uncomfortably.

"It is, and that's not even the craziest part. Aurora was going to be placed into a group home, but they were all full, so she was sent to juvie instead. I'm sure Ms. Davis—her social worker—would let her rot in there if she could." Sirius started digging a hole in the sand with his foot. *Wow, it feels good to be able to tell Felix what has been going on.*

"Juvie, as in jail for kids?" Felix asked. "That really is crazy, and so are you."

"I can't argue with that," Sirius laughed. "This whole situation is *assurda*."

"Are you sure you thought this out? Kids, especially teenagers, can be difficult and a lot of work."

"You make it sound like it's a bad thing?"

"I guess it depends on how you look at it. Do you really want to lose your freedom?"

"I'm not going to lose anything. I'm gaining a family," Sirius explained. "Right now, Aurora's needs are greater than mine. She needs family—a real home."

"I think she needs more than a family. She's going to need a therapist and counseling after being in jail and everything else you say she's been through. You sure you want to deal with her and her baggage for the next five years?" Felix questioned.

"You know family is forever, and not just until she turns eighteen, right?"

"Hey—I'm just saying. I know when you make up your mind, no one can change it; but don't say I didn't warn you."

"I don't think being Aurora's father is going to be as bad as you make it out to be," Sirius said.

"I hope you're right. She's going to be your ball and chain," Felix teased.

"Felix, you could be more—I don't know—supportive?"

"Nah, I need to get you prepared for raising a hormonal teenager."

"I'll remember that." Sirius laughed.

"Good, now let's get out there. Those waves are perfect!" Felix pointed to the sparkling ocean.

"Agreed," Sirius responded, as he and Felix stood up, grabbed their surfboards, and started to jog to the water. "*Chi è?*" he grumbled, as he heard his phone ring and walked back to his stuff.

"Yo, Sirius, what's the hold up?" Felix yelled, already at the water's edge.

"Nothing! Just a call I need to take," Sirius called back over his shoulder.

"Dude, let it go to voicemail," Felix hollered over the sound of the waves, as he was already waist-deep into the water.

"I can't! It's important," Sirius shouted back to his friend, hoping he would just enjoy the waves for them both until he could finish the call. "Hello?" he answered.

"Hi Sirius, this is Warden Sanchez."

"Hello Warden, how is everything?" Sirius asked.

"Everything is fine. I just wanted to give you an update concerning Aurora's physical."

"I see. How did it go?"

"Well, for starters, the information you gave us was accurate. Dr. Deleon found scars all along her back but no bruises; the doctor thinks that the bruises you saw have faded. She also found some inconsistencies in her original medical chart, especially concerning her height and weight," Mr. Sanchez explained.

"Wow, that's a lot. Uh, how did Aurora react when it was discovered?"

"She kind of shut down, and she got really quiet," Mr. Sanchez responded.

"Did she say anything about it?"

"She refused to talk about it; Dr. Deleon thinks she's scared of someone."

"Other than not wanting to talk about the situation, how has she been?" Sirius asked, concerned.

"Aurora has been doing well. There's been nothing out of the ordinary."

"That's good to hear," Sirius responded. "Has she been staying out of trouble?"

"Yeah, for the most part, I'd say so. She's making a few friends here, which is good for her too. I just wish she would feel more comfortable talking about her past."

"Well, I'm sure she will—with time—especially now that she knows she will be out of the system after juvie."

"I hope so, but she doesn't seem to trust anyone here, not even her friends."

"That's sad; I was hoping she would open up a bit to her peers." Sirius watched Felix catch a wave.

"Sirius, I was thinking maybe it would be a good time for you to come here. I'm curious if Aurora will open up to you; maybe you can discover something about her past."

"Yeah, that's a good idea. When would be a good time?" Sirius asked.

"The sooner the better," Mr. Sanchez responded. "I'll just have to figure out how to give you guys the privacy you need."

"That would be appreciated," Sirius answered.

"Well, I know you want to be as discreet as possible."

"I do, because I can guarantee that you don't want the paparazzi trespassing all over the grounds."

"You're right about that. That would cause more than just a little disturbance."

"Anyway, is there a day and time you were considering?" Sirius waved back at Felix, who was waving at him to join.

"That depends on your schedule. You can come during normal visiting hours; then you two could visit in my office. The only thing is—we would have to get you in here without being seen by any of the girls. The other option is coming early in the morning or in the evening during lockup. That might be the best option," Sanchez explained.

"How early?"

"Earliest would be 6:00. You would give you about an hour to visit, since breakfast is at 7:00."

"That should be fine," Sirius stated.

"Great, we'll plan on that. Hopefully you can get up early enough," Mr. Sanchez teased.

"That shouldn't be an issue. Getting up early is part of my normal routine, so it's all good."

"Now, the best day for you to come would be a Saturday or a Sunday. I hope that won't be a problem."

"No problem at all, I'll make it work. So would next Sunday the 24th be too soon?" Sirius questioned.

"No, that will be fine. As I said, the sooner the better. I'll email you all the details."

"Great, I'll be there bright and early," Sirius stated.

"Yes, and I will let Aurora know to expect you next Sunday."

"Alright, and can you give Aurora a message for me?"

"Sure thing."

"Just let Aurora know that I'm very much looking forward to seeing her on Sunday. I don't want her to think I'm visiting because I am obligated. I want her to realize that it's because I want to see her and spend time getting to know her," Sirius explained.

"Will do."

"Thanks, I'll be looking forward to your email and seeing you on Sunday. *Ciao*," Sirius replied, as he pressed the end call button on his phone before tossing it on his towel and running into the ocean, surfboard in hand.

"Hey, Sirius, it took you long enough," Felix stated loudly, having just caught a second wave to the shore. "So what did the kid do?"

"What do you mean?" Sirius asked, wading into the water.

"Well, I'm assuming the center would call you if she got herself into trouble or something."

"Warden Sanchez probably would, but she's fine. We were just planning a time for me to go there to see Aurora." He and Felix paddled out on their surfboards, bobbing over incoming wave ripples.

"Can't you go there and see her anytime you want?" Felix looked over at Sirius.

"I wish, but there are rules and guidelines you need to follow. Also, we want our visit to be very discreet. I don't want any of this getting out on social media, not until Aurora's adoption is finalized."

"Fine, I still think you're nuts. After this, you both are going to need a therapist," Felix announced.

"Thanks Felix, I know I can always count on you to be an optimist," Sirius joked.

"Hey, just refer to me as your life consultant—someone who tells you when you are doing something crazy and telling you the truth of how things are going to be," Felix explained. "Now, I don't know about you, but I'm gonna catch this incoming wave," Felix yelled, as he squatted on his board and waited to catch the wave to shore.

"I may be crazy, but I know it's the right thing to do. I will do what I believe is right and have faith in the ultimate good," Sirius chanted out loud to his friend who wasn't paying attention. "Hey, Felix, *aspettami*! Wait up!" Sirius yelled out to him, standing up on his board and catching the tail end of the wave. Riding his surfboard to shore, he continued to silently chant his mantra, knowing everything would turn out alright—or so he hoped.

(Monday, March 18ᵗʰ)

As Aurora sat in the classroom, she began to daydream about one of her horrible childhood memories.

"*Aurora, go back to your room! This is family time,*" Uncle Cain screamed at her.

"*I am family!*" Aurora yelled back.

"*No, you're not. You are my stupid little sister's mistake. Now, go to your room before I make you!*" Aunt Lyssa threatened.

"*Mom, can we watch the movie already?*" her cousin Molly complained.

"Of course, darling! Now go get the popcorn from the kitchen while I deal with your cousin," Aunt Lyssa smiled at her favorite daughter.

"Yes, Mother," Molly replied, skipping to the kitchen.

"Aurora, go to your room." Aunt Lyssa frowned.

"No, I want to watch the movie too. Please, Auntie," Aurora begged.

"Why is she still here?" Molly questioned as she returned to the living room.

"Don't worry, darling, I'm going to get rid of her," Aunt Lyssa answered.

"Get rid of me?"

"If you don't do as you are told, that is exactly what will happen. I'll give you to a family who actually wants you," Aunt Lyssa responded. "Now go!"

"Yes, Auntie," Aurora cried, as she started to walk toward the steps.

"Aurora, wait," Uncle Cain yelled, watching Aurora come to a halt and turn towards him. "Lyssa, honey, just let her watch the movie," he said to his wife.

"No, I will not give in to her tantrum," Aunt Lyssa complained.

"Honey, we'll deal with her tomorrow. For now, just leave her be. It's not worth ruining our peaceful evening over," Uncle Cain stated.

"And what's your idea of dealing with her? She may be a menace, but we can't exactly lock her in her room 'til she's eighteen," Aunt Lyssa replied.

"I'll tell you tomorrow," Uncle Cain said. "Aurora, you may stay here and watch the movie with us."

"Really?" Aurora asked, excitedly.

"Yes," Uncle Cain answered, as Aurora walked over to the couches and went to sit down.

"Who said you can sit with us!?" Aunt Lyssa shrieked.

"Uncle Cain said I can watch the movie," Aurora declared.

"He said you can watch the movie, not that you can sit with us. Go sit on the steps!" Aunt Lyssa ordered, grabbing her niece by the arm and dragging her towards the steps.

"I don't want to!" Aurora pulled back with all her strength.

"If you want to watch the movie, you sit on the steps," Aunt Lyssa replied in a menacing tone.

"But it's too far! I won't be able to see," Aurora complained, bursting into tears as her aunt threw her down on the first of the steps. She started getting back up when she heard her uncle's dead-cold voice, making her freeze in her movements.

"You will be able to see fine," Uncle Cain said. "You must sit on the steps if you want to watch the movie. If not, you will go to your room and go to bed." Her uncle gave her a look that sent chills all over her body.

"Fine," Aurora sniffled, covering her face with her hands, trying to hide her frustration and anger. She didn't want to lose the privilege of watching the movie altogether, but she knew if—

"Aurora! Aurora!" Mrs. Sterling yelled, pulling Aurora back to the present from her childhood memory.

"Yes, ma'am," Aurora answered, jerking her head towards the teacher, who looked at her expectantly.

"Aurora, pay attention, Now, can you tell the class who said the famous words: 'Give me liberty, or give me death'?"

"Doubt she can." Aurora heard someone behind her snicker. Mrs. Sterling pursed her bright red lips and frowned at the offending student.

"Patrick Henry," Aurora answered confidently.

"Excellent," her teacher praised Aurora, smiling at her from the front of the classroom. "That's all for today, class. Be sure to study for your test on Wednesday. Enjoy the rest of your day!" Mrs. Sterling opened the classroom door, signaling the end of social studies class. As usual, she waited at the door to say goodbye to all her students before the door closed and classes were finished for the day.

"Finally!" Aurora heard Sandra declare. "Hey, Aurora, you ready for the test?" Sandra bounced over to her desk, where Aurora was still sitting.

Aurora looked up at Sandra, who was doing a little hip-hop dance. "Sandra, please explain to me—why are you so excited?"

"School is done for today!" Sandra finished her happy dance with a pose of hands in the air and a spin. "I'll be so glad when summer is here! There will be no school, and I should be released by then."

"Good for you," Aurora mumbled, rising from her desk and collecting her social books to bring them back to her cell to study for the test.

"Girl, what's your problem?" Sandra asked.

"Uh, it's nothing." Aurora walked past Mrs. Sterling with Sandra right behind her.

"I don't get a goodbye, Mrs. Sterling?" Mrs. Sterling asked the two friends in mock offense as they walked past her, rolling their eyes. "Have a nice afternoon, girls! Stay out of trouble, and don't forget to study for the test!"

"Bye, Miz Sterling," Sandra called over her shoulder, poking Aurora in the side to respond.

Aurora said the obligatory, "Goodbye, Mrs. Sterling!"

Sandra wrapped her arm around Aurora's shoulder as soon as they turned the hallway corner to head back to the common room. "Liar! It ain't nothing! You are so moody today. What's up? You were hardly paying attention in classes, and you actually like school."

"I was just daydreaming, I guess. It felt more like a nightmare though." Aurora and Sandra entered the common room, which was packed full of girls already who had also finished their final classes for the week.

"Okay, details. What was the nightmare daydream thing about?" Sandra questioned, sitting down next to Aurora on the only empty couch in the common room.

"It was about my past." Aurora sighed quietly. "It was when I stayed with my aunt and uncle."

Sandra raised her eyebrows in surprise. "You never said you had family, 'Ora! I thought you were an orphan—like a real orphan—and that's why you were in the system."

"They aren't my family, not anymore. They lost that right when they threw me on the streets," Aurora shakily said. *"I can't believe how it still feels like yesterday; I just can't seem to get over this part of my past."*

"Really? Why? What happened?" Sandra looked at her friend compassionately.

"I really don't know why. The night before they wanted to watch a movie, and they refused to let me watch it with them. They made a big deal out of it, and then all of a sudden, my uncle changed his mind. It was so strange." Aurora took a deep breath, trying not to cry. "The next day, he told me to grab my stuff and to get in his car." Aurora paused for a moment, closing her eyes.

"Why did he do that?" Sandra questioned, prompting her to continue.

"I didn't understand at the time—I just knew it was bad," Aurora explained in a raspy voice, looking at Sandra with tears in her eyes. "We were in the car for a long time; it felt like hours. We came up to this church, and then he yelled at me to get out of the car. I got out, and he just drove off, leaving me there on the street."

"Wait a sec—he just, like, straight up abandoned you? That's crazy." Her brown eyes opened even wider than before.

"Yeah, he did," Aurora said, wiping away her tears with the palms of her hands. "I was so scared. I—I didn't know what to do."

"How old were you?" Sandra's normally loud voice sounded softer than usual, as if she was trying to give Aurora some kind of comfort.

"Eight years—" Aurora started to answer.

"Sandra!" The girls heard a voice shout above the commotion of the common room right behind them.

"Counselor Hansen," Aurora said, standing up quickly to turn around and face the counselor, who was missing her normal energetic smile. "What are you doing here?"

"I work here," Mrs. Hansen answered, chuckling.

"She meant here in the common room. Shouldn't you be in your office?" Sandra questioned curiously, as she stood up next to Aurora.

"Well, I actually came here to talk to you, Sandra. You missed our counseling session this past Friday," Mrs. Hansen said, crossing her arms and staring Sandra down in disappointment.

"Oh, my bad," Sandra responded, twirling a curl around her finger.

Mrs. Hansen shook her head at Sandra's teenage antics and looked at Aurora. "Before I take Sandra with me for her make-up session, I have to be honest—Aurora, I overheard some of your story of what happened with your uncle. Why have you never said anything about that in our counseling sessions?"

"Because it's none of your business," Aurora snapped.

"Well, you know I can try to help you with whatever you are feeling if you would just talk to me," Mrs. Hansen said.

"Help me? Why does everyone think I need help? I don't need to be fixed!" Aurora looked at her counselor boldly.

"The stuff you have been through—" Mrs. Hansen paused. "Aurora, I don't want it to tear you down anymore."

"The stuff I have been through has made me stronger. When will everyone get it through their heads? I'm not broken, so stop trying to convince me that I am!" Aurora insisted.

"We will talk about this another time, Aurora. Now is not the place or time. Also, a little word from the wise: if you don't want people to overhear your conversations, I suggest you don't talk so loudly." Mrs. Hansen scolded, as she turned to leave the room. She called back over her shoulder, "Sandra! We need to have our chat today, or I will have to mark down that you missed. Don't forget our meetings are mandatory." Mrs. Hansen kept walking, assuming Sandra would most likely follow.

"Yeah, I know," Sandra whined as she followed Mrs. Hansen. "See ya later, 'Ora!"

"See you later," Aurora responded, a little annoyed after Mrs. Hansen's comment about talking more quietly. She watched Sandra scurry out of the room and breathed a prayer that her friend's meeting would go well. The counseling sessions were never fun, and they didn't seem to make a difference. "Please God, have everything work out for me," Aurora prayed quietly to herself, for what seemed like the millionth time. She certainly hoped her future with Sirius Marino would be better than the last five years of her life.

Chapter 10

Sunday, March 24th

"Good morning, Sirius! Welcome to Turning Point Juvenile Detention Center," Warden Sanchez greeted him discreetly at the back entrance of the facility. The center reminded Sirius of a stronghold, with cold-gray, concrete walls enclosed by a high barbed-wire fence; he had no idea what to expect, other than Aurora's descriptions over the phone.

"*Buongiorno*! Thank you, it's good to finally get here," Sirius responded, giving the warden a warm handshake and a brief smile from beneath his dark baseball cap and tinted sunglasses. He had tucked his shoulder-length curls into a man bun and hidden them under the cap for extra protection against being recognized.

"How was your flight?" Warden Sanchez unlocked the heavy metal door with a key code, and motioned Sirius to enter ahead of him.

"It went as well as expected," Sirius answered, waiting for the warden to close the door behind them.

"That's good. Well, I'm glad you were able to make it out here today, especially this early in the morning."

"Me too," Sirius agreed, as he removed his sunglasses but kept his cap on, just in case an uninformed guard walked by.

"I think it will be very good for Aurora to see you here today," Warden Sanchez said, positively. "She's in the common room. I figured that would be the best place for you two to chat, since it will be more comfortable than in the smaller visitation room."

"Sounds good, please lead the way," Sirius commented, eager to see his future daughter. "How has she been this past week?"

"She's been doing well; mostly staying out of trouble, getting her school work done on time," Mr. Sanchez responded as he and Sirius walked through the back corridor and down a few other hallways, until they reached the front reception desk.

"Hello, Warden Sanchez," Ms. Jacobs, a short, middle-aged receptionist greeted him cordially.

"Hi Ms. Jacobs, this is Sirius Marino. Can you help him get signed in?"

"Oh, of course, anything for one of my favorite celebrities," Ms. Jacobs replied enthusiastically.

"Thank you." Sirius smiled, seeing that she was more than a little starstruck at the mention of his name.

"Sirius, I will leave you in Ms. Jacob's capable hands. She'll show you what you need to do and what papers you'll need to fill out," Mr. Sanchez explained. "Sorry for all the hassle, but I'm sure you know that there is a process to visitation."

"It's no problem, and I realized that when I saw the long list of what-to-do and what-not-to-do when I registered online." Sirius laughed.

"Glad you are up to date on everything," Mr. Sanchez responded.

"Me too! It will make the process quicker," Ms. Jacobs agreed, and gathered the needed forms to give to Sirius.

"Then I'll leave you to it," Mr. Sanchez responded. "Sirius, I'm going to go talk to Aurora really quickly, just to make sure she's okay. I'll see you in the common room."

"Alright," Mr. Sanchez heard Sirius answer, as he walked through the doors to the hall leading to the common room. Warden Sanchez saw Aurora reading in her usual spot, sitting on the floor along the back wall.

"Good morning, Aurora," Mr. Sanchez called out, walking up to Aurora.

Aurora looked up from her book. "Good morning, Warden Sanchez."

"How are you feeling?" He looked at her kindly.

"Is that referring to my health, or how I feel about today's visit?" Aurora asked, trying not to sound as annoyed as she felt. She was excited for her visit with Sirius, but that didn't mean she wanted to discuss her feelings with anyone other than God or her journal.

"I guess both," Mr. Sanchez answered, chuckling at Aurora's spunk.

"I'm good." Aurora cleared her throat and got up to sit on one of the common room couches.

"Are you nervous?" Mr. Sanchez asked, taking a seat opposite from her.

"No," Aurora responded, twiddling with her book cover.

"Okay, good, and I do want you to know that everything will be fine," Mr. Sanchez tried to sound reassuring.

"I hope you're right," Aurora said under her breath.

"*Buongiorno,*" Aurora heard Sirius call out, and looked up to see him enter the common room.

"Sirius, how did the check-in process go?" Mr. Sanchez asked.

"Kind of tedious, but fine. I don't think I've ever been patted down before." Sirius laughed uncomfortably. "That was interesting."

"Not even at the airport?" Mr. Sanchez asked.

"No, never," Sirius said.

"You have to be patted down at the airport?" Aurora questioned, looking from Sirius to the Warden and back to Sirius.

"Sometimes people do. Most times, TSA has people go through metal detectors," Mr. Sanchez answered.

"What's TSA?" Aurora continued.

"It's the airport security," Sirius responded.

"Why is there so much security?" Aurora asked.

"Well, I'm sure Sirius here can answer whatever questions you may have about that, seeing how he flies all the time," Mr. Sanchez said. "In the meantime, enjoy your visit."

"*Grazie*, we will," Sirius answered as he and Aurora watched Warden Sanchez leave. "So, Aurora, it's really good to see you again."

"It's good to see you too," Aurora replied, as she looked him up and down. He looked different from the last time she saw him. When she saw him at the precinct, he was dressed in a really nice dark purple suit. Today, he was dressed in comfortable clothes—dark jeans with a dark blue t-shirt and a baseball cap.

"What are you reading?" Sirius asked, sitting on the couch facing her.

"It's—um—the *Chronicles of Narnia: The Lion, The Witch, and the Wardrobe* by C.S. Lewis." Aurora held up the book so Sirius could see the faded cover.

"Good book! How do you like the story?" Sirius smiled, remembering when he had discovered the world of Narnia as a kid himself.

"It's great," Aurora answered, smiling faintly. "I wish I could escape to a world like Narnia, minus the White Witch."

"Yeah, that makes sense. How far did you get?" Sirius leaned forward, showing interest. He was glad to know his future daughter was a bookworm. *At least we have one other thing in common besides a rough start in life,* Sirius thought.

"Uh, I'm at the part at the Stone Table."

"Nice, you're getting to the epic part."

"Epic?"

"Yes, I would give you details, but I won't spoil it for you."

"Oh, okay," Aurora answered, closing the book and putting it to the side.

"So how have you been, Aurora?"

"I've been fine," Aurora replied but her striking green eyes said otherwise.

"Just fine? How's life in, well, the center?" Sirius asked.

"You mean jail, or juvie," Aurora said, laughing and breaking any last feelings of awkwardness surrounding the visit. "You can say it; you know—it's not a bad word."

"Alright, alright," Sirius laughed. "Let me rephrase: how's life in juvie?"

"Eh."

"Eh? Oh come on, what kind of answer is that?"

"I don't know," Aurora shrugged.

"Well, I don't think 'eh' is an actual word, so you got to give me something better than that. Like if you could sum up life here in one word—what is it?"

"Umm, boring," Aurora answered, saying the first word that popped into her head.

"Boring? Wow, really?"

"Yeah, it's the same thing every single day. I wake up, clean up my cell, go down to breakfast, have school, lunch, more school, down time, dinner, lockup, and then lights out. Boring is an understatement." Aurora rolled her eyes.

"That does sound quite monotonous," Sirius agreed empathetically.

"It's so, so incredibly dull. I can't wait to get out of here."

"Hopefully, you'll be able to get out soon."

"I'd better! Umm, I mean—I hope so too. I don't know how much longer I can stand being here."

"What's the first thing you want to do once you get out of here?" Sirius asked, trying to steer the conversation into a more positive direction.

"I don't know. I never thought about that."

"You haven't?"

"Nope, all I care about is getting out," Aurora stated.

"Well, that's something you may want to think about," Sirius advised, with a twinkle in his eye.

"Oh, okay," Aurora answered quietly. *Maybe Sirius is the real deal. He seems to be a kind and genuine person. Someone I can finally trust.*

"Tell me something," Sirius said, breaking the silence. He knew that they had limited time for their visit, and he wanted to learn as much about his future daughter as possible before he had to leave.

"What?" Aurora looked at him quizzically.

"Anything that you want me to know or anything you want to share."

"Like what?"

"Like what's your favorite thing to do?"

"Oh, um, I don't really have a favorite thing to do. I guess read," Aurora held up the book for emphasis.

"That's it? You didn't enjoy any sports or clubs when you went to school outside of juvie?"

"I wasn't really in the 'in-crowd,' so no, I wasn't part of any clubs. I did my best to avoid being used as a punching bag."

"You mean your fellow students? Why didn't you go to the head-master?" Sirius questioned with concern.

"Headmaster?"

"Sorry, I mean principal," Sirius corrected himself.

"Oh, okay. And I never told anyone, because he wouldn't have believed me; he never did. He always assumed I was the one to start anything related to trouble."

"Why would he do that?"

"I don't know. He always said, 'Not surprising behavior for a brat from the wrong side of the tracks.'"

"I'm sorry you were treated that way. It's rubbish."

"Rubbish? What does that mean?" Aurora asked, trying to figure out Sirius' accent.

"Umm, it depends. It can be referred to as a person who is worthless or useless, or it can mean something said that is untrue or nonsense. In this instance, I meant that this situation is complete nonsense," Sirius explained.

"That makes sense. But why didn't you say just what you meant? Like why do you talk like that?"

"Oh, Aurora." Sirius laughed. "I'm guessing you don't watch a lot of television."

"Not a lot, I...I was hardly ever allowed to. Why?"

"Have you heard of *The Con Artist* or *The Curse of Tragic Jack*?" Sirius asked.

"Yeah, you played in both. I remember watching *The Con Artist* with my dad. My mom was so mad he let me watch a rated PG-13 movie." Aurora laughed, remembering a happier time. "I'll never forget the look on her face when she came home and saw us watching it. The funny thing is she didn't even turn it off on us like usual—she let us finish watching it."

"Well, it's not exactly a suitable movie for a little kid. I don't think I would have let you watch it either. Anyway, then you do know who I am." Sirius looked at Aurora with a newfound curiosity.

"Yeah, you're a celebrity—a movie star. So what?"

"But do you know where I'm from?" Sirius asked, wondering if Aurora was perceptive enough to have pin-pointed his accent.

"Umm, Hollywood, California, I guess," Aurora suggested. "Isn't that where all you stars are from?"

"That's partially right. I currently live in Malibu, California, but I'm originally from Italy—Sianna, Tuscany."

"You're Italian?"

"Italian by birth and by upbringing. Now I would be considered Italian-American, because I am a US citizen. If I was still an Italian citizen, I don't think the state of New York would allow me to adopt you so easily. Anyway, enough about my background for now, what about you? Where are you from?" Sirius leaned back on the couch and spread his hands over the back of the couch, making himself more comfortable.

"Summit, New Jersey," Aurora answered without hesitation.

"How did you end up in New York?"

"I was sent to live with my aunt and uncle. I didn't stay there long though. I lived with them until they kicked me out and threw me into the system."

"*Oh mio*, why did they do that?"

"I don't know. My aunt and my mom never got along—I think my aunt was jealous of her. Don't know why, though."

"Did they really kick you out?"

"Yeah, they actually abandoned me in front of a church," Aurora answered. Tears welled in her eyes, but she hoped the tears wouldn't fall. She refused to cry because of what they did.

"I'm so sorry. I'm curious—what happened to your parents?" Sirius asked carefully, aware that he was encroaching on emotional territory, being an orphan himself.

"They're dead," Aurora replied quietly.

"I'm sorry. How did they die?"

"Car accident. They were hit by a drunk driver."

"Sounds familiar," Sirius said under his breath, so Aurora wouldn't hear. "Aurora, I am truly very sorry for your loss," Sirius said empathetically. He reached out and put his hand over hers in an attempt to comfort her.

"Why are you sorry? It's not your fault," Aurora stated bluntly, taking a deep breath and pulling her hand away from under his.

"*Verissimo*, true, it's not, but I'm still sorry that you lost your parents. It's very painful at any age."

"What does verecemo mean?" Aurora asked.

"It's *verissimo*," Sirius laughed. "It's Italian, meaning very true."

"So I'm guessing you speak Italian?"

"*Si, parlo fluentemente italiano*. I speak it fluently." Sirius smiled, chuckling.

"Umm, have you lived anywhere else?"

"Yeah, London for some schooling—that's probably where I picked up some of the lingo," he laughed.

"London? As in England?"

"*Sì*, yes, that's right," Sirius answered.

"That is so cool," Aurora commented. "Mr. Marino, can I ask you something?" Aurora questioned, bringing her knees up to her chest.

"Sure," Sirius answered.

"Why are you doing this?"

"Doing what?" Sirius asked, with a puzzled look on his face.

"You know—adopting me? Why do you want to deal with all that drama?" Aurora questioned.

"You know Aurora, our stories aren't very different. We are actually very much alike."

"What's that supposed to mean?" Aurora asked.

"Well," Sirius started, taking a deep breath before he continued. "It was just before my sixth birthday. My parents and I were walking home from midnight Mass; we didn't live far from the church. It was a beautiful night. On our way home, it started to snow. It was magical because it hardly ever snowed there," Sirius explained, smiling as he thought about it.

"Midnight Mass? That's Christmas Eve, right?"

"*Sì*."

"I'm guessing there's more to the story," Aurora suggested.

"Yeah, there is," Sirius replied softly. "On our walk home, we were approached by a man. I didn't know what was going on, but I wasn't scared at first, because I was with my parents. I knew they would protect me no matter what. I wasn't truly afraid until I saw what he had."

"Saw what?"

"The man had a knife. He pulled it out and, well..." Sirius started to say, as he looked at the look of shock on Aurora's face.

"Did your parents survive?"

"No, they died," Sirius said, as tears welled up in his eyes and fell down his face. "It was one of the worst days of my life; I still miss them every day. After that, I was sent to live with my grandparents and then my aunt and uncle in Tuscany."

"I'm sorry," Aurora said sympathetically, as she let her own tears run down her cheeks. She grabbed a tissue from the table between the two couches, and wiped the tears off her cheeks.

"Aurora, let me tell you a little something about life: it doesn't always work out the way we hope or plan. It will unfold as it should. Life is painful, messy, and hard, but it can also be beautiful, and it's most definitely worth it," Sirius explained. "Do you understand?"

"Yeah, but that still doesn't really explain why you're doing this."

"Yes, it does. Aurora, you need a home. You need to be with family who cares about you. A place you can experience love and compassion; a place you can grow and experience life without anyone holding you back. Does that make sense?"

"I guess," Aurora answered.

"I was lucky, Aurora. I had my family to take care of me. They sacrificed so much for me, and what I'm doing now is trying to live how my parents would have wanted me to live. I'm doing what I believe they would have wanted and encouraged me to do—to help you as my family helped me."

"So, what's going to happen, like after the paperwork and everything is done?" Aurora asked nervously.

"Once the adoption is finalized and you are released from juvie, you'll come to live at my home in Malibu with me." Sirius smiled reassuringly.

"But what happens once I age out?" Aurora asked. She had to make sure that this was a family for life, and not a temporary quick fix for publicity.

"Age out?" Sirius looked at her puzzled.

"Yeah, when a foster kid turns eighteen, they age out of the system. Sometimes there are policies to help them until they become a certain age, but most times, kids are thrown out onto the streets. So what will happen to me?"

"Aurora, we'll be family, and I won't stop being your family once you turn eighteen. It doesn't work like that for me. Family is for life! That is, unless you don't want to be adopted, and that decision is entirely up to you."

"I want to be adopted. I always wanted that, but sometimes it doesn't work out." Aurora sighed. "I just want everything to work out this time."

"This time? You were to be adopted before?"

"Yeah," Aurora said quietly.

"Why weren't you?"

"I don't know. A few years ago, I was placed with this family. It was the best placement I've ever had," Aurora answered, feeling tears in her eyes. "They were going to adopt me. When I was there, they had a baby. I was so excited to have a family with a younger sibling I could watch grow. Then it all ended—Ms. Davis pulled me out a week later."

"Why did Ms. Davis pull you out?" Sirius looked shocked.

"I'm not sure; Ms. Davis told me that they had their own family now, and they didn't want me anymore."

"I'm sorry, Aurora," Sirius replied. "I want you to know that I won't be backing out, and nobody, not even Ms. Davis, is going to change my mind."

"You sure?"

"Aurora, I'm one hundred ten percent sure, and I promise I will do whatever it takes to see this adoption through."

"Thanks," Aurora answered. "Mr. Marino, what do you want me to call you? I mean you are adopting me. Isn't that going to make you my father?"

"I hate to interrupt you two," Warden Sanchez called out, walking into the common room. "It's ten minutes before seven. It's almost time for breakfast, so if you don't want this entire facility to know you are here, I suggest you start to make your exit."

"Okay, sorry Aurora," Sirius said, standing up. "It looks like we need to postpone this conversation until next time."

"When can you come back? Soon?" Aurora questioned, as she stood up next to Sirius.

"That's something Mr. Marino and I will discuss," Mr. Sanchez stated. "In the meantime, you can call him during free times."

"I can?" Aurora asked excitedly.

"Yes, and I'm sure Mr. Marino would also like that," Mr. Sanchez commented.

"I would indeed," Sirius acknowledged. "Aurora, call me whenever you want. If I don't answer and I'm busy, leave a message and try again another time."

"Maybe not too often, Sirius is very busy," Mr. Sanchez interjected.

"Not too busy for Aurora. If I'm to be her father, then I need to be available for her at all times," Sirius said to Mr. Sanchez. "Aurora, listen, don't worry about being a bother. If you are permitted, call me whenever you want for any reason. Understand?"

"Yeah," Aurora answered.

"Alright, now, I'd better get out of here, or we are going to be all over the media," Sirius remarked.

"That sounds like a good idea," Mr. Sanchez responded.

"Well, Aurora—it's great to see you again, and I will see you really soon." Sirius offered her a parting handshake which she took with a smile.

"Okay," Aurora said, as she watched Sirius and the Warden turn away from her and walk out of the room. "Sirius! Wait!" she called out, as she ran to catch up with them.

"What is it, Aurora?" Sirius asked.

"Aurora, he needs to get out of here," Warden Sanchez interrupted. "Also, you need to get to your cell. We don't want the other girls to know that you had a visitor."

"Alright." Aurora sighed as she turned to leave.

"We have some time, Warden," Sirius replied to him. "Aurora, hold up. What is it?"

"It's nothing. I just wanted to ask you something. How do you say 'see you soon' in Italian?"

"It's—*a presto*," Sirius chuckled.

"Okay, *a presto*, Mr. Marino," Aurora said.

"*A presto bella*," Sirius responded, as he turned to leave.

"*Bella?* What does that mean?" Aurora asked.

"It means beautiful," Sirius called back as he exited the room, flashing her a smile.

"Bye," Aurora called out, just before she dashed down the hall back to her cell. She made it to her cell just in time before the buzzer went off and the cells opened. As the cells opened, she acted as if she had just walked out, as though she had been there the entire time.

"Hey, Aurora, you look happy," Lexi mentioned, as she walked out of her call and approached Aurora.

"I am," Aurora replied.

"That's surprising. You usually look gloomy. What changed?" Lexi stifled a morning yawn with the back of her hand.

"Nothing, I just have a good feeling," Aurora stated mysteriously, as they got into the line with the other girls and headed to breakfast.

As Aurora headed back to her cell, Sirius rushed out of the detention center to avoid being seen. Once he was in his rental car, he let out a sigh of relief. *What a wonderful visit,* Sirius thought to himself, as he pulled out of the detention center and made his way back to the airport for the long flight back home. He had a lot of things he needed to get done before Aurora came home, and he wanted to get a head start on everything. *Today went so well, and I'm so glad we had this time to bond. I have a feeling everything is going to be alright.*

Chapter 11

Tuesday, March 26th

"YOU IDIOT!" SIRIUS TENSED as he heard Sierra's shrill voice. "How dare you treat me like this?!" she yelled.

"Sierra, I don't get why you are so mad," Sirius responded, trying to sound calm. He hoped his calmness would somehow magically calm her down, so she would lower her voice. It was starting to draw too much attention from tourists and the regular park goers.

"Of course you don't. You are such a guy!" Sierra pouted, her long eyelashes fluttering.

"Well, I'm glad we cleared that up." Sirius laughed sarcastically.

"Don't you dare make fun of me!" Sierra's black oval-shaped eyes flashed angrily.

"I'm not! Sierra, you called *me* because you wanted to talk, so I agreed to come out here. Will you please *talk* to me?" Sirius ran his fingers through his hair, exasperated with the petite influencer who was yelling at him at the top of her lungs. She was gorgeous and smart, but right now that was the last thing Sirius cared about. All he wanted to do was end whatever relationship he had started with her, especially now that he was seeing her true unpleasant personality.

"No, just forget it! There's nothing to talk about. I thought you liked me; we got along really well on our date a few months back. Then after that, you ghosted me!" Sierra scoffed.

"Sierra, will you please calm down?"

"Calm down!?" Sierra's pale cheeks started turning a shade of red to match her scarlet lipstick.

"Yes, we really don't need to have any more attention drawn to us," Sirius answered, glancing around nervously, and seeing a tourist snap a picture in their general direction. "I really don't want this conversation to be on some gossip site."

"I don't care! We are outside, and there's no one around. I don't need to calm down. I can be as loud as I want!" Sierra announced, crossing her arms angrily and holding her head high.

"Sierra, I'm not sure if you noticed, but we are in the Lake Hollywood Park. There are tons of people around, and I really don't think we need to cause a public disturbance over something so silly. We don't need the police to be called on us, and we definitely don't need the paparazzi getting the details of our private conversation," Sirius explained.

"Wow, you are such a jerk! All you care about is yourself!" Sierra exclaimed. "You know, you never even tried to get in touch with me after our date."

"I did call you, but you didn't answer," Sirius defended himself. "If you did, you would have known I was working on that movie in Spain. I was in a different time zone, as well as very busy."

"Well, you should have at least asked me to come with you. I would have supported you as your girlfriend," Sierra said in a softer tone, reaching out to hold Sirius' hand.

"Girlfriend?" Sirius questioned, quickly pulling his hand back. "Sierra, let me make one thing very, very clear—you are not my girl-friend."

"Excuse me," she interrupted, stomping her high-heeled foot like a little child. "Yeah, I am!"

"No, you're not." He ran his hand over his face wearily and contin-ued, "Sierra, please, listen to me. We had *one* date—*un appuntamento*, and to be honest, it was nice; but I'm not ready to make any kind of commitment right now—neither to you nor to anyone else."

"And why not?" Sierra crossed her arms over her pink mini-dress, and glared up at Sirius.

"It's because...um....it's just not a good time. I have other obliga-tions that I really need to focus on, and I don't need any distractions."

"Let me get this straight—you have things that are more important than me?! What is it? Another movie? A television series? Is your career really more important than me?" Sierra looked like she was about to cry.

"That's not what I said."

"Whatever, it's fine. I get it," Sierra growled in frustration. She grabbed her designer purse with her perfectly-manicured fingers and walked away in a huff. "Have a great life!" she yelled back at Sirius.

"Fine," Sirius yelled back, as he walked to a shady spot under a tree and sat down in the grass. "This is *pazzesco*," he thought to himself, feeling relieved that he hadn't committed to a serious relationship with her. At this point, the only stress in his life came from Ms. Davis and her nagging agenda. Feeling a headache coming on, he put his hand to his head and thought of a mantra. "This shall pass. I have the strength to overcome this challenge and emerge stronger than before." He took a deep breath and felt somewhat better; thankfully, his mantras and his faith in Buddhism had never failed him. He had converted to Buddhism in college and never looked back. It was something that kept him grounded. *Well, until recently; now it seems like the mantras aren't helping as much as they once did.*

"Ugh, please do not be Ms. Davis," he groaned, as he heard his phone ring and pulled it out of his pocket. "Hello," he answered. He listened to the recording that played. "Yes, I'll accept the charges," he said into the phone. "Aurora!" he greeted, smiling as if she could see his smile through the phone.

"Hi, Mr. Marino." Aurora's voice sounded happy.

"*Ciao,* Aurora, it's good to hear your voice. How are you?"

"I'm fine. Just counting down the days till I'm out of here."

"I'm sure you are. Have you figured out what you want to do once you are out?"

"No, not yet," Aurora replied.

"I'm sure you'll think of something." Sirius got up and started to walk around to let out his negative energy, as he was still annoyed from his encounter with Sierra. He was trying very hard not to let that influence his conversation with his future daughter.

"I guess. Are you busy?"

"No, I have nothing going on right now. Why?"

"I just wanted to make sure you were free to talk. I didn't want to interrupt anything."

"Well, I'm free to talk for as long as you are able."

"Great, so—um—what have you been doing?" Aurora asked.

"Mmm, let me see—I took a flight back home right after our visit, and I've just been starting to get things situated here for when you come home," Sirius explained. "Now, why don't you tell me about your day?"

"Why? Nothing interesting ever happens here; it was a normal, boring day in juvie. The highlight of my day so far has been talking to you." Aurora laughed. "Your day has to be more interesting than mine."

"From what you said the other day, it sounds more monotonous than boring, but I get it." Sirius chuckled. "My day hasn't really been too interesting either."

"What does monotonous mean?" she asked.

"Well, every day you have the same routine, so that's repetitive or monotonous."

"That makes sense," Aurora commented. "So, don't you have a crazy life in Hollywood?"

"It can be depending on the day, but my life isn't too crazy, especially if I'm not doing any projects."

"Are you doing any?"

"Any what?" Sirius asked.

"Aren't you doing any projects right now?"

"No, I'm going to take a little break until—well—your adoption is finalized."

"So it's my fault you're not doing your job?" Aurora questioned, sounding anxious.

"Not at all, Aurora. I have just done a lot of projects in a row without any time off, so I'm taking advantage of this opportunity to rest and relax."

"Rest and relax? Dealing with Ms. Davis and my teen drama is relaxing for you?"

Sirius laughed. *I like that Aurora has a good sense of humor,* he thought before responding. "Dealing with Ms. Davis, no, that's definitely not relaxing. Her presence alone has been giving me a headache, but dealing with your drama is not too big of a deal. In fact, you haven't caused any."

"I guess not, but I'm sure I'm causing you stress you never had to deal with before—like worrying about me."

"Aurora, you are making yourself sound like some kind of burden, and you're not. Also, you aren't causing me any stress."

"Are you sure?"

"I'm positive," Sirius reassured her. "Actually, it's kind of nice worrying about someone other than myself."

"I think you're just saying that to be nice."

"No, I'm not. I'm being absolutely serious, and I think it's now my job to worry about you, since you'll be my daughter," Sirius teased back.

"I guess so." Aurora laughed. "So, as your daughter, am I allowed to worry about you?"

"Well, you shouldn't have to."

"Why can you worry about me, but I can't worry about you? Isn't that hypocritical?"

"Hypocritical, huh?" Sirius laughed. "Aurora, that's not what I meant. You are allowed to worry about me, but you shouldn't have to worry about a full-grown adult. I'm going to be the parent. It's my responsibility to take care of you—that's my full-time job if you want to think about it that way. Acting is my second job of importance."

"That makes sense. So...has Ms. Davis caused you any problems?"

"Aurora, please don't worry about that. You should worry about other things."

"Like what?" Aurora questioned.

"Like doing your school work or thinking about what color you want your room painted, stuff like that."

"But Mr. Marino, what if she leaks information to the press?"

"She's not going to do that," Sirius said firmly.

"How do you know? She can cause big problems for you."

"I'm sure she can try, but it's nothing I can't handle. Anyway, I don't think she's going to be bugging us anytime soon."

"Why do you say that?"

"Because I threatened to sue her for harassment."

"Can you actually do that?" Aurora sounded shocked.

"Yes, I can if she continues to make up lies about me and spread rumors."

"Oh, okay."

"Aurora, can you do something for me?"

"Umm, yeah, sure," Aurora answered.

"If you ever are going through something, or if you need to talk to someone, can you come to me and be honest about it?"

"Umm, I don't know." Aurora sounded guarded.

"Aurora, I want you to feel safe and comfortable talking to me, no matter what it is."

"Alright," Aurora answered quietly.

"Alright? Does that mean you'll talk to me?"

"Yeah, I don't mind talking to you. I mean, we have similar pasts—you get me more than most adults."

"That's true, and you don't want to keep your emotions bottled up, because it's not healthy for you," Sirius explained.

"Okay, from now on, I'll try to talk to you about what I'm feeling."

"Alright, I'm glad to hear that." Sirius leaned against a tree in the park.

"So, I asked this on Sunday, and you didn't have the chance to answer. What do you want me to call you?" Aurora asked.

"Aurora, you can call me whatever you want. Whether it's Sirius or Dad or whatever you feel comfortable doing," Sirius explained.

"What's Dad in Italian?"

"Umm, it's *papà*."

"So you don't care what I call you?" Aurora asked.

"Not really, as I said, it all depends on what you feel comfortable with," Sirius answered.

"Okay," Aurora started.

"Hey, Aurora! It's dinner time, you coming or what?" Aurora heard Lexi yell.

"Yeah, I'm coming. Hold on a minute!" Aurora answered her friend. "I guess I need to go," she said into the phone.

"It does sound that way. Have a good night, Aurora."

"Thanks, you too. Bye, Mr. Marino," Aurora replied as she hung up the phone.

"*Ciao*, Aurora," Sirius responded softly, smiling to himself, as he put his phone in his back pocket.

"Who's Aurora!?" Sirius heard someone yell behind him. He quickly turned around, his brown eyes widening as he saw Sierra stomp towards him.

"Sierra, what are you doing here? I thought you left!" Sirius started to panic, hoping she hadn't heard anything about the adoption.

"So—who is she?" Sierra questioned, her arms crossed and eyes blazing.

"Who?"

"Aurora. Who is she? Is she the new girl you've been seeing? Is that why you dropped me so fast?"

"You are not serious," Sirius mumbled, holding his head and feeling a headache coming on again.

"Come on Sirius—admit it!"

"Admit what? Have you been listening this entire time?"

"Maybe...so what if I was? How else am I going to know if you have been lying and seeing someone else?"

"This is ridiculous! How many times do I have to say this? I'm not seeing *anyone*!"

"Well, why else would you not want to be with me? It has to be because you found someone else!" Sierra stepped in closer to Sirius until they were almost nose to nose. She jabbed his chest with her sharp fingernail. "Who is this Aurora? Is she more famous than me? Is she prettier than me?"

"No, Sierra, you don't understand anything," Sirius said, brushing her hand off of his chest. "I'm telling you the honest to goodness truth. I haven't been seeing anybody—not you, not anyone."

"Then who's this Aurora? Someone you are thinking of dating?"

"No, not even close," Sirius answered, shaking his head, and thinking of something to say to get Sierra off his back. "If you must know, Aurora is a relative."

"I thought it's common knowledge you don't have any family."

"What does that matter?"

"Well, if you don't have any family, you can't have any relatives," Sierra said slyly. "You are such a liar!"

"Where did you hear that, the media? Smart, they are super reliable." Sirius laughed, hoping she would let it go.

"I don't believe you. So, what does this girl, Aurora, have that I don't?" Sierra glared angrily.

"There's really no point," Sirius grumbled. "Even if I wanted to explain it, I doubt you would listen to a word I'm saying."

"What are you insinuating!?" Sierra screamed at him.

"That you have selective hearing," Sirius answered, raising his voice a notch.

"I do not!"

"You do, and I really don't appreciate you screaming at me over an argument that is incredibly juvenile. *Questo è ridicolo*!" Sirius turned away from her and started to walk away.

"How dare you!" Sierra gasped. "Hey! Where do you think you're going?"

"Leaving!" Sirius yelled back, and started walking faster.

"Hey! Don't you dare walk away from me! You'll be sorry!" Sierra threatened.

"I doubt that," Sirius said under his breath as he walked back to his Maserati. "This shall pass. This shall pass. This shall pass," he repeated to himself. He regretted coming out here to talk to Sierra; he didn't realize she would be such a big problem. He really hoped he was done dealing with her after today.

(Thursday, March 28ᵗʰ)

"Brianna, where have you been?" Dr. Deleon questioned Dr. Morton as she walked into the office.

"Hi, Angela—I wasn't sure if I was going to see you today or not," Dr. Morton responded, as she put on her doctor's coat.

"Well, seeing as I took over your duties during your personal time away, I've had to be here more than I would like," Dr. Deleon teased, smirking at Briana. "So, where have you been?"

"I told you before, I had a family emergency. It took a little longer to deal with than expected. I'd rather not go into details right now though," Dr. Morton explained.

"I'm sorry about your situation; I hope everything turns out alright," Dr. Deleon said kindly. "When you were away, there was a situation that came up."

"What happened?" Dr. Morton asked, glancing at Dr. Deleon.

"Well, you need to see Warden Sanchez immediately."

"Why? What happened?"

"It may be better if he told you." Dr. Deleon sighed.

"Very well." Dr. Morton rushed out the door, her straight, short blond hair bouncing on her shoulders as she walked out of sight.

"Alright," Dr. Deleon mumbled under her breath as she watched Dr. Morton rush down the hall, closing the door behind her. Dr. Deleon quickly sat back down at her desk and picked up the phone, dialing the extension to Mr. Sanchez's office. "Mr. Sanchez," she said into the phone urgently.

"Hi Dr. Deleon, is everything alright?" Mr. Sanchez asked, his voice crackling over the speaker.

"Not really—I'm calling to warn you. Dr. Morton is on her way to your office," Dr. Deleon replied.

"Did you tell her what was going on?"

"No, I told her that we had a situation come up when she was away, and you needed to see her immediately. She didn't seem very happy."

"Thanks for giving me the heads-up," Mr. Sanchez said, hearing someone knock on his office door. "That's probably her now."

"Of course, I thought you should know."

"Thanks again, Dr. Deleon," Mr. Sanchez answered, hanging up the phone and hearing a second knock. "Come in!"

"Mr. Sanchez, I heard you wanted to see me. So, what is it?" Dr. Morton asked mindfully, as she entered his office and closed the door.

"Yes, please sit down," Mr. Sanchez replied, gesturing to the chair across from his desk.

"Is everything okay?" Dr. Morton asked. She sat down quickly and took a deep breath, obviously bracing herself for whatever was going to happen.

"To answer your question, no. Everything is not alright," Mr. Sanchez said harshly. "I'll get straight to the point. Do you remember doing Aurora Bennett's intake physical?"

"Oh, umm, I don't believe it was me who did it, but I could be wrong. It was such a long time ago," Dr. Morton said nervously.

"Well, here is the hard copy," Mr. Sanchez responded, taking out a file from his desk and handing it to her. "There are several inconsistencies on it."

"What kind of inconsistencies?"

"I suggest you take a good look at it. First of all, there is no record of any scars or bruises. Second, it shows the height and weight for an average thirteen-year-old girl. Lastly, there is no record of Ms. Davis being present."

"Okay, so what does this have to do with me?" Dr. Morton asked, picking up the file and scanning through the information.

"I'm curious to know as to why there are so many inconsistencies."

"You should ask Dr. Deleon, seeing as she was the one who was present," Dr. Morton explained, pointing to Dr. Deleon's signed name.

"That's the problem. Dr. Deleon was not here that day. I have it on good authority that she was out of the state with family."

"That's not possible," Dr. Morton mumbled, as she placed the file back on the desk. "Then why is her name signed?"

"I was hoping you could tell me."

"Me? Why me?" Dr. Morton asked nervously.

"Dr. Morton, you are the only other one who would have been here. So what happened?" Mr. Sanchez questioned, staring at Dr. Morton intensely.

"I don't know...". Dr. Morton started to say.

"Don't know what? Don't know of a good story to get you out of this mess?" Mr. Sanchez seethed. "I suggest you tell me the truth, or you will not only lose your job but will also be brought up on criminal charges."

"You can't do that!" Dr. Morton stood up and banged her hand on the desk.

"Actually, I can," Mr. Sanchez threatened, holding up the file and waving it in front of Dr. Morton.

"Mr. Sanchez, please—"

"No—explain! Now! Before I have you escorted out."

"Okay, okay, I'll explain everything," Dr. Morton said, looking panicked.

"Very well, I'm listening." Mr. Sanchez seated himself again and took out his notebook to take notes, while Dr. Morton remained standing.

"I'm the one who did the initial intake exam for Aurora. I was writing out her chart based on what I observed—with the scars, bruises, and her accurate height and weight. After I was finished, I called for Officer Edwards to escort her to her cell."

"So just to be clear—you *were* here that day?" Mr. Sanchez asked.

"Yes, I was," Dr. Morton admitted.

"What happened to the original chart?"

"I shredded it."

"How did that come about?"

"Well, as I was finishing up Aurora's chart, Ms. Davis walked in. She asked me to alter her chart to what it is now," Dr. Morton confessed, looking somewhat ashamed.

"Did she say why?" Mr. Sanchez scribbled down some notes and looked up again.

"No, she didn't. I didn't want to do it, but she threatened me! She said she had something on me that would ruin my career, and she threatened to tell my secret if I didn't do as she asked."

"What was the secret?" Mr. Sanchez questioned.

"I'd rather not say. It's something in my personal life, but it could ruin my life—personal and professional. I couldn't let that happen, so I did what she wanted."

"That's not good enough. You need to tell me, or I won't be able to help you."

"You can't help me," Dr. Morton said hopelessly.

"Alright. I respect your right to privacy about your personal life. But what I really need to know—do you know if Ms. Davis has done this before? I find it strange she would try to ruin her career just to hide the injuries of one girl."

"I'm not sure. This is the first time I have ever dealt with her," Dr. Morton answered. "There is someone you can talk to, though—Dr. Andrew Grace. He was here before me, and from my knowledge, he has dealt with her multiple times in the past."

"I do remember him. I also remember he quit very abruptly," Mr. Sanchez responded.

"Do you think Ms. Davis asked him alter the girls' charts?"

"I don't know. If she had something on him, she might have," Mr. Sanchez stated.

"So what now?"

"Well, I'm going to talk to Dr. Grace and see what he has to say."

"I meant about me. I'm assuming I no longer have a job here," Dr. Morton said nervously.

"That is correct."

"Is there any way I can keep my job?" Dr. Morton pleaded.

"I'm afraid not. You have made a serious error in judgment, and I cannot condone this behavior. Dr. Morton, I'm truly sorry; I wish this could have gone a different way."

"I understand, Mr. Sanchez," Dr. Morton replied.

"Okay, now, just wait a moment while I call Officer Walters," he said to her, picking up his walkie-talkie. "Walters, I need you to come up here and escort Dr. Morton to her office to pick up her personal belongings and then escort her out of the building."

"Is this really necessary?" Dr. Morton asked.

"It is. Now, may I have your keys, please?" Mr. Sanchez held out his hand, as Dr. Morton handed over the keys. "That should be Officer Walters," he said as he heard a knock on the door. "Come in."

"Mr. Sanchez," Officer Walters nodded to the Warden. "Are you ready, Dr. Morton?" she asked Dr. Morton.

"I am. Goodbye, Mr. Sanchez," Dr. Morton sighed.

"Goodbye, Dr. Morton," Mr. Sanchez responded, as he watched Officer Walters escort Dr. Morton out of his office. "I wonder what Dr. Grace has to do with this," he thought, as he opened up the BINGE search engine on his computer and typed in 'Dr. Andrew Grace.' He looked at the screen and clicked on the link 'People Finder.' As he waited for the search to load, he tapped his fingers on his desk. "What do we have here?" he asked himself. He looked through the information and came across something on the public records that made his eyes go wide—Dr. Grace had filed for bankruptcy. "That's interesting," he said as he scanned the rest of the page. "He lives lavishly for many years; then files for bankruptcy; and then he is never heard from again. I wonder..." he thought, picking up his phone and dialing Mr. Marino's number.

"Hello?" he heard Sirius say.

"Hi, Mr. Marino, this is Warden Sanchez. Is this a good time?" Mr. Sanchez asked.

"Yes, it's fine," Sirius replied. "Is everything alright?"

"It is," Sanchez admitted. "However, I came upon a small problem, and I'm not sure how to look into it without causing a ruckus, especially when I don't know who I can trust in my own facility."

"I see," Sirius commented.

"Sirius, do you know of anyone in the justice community, like in the FBI or someone who works in criminal investigations?"

"The FBI?" Sirius asked, shocked by what he had just heard. "Why?"

"Is there anyone you know who could find anything out?"

"I don't know of anyone in the FBI or any other federal agency. However, I have a friend who's a private investigator. I've been talking to him about this situation," Sirius responded.

"A private investigator? That would help a lot, but I don't know if I can afford that. I can't use funds from the detention center, and I can't afford to take it out of my personal account," Sanchez explained apologetically.

"Mr. Sanchez, I'll take care of it."

"I can't ask you to do that, Sirius."

"You are not asking; I'm offering, and I've already had him look into some things. All of this is coming up because of Aurora, and the only reason you looked into any of this is because I mentioned Aurora's scars and bruises. Something is going on here; we both see it. As Aurora's future guardian, I feel obligated to dig deeper."

"Are you sure?"

"Absolutely, don't worry about it."

"Thanks, Sirius. I really appreciate it."

"As I said, it's no problem at all; I'll email you his information," Sirius stated. "I'll let him know to send me the bill, so you don't have to worry about it."

"Thanks, I appreciate it."

"Good luck. *Ciao.*"

"Bye," Mr. Sanchez responded, hanging up his phone. "I really hope this PI can find something out," Mr. Sanchez thought, as he got back to his work.

(Friday, March 29th)

"Hey, 'Ora! What's happening?" Sandra asked her, walking up to where she sat on one of the couches in the common room.

"Oh, you know—stuck in here, same as you," Aurora laughed. "Why? Is there something interesting happening that I should know about?"

"No, nothing interesting ever happens here unless there's a fight or a crazy rumor going around," Sandra said slyly, sitting down next to Aurora.

"Alright Sandra, what's going on?" Aurora sighed, rolling her eyes.

"Well, Lexi told me that you may have been on the phone the other day. That true?"

"Yeah, so what?" Aurora asked.

"Aurora, the only people we are allowed to call are parents, other family members, or legal guardians. Your parents aren't around anymore, and your last legal guardian would never check in on you from what you've said. So, who were you talking to? Have you decided to talk to your aunt and uncle?"

"No way! I would never talk to them again, not even if you paid me!" Aurora exclaimed.

"I wouldn't either, especially after the way they treated you," Sandra agreed. "Then who were you talking to?"

"Umm, no comment."

"Why not?"

"I mean, I don't want to say," Aurora corrected herself.

"Okay, why not?"

"Because I don't want to jinx it or anything. This—umm—home might not happen; they are concerned about my past."

"Aurora, who wouldn't want to foster you?" Sandra asked. "I get you have a crazy past, but so what?"

"I'm not that special," Aurora said, trying to distract Sandra from the topic of guardians.

"I never said you were special," Sandra teased.

"Wow, thanks a lot," Aurora scoffed in mock hurt.

"I'm teasing, but seriously, you are one of the nicest girls I know. You're actually too nice so you had to be locked up!" Sandra laughed at her own lame joke.

"Thanks—I think. Was that a compliment or an insult?"

"Take it as you will," Sandra suggested freely. "Anyway, Ms. Davis must be causing trouble for you, as usual."

"Yeah, I wouldn't put it past her. I think talking trash about us kids is her favorite pastime."

"You got that right," Sandra agreed. "So, who are these foster parents? Anyone you've heard of before?"

"Sandra, I really don't want to talk about it. I don't want to jinx it."

"Since when do you believe in jinxes?"

"Since right now," Aurora said convincingly.

"Are you really freaking out about this?"

"I'm not freaking out, just a little worried," Aurora said, standing up.

"Well, don't be," Sandra assured her. "Anyone would be lucky to foster you. If not, they are crazy and don't deserve to be foster parents!"

"Thanks, Sandra. Anyway, it's almost time for lockup. We need to get to the hall for lineup," Aurora said, making her way to the hall.

"Ugh, this is so annoying," Sandra muttered as she went to catch up with Aurora. "We have to line up for meals, for the common area, and for lockup. Can't they just trust us to roam around on our own?"

"It is annoying, but it's procedure. We'll get out of here one day, and hopefully never have to deal with this stuff ever again."

"I can't wait!" Sandra said, loudly.

"Sandra, shhh," Aurora shushed her.

"What?"

"No talking in line," Aurora whispered. "Do you want to get us into trouble?"

"No," Sandra mumbled.

"Good. Neither of us can afford that."

"Girls, quiet! No talking!" the guard yelled at them. "Now, let's get going." Aurora and Sandra walked with their group to their cells for lockup.

Stepping into her cell, Aurora took a deep breath, as the door slammed shut and locked. "I don't think I'll ever get used to that," Aurora whispered to herself. She sat down on her cot and prayed, "God, please help me. I can't lie to my friends, but I promised Mr. Marino I wouldn't tell anyone about the adoption. What should I do?"

Chapter 12

Saturday, March 30th

"What do you two wanna do once you get out of here?" Aurora asked her friends, leaning back on the couch in the common room.

"I have no idea," Lexi yawned, tired from the boring week of classes.

"How do you not know?" Sandra questioned.

"That's because I'm not outta here yet; once I am, then I'll figure it out," Lexi shot back at Sandra.

"That makes sense," Aurora interjected.

"No, it doesn't. You should have a plan!" Sandra declared loudly enough for the entire common room to hear.

"I have a great plan," Lexi reassured her, rolling her eyes. "*Not* gonna do anything illegal. I don't wanna come back here ever again!"

"I like that plan," Aurora answered confidently. "It's the best one I've heard all day."

"Yeah, I guess," Sandra mumbled.

"So what's your plan, Sandra? I'm assuming you have it all together," Aurora teased.

"Of course I do, girl! I'm moving into the mall permanently." Sandra smiled.

"Why am I not surprised!" Aurora exclaimed, her green eyes twinkling.

"Because that's all she talks about," Lexi added in mock annoyance, flicking a long black braid she had just finished braiding over her shoulder.

"That's true," Aurora agreed.

"No, it's not!" Sandra argued, pouting.

"Yes, it is. The mall is better than a forever family for you! You would move in there for real if you could," Aurora teased.

"I guess you're right," Sandra giggled.

"Oh, no." Aurora frowned as she saw who was walking in their direction.

"What's wrong?" the girls asked with concern.

"What are you losers talking about?" Myra asked, interrupting their conversation.

"None of *your* business, Myra," Sandra snapped.

"Hey! You don't need to be so rude," Myra lashed out, crossing her arms across her chest.

"Maybe if you weren't so obnoxious interrupting our conversation, Sandra wouldn't have to be so nasty!" Aurora snapped back, standing up defensively.

"You wanna know something? You better watch your back, Aurora Bennett." Myra smirked, her icy blue eyes looking dangerous.

"Seriously, Myra." Lexi sighed, tugging Aurora to sit back down. "If you are looking for a fight, go bug someone else."

"Yeah, the last time you messed with us; you got your butt kicked!" Sandra added.

"That's because it wasn't a fair fight! It was me against the three of you," Myra argued.

"No, it was you against Amy. Aurora and I were trying to keep you two apart," Lexi clarified, rolling her dark brown eyes in annoyance. "Can you just go away?"

"But I'm doing Aurora a favor," Myra said, looking at Aurora intensely.

"Oh yeah? What kind of favor?" Aurora questioned sarcastically.

"Just thought I'd let you know that your best friend is currently in intake," Myra said mockingly.

"You have a best friend that we don't know about, Aurora?" Lexi teased.

"I guess so," Aurora laughed. "Myra, you are gonna have to spell it out for me, because I have no idea who you are talking about."

"You'll find out eventually," Myra said mysteriously, placing her hands on her hips.

"Seriously!? Will ya just tell me what's going on?" Aurora asked, as she was mostly irritated but was also starting to feel anxious. *There are too many people from my past that I would rather not meet in juvie.*

"You know, I should help you out, but I don't think I will. I'll just let you freak out about it," Myra laughed. "Hey, let me know if you figure it out."

"Why would she freak out?" Sandra questioned, giving Myra a death-glare. "I thought you said that they were friends."

"Did I? My mistake." Myra grinned.

"Then—am I friends with this person or not?" Aurora questioned, trying to get a feel for whether or not Myra was bluffing.

"I've already said too much," Myra answered.

"Seriously!?" Sandra nearly shouted. She stood up and faced Myra with her fists doubled up, ready to pick a fight on behalf of her friend.

"Don't provoke her, Sandra." Aurora grabbed Sandra's arm and pulled her back. "All she wants is attention. Don't give in to her insanity!"

"I'm not crazy, Bennett!" Myra seethed, her eyes narrowing.

"Myra, get lost," Aurora insisted.

"And what if I don't?" Myra questioned, pushing Aurora's hand away.

"Girl, are you looking for a fight? If so, keep it up. If not, beat it!" Lexi yelled at Myra.

"Whatever," Myra mumbled, seeing Officer Walters look in their direction; she quickly backed away from the three girls and walked off to avoid getting into trouble.

"What on earth was that about?" Lexi asked, looking at Aurora with wide eyes.

"I have no idea," Aurora answered. "But I'm sure we will find out soon enough."

"Let's forget about Myra and her insane, empty threats. What's your plan, 'Ora?" Sandra asked.

"What plan?" Aurora asked, still worried about what Myra had said.

"You know, the plan you have for when you get out; what do you wanna do?" Lexi asked.

"Not you too," Aurora mumbled under her breath.

"What do you mean by that?" Sandra questioned.

"Nothing," Aurora answered too quickly.

"Don't lie, 'Ora. It's definitely something. Does it have anything to do with your next foster parents?" Sandra asked excitedly.

"Wait a sec—you have new foster parents?" Lexi whispered.

"Sandra! I asked you not to say anything," Aurora grumbled angrily.

"Well...I didn't think it applied to Lexi! Sorry, my bad," Sandra said in a somewhat quiet voice.

"What's going on?" Lexi asked, crossing her arms and looking first at Aurora and then at Sandra.

"Aurora is worried about her new foster parents—she's afraid Ms. Davis is going to ruin it for her and make them bolt," Sandra explained, as she held her hand up to her face so that no one can see what she's saying.

"That makes sense, based on Ms. Davis's track record," Lexi agreed.

"You know what? Next time I'm not going to tell you anything—either of you," Aurora complained, rolling her eyes.

"Sorry! Didn't know it would be such a big problem," Sandra said apologetically.

"It's fine," Aurora sighed, giving Sandra a side hug. "Just keep it between us, and don't tell anyone else, please."

"My lips are sealed," Lexi agreed, zipping her lips with her fingers.

"I guess I can keep my big mouth shut, since you two are my only friends here," Sandra said, laughing at herself. "But what's the big deal? You shouldn't be this worried about your next foster parents."

"Yeah, just try to chillax," Lexi added helpfully, lounging back on the common room couch.

"I know. It's just you both know how Ms. Davis is. She has caused so many issues—not just in my life but for others too. I don't want anything to go wrong," Aurora explained.

"Wow, this must be one great placement," Lexi answered.

"I don't know too much about it, but um, it could be. I just don't want to get all excited about it, and then have everything come crashing down, like usual," Aurora said.

"That makes sense, but 'Ora, you need to stop worrying. It will be fine," Sandra replied, squeezing her friend's hand.

"Yeah, I guess," Aurora sighed, squeezing Sandra's hand back and glancing up at the common room clock. "Oh no! Darn it!"

"What's wrong?" Lexi asked.

"Uh, nothing, I just forgot that I have a meeting with Mrs. Hansen," Aurora explained, jumping up from the couch.

"So what? Since when have you cared about going to your counseling sessions?" Sandra questioned suspiciously.

"Umm, it's because I got my placement; I just want to do everything right."

"Whatever, girl, do what you gotta do," Lexi answered.

"Have fun!" Sandra said loudly, waving goodbye.

"I'll try," Aurora replied over her shoulder as she walked towards the common room exit. She signed out with Officer Walters and quickly sprinted down the hallway to Mrs. Hansen's office. As she slowed down to walk, she prayed that everything would go well. She took a deep breath as she approached the door, and then she knocked.

"Come in," Mrs. Hansen said cheerfully.

"Umm, Mrs. Hansen," Aurora said, walking into the room and quickly closing the door behind her.

"What can I do for you, Miss Bennett?" Mrs. Hansen smiled kindly.

"Um, I have a problem, and I didn't know what to do."

"I see. What's the problem?" Mrs. Hansen gestured for Aurora to take a seat on the chair in her office.

"Some of my friends caught me talking on the phone, and they figured out that I have a placement. I couldn't tell them anything, because I promised Mr. Marino I wouldn't. I just don't know what to do," Aurora explained.

"I may be able to help you out with that."

"What do you mean?"

"Well, the thing is, Warden Sanchez and I figured this would happen. We talked about it after Mr. Marino came to visit you, and we decided if you wanted to call him you could call him on my office phone, anytime you want."

"Seriously?" Aurora's eyes widened, and her heart skipped a beat.

"I am," Mrs. Hansen answered, chuckling.

"That's great!" Aurora exclaimed, loudly. She wanted to jump up and down with excitement. *Maybe things are looking up after all!*

"Good morning, *zia*. Well, I guess it's afternoon for you." Sirius laughed. "How are you doing?"

"I'm quite fine, thank you. Are you home?"

"No, I'm actually in my car, waiting for Felix and Bridgette to show up. They want to do a yoga class with me. Bridgette thinks it will help me relax."

"That sounds like fun!"

"Oh, yes, so much fun," Sirius chuckled sarcastically. "So why are you calling, *zia*?"

"I just wanted to call to give you a heads-up," Aunt Liv answered.

"Heads up for what?" Sirius asked, sitting up straighter in his Maserati.

"It's just I'll be paying you a visit."

"*Aspetta*! What? When?" Sirius questioned.

"Well, I knew what you'd say if I told you beforehand, so I'm at a hotel in Zürich. Tomorrow morning, I have a flight for Los Angeles," Aunt Liv explained.

"Are you joking?"

"I'm not. I took a train from Rome to Zürich, so I can enjoy some time here. Then tomorrow, I have a flight to Los Angeles. I should be getting to L.A. tomorrow afternoon around two o' clock," Aunt Liv explained. "I was hoping you would be able to pick me up in one of those nice, sporty Italian cars you keep for your favorite aunt."

"Of course I can do that for you," Sirius laughed. "So, what made you decide to come for a sudden visit?" He reclined his car seat to a more laid-back position.

"Well, I assumed that preparing for a teenager to live with you would be the last thing on your mind. I'm sure you are more concerned about other things like dealing with that crazy lady—I even forgot her name."

"So...?"

"So, I thought I'd come to help you get ready," Aunt Liv said excitedly.

"Okay, but Aurora's not even here yet. There's probably no hurry. Her release date is a little more than a month away."

"Sirius, you should at least be somewhat prepared! Aurora should have some clothes, shoes, and other important items that girls need. I'm sure you would rather not shop for all that, especially since you are keeping the adoption quiet."

"This is true," Sirius agreed.

"And what about her room?"

"What about it?"

"She is a teenage girl. I think she would find her room very boring if it was just plain white," Aunt Liv commented.

"*Zia* Liv, I doubt Aurora has ever had her own room, except for maybe her current living situation, so I don't think she will care too much."

"Well, you should at least paint it her favorite color. You do know what her favorite color is, don't you?"

"I don't think it ever came up," Sirius answered.

"Of course, it didn't. It would be *very* good if you could find out and let me know."

"I will, and I suppose you want to be the one to decorate her bedroom?" Sirius grinned, already knowing his aunt's response.

"Of course, anything for my future grandniece; well, I suppose she'll be more of a granddaughter. It will be fun."

"I think you are going to be the worst at spoiling that girl."

"Absolutely! I think Aurora deserves some spoiling, especially after everything she's been through. Don't you agree?" Aunt Liv asked softly.

"*Sì*," Sirius agreed. "Unfortunately, I don't know much about her likes and dislikes, except that she likes to read books."

"Well, that's something at least—oh, I got to go! I'm meeting some friends, so I will see you tomorrow. *Ti amo!*"

"Okay, have fun. Love you too." Sirius hung up the phone. "Now to meet up with Felix," he thought out loud. Sirius heard his phone ring just as he was just about to exit his car. Looking at the phone, he saw it was the number for the detention center. *It's probably Warden Sanchez.* "Hello?" Sirius asked, answering the call.

"Hi, Mr. Marino," he heard Aurora say cheerily on the other end of the line.

"*Buongiorno,* Aurora," Sirius replied, stifling a yawn.

"Did I wake you?" Aurora asked.

"No, you didn't. I've actually been up for a little bit," Sirius replied.

"I'm surprised you normally sleep so late. I would have thought that you would be up earlier."

"Oh, Aurora," Sirius chuckled. "Did you forget I'm in California?"

"So?"

"There's a three-hour time difference. It's 8 a.m. here," Sirius answered.

"Oh, I forgot about that. Sorry I called so early." Aurora sounded apologetic over the phone. "I hate getting woken up by the wake-up call here at the center."

"It's fine, Aurora. As I said, I was already awake," Sirius said, reassuring her he wasn't irritated. "How are you doing today?"

"I'm okay, I guess. I just wanted to talk—if you have time."

"I always have time for you." Sirius glanced outside his window—no Felix or Bridgette in sight.

"Great! What are you doing?" Aurora sounded genuinely curious.

"I'm actually sitting in my car, waiting for two of my friends to show up," Sirius answered.

"Oh, what are you guys gonna do?"

"Uhh, they decided to get me out of bed at the crack of dawn, so I can take this sunrise yoga class with them," Sirius said.

"That sounds fun. I think?"

"It will be interesting if nothing else." Sirius chuckled. "Was there something specific you wanted to talk about, Aurora?" Sirius felt that there was something bothering her.

"Kind of—my friends are bugging me about my placement," Aurora answered.

"Why are they bothering you?" Sirius adjusted his seat to the upright position again to be more alert for this conversation.

"The other day, they found out I was using the phones in the common room," Aurora explained. "The thing is, we can only use those phones to call family or potential placements. Thankfully, I told the counselor, Mrs. Hansen, about my dilemma, and she said I could use her office phone to call you, as long as she isn't busy."

"Well, that's good."

"I guess, but I think my friends might have connected the dots." Aurora sighed, sounding worried.

"Ah, I understand now. Because they caught you using the phones, they figured out you have a placement, and now they want to know all the details."

"Yeah. They were so nosy. They kept asking me all these questions, but I can't tell them anything," Aurora groaned. "I dodged their questions for now. I just told them I didn't want to talk about it, because I was worried that Ms. Davis would mess things up."

"That was smart," Sirius encouraged.

"I guess. I just really hate lying to them especially since they're my only friends here."

"I understand. Aurora, do you think you could trust them with the truth?"

"Mmmm...probably not."

"Alright, you need to trust that."

"What do I need to trust?"

"Yourself—you need to trust yourself," Sirius paused. "Aurora, I'm sure you know that feeling—the feeling when you are second-guessing yourself because you know it's a bad idea. I want you to trust that instinct."

"So what if I did trust my friends?"

"Then I will have to trust you to make a wise decision based on your instincts, but I also need you to trust me."

"I do trust you. Well, I think I do. Anyway, it wouldn't be smart to tell them. If I did, everyone in the center might end up knowing."

"Then I guess you have your answer," Sirius replied, smiling.

"Mr. Marino, can I ask you something?"

"Of course, you can ask me about anything."

"Okay, I was going to ask you last time, but I didn't have a chance. To be honest, I was a little nervous."

"What is it, Aurora?"

"That Sunday, when you were talking about your parents, you mentioned you were going home from Midnight Mass. Does that mean you're Catholic?"

"Umm...no, I'm not. I was raised Catholic, but I don't practice Catholicism anymore. Why do you ask?" Sirius was genuinely surprised by Aurora's question.

"Are you religious then? Or are you an atheist?"

"I'm a Buddhist," Sirius answered. "What about you?"

"I don't know." Aurora hesitated.

"Don't know what?" Sirius questioned, wondering why she got hesitant all of a sudden.

"I don't know if I want to say," Aurora said quietly.

"Aurora, you were the one who brought it up."

"I know," Aurora sighed.

"What's the matter?" Sirius asked. "Why are you sounding scared? You did say you would talk to me about anything."

Aurora could hear the concern in his voice. "Because there's stories. Stories about foster families not letting their foster kids—you know—practice their religions."

"Aurora, I think I get what you are saying," Sirius replied kindly. "Is that what you are concerned about?"

"I guess."

"Did something happen to you? Did someone in a former home prevent you from practicing your faith?"

"Kind of, but something really bad happened to a friend of mine." Aurora paused, prompting Sirius to talk.

"Aurora, you can tell me—whatever it is. What happened?"

"Her name was Yasmine. We went to school together. She was a devout Muslim, but she was placed with a family who hated all religions. I knew them; there were a lot of crazy rumors about that family."

"What kind of rumors?"

"That family was nuts. They were completely against practicing any religion, and a lot of the kids who were placed there ran away. They treated Yasmine terribly; they took away her Qu'ran, her hijab, and her prayer rug."

"That's not right. They should have been reported," Sirius responded in a shocked voice.

"It was a terrible situation, and Yasmine was miserable. They tried to make her into someone she wasn't, and she ended up hating her life," Aurora said sadly.

"Is she still with that family?" Sirius questioned. "Do you still talk to her?"

"No one can help her—not anymore," Aurora's voice cracked on the other side of the phone, and it sounded as if she was trying to hold back tears. "She's dead."

"I'm so sorry, Aurora. Do you know what happened?" Sirius was stunned.

"Yasmine ran away. She told me she was going to go to her old mosque. Apparently, the mosque's imam had connections in Israel and Jordan and other places. She hoped to somehow find a way to get to her extended family who still lived in Jordan. That was her plan, anyway," Aurora explained, sniffling. Sirius could tell she was crying on the other end.

"How did you find out about Yasmine's death?" Sirius asked softly.

"I was at school, not long after Yasmine left, and they made an announcement. They told everyone and had a moment of silence, honoring Yasmine. I don't know the details of how she died—just that the cops found her body."

"Oh Aurora, I'm very sorry for your loss," Sirius responded. "Did anything like that ever happen to you too?"

"Yeah, the reason I know so much about her is that I was with the same family for a few weeks. They took something really important from me." Aurora sniffled.

"What did they take?"

"They took my Bible; it was our family Bible. It was one of the few things I was able to take with me to all my different placements that no one wanted to steal, until I got to that family."

"I'm so sorry. Aurora, I want you to know I will never do anything like that. If religion is a big part of your life, then no one should take that away from you."

"Really?"

"Yes, really, and I'm assuming it was illegal for them to do that—well, according to the foster care system guidelines of New York."

"Why do you say that?"

"Well, that's because freedom of religion is a right that we have as Americans. It's the first amendment of our United States Constitution. We have the right to worship freely, the right of the press, and the right of free speech. No one should take away your rights," Sirius explained.

"I thought you said you were Italian," Aurora unexpectedly interjected.

"I am. I was born in Italy, but I'm also an American citizen now. Remember?"

"That's right...so, you're technically Italian-American?"

"Yes. I officially became a citizen several years ago—actually, on my twenty-eighth birthday. Right now, I have dual citizenship, so I'm an Italian by birth and an American by choice."

"That's really cool."

"It sure is! I love being part of both countries, especially with their traditions," Sirius stated. "So, was that your only concern?"

"Yeah, I just didn't know if you would allow me to practice my religion, so that's why I didn't say it at first," Aurora admitted.

"Of course, I will. As I said, it's your religion; you can practice it, and I will never tell you to do otherwise or to change because of my personal beliefs."

"Thanks, Mr. Marino," Aurora answered, sounding relieved on the other end.

"I hope I have calmed your nerves about that. Now, how has everything else been?" Sirius looked out his car window again—no Felix or Bridgette yet. *I hope they are even later than usual, because I would like to continue this conversation.*

"Everything's fine," Aurora stated.

"So what have you been up to?"

"Not much, been praying a lot—I think that's what is keeping me sane. There's just a lot to deal with here."

"That makes sense," Sirius commented. "Is there anything else on your mind?"

"Yeah. There's this girl Myra—she said something interesting to me today. I'm kinda worried about it."

"Why? What did she say?"

"Well...Myra and I don't exactly get along; she's a real creep to me and my friends. Anyway, she came up to us and said something about how my 'best friend' is currently in intake. I told Myra she would have to explain, since I had no idea what she was talking about. Then she just started to be really annoying; she finally walked away after she saw a guard looking over at us."

"Hmmm, that's interesting. Do you think what she said has any validity?"

"I don't know; Myra isn't our friend. I think she was just trying to stir up trouble, but I wonder if someone I know from one of my previous homes is really here."

"Alright, just be very careful, Aurora. If anyone threatens you, please tell someone at the center immediately, or ask to call me. I don't want anything to happen to you." Sirius felt a sudden protective urge; something he had never experienced before.

"I'll be alright. If I learned one thing from being here, it's to keep your head down and your mouth shut. It's the best way not to get beat up or shanked." Aurora laughed.

"Oh my, just please take care of yourself, and be cautious and safe," Sirius warned. "*Fratello*!" Sirius jumped, as Felix banged on his window.

"Hey, dude! What are you doing?" Felix yelled, his face pressed up against the car window glass.

"Hold on, I'll be right there, you lunatic," Sirius mocked.

"What's the matter?" Aurora questioned, sounding slightly panicked. "Are you okay!?"

"I'm fine. My friend Felix apparently thought it would be funny to try to give me a heart attack by banging on the car window when I wasn't paying attention!" Sirius glared at Felix and pointed to the phone, signaling his friend to back off. "Anyway, I need to go, before he decides to try to pry the phone out of my hand and drag me out of my car," Sirius explained.

"Would he really do that?" Aurora laughed.

"He just might."

"Wow, okay. Hey, Mr. Marino? Please try not to worry too much about me."

"I'll try not to, *bella*. Anyway, call me anytime," Sirius responded. "Oh—one more thing I need to ask you, so my Aunt Liv doesn't do me in. What's your favorite color?"

"Umm, blue, I guess. Why?"

"I'll explain later," Sirius answered.

"Umm, okay, TTYL," Aurora said the acronym as she hung up the phone.

"*Ciao*, Aurora," Sirius said. "Hey, why did you two drag me out here at the crack of dawn and then show up late?" Sirius questioned, as he got out of his car and walked up to Felix. Both of them laughed, seeing the look of frustration on Sirius' face. They were always late for every appointment thanks to Bridgette's morning make-up and hair routine, and as usual, she was the picture of perfection, even this early in the morning.

"Sirius, I thought you liked yoga." Bridgette smiled.

"I do, but it's usually something I do alone for meditation," Sirius explained, locking his car door and starting to walk towards where the class was being held in the park.

"Well, think of it as a group meditation session to help you mellow out any uneasy vibes," Bridgette replied, jogging ahead of the men to complete her warm up. "See you boys there!"

"Mellow out uneasy vibes?" Sirius questioned, turning to Felix. "Is she serious?"

"Hey, don't look at me! This was all her idea," Felix defended himself, pointing at his fiancée, who was gracefully jogging towards a line of trees and some other people doing downward dog.

"Why are you supporting this craziness?" Sirius asked.

"Dude, if I were you, I'd just go with it! It's so much easier that way," Felix answered. In a joking manner, he put his arm around Sirius' neck, putting him in a headlock.

"Karma is going to kick you to the curb." Sirius grunted, struggling out of the headlock, and pushing Felix away. "Seriously, Felix—did you mention anything to her about my life-changing decision?"

"No way, do you really think I would do that to you?" he asked sincerely.

"Of course not, I trust you like a brother. I'm sure Bridgette is just trying to help decrease my stress level in her own strange way, which I don't think is actually going to help." Sirius rubbed the back of his neck, trying to work out a few stress knots.

"Do you want to tell her that?" Felix teased.

"Mhmm, I might be crazy—just not that crazy," Sirius scoffed. "How about *you* say something?"

"Nope! I'm not going to mess with her so-called 'brilliant idea.'" Felix laughed. "Anyway, you know she is just worried about you. She thinks of you like an older brother."

"That's true. We have known each other a very long time. I am grateful Bridgette cares so much for this lonely old bachelor."

"Hey! Are you guys coming or not!? The class is about to start," Bridgette yelled out to them.

"*Arriviamo*; we're coming!" Sirius yelled back. "Well, let's get this over with," he said, looking at Felix grinning.

"Hey, at least your stress can't get any worse from doing some yoga," Felix responded.

"Oh, Sirius!" they both heard a sweet voice call out. Turning towards the voice, they saw Sierra's sprightly form in a hot pink yoga outfit, walking briskly toward them from the parking lot.

"Oh no..." Sirius groaned.

"So, I was wrong." Felix laughed. "Your stress is going to get sooooo much worse." Felix's laughter got louder the closer Sierra got to them.

"Did I mention that Sierra has gone from a pest to completely irritating?" Sirius whispered, not wanting Sierra to hear.

"Yep," Felix answered back in a whisper.

"I think she just leveled up to stalker!" Sirius mumbled.

"You are *doomed*," Felix replied, working hard to breathe in between laughing.

"It's *not* funny," Sirius grunted.

"What's not funny?" Sierra asked sweetly as she came up to them, her perfectly white sneakers and blond hair fairly sparkling in the morning sun.

"Oh, nothing," Felix quickly answered, choking back a laugh.

"Hello, Sierra. What are you doing here?" Sirius questioned, crossing his arms.

"Oh sweetie, you know I love yoga! It's so calming," Sierra said cheerfully, touching Sirius' forearm possessively.

"Oh yeah, since when?" Felix chuckled.

"I wasn't talking to you, Felix," Sierra replied harshly in Felix's direction.

"And that was a rhetorical question," Felix mumbled under his breath.

"What was that?" Sierra's eyes narrowed, grabbing Sirius' arm in a lock grip.

"What was what?" Felix asked. "Did you hear something, Sirius?"

"Nope." Sirius laughed, and pulled his arm gently away from Sierra's iron grip. *For a tiny woman, this lady has got a ridiculously strong grip!*

"So what's the hold up?" Bridgette interrupted, fixing her bun while walking back to Sirius and Felix. "Oh, hi Sierra! What are you doing here?"

"I'm here to take the yoga class, of course," Sierra said, changing her tone to a more pleasant one again.

"How wonderful! The more the merrier," Bridgette answered.

"Great, this will be so much fun!" Sierra replied, looking at Sirius adoringly.

"Felix, a little help." Sirius coughed, hoping to cover up what he said.

"Hey, Bridgette, let's set up our yoga mats on the lawn while these two have a pleasant conversation," Felix said, giving Sirius a thumbs up as he led Bridgette away.

"Felix! That's not what I meant!" Sirius yelled after him. He turned to Sierra. "What are you really doing here?" he questioned her, his eyes narrowing at the petite blond in front of him.

"I told you, I'm here for the yoga class," Sierra answered innocently.

"Sure you are. The real question is, how did you know I was going to be here?"

"Oh Sirius, I didn't!" Sierra acknowledged. "Why don't you believe me?"

"Because you've given me no reason to trust you," Sirius said bluntly as he walked away.

"Sirius, wait!" Sierra ran after him to catch up with his long strides.

"What do you want, Sierra? I've told you before, I want nothing to do with your drama," Sirius explained calmly, turning back to her.

"I just want to talk."

"Sierra, we have talked. Well, I've talked, and you've screamed. Having a conversation doesn't work that way. If you want me to listen to you or consider what you have to say, you have to first listen to what I am saying. Having a conversation is a two-way street."

"You're right, and I'm sorry about how I acted the last time we met. Can I just get a do-over? Can we please try to have one of what you consider a real conversation?" Sierra asked, looking at him with large puppy eyes.

"I don't know."

"Come on, Sirius; I truly am sorry!" she exclaimed. "I didn't mean to act that way the last time we talked. I don't know what came over me. Maybe I was just jealous about the woman you were talking to because I didn't know it was a relative. I won't be as crazy from now on—please."

"Alright, alright, if you really want to talk, we can. But just as friends," Sirius relented.

"Then maybe we can grab coffee after the yoga class," Sierra said, smiling perkily.

"No, not this time, Sierra. I have something important I need to do after this class."

"Like what?" Sierra questioned scornfully.

"Excuse me?"

"What is more important than fixing our relationship?" Sierra seethed.

"Are you seriously starting this again?" Sirius questioned. "Sierra, we don't have a relationship. You are an acquaintance—nothing more, nothing less."

"Why don't you want to be my boyfriend? We are perfect for each other, Sirius!" Sierra pouted. "I don't know why you would want to jeopardize your career by not being with me—a world-renowned influencer! Unless...you have been seeing someone else, and you are the one lying to me! What was her name again, that girl on the phone? Amanda? Anastasia?"

"Are you threatening me? First, you try to pressure me into a re-lationship, and when I turn you down, you threaten me—such an ingenious plan." Sirius couldn't help but laugh at her ridiculous ideas.

"How dare you laugh at me? I can make your life miserable," Sierra threatened.

"Okay, good luck with that," Sirius responded, backing away and rolling out his yoga mat on the lawn. "Enjoy the yoga class—far away from me, please!"

"You're such an idiot!" Sierra screamed at him, turning around and stomping off in the opposite direction.

"Hey, Sierra! The yoga class is in this direction," Felix called out to her as he made his way back to Sirius, pointing towards the rest of the class. "Uh...guess you guys didn't have a pleasant conversation?" He pointed to Sierra's retreating form.

"Not whatsoever," Sirius answered, shaking his head wearily. They watched Sierra huff toward the parking lot as fast as she could, her blond ponytail bobbing angrily.

"What happened?"

"She didn't want to take no for an answer." Sirius sat down on his yoga mat and crossed his legs.

"Wow! That girl is nuts." Felix laughed and sat down on his own mat.

"That's a nice way to put it."

"I'm guessing you two aren't going on another date anytime soon?"

"Not a chance," Sirius grumbled.

"Well, at least you won't be dealing with two crazy ladies, because I'm thinking what's-her-name is going to be a handful," Felix remarked.

"I don't know about that. I have a feeling Ms. Davis is going to be the true handful until the adoption is finalized, and after that, I'll get grief from everyone else—everyone but her," Sirius explained.

"Umm, I'm confused. Are you referring to 'her' as Sierra or Aurora?" Felix asked, going into downward dog position after seeing the yoga instructor start the popular yoga warm up pose.

"Who do you think?" Sirius followed suit.

"Aurora," Felix answered. "Am I right?"

"*Sì*," Sirius replied, focusing on the next yoga pose.

"Sirius, what took so long for you to join? We've been at this for a while already, and where's Sierra?" Bridgette questioned.

"Answer to your first question is Sierra, and the second is—she left. Thank goodness," Sirius mumbled.

"Oh, okay," Bridgette replied. "By the way, couldn't help overhearing your conversation just now. Who's Aurora?"

"Ugh." Sirius sighed.

"Did I say something wrong?" Bridgette asked, looking concerned.

"Nope—just don't worry about it, honey. Sirius is dealing with the after-effects of Sierra-toxicity," Felix said, trying to keep a straight face.

"Okay, got it! Sorry I said anything," Bridgette replied, before going back to her yoga pose.

"It's all good. Let's just get this over with." Sirius laughed as he breathed a sigh of relief. He was thankful Bridgette had dropped the question about Aurora's identity after Felix spoke up. Hopefully, Bridgette would be a huge support for both him and Aurora after the adoption was finalized. Aurora would definitely need a few positive female figures in her life. *I hope Bridgette can be like an older sister or maybe even an aunt for Aurora.*

As Sirius breathed in and out deeply, releasing the stress of his latest Sierra encounter, he couldn't help but smile at the thought of having a family of his own. Their chance for a family came about in an unexpected way and would be small and a little broken, but perfect for him and Aurora—a family was what they both needed right now.

Chapter 13

Monday, April 1st

"Sɪʀɪᴜs! Sɪʀɪᴜs, ᴅᴀʀʟɪɴɢ, ᴀʀᴇ you home?" Aunt Liv yelled as she walked through the entryway, closing the door behind her.

"Yes, Aunt Liv, I'm up here!" Sirius yelled from the upstairs hall of his California mansion.

"Good morning, darling," Aunt Liv said. She walked energetically up the stairs and met Sirius in the hall, giving him a kiss on the cheek. "First, please tell me you have coffee. Second, what are you doing up here?"

"Well, to answer your first question, it depends if you mean American coffee or *caffè*." Sirius teased.

"*Caffè*, of course! Well, more specifically, I'd love a cappuccino. I don't know how Americans can drink that terrible coffee they love so much. You wouldn't find that in any Italian home, especially not mine."

"I'm aware. You know I always have your favorite espresso ready for you when I know you are going to make an appearance. What kind of nephew do you think I am?" Sirius put his arm around his aunt and gave her a reassuring squeeze.

"This is why you are my favorite nephew!" Liv said proudly.

"*Zietta*, you are aware I'm your *only* nephew, right?" Sirius asked jokingly as he walked into the first bedroom on his left with Aunt Liv right beside him.

"Yes, of course, so back to my question. What are you doing up here?" Aunt Liv asked.

"I'm figuring out what to do with Aurora's room."

"That's smart. You know that is my main reason for being here, so we can get everything situated for Aurora's homecoming. Also, thank you again for picking me up at the airport, and on time too," Aunt Liv commented happily.

"You're welcome—you know it's no problem." Sirius smiled at her, thankful that she was there. "You know, I think we should start getting this room situated today."

"Why so quick?"

"I just have a feeling that her room needs to be done sooner rather than later."

"Do you think something is wrong?" Aunt Liv asked, her brows furrowed.

"I don't know," Sirius answered. "But I think something feels a bit off; I just don't know what it is."

"Well, follow your gut. You always have, and it's never steered you wrong. Now, back to Aurora's room. Any idea what you are going to do in here to make this look like a girl's room and something Aurora will love?" Aunt Liv glanced around the empty bedroom.

"I'm going to see Aurora soon, so I'll get some more ideas as to what she will want her room to look like then. Hopefully, I can worry less about feeling like something is off."

"Well, just hang in there. There's not much you can do about that now."

"That's true," Sirius stated as he walked over to the large window and looked at the view of his Italian gardens below.

"That girl is going to feel like she is in heaven when she gets here," Aunt Liv commented.

"I'm sure she will, especially after everything she's told me about her previous foster homes. So, what do you think about the room for her?" Sirius questioned, gesturing to the walls around him.

"I think it's a nice location and size. However, it lacks color and furniture."

"Yes, it does," Sirius laughed, looking at the cream-colored walls and beige carpet. "But I was referring mostly to the layout of the room. What are you thinking?"

"Hmm…about the furniture, I think a queen-sized bed would look really nice along that wall with end tables on either side. Of course, she'll need a nice dresser with a large mirror; and we can't forget bookcases, because we know how much she likes to read."

"Well, she also should have a desk, so she has a place to do her schoolwork. I was thinking of having two large bookcases."

"Umm… don't you mean you're thinking about having four book-cases?" Aunt Liv raised her eyebrow, and looked at her nephew with a twinkle in her eye.

"Really, Aunt Liv? I was thinking it would more like this." Sirius pulled out his phone, showing her a picture of the bookcase desk he was thinking of purchasing. "Three of the bookcases will technically be connected to her desk, so that's one big piece, and there will be a bookcase on the opposite side of the dresser. That's two."

"Your math is flawed. One plus one plus one is three, and if you add the other one, that's four," Aunt Liv said.

"Those three on the one wall will be one unit. It's like they equal the value of x."

"Seriously?" Aunt Liv questioned, her eyes widening.

"Yes, it's called math, or algebra." Sirius laughed.

"Well, aren't you a *mattacchione*?"

"Oh, Auntie, I thought you loved my jokes," Sirius teased.

"Only when they're funny!" Aunt Liv protested.

"Well, you and *zio* raised me, so the blame for my terrible jokes comes from you two!"

"Alright, fine, whatever you say. Have you made any decisions regarding Aurora's life for after she gets here?"

"Like what?"

"Have you decided where Aurora is going to attend school? What about her current grades? Will she need extra help to get ahead? Are you going to employ a nanny to assist you? There's a lot to think about," Aunt Liv said in a gentle but assertive tone.

"Yes, I have looked into all of that. I'm thinking of having her go to Horizon Acres School. I've made sure she has all of the tools she needs to succeed there. I also found a certified counselor at a local church, if she wants to talk to someone about anything." Sirius thought back to the conversation he had with Aurora. *I will do everything in my power to make sure Aurora has everything she needs to succeed at life.* Aunt Liv's surprised voice pulled him out of his musings.

"A counselor? At a church? What church have you been to recently?"

"Yes, at a church, I went to Calvary Bible Church. They have counseling services there. As I said before on our way back from the airport, I want Aurora to be able to talk to someone who can listen to her and give her good life advice for as long as she wants. She's been through so much trauma—from her parents dying to being abandoned by her relatives to being thrown from foster home to foster home, and now she is in a juvenile detention center only because all of the group homes were full. Well, that's according to Ms. Davis. Who knows if that's the real reason?"

"That poor girl." Aunt Liv sighed. Looking at Sirius, she asked, "What about this private detective that you told me about? Have you heard anything from him?"

"*Sì*, I have. Ms. Davis has been involved in many illegal activities with no one in the foster care system stopping her because of her excellent bribery skills."

"Well, we already know she isn't a saint," Aunt Liv said sarcastically.

"She most definitely is not, but there's a big difference between doing something unethical versus something illegal."

"Is it that bad?"

"Let's just say if she gets caught, she will be going to prison for a long, long time. She seems to be putting children in horrible homes on purpose, and these foster homes aren't even real homes. It's all a ruse."

"And?"

"According to the detective, she's trafficking these foster kids," Sirius stated. As he shared the truth with his aunt, his heart broke for the many innocent children who had suffered.

"Who would believe a social worker—someone who is supposed to help children—would do terrible things to the children in her care?" Aunt Liv stated with her big brown eyes filling with tears.

"I think that's the point. Who would believe it?" Sirius asked. "Thankfully, the warden, the prison counselor, and even a few police officers don't trust her; and they are also pursuing their own investigation."

"Well, I suppose they can testify against Ms. Davis if this goes to court."

"I really hope she doesn't get a full trial. I want her to plead guilty and be locked up before any more kids get hurt."

"I hope so too, Sirius," Aunt Liv agreed. "Anyway, on a happier note, I can't wait to go shopping for Aurora's room décor."

"Fantastic!"

"Did you find out what her favorite color is?" Aunt Liv asked.

"*Sì*, blue; *credo*."

"Wonderful, this is going to be so much fun!" Aunt Liv exclaimed.

"I'm glad you're thrilled, but I think you may want to wait for her with some decision."

"Oh, don't worry—I figured we would just paint the walls and have it all ready for her to add some finishing touches. It will be more fun that way."

"I'm sure she'll love that," Sirius replied, smiling at his aunt's enthusiasm.

"Mmm, I just want Aurora to feel safe and at home here," Aunt Liv said. "I want her to feel special."

"She's been through a lot. I don't just want her to feel special—I want her to feel loved. That's a feeling I'm sure she hasn't felt in a long,

long time. Now, let's go down and continue this conversation over cappuccino."

"When did you become so wise?" Aunt Liv questioned softly, following him out of the bedroom back into the hallway.

"I have a great family who inspired me to become a wise old man."

"You're going to be a great dad, Sirius."

"I hope so," Sirius answered. As Sirius and his aunt walked towards the kitchen for Aunt Liv's cappuccino, Sirius reflected, *Aurora has been through so much. I just want Aurora to be happy and loved. She needs all the love my family can supply, so maybe someday she can feel complete.*

(Tuesday, April 2nd)

"Have I mentioned how much I hate this place?" Sandra whined, gesturing around the cafeteria of the juvenile detention center.

"Uh, yeah, just about a hundred times a day," Aurora answered. "Is there a new reason?"

"Yeah, the food stinks," Sandra complained loudly.

"That's not new," Lexi pointed out.

"You make it sound like I mentioned it before," Sandra said.

"You have—waaay too many times," Aurora sighed dramatically. "You really need to come up with something more creative. Maybe use some more adjectives."

"Ha-ha-ha, not funny! Especially since you aced that dumb gram-mar test. Why do we even need to know any of that useless stuff?" Sandra complained.

"So you can sound smart during job interviews," Aurora answered, grinning at Sandra. "How did you do on that test?"

"Uh, don't ask. I hate school!" Sandra said.

"You know if you studied more in your free time, maybe you would ace tests more often," Aurora suggested.

"Yeah! Instead of watching your reality TV shows," Lexi added, grinning mischievously.

"Hey! You didn't do great on that test, either, Lexi," Sandra pointed out.

"You don't need to rub it in," Lexi said.

"Yeah, you really shouldn't," Myra interrupted, walking over to their table from a nearby desk. "Especially since we can't all be as smart as little 'Miss Perfect.'"

"I never said I was perfect," Aurora replied calmly. "And you are bugging us, because?"

"Because she can," another voice declared boldly. The three girls looked over to see a scrawny girl with bright pink hair walk casually to their table.

"Oh, crud," Aurora murmured under breath.

"Hey, loser! Did ya miss me?" the pink-haired girl sneered.

"Hi Mara, it's great to see you too," Aurora said sarcastically.

"You two know each other?" Sandra questioned, eyes opened wide.

"Unfortunately," Aurora said, gritting her teeth. *God, please don't let Mara or Myra see how scared I am, and please don't let me have a panic attack right now.* Aurora could feel her heartbeat start to quicken.

"Unfortunate for you—not for me," Mara sneered.

"Hey, Mara, you should take her down a peg." Myra laughed wickedly.

"Wow, now we have a Myra and a Mara. What are the chances of that?" Sandra laughed. "Hey, are you two going to start a club?"

"Shut up!" Myra yelled, pulling her fist back. Before Myra could throw a punch, Mara grabbed her arm and pulled her back.

"Myra, stop!" Mara said, as loud as she could without notifying the guards on duty. "Leave them be."

"What!? Come on, girl! We need to show them who's boss!"

"No!" Mara said sternly.

"But why?" Myra whined.

"Because I said so. My war is with Aurora. As long as those leeches don't get in my way, they won't get hurt," Mara explained. "I would watch your back, Bennett. You'll get what's coming to you."

"Hey, skinny girl, get lost!" Lexi said, as she stood up and took a step towards Myra and Mara, clenching her fists.

"Lexi! Stop! Do you wanna go to solitary?" Aurora jumped up from her chair to get in front of Lexi to stop her from doing something she might regret. "Mara, just walk away. It's not worth getting in trouble over."

"You can't tell me what to do, Bennett," Mara taunted, jabbing a finger at Aurora's chest.

"Not trying to. Just stop acting like a brat before you get sent to the infirmary or solitary." Aurora brushed Mara's hand away.

"I can act however I want in here!" Mara yelled.

"Fine! You wanna be this way? Then go ahead and be crazy, but no one here is interested!" Aurora yelled back. "Your battle is with me, so leave them alone."

"I will, as long as your freakish friends stay out of my way," Mara sneered.

"Good, now I suggest you back away from us before one of those guards sees you and decides you're up to no good. I don't think you want to be labeled a troublemaker the first few days you are here," Aurora suggested. Her voice sounded confident, but she was shaking internally. *Pull yourself together, Aurora*, she said to herself.

"Whatever, I'm not worried. But I'll leave you alone—for now. I can't risk having either of us being thrown in solitary; then I can't have my fun," Mara explained, grinning evilly.

"Mara, you better hope they put one of us in solitary, because if you mess with me or my friends, you will be sorry. I'll make sure of it!" Aurora threatened, her green eyes flashing at her old nemesis.

"Really? You didn't scare me before, and you don't scare me now. You're pathetic," Mara said, glaring at Aurora with her arms crossed.

"You should be a little scared, Mara. You don't have your lawyer mother to bail you out. She can't save you this time!"

"Go to..." Mara started to yell, turning away from Aurora and her friends.

"You wish," Aurora interrupted.

"Watch your back, Bennett! I'm coming for you!" Mara fumed as she stomped away, pulling Myra with her.

Aurora sat back down at the table and took a deep breath. "Hey, girls—do me a favor and stay far away from her."

"Aurora, what's going on? How do you know Mara?" Lexi questioned.

"It's a really long story," Aurora said, sighing.

"What's the short version?" Sandra asked.

"Mara is the biological daughter of one of my previous foster families," Aurora said. "She really hates me."

"What did you do to invoke her wrath?" Lexi asked.

"Nothing—she just hated me from day one. In fact, I don't know who's more evil—Mara or her mother. They both made my life miserable, but I never did anything to either of them. I was nothing but nice to them. My mom always said: 'Kill them with kindness.' But it always seemed to backfire and make them madder when I didn't react."

"Wow! That's nuts," Lexi said.

"Yeah, it is. That girl is a witch!" Aurora declared.

"So, she's not just mean, she's also crazy?" Lexi asked.

"Umm, no. Well, yes, she is. But what I mean is—she's a witch. She's into all of that dark stuff. She even threatened to put hexes on me once," Aurora explained.

"Please tell me you're kidding," Sandra said.

"Nope, she's scary. Anyway, she has caused me a lot of issues. She blamed me for things I didn't do—illegal things; and she eventually got me kicked out of the house," Aurora continued to explain. "That girl is the queen of manipulation."

"Oooh, that's bad. That's really bad," Sandra said, her eyes popping.

"You think? I'm dead," Aurora cried, putting her head in her hands.

"So, what are we gonna do?" Lexi asked.

"What do you mean, we?" Aurora said, looking up at Lexi.

"She means we're not letting her get to you," Sandra said in a protective tone.

"Yeah, if she wants to hurt, she's going to have to go through us!" Lexi agreed.

"You guys can't do that. I'm not going to let you." Aurora felt tears of gratitude well up in her eyes, but the whole encounter had shaken her up, making her stomach churn.

"Yes, we can, and you don't have a choice," Lexi demanded. "Friends don't let friends go down without a fight, especially with someone as creepy as Myra or Mara."

"I don't know. Umm...Lexi, Sandra, I gotta go. I think I'm gonna be sick," Aurora squeaked out, jumping up from the table and dashing to the hall. She had just gotten past the door before someone grabbed her arm and pulled her back. "Let me go!" she yelled, trying to pull free, thinking it was Mara.

"Hey! Bennett! Where do you think you're going?" she heard a voice ask.

Oh, thank God it's only Officer Walters, she quietly prayed. "Please, Officer Walters, let me go!"

"Bennett, get back to your table. You have ten more minutes of meal time."

"Please, I need to use the bathroom," Aurora cried, tears streaming down her face. "I'm going to be sick."

"Alright, alright," she said, letting her go. "Go ahead. Just hurry up."

"Yes, ma'am, thank you," Aurora answered before speed-walking down the hall to the bathroom. She stormed through the door and into one of the stalls. Bending over, she retched into the metal toilet bowl in front of her.

"What do I do now?" she asked herself out loud. "Ugh, I probably should tell him about this; he's not going to be happy." She thought she was going to be sick again when she suddenly felt someone holding her hair back. She quickly got up and pulled away from whoever was behind her and grabbed a paper towel from the sink and wiped her face clean. She looked up to see Lexi and Sandra standing in front of her.

"You okay?" Sandra finally asked empathetically.

"Yeah, I guess," Aurora answered nervously.

"What was that about?" Lexi questioned.

"It's nothing."

"It doesn't sound like nothing. And who were you talking about?" Lexi asked.

"What do you mean?" Aurora pretended not to know whom Lexi was referring.

"You said 'I should tell him' and 'he's not going to be happy.' Who are you talking about? Not the warden, right? Does it have to do with the family you are going to be placed with?" Lexi continued to ask.

"I really wish you hadn't asked about that."

"Why? What is going on? Why won't you tell us anything? You must be afraid of something other than Mara and Myra," Sandra suggested.

"I'm not afraid. It's just complicated." Aurora sighed, leaning against the bathroom wall.

"Aren't we your friends? Can't you trust us? Explain, Aurora," Sandra demanded.

"I'm not supposed to," Aurora answered, as she slid down the wall and sat on the grungy bathroom floor. Lexi shuffled to Aurora's side and sat down next to her.

"Seriously, Aurora, just tell us," Lexi said softly, putting her hand on Aurora's shoulder.

"Okay, fine!" Aurora conceded. She threw her arms up in the air in frustration. "But you girls can't say anything."

"We won't," Sandra said, as she sat down on the other side of Aurora.

"No, you guys have to swear you won't tell anyone. This is a really big deal. I may never have another opportunity like this in my life. I don't want to mess it up, and that witch Ms. Davis is trying whatever she can to stop it," Aurora explained.

"Aurora, we swear. What's going on?" Lexi questioned.

"Okay, you guys know that before I came here, my friends and I would pickpocket, so we had money for food and to escape those bad foster homes, right?"

"Right," the girls confirmed in unison.

"Well, the night before I was brought into juvie, I got caught pick-pocketing."

"By the police?" Lexi interrupted.

"Not exactly...umm...I got caught by someone else. He—umm—let me go. He followed me to the school and then to the police station."

"That's really creepy. Why was this guy following you?" Sandra asked.

"To make sure I was safe. I mean—I was out really late, like 1 a.m. It makes sense why he'd be concerned. Then I went to the school to sleep instead of to my foster home. So in a way, I understand," Aurora explained.

"True, but when you're a foster kid in a bad home, that's life. It's a normal thing to be out late," Sandra said.

"Yeah, well, he didn't grow up like that, from what I know."

"So why bring him up? What does he have to do with anything?" Lexi questioned.

"Umm, because he is the one trying to adopt me," Aurora admitted.

"What?!?" Sandra and Lexi questioned, looking at Aurora and each other in shock.

"Yeah, I kind of figured that would be the reaction, but that's not all. It's not just the fact that he's adopting me. It's because of who he is."

"What do you mean?" Sandra asked.

"He's kind of somebody."

"Somebody—such as?" Sandra continued.

"Well, you both know him or know of him."

"Umm...how do we know 'of' him?" Lexi questioned.

"His name is Sirius Marino," Aurora said quietly.

"What!?!" they exclaimed, more loudly than before.

"Yeah, I know. It's crazy." Aurora laughed nervously.

"Oh, come on, tell us who's really adopting you," Sandra stated.

"I did. It's Sirius Marino," Aurora confirmed in a whisper.

"Aurora, are you serious?" Lexi asked.

"Yeah, I wouldn't have told you if I wasn't, and the reason I didn't tell you guys earlier was because he didn't want anyone to know," Aurora explained, looking back and forth between the two girls. "What? Say something."

"Oh my goodness, that's insane," Lexi said.

"Hold up, let's say you are telling the truth, and not to be mean or anything. But why would he want to adopt you?" Sandra questioned. "I mean he is a movie star, and you are a foster child, unless he's doing it for attention."

"That's a possibility. Have you thought of that, Aurora?" Lexi added.

"I thought that too, but he said that attention wasn't the reason. In fact, he is trying to keep it out of the media. He said something along the lines of he doesn't want the paparazzi showing up here."

"Wait, he told you that?" Lexi asked. "When?"

"Umm, when he came here to visit me."

"He was here? When!?" Sandra exclaimed, jumping to her feet.

"Not too long ago, and he is the one I've been calling," Aurora admitted. "He seems to be sincere, and I think he actually cares about what happens to me. I mean, he wasn't happy about me coming here, and he can't stand Ms. Davis. He's been dealing with her continuously and going to court to fight her, which means he's fighting for me. If he was just doing this for attention, I don't think he would deal with all that added stress."

"Okay, you've got a point," Lexi said. "And we understand why you didn't say anything."

"Yeah, we get it," Sandra agreed.

"Good, and you won't say anything, right?"

"Of course not," Lexi responded.

"Our lips are sealed," Sandra added.

"Okay, and let's not talk about this around the others, alright?"

"No problem," Lexi confirmed.

"Alright, now that we know what's going on, let's get out of here before someone sends a guard in here. I don't need to get in trouble for breaking rules again," Sandra declared.

"Good idea," Aurora agreed. "We'll have another secret meeting some other time; then I can tell you more."

"Oooh, I love gossip," Sandra remarked.

"We know," Lexi and Aurora said in unison, as they all left the bathroom and headed to the common room for free time. Aurora felt so relieved after telling the girls about Sirius. *I feel like I can breathe again. Hopefully, everything will continue to look up.* "Hey girls, I think I'm going to use the phones."

"Why?" Sandra asked.

"I need to talk to—you know; I should tell him about Mara," Aurora stated. "Hopefully, she won't do anything that will make me stay here longer than I have to."

"Okay, have fun," Lexi replied.

"Yeah, enjoy your time! We'll make sure no one bothers you," Sandra added.

"Thanks girls," Aurora replied. She quickly walked over to where the phones were. "Please, be home. Please be available," she said quietly, as she dialed his number and listened to it ring. She heard Sirius greet her after the second ring. "*Buon pomeriggio*, Aurora, how are you?"

"Hi, I'm fine," Aurora said, as she played with the wire connected to the phone. "How about you?"

"I'm doing well," Sirius answered. "Aurora, do you mind if I put you on speaker phone? My aunt is here, and she wants to say hi."

"Umm, sure, that's fine," Aurora said, a little flustered.

"Alright, *bella*, you're on speaker now," Sirius replied.

"Hi Aurora darling, this is Aunt Liv. I'm Sirius' aunt."

"Ohh, hi!" Aurora exclaimed.

"I just wanted to say *ciao* and see how you are doing," Aunt Liv stated. "Also, I was wondering what are your favorite colors. We are working on your room, and I wanted to know what colors we should use."

"Umm, blue and purple," Aurora answered. "But you could just leave the walls white. It doesn't matter to me."

"Oh, alright, what would you rather?"

"I'm not sure...nobody has asked me that before. I guess my favorite would be light blue."

"Very well, I have another question for you; what activities do you enjoy?" Aunt Liv asked.

"Umm, I like to read, and I enjoy writing."

"Anything else?" Aunt Liv asked.

"I like ballet; I always wanted to take ballet classes," Aurora answered.

"Okay, wonderful, that was very helpful!" Aunt Liv exclaimed. "It was really nice talking to you, and I can't wait to meet you in person. Now, I'll let you and Sirius get back to your conversation while I start designing your room."

"It was really nice talking to you too, and I can't wait to meet you either," Aurora said excitedly.

"Bye Aunt Liv," Sirius said loudly. "So how is everything, Aurora? Are you okay? It's not like you to call me two days in a row."

"Umm, not really—you know how you said I can tell you anything."

"Yeah, of course. What's wrong?"

"I need to tell you something," Aurora said, trying not to cry, but failing. "Remember yesterday when I said that girl Myra was bugging me and my friends about how my best friend is currently in intake?"

"Yeah, I remember."

"Well, umm, I know who it is now. It's this girl named Mara. I know her from before; she's the biological daughter of one of my previous foster families. She really hates me with a passion."

"That's not good. Did she say anything to you?" Sirius asked.

"Yeah, she said—umm—she said she's coming for me. *Papà,* I'm–I'm really scared," Aurora stuttered. "I don't know what to do."

"Hey, *bella,* calm down; everything is going to be okay," Sirius started. "First, you need to say something to Warden Sanchez and the counselor. Second, just try to keep your head down. In the meantime, I'm going to see what I can do about this."

"What can you do? I'm stuck here for thirty more days." Aurora couldn't help but cry, letting the tears fall down her face.

"Aurora, don't worry about that. For now, just talk to Warden Sanchez and Mrs. Hansen. They will know what to do."

"I can't do that," Aurora continued to cry.

"Why not?" Sirius asked.

"You don't understand. If I say anything, I'll be labeled a snitch. Then it won't be just her that comes after me," Aurora rambled, starting to freak out.

"Aurora, listen to me. I know you're scared, but you have to say something to someone. At least promise me you will talk to the counselor. If you don't, I'll have to contact Warden Sanchez."

"Alright, alright, I'll do something. Just please—please don't say anything to anyone," Aurora pleaded.

"*Bella*, if you aren't going to say anything, then I need to. One of us has to be the responsible one. If I say something, then you won't have to do anything. You won't get labeled. You have to trust me," Sirius explained.

"Fine, it's fine. Hopefully nothing bad will happen until my release," Aurora stated. "*Papà*, do you know what's going to happen after I get released? No one has told me anything."

"I'm not sure. From my knowledge, you'll be placed with me. I haven't heard anything else. As I said before, just trust me. Everything will work out."

"Okay, I do trust you; you're the only one who has actually cared."

"Well, I'm glad you trust me. Just for now, be careful. Keep your head down," Sirius explained. "Perhaps say a few prayers."

"I do pray, *papà*—all the time. I'm just really scared."

"I know you are, and that's okay. But you shouldn't have to feel that way. Again, just be careful."

"I will. Anyway, there's something else you should know."

"What is it?" Sirius asked.

"I kind of had to tell my friends about everything—well—almost everything," Aurora admitted. "I'm sorry. They were concerned about me, and I just had to tell them the truth."

"Aurora, it's fine. I understand. You did what you felt you had to do."

"Really?" Aurora asked.

"Yes, of course. However, now that more people know, there is a better chance that this could leak out to the media. Once the media knows, the whole internet knows," he said. "It may not happen, but it could."

"So you're not mad at me?" Aurora asked.

"No, absolutely not, I'm not upset; I'm not mad. I am just concerned."

"Why are you concerned?" Aurora questioned cautiously.

"Aurora, darling, you are new to this world—my world. The paparazzi and the media can be a real nuisance; they have a habit of taking a story and twisting it to fit whatever narrative they want. It's not right, but it's what they do. That's how they sell magazines; it's how they get views on their websites. I just want you to be aware," Sirius explained.

"Will it always be like that?"

"Yes, and when the world does find out about you, it's going to be crazy for a while. So crazy, that we will want to keep our heads down for a bit; just until they find someone else to exploit."

"That makes sense," Aurora agreed.

"Are you okay?"

"Yeah, I think so; and I trust you to help me through it all. You will be there for me, right?" Aurora asked.

"Of course, I would never abandon you. Aurora, I will be there for you always," Sirius promised.

"Okay, anyway, I should go. My friends are waiting for me."

"Okay, be careful. Be good. I'll see when I can get over there to visit you," Sirius replied.

"Sounds good," Aurora responded. *"Buonanotte papà."*

"Oh wow! Someone is learning Italian," Sirius chuckled.

"Yeah, I thought I would spend some of my free time learning the language." Aurora smiled to herself.

"That's great. Well, have fun with that. *Buonanotte bella*."

"*Ciao, papà*," Aurora replied, just before hanging up the phone. She hoped he was right—that everything would be fine, but something was telling her this was going to be a long and difficult journey.

Chapter 14
Thursday, April 4th

Aurora stood near her cell door, waiting for the heavy metal door to automatically unlock and open. *Here we go—another day in juvie, whoopie.* As the door opened, she walked into the hall and lined up with the other girls. She was so tired of all the procedures and regulations. Stand up straight, no leaning against the walls, no talking in line, no talking to friends; keep your hands and feet to yourself, and no high fives or hugs with friends. After being in juvie for a month, Aurora was already exhausted. She felt bad for those who had to stay longer, especially those in similar situations as herself.

As she stood in line waiting, she looked down at her feet making sure she was standing up straight with her hands folded behind her back, just as the rules specified. There was no way she was going to get into trouble for not following instructions, especially since her release date was right around the corner.

"Aurora…" an eerie voice whispered.

"Aurora…" the voice whispered again.

Aurora looked around, seeing if she could spot any of her friends close by who might be messing with her. She scanned the line, until she found them standing at the end of the line, minding their own business. She turned back forward and figured she was just hearing things.

"Aurora..." the eerie voice said once again.

She turned to face the girl standing behind her. "Did you hear that?" she asked her, as quietly as she could.

"Shhh, no talking. Do you want to get us in trouble?" the girl snapped at her.

"Sorry," Aurora responded, turning to face forward again. Aurora shook her head. *Maybe I'm losing it.*

"Hey, loser!" she heard the eerie voice say in a slightly louder tone. She shuddered, knowing exactly who it was now. She looked behind her and saw Mara glaring at her. *If looks could hurt, I would be seriously injured right now.* She was about to say something to her when the guard on duty told them to start walking to the cafeteria. As they made it to the large cafeteria, she made a beeline for one of the tables, hoping to evade Mara just long enough for her friends to join her. She quickly found an empty table and sat down, hoping Mara would go straight into the single file line for breakfast. Aurora looked behind her, and to her dismay, saw Mara heading in her direction.

"There you are, Aurora," Mara said, almost sweetly.

"Was I missing?" Aurora asked sarcastically.

"You know it was a good thing I caught up to you, or we would have missed this special time together," Mara said, sitting down at the table across from Aurora. She smirked wickedly.

"Do you have anything better to do than bug me? Why can't you just leave me alone?" Aurora questioned, clenching her fists.

"Because this is just too much fun," Mara sneered.

"Lucky me," Aurora mumbled. "What do you want?"

"That's for me to know," Mara bullied.

"Wow, that's informative," Aurora said, rolling her eyes.

"Hey, Mara!" Aurora looked over to see Lexi and Sandra walking quickly over towards the table. Sandra was practically yelling across the noisy cafeteria. "Take a hike, Mara! Aurora might let you annoy her, but we won't. So go away! Now!"

"Fine," Mara said, as she stood up from her seat. She went over to Aurora and leaned over her, so she could whisper in her ear. "I'll see you later, girly."

"Go away, Mara!" Aurora insisted, pointing toward the other side of the room.

"Alright, I'm going." Mara turned abruptly and walked over to join Myra and her friends.

"You okay, 'Ora?" Sandra asked, as soon as Mara was out of earshot.

"Yeah, she's just being really creepy," Aurora said.

"What did she say?" Lexi asked, glaring at Mara's departing form.

"Umm, she was just trying to scare me earlier. She was following me, so I came in here as fast as I could. I was hoping she would go straight for the food instead of bugging me, but I was wrong," Aurora explained.

"We saw that," Lexi stated, sitting down next to Aurora with her tray of French toast, oatmeal, and raisins.

"You did?" Aurora questioned.

"Yeah, so we got you breakfast," Sandra said, putting her tray on the table before sitting down.

"I'm surprised they let you do that," Aurora mumbled, eyeing the food on the tray.

"Me too," Sandra agreed. "Maybe they know who is—you know—adopting you."

"I doubt that, but thanks." Aurora grabbed her bowl of oatmeal from the tray and took a small spoonful. Her encounter with Mara had killed her appetite. She thought about how her mornings would be in the near future with her *papà*. It made her happy to daydream about it. She just had to survive a few more weeks of Mara's bullying before getting out of her current nightmare for good. "Hopefully, Mara will leave me alone now," Aurora said biting a piece of toast. "Then when I leave here, I'll never have to deal with her again."

"Girl, you should fight back! If she pushes you, push back harder," Sandra said, sipping her cup of orange juice.

"I really don't wanna get thrown into solitary, Sandra. Also, you-know-who won't be happy with me if I do that. I kind of promised him I would stay out of trouble," Aurora replied.

"That makes sense, and you know, we're glad you have someone on the outside that cares about you," Lexi said.

"Yeah, I kinda wish I had that too. You're lucky. Actually, you're really lucky," Sandra said in a hushed voice, not wanting those around them to get curious.

"Who are you losers talking about?" Myra questioned, walking up to the table with her arms crossed.

"None of your business, Myra," Aurora said. *Oh God, please help me to be able to deal with Myra and her craziness.*

"Are you being adopted out of the system or something?" Myra asked, not backing away.

"She said it's none of your business!" Lexi raised her voice.

"Wow…I can't believe someone actually wants to adopt you. Don't they know you're just a good for nothing piece of trash? They'll probably throw you back into the system in less than a month," Myra sneered.

"Go away, Myra!" Aurora yelled. "We just told your creepy name-twin to go away, and the same goes for you."

"Hey, she was just asking a question," Mara said, as she walked up behind Myra.

"It didn't sound like just a question," Aurora said, mocking Mara's tone.

"Well, it was!" Mara seethed.

"Really? Because it sounded like an insult! Now, go away, or you're gonna regret it," Lexi threatened, glaring at Mara and Myra until they looked away.

"Whatever!" Mara turned to walk away but stopped right behind Aurora. She laughed loudly, striking Aurora on the back of the head and pushing her face into her bowl of oatmeal.

"You have got to be kidding me!" Aurora exclaimed.

"Oops, clumsy me," Mara said sarcastically.

"Go away!" Aurora jumped up from her chair and stood in front of Mara, invading her personal space. "Back up, or I'll make you." Aurora watched Mara back up so she can get by; but when she tried to pass, Mara tripped her, causing her to slam into the floor.

"Mara!" Lexi and Sandra yelled in unison, jumping up from their seats and going straight to Aurora, so they could save her from her tormentors.

"You should watch where you're going, Bennett," Myra teased, laughing hysterically.

"You may want to watch what you're doing!" Aurora said loudly, as she stood up from the ground with her friends' help. "You never know who may be watching." Aurora looked around the room, realizing that they had the attention of those around them.

"You better not be threatening me!" Mara yelled, getting in Aurora's face.

"I'm not—just warning you. Look around. We caught the attention of almost everyone around us, and it looks like you caught the attention of the guards," Aurora pointed out, watching a guard come up behind Mara.

"Is there a problem here?" Officer Anderson asked, as he marched over to the group. Mara and Myra slowly turned around and came face to face with the ill-tempered guard.

"Hello, sir, we're just having a friendly chat," Mara said sweetly.

"A chat, huh? It doesn't look like it's just a chat, and it certainly doesn't look friendly," Officer Anderson pointed out.

"Well, it is. If you were paying attention, you would know that. Right, Aurora?" Mara asked her.

"Aurora, is that what happened?" Officer Anderson questioned.

"Umm, yeah," Aurora answered, seeing that the guard hadn't witnessed any of the bullying. She assumed he probably just heard the commotion and came over to deescalate the situation before it became physical.

"Are you sure, Aurora?" Officer Anderson asked her again.

"Yeah. But if you don't believe me, just check the cameras," Aurora quickly added. She glanced at Mara, who scowled at her.

"Alright, then, I will," Officer Anderson said.

"Good," Aurora stated.

"I don't think that's necessary," Mara intervened.

"I do, and Miss Brown, I suggest you lose that attitude of yours; if you don't, we're going to have an actual problem," Officer Anderson warned.

"Fine," Mara mumbled.

"Good, and the same goes for the rest of you!" Officer Anderson shouted at the girls before walking away.

"Yes, sir," the group said in unison, not wanting to get into any trouble.

"I suggest you stay out of my way, Mara," Aurora warned. "You just got a free pass, but the next time you mess with me, I won't let you get away with it."

"Whatever, you just better watch your back," Mara seethed, as she grabbed Myra's arm and pulled her away from Aurora and her friends.

"I'm not afraid of you, Mara—you or your evil twin!" Aurora said, finding an inner courage she didn't even know she possessed.

"We'll see about that," Mara warned.

"Are you okay, Aurora?" Sandra asked, putting her hand on Aurora's shoulder.

"Yeah, I'm fine," Aurora confirmed.

"Are you sure?" Lexi questioned.

"Yeah, I'm sure. We just have to be really careful what we talk about when we're not in private. You don't know who could be listening," Aurora said, sighing loudly.

"Not a problem," Lexi agreed, sitting back down at the table with Sandra by her side.

"Yeah, we don't want anyone knowing things that's none of their business," Sandra added. "But can you tell us how that phone conversation went?"

"Sandra, are you serious? You just said that—" Aurora started, before Sandra interrupted.

"I know, I know. I didn't mention names. Just how'd it go? Did you say anything about Mara?"

"Yeah," Aurora mumbled quietly. "I mentioned it. He's concerned; he doesn't want me getting hurt."

"He and us both—we don't want anything to happen to you either," Lexi confirmed. "Did he say anything else?"

"He said I should tell someone about the bullying," Aurora confided.

"Well, you probably should," Sandra replied.

"What!?" Aurora questioned, shocked her friends would even suggest that. "I'm not a snitch," Aurora insisted.

"We know, but this is serious. It's not just a random bully; this is Mara. You know her from your past. Who knows what she will do? I mean, she hates you. We can tell she really, really hates you!" Sandra exclaimed.

"Sandra is right. What if she tries to do something?" Lexi wondered.

"Like what?" Aurora asked.

"Like, what if she tries to end you?" Lexi questioned.

"I don't think she would do that," Aurora stuttered, as she fiddled with her fingers.

"Why wouldn't she? She has nothing to lose. She's in jail for who knows what. What's stopping her if she really wanted to kill you?" Lexi asked.

"Nothing, I guess," Aurora mumbled.

"You see? You have to tell someone," Sandra urged.

"Alright, alright, I will."

"Good," Lexi responded, and she looked down the hall and paused. "Hey girl, there's Mrs. Hansen! Go talk to her."

"Now?" Aurora asked, looking exhausted.

"Yes, now, what if something happens? You need to talk to her!" Sandra agreed.

"Fine, I'm going. If anything does happen, it's your fault," Aurora stated, teasingly.

"Oh, okay, we get it," Sandra said.

"Yeah, anyway, you better catch up before she gets too far down the hall," Lexi added.

"Alright," Aurora mumbled, before running up to Officer Anderson, who was watching the mess hall. "Excuse me, sir, can I go talk to Mrs. Hansen for a minute?"

"Miss Bennett, it's time for breakfast, and then you have to go to classes. You can talk to her later," Officer Anderson said.

"Please, it's really important—like mental health emergency important," Aurora said quickly, hoping the guard would believe her.

"Do you really have to talk to her now?" Officer Anderson questioned, looking agitated by her request.

"Yes, please," Aurora begged.

"Fine, just hurry up." He sighed.

"Thank you!" Aurora yelled, as she ran down the hall. "Mrs. Hansen, wait up!" Aurora ran up to her and stopped short before she could run into her.

"Aurora Bennett, what are you doing out here? Shouldn't you be eating breakfast?" Mrs. Hansen asked.

"Yeah, but I kind of lost my appetite," Aurora said, glancing back at the mess hall before looking at Mrs. Hansen again.

"What's wrong, Aurora?" Mrs. Hansen commented.

"It's—umm—that new girl, Mara. She has been causing me some trouble," Aurora said, nervously playing with her thumbs.

"Aurora, did you do anything to antagonize her?" Mrs. Hansen questioned.

"No, of course not," Aurora stated frantically. "I know her from before—she's the kid of one of my old foster parents."

"Okay," Mrs. Hansen commented.

"She's always did things to get me in trouble, but now that she's here, it's continuing," Aurora explained. "I thought that you should know."

"All right, well, I'm glad you told me," Mrs. Hansen stated.

"Well, I kind of had to. I made a promise to someone," Aurora admitted.

"I'm guessing that someone is Mr. Marino," Mrs. Hansen stated.

"Yeah, it was *papà*, and Sandra and Lexi—they all convinced me."

"*Papà*?"

"Yeah, you know—I thought I should start calling him that, since he's going to be my dad," Aurora said.

"That makes sense," Mrs. Hansen commented. "You have a smart dad."

"I suppose," Aurora said.

"You really do," Mrs. Hansen confirmed. "And thank you for coming to me, Aurora. Now, I suggest you get going before you miss your class. Something tells me you're going to have a busy day."

"Alright," Aurora answered, as she watched Mrs. Hansen walk down the hall to her office.

"Snitching on me, loser?" she heard Mara say behind her. Aurora nearly jumped out of her skin.

"Mara, what are you doing out here!?"

"I thought it was weird when you left the mess hall the way you did, so I thought I would see what you were up to," Mara explained.

"Wonderful, now get out of my way," Aurora said coldly.

"You should be nice to me," Mara warned.

"Why is that? We hate each other, and that's never going to change—no matter what."

"That's not true. You will, because if you don't, I'll tell everyone about your dad," Mara threatened.

"What are you talking about? I don't have a dad," Aurora said, attempting to walk past Mara.

"Yes, you do," Mara stated, as she roughly grabbed Aurora's arm and pushed her back. "That's right. You don't call him 'dad' or 'daddy.' You call Sirius *papà*, right?"

"What did you say?" Aurora could only stare in shock at what Mara had just said.

"You heard me. Aurora Bennett's adopted father is *the* Sirius Marino—the movie star. Wow, wow, wow! How did a loser like you manage that? How did you even meet him?"

"That's none of your business," Aurora warned. "Now, get out my way! Leave me alone! Or you will regret it!"

"Aww, I don't think your new dad will like it that you're threatening me. I wonder what it would take for him to abandon you, like your aunt and uncle did," Mara said.

"Leave me alone!" Aurora yelled, hoping she would get the attention of the guards.

"No way," Mara scoffed. "If you don't want trouble, you'll do whatever I say."

"You're insane; that will never happen!" Aurora shouted, as she pushed by Mara. Mara quickly grabbed her by the arms and slammed her into the wall, causing her to fall to the ground. "Ouch! Mara, leave me alone!"

"If that's how you're going to be, then it's your funeral." Mara loomed over Aurora. "Think about it—when everyone in the center finds out, they'll treat you differently. You should know what can happen when these girls get jealous," Mara warned. "When that happens, you won't be just my punching bag."

"I don't care! I've survived worse than you," Aurora said as she got up from the floor.

"You should. I'll make sure you'll regret it if you don't," Mara threatened. "Maybe I'll even put a hex on you."

"Go ahead," Aurora said, pushing past her and walking away as fast as she could.

"You'll be sorry!" Mara screamed down the hall.

"Whatever!" Aurora yelled back, running down the hall to the mess hall to be with her friends. As she got there, she saw that all the girls had lined up to go to classes. She quickly got in the back of the line with Sandra and Lexi. "Girls," Aurora whispered, as loud as she could without any of the guards hearing her. "9-1-1, we have an emergency."

"What is it? What happened with the shrink?" Sandra questioned quietly.

"Mara knows," Aurora whispered.

"What do you mean she knows?" Lexi asked.

"Mara knows about him," Aurora clarified.

"How?" Sandra and Lexi asked together.

"She—she heard me talking to Mrs. Hansen. We may have brought it up, and she heard us," Aurora said. "Oh my gosh, I think I'm going to be sick."

"That's not good," Sandra said.

"Sandra, shut up," Lexi scolded. "Aurora, are you okay?" Lexi asked her, noticing how pale her face had just become.

"No, what do I do, girls? I'm scared," Aurora admitted, as she felt an unsettling chill creep up her spine.

"Girls!" they heard a guard yell at them. "Quiet! No talking in line!" The three girls immediately stopped talking. They watched as the guard turned away from them and went to yell at someone else for leaning against the wall.

"Aurora, you need to tell him," Sandra whispered to Aurora, as quietly as possible.

"I know," she whispered back.

"Let's go, girls!" the guard barked at them. Aurora and the girls immediately started walking in the line. When they arrived to the classroom, they took their seats and waited for the teacher to begin the lesson. As Aurora sat there, she couldn't stop shaking. Mara knew her secret—a secret she promised her *papà* she would keep.

What will he say? Will he be angry with me? Will he be angry enough to abandon me, like Mara said? No, he wouldn't do that; he actually cares for me. But still, what do I do?

She sighed quietly, trying not to draw any attention to herself. Aurora realized what she had to do—she had to tell him, no matter what the consequences would be. She just hoped she could get through this in one piece.

She could barely pay attention in class; she was way too nervous. She could feel Mara watching her. As soon as the class ended, she ran to the bathroom and quickly went to one of the metal sinks to splash cold water on her face. She looked at herself in the mirror, and her face was white as a ghost. She took some slow, deep breaths as she prayed to God, asking and begging Him to help her.

The bathroom door opened and slammed shut, making her jump. She heard footsteps heading her way. Afraid it was Mara, she quickly ran into one of the stalls. Aurora locked the stall door and sat on the toilet, waiting for the room to clear out. She heard a bunch of voices—talking and giggling about random stuff but mostly complaining about life in juvie. After a bit, all of the noise ceased. She was about to leave the bathroom stall when all of a sudden, she heard the bathroom door open and close again. She froze in fear, praying it wasn't Mara or Myra.

"Hey, Aurora," she heard someone say. Aurora couldn't speak; for some reason, she couldn't figure out who it was. "Aurora, where are you?" she heard the voice ask.

"Aurora, it's us—Sandra and Lexi."

Aurora took a deep breath, relieved it was her friends. "I'm in here," Aurora said quietly. She slowly unlocked the stall door and gently pushed the door open. "Hey," she squeaked, glancing at them.

"Are you okay? We saw you run out of the classroom, and we figured you came in here," Sandra said.

"No, I'm not okay. But what else is new?" Aurora stated.

"You'll be fine," Lexi said to her.

"You're kidding me, right? Girls, I'm dead," Aurora said.

"I doubt you're dead," Sandra said.

"No, I am. You even said so," Aurora said.

"I was just giving you the worst-case scenario. I didn't think it would really happen," Sandra commented, hoping Aurora would believe her.

"No, she is going to tell everyone. Who knows how everyone is going to treat me after that?" Aurora questioned.

"No one is going to hate you, except maybe Mara and Myra," Sandra said.

"I really hope you're right." Aurora sighed.

"We are. Anyway, let's get to class. We can't be late," Sandra replied.

"Yeah, come on, Aurora," Lexi stated, grabbing onto Aurora's arm and pulling her along.

"You guys go ahead," Aurora pulled her arm back. "I'll be there in a minute."

"Are you sure?" Lexi asked.

"Yeah, I'm fine. I'll be right behind you," Aurora assured them. As Aurora watched them leave the bathroom, she leaned against the sink and took a deep breath. After a couple minutes, she went to the door and slowly opened it. When she saw no one around, she ran out of the bathroom and headed into the hall to her next class.

"Oh, looooser!" she heard Mara's piercing voice.

She quickly turned to face her and asked, "What do you want?"

"You know what I want," Mara stated.

"Yeah, I do, but I'm not doing anything for you," Aurora said, clenching her fists.

"You should. I'll make sure you'll regret it if you don't," Mara threatened. "I'll tell everyone about him. Maybe I'll tell everyone that he's more than just your daddy."

"You wouldn't dare," Aurora seethed.

"Just watch me. I'll make your life worse than hell," Mara threatened again.

"You know what? Go right ahead," Aurora said, pushing past her and trying to run away from her tormentor as fast as possible.

"Hey! I'm not done talking to you!" Mara yelled, grabbing Aurora from behind and throwing her against the wall. Aurora fell back, slamming her head against the wall and hitting the ground with a thud.

"Mara! Leave me alone," Aurora shouted, as she put her hands to her head, hoping the room would stop spinning. The only thing Aurora could think to do was pray. *Jesus, please help me. Protect me from Mara. Help me be strong.*

"What are you going to do about it, loser? Or maybe I should call you Jezebel? Isn't that how you got the movie star's attention?"

"Shut up!" Aurora yelled back as she jumped to her feet. She staggered but quickly regained her balance. Then she shoved Mara into the wall behind her. "I kicked your butt before, and I can do it again.

Don't mess with me!" Aurora yelled, as she watched Mara grip her side.

"You'll be sorry!" Mara screamed.

"Whatever," Aurora commented. Trying to walk away, Mara kicked her legs out from under her, making Aurora fall to the ground in a heap. As Aurora tried to get to her feet, Mara's fist slammed into the side of her head, catching her completely off-guard.

Mara continued to take advantage of Aurora, throwing punches all over her body. Aurora quickly turned over to protect the front of her. She felt like she was being attacked by multiple girls, until it suddenly stopped.

"Knock it off!" she heard a voice yell. "Take these three to solitary!" Aurora heard that same voice say. She tried to get a good look at her Good Samaritan, but she could hardly see straight from being struck in the head so many times.

Suddenly, she heard Mara scream, "I will get out of solitary, loser! And when I do, I will get even!"

As she trembled in fear, Aurora felt someone pick her up. She tried to stay as still as possible, since it hurt too much for her to move around. Just before she lost consciousness, she prayed. *Jesus, help me.*

Chapter 15
Thursday, April 4th

SIRIUS WAS JOGGING DOWN the path behind the homes in his gated community when he felt his phone buzz. After checking his caller ID, he saw it was his PI. *Finalmente! I hope he found something good,* he thought to himself as answered his phone. "Hello?"

"Mr. Marino, it's Jack."

"Hey, Jack, please tell me you have something," Sirius said.

"Yeah, I do," Jack responded.

"That's good to hear. What did you find out?"

"It's not good. It looks as though Ms. Davis is running some kind of trafficking ring."

"Wow," Sirius commented. "I was hoping that wasn't the case. Are you sure?"

"I'm positive. All I had to do was follow the money. It seems Ms. Davis has been paying everyone off—the doctor at the juvenile detention center that left years ago and the doctor that was recently fired."

"That's not surprising."

"No, it's not, unfortunately," Jack stated. "I also found some police officers and social workers who may be involved, and of course, no one is saying anything; but it seems Ms. Davis is connected to everyone involved."

"That also doesn't surprise me, considering Ms. Davis tried to bully me into backing down," Sirius stated. "Did you find out how she can afford to pay those people off, or what kind of information she had on the others?"

"No, I haven't, but I'll keep looking into it. Don't worry," Jack said assuredly. "I hope the information I found is helpful to you."

"It is; I'm going to put a stop to the trafficking, or at least try. But first things first, Aurora needs to get out of that center. It's a dangerous place for her to be right now," Sirius explained.

"What do you know, Mr. Marino?"

"Nothing really, I just have a bad feeling; in fact, I've had a bad feeling for weeks."

"Have you talked to the warden about it?" Jack asked.

"Of course I have, but he assured me that everything is fine, seeing as they have procedures as well as a no bullying and fighting policy. Like that's going to make a difference."

"Well, hopefully, you'll get her out of there soon." Jack agreed sympathetically.

"That's the plan," Sirius stated. "By the way, did you find out how Ms. Davis got the information on that police report?"

"I'm guessing you are referring to the document she's trying to use to make you look unfit."

"That's the one," Sirius confirmed. "That report is supposed to be sealed. There's no way she should've gotten her hands on it, even the judge is stumped."

"Probably the same way she has been getting away with everything else—paying someone off," Jack suggested.

"Wonderful," Sirius mumbled. "Were you able to find anything else?"

"Unfortunately, no, but I'll keep digging. I'll keep you updated. For now, I need to update the warden."

"Okay, sounds good, and thanks again for looking into all this. I know you're technically retired," Sirius said.

"It's fine, and I do owe you one. Anyway, got to go." Sirius heard Jack hang up the phone.

"*Ciao.*" Sirius sighed as he started to run back to his house. He needed to clear his head; that conversation made him feel sick. How could someone who is supposed to be taking care of kids do that? It was absolute *ridicolo*. He had no idea how he was going to stop Ms. Davis. Sirius took some deep breaths and chanted, "This challenge is temporary, but my strength and resilience are permanent. Trust in the journey," he mumbled, trying to push the situation from his mind. He was deep in thought when he heard a familiar voice yelling his name.

"Hey, Sirius! Wait up!" Felix yelled as he ran to catch up with Sirius and grabbed him from behind.

"Felix, what are you doing here!? Do you have a death wish?" Sirius asked. He turned to Felix. "You were lucky I wasn't using my earpods; I wouldn't have known it was you. You could have ended up with my fist in your face."

"Sorry, do you know how hard it is keeping up with you? Man, how can you run so fast?" Felix said, panting hard and doubling over in pain.

"You know if you worked out regularly, you could actually keep up with me," Sirius joked. "So, why are you here? Don't you have a home across the country in New York?"

"Yeah, but Bridgette and I—well, Bridgette thought you needed to have some fun."

"Blaming this on her?"

"Sure, why not? Hey, it's an excuse for us to come out here and have a big *festa*," Felix explained.

"It's good to know I can always count on you guys." Sirius laughed, as he and Felix started to walk back to Sirius' house.

"Of course you can! What kind of friends would we be if you couldn't?" Felix joked. "Come on, let's go. We have the makings for some great drinks; we even have stuff to make spritzs."

"*Festa* and spritzs, huh? You're starting to sound a lot more Italian," Sirius laughed. "You know, that's not a bad thing."

"How's everything with the adoption going, or do I even want to ask?"

"You wouldn't believe it," Sirius mumbled.

"Man, that Ms. Davis is really causing you trouble—I mean, I can't believe she took you to court!"

"Yeah, she's something else."

"Well, at least there's nothing she can use against you! You're clean as a whistle," Felix said.

"Am I really?" Sirius asked sarcastically.

"Umm, yeah, unless you've done something I don't know about."

"Nope, you know what I know," Sirius groaned. "Thankfully, she has nothing. Ugh, that woman is driving me crazy."

"So you've mentioned. Did you say any mantras?"

"Yes, of course. I was just saying one when you interrupted my jog," Sirius commented, elbowing Felix in his side.

"Is that still helping you deal with life?" Felix asked teasingly.

Sirius smirked at Felix's comment. "Honestly, Felix, the mantras are not helping like they used to. It makes no sense."

"I wouldn't stress about it too much. Now, let's get to your house. Whoa!" Felix stopped short, and his eyes opened wide with shock.

"What?" Sirius asked.

"What's with the piranhas in front of your gate?" Felix questioned, pointing to the large steel gate in front of Sirius' house.

"You have got to be kidding me," Sirius seethed. "Not the paparazzi! What are they doing here!?"

"Do you think it's because of—you know?"

"Because of Aurora?" Sirius asked.

"I mean, Sierra *did* say that you would be sorry. Do you think she said something to the media?" Felix wondered.

"Hey! There he is!" one of the paparazzi yelled before Sirius could respond. All of the paparazzi came rushing up to them with cameras flashing in their faces and shouting at them with demands to look their way.

"Sirius! Sirius, is it true? Are you involved with a younger woman?"

"What's her name? Amanda?"

"Did you officially break up with Sierra? What happened between you two?"

Felix and Sirius tried to push their way through the crowd toward the side of the property, but their voices were drowned out by the reporters. "Hey! That's enough! This is private property! Now get out, or I'm calling the police!" Sirius yelled at the top of his lungs.

"Leave! Now!" He watched as the group of reporters backed away at his booming voice. Just as they were given room to breathe, Sirius and Felix took off towards the back of the house.

"Dude, get us in!" Felix yelled, looking back over his shoulder and seeing some of the flashing cameras still in pursuit.

"I'm working on it," Sirius said. He punched in the code and unlocked the digital lock on the large steel gate. As soon as the gate was open, they rushed inside and slammed the gate shut, locking it.

"Is it locked?"

"Yeah, yeah," Sirius replied.

"That was nuts!"

"This is bad," Sirius mumbled, as they made their way into the house through the back door.

"Hey! You two! What's going on? What's with the circus out there?" Bridgette questioned.

"Oh, hey baby, what do you mean?" Felix asked, playing dumb.

"Don't do that! You know what I mean. Now, what's going on? What's with the piranhas?"

"Umm, Sirius," Felix started, elbowing him in the arm to get his attention. "We—I mean, you should probably tell her."

"I know." Sirius groaned.

"Tell me what? What did you two do?" Bridgette asked them accusingly.

"Why do you think I was involved?" Felix questioned.

"Because it's always you, so start talking. Or I might just clonk you over the head with a frying pan," Bridget threatened.

"Okay, okay, Sirius please tell her—before she resorts to violence," Felix said, folding his hands in a prayer position.

"Fine, it's just a crazy story. You might want to sit down for this," Sirius prepared her.

"Okay, I'm sitting," she said, as she sat down in a nearby chair. "Now, I suggest one of you start explaining." Bridgette folded her arms over her chest and glared at both of them, waiting for one of them to speak.

"Well, there's no good way to say this—Sirius is nuts," Felix teased.

"Really, Felix," Sirius scolded, slapping him playfully on the back of his head. "Ignore him; Bridgette, the truth is, I'm in the process of adopting a kid from the foster care system in New York."

"Say what?" Bridgette asked, her eyebrows raised in shock.

"You heard him—he's going to be a father!" Felix said enthusiastically, slapping Sirius on the back.

"Felix, quiet!" Bridgette yelled at him. "Sirius, please tell me you're kidding."

"I'm not," Sirius said.

"Why would you want to do something like that?" Bridgette questioned.

"Wow! I did not think that would be her reaction," Felix said with astonishment, looking over at Sirius apologetically.

"Bridgette, really? I thought I would get more support from you," Sirius said.

"Sorry, it's just that the paparazzi out there put me on edge. They ambushed me when I was unloading the car from shopping. My bad for leaving the gate open for too long." Bridgette sighed.

"Oh *Mama Mia*, *questo è pazzesco*," Sirius mumbled.

"Dude, this being crazy is an understatement," Felix pointed out.

"Is that why they are here? Because of the adoption?" Bridgette asked.

"I don't think so. There seems to be more to it than that. Outside, they were asking who I was dating; there was no mention of the adoption," Sirius declared. "I think they are on a wild goose chase, by guess who?"

"Who?" Bridgette asked.

"Ooohhh, I know—this has to be Sierra's doing," Felix said, grinning.

"Why do you say that?" Bridgette asked.

"Do you really need to ask?" Felix gave her a look.

"He's right. It was before that yoga class. After I told her to get lost for the hundredth time, Aurora called me," Sirius explained. "And as soon as I hung up, I had to deal with Sierra again. She apparently overheard part of our conversation. She thought Aurora was someone I was interested in romantically."

"Is Aurora able to call you? From you-know-where?" Felix asked.

"Yes, she is," Sirius confirmed.

"Hold up, who's Aurora?" Bridgette questioned, looking at the guys. "Come on guys, no more secrets."

"That's the girl Sirius is adopting," Felix said.

"Okay, and where is she?" Bridgette questioned again.

Felix answered, "That's the tricky thing. The 'you-know-where' refers to the juvenile detention center where she is being held."

"The kid you're adopting is in jail?" Bridgette questioned Sirius. "Why? What did she do?"

"Nothing!" Sirius answered. "She's being held in juvie because all the group homes were full, and it doesn't help she has a reputation for running away."

"Oh my goodness, *tu sei pazzo*," Bridgette said slowly, obviously still in shock.

"I think we have already established that I'm crazy," Sirius said. "Anyway, I told Sierra she was way off track, but she threatened me. She said she would ruin me. She probably assumed I was dating a younger woman."

"Wow, I've said it before, and I'll say it again. She is nuts," Felix confirmed.

"Psycho is more like it," Bridgette commented.

"You didn't believe me when I tried to tell you both this before," Sirius said. "Anyway, there's more to the story."

"What do you mean?" Bridgette asked.

"It's just—at the detention center where Aurora is, there is this girl. She knows Aurora from a previous foster home, and apparently, they don't get along. In fact, this girl went out of her way to threaten Aurora," Sirius explained.

"That's so scary—that poor girl," Bridgette said.

"Is she worried?" Felix asked.

"Yes and no. Yes, because this girl certainly has it out for her; and no, since the detention center has a no fighting and no bullying policy," Sirius said, wearily running his hands through his hair.

"Well, that's good," Felix said.

"Yeah, it is. Hopefully, everything will be fine."

"You don't sound too confident." Bridgette observed Sirius as he nervously fiddled with his phone.

"I guess it's more wishful thinking, but still, she should be fine," Sirius stated. "Oh no," he mumbled, looking down at his phone as it lit up.

"What now?" Felix asked.

"It's the detention center," Sirius commented.

"Is that bad?" Felix probed.

"No idea. Guess I need to go deal with this first before I start doing some damage control," Sirius stated.

"You do that. We'll finish setting up," Felix reassured him.

"Wonderful," Sirius said sarcastically. He walked down the hallway and went upstairs to his room, so he could have some privacy. "Hello?" he said, answering his phone.

"Hi Sirius, it's Mr. Sanchez," he heard the warden's voice say.

"I figured. How is everything?" Sirius asked.

"Not great, that's why I'm calling," Mr. Sanchez commented. "I'm sorry to have to tell you this, but Aurora was attacked."

"What happened?! Is Aurora okay?" Sirius inquired.

"Right now, she's asleep. She's got some bad bruising, but that's it. It's a miracle she's not hurt worse," Mr. Sanchez assured him. "I'm assuming she's told you about a certain girl."

"She has."

"Well, she's the one who attacked Aurora." Mr. Sanchez sighed.

"Ugh, that girl is going to be trouble," Sirius mumbled under his breath.

"There's more," Mr. Sanchez said.

"Why doesn't that surprise me?" Sirius asked. "What is it?"

"The girl who attacked Aurora—she knows," Mr. Sanchez said.

"She knows what?"

"She knows that you are adopting Aurora."

"How did this happen?"

"Aurora went to talk to the counselor about this girl. Mrs. Hansen apparently brought up your name and how you're adopting Aurora. That's how she found out. This girl is trying to get at Aurora, by threatening to tell the whole center. That's what the security cameras show," Mr. Sanchez explained. "I'm really sorry about this."

"It's fine. It's not your fault; it's not anyone's fault really," Sirius said as he lightly rested his head on the wall.

"Well, I'm glad to hear that. I'm going to try my best to keep a lid on things. For now, the girl is in solitary confinement, so she won't be able to do anything."

"Is there a chance she already has?" Sirius asked.

"Maybe, but I doubt it. I think it would be around the center by now if she did."

"That's true. I just can't believe one girl can cause so much trouble."

"Here's the thing, I watched the attack on the security cameras, and she wasn't the only one who attacked Aurora," Mr. Sanchez said. "Apparently, a few other girls sneaked out of the classroom. After watching the attack, wow, an attack that brutal should have caused other injuries, like a severe concussion, broken bones, or worse. The thing I'm not sure about is if it was planned or if it was just a random attack because of her hate for Aurora."

"It sounds too organized not to be planned," Sirius commented.

"That's exactly what I was thinking," Mr. Sanchez agreed. "Anyway, Aurora is in the infirmary; she's not awake yet. When she feels up to it, I'll have her call you. She'll be on bed rest until at least tomorrow morning or until she's feeling better."

"Sounds good."

"Also, before the big attack, she and Aurora pushed each other around. They both know that this center is a no fighting and no bullying zone. Seeing as they both broke the rules, they will both be put on kitchen duty cleanup after dinner as their punishment," Mr. Sanchez explained.

"Both of them? In the same room, together? Are you sure that's a good idea?" Sirius questioned.

"Yes," Mr. Sanchez answered. "I know what you're thinking, but they need to learn to get along. Hopefully, this will help them do just that."

"Thanks for letting me know."

"No problem, Sirius. I have to go now. I have a pile of paperwork to do because of this mess," Mr. Sanchez complained.

"Oh, good luck, I think you're going to need it." Sirius stated. "*Arrivederci*!"

"That I will, bye," Mr. Sanchez said before hanging up the phone on his end.

"Is the universe just against me today?" Sirius asked out loud, fed up with the day he was having. *First, I have the conversation with Jack, the PI; then the paparazzi bombarded me in front of my house; and now, I just received news that Aurora has been attacked by her nemesis and is in trouble for fighting back.* "This is just fantastic," he said as he put his phone in his pocket.

Aurora getting hurt weighed heavily on his heart. At least she was fine—physically, anyway. The media was the pressing issue at hand. The best-case scenario would be for him to tell the media in his own time, and they would eventually go away like they always did. Unfortunately, this wasn't about that. A rumor about him dating someone was not good, and they would bother him until they found out what they wanted to know. He wanted to keep the adoption private, but if they watched him closely enough, they would find out sooner than he wanted them to. "I have to get this under control," he thought out loud, heading back downstairs.

(Thursday, April 4ᵗʰ)

Aurora blinked her heavy eyelids as she woke up. The last thing she remembered was being carried to the infirmary after being attacked by Mara. She squinted, waiting for her eyes to adjust to the bright light as she slowly tried to sit up. "Oww." She sighed, putting her hands to her head. Her head throbbed, and her body ached.

"Miss Bennett," she heard a voice say. She looked over and saw Dr. Deleon walking towards her cot. "Please lay back down. You don't want to make yourself sick."

"No problem, Doc," Aurora replied, groaning in pain.

"How are you feeling?" Dr. Deleon asked.

"It feels like I got hit by a truck," Aurora mumbled.

"Well, I doubt that, seeing how you would be in worse shape if that was the case. However, I'm sure you are in a lot of pain."

"I still think it hurts like getting hit by a truck."

"Well, I'm glad you still have your sense of humor," Dr. Deleon replied. "You are fortunate; an attack like that could have given you a major concussion as well as a few broken bones."

"How does that make me lucky?"

"Even though you could have had those injuries, you don't. All you have is some bruising, and you don't seem to have a concussion. However, it may be too early to diagnose, so I need you to stay here overnight," Dr. Deleon explained.

"Ugh, how long have I been here?"

"Less than two hours." Dr. Deleon glanced at her wristwatch to confirm the time.

"I'm guessing that's a good thing, right?"

"It seems to be, but only time will tell. For now, try to get some rest, but don't go to sleep yet, just in case you do have a minor concussion," Dr. Deleon warned.

"All right." Aurora sighed.

"Also, Warden Sanchez is planning on coming here in a bit. He's just finishing up some things, and then he'll head down here—probably in the next few minutes."

"Why?"

"Just to check in on you. Since you are awake, I'm sure he'll want to talk to you about what happened."

"Okay," Aurora responded.

"Well, I'll be right over here if you need anything." Dr. Deleon pointed to her desk on the other side of the room.

"Thanks." Aurora sighed, trying to relax. She was plagued with thoughts about her encounter with Mara. She then realized that Mara knows about Sirius Marino and suddenly felt sick to her stomach.

The sound of a door opening and closing pulled her from her thoughts. "How is she?" she heard Warden Sanchez ask the doctor.

"She seems fine. She's awake. She says she's in a lot of pain, but that's to be expected from all the bruising. Thankfully, she doesn't seem to have a concussion. However, I would like to keep her overnight for observation," she heard Dr. Deleon say.

"That will be fine. I'm guessing she's feeling well enough to have a conversation," Warden Sanchez inquired.

"She should be. Go right ahead." Dr. Deleon nodded in Aurora's direction.

"Thanks," Mr. Sanchez said. Aurora closed her eyes, trying to calm herself down. She could hear his footsteps grow louder as he walked closer toward her cot. "Miss Bennett, how are you feeling?"

Aurora opened her eyes and turned her head toward the warden. "I'm in pain, but I'm fine. I've been in worse situations," Aurora answered.

"Well, I'm glad you are feeling alright," Mr. Sanchez responded as he grabbed a nearby chair and moved it to the edge of her bed. He quickly sat down. "I would like you to tell me what happened."

"Didn't Mara already tell you?" Aurora asked.

"She did. I also checked the security cameras to confirm her story. Unfortunately, what she had confessed didn't match what was shown on the cameras. I was hoping you could fill in the blanks," Mr. Sanchez explained.

"What do you want to know?" Aurora asked.

"First off, who started it?"

"Mara did," Aurora responded. "She got in my face. When I didn't fight back, she pushed me, so then I pushed back, hoping she would back down. But it just made things worse. That's when she started attacking me."

"I see. Why did you think she wanted to get into your face? Did you antagonize her?" Mr. Sanchez questioned.

"No, sir," Aurora responded.

"Alright, then why? Why were you two in the hall in the first place?" Mr. Sanchez asked.

"I was in the hall first," Aurora admitted. "Officer Anderson let me go into the hall, so that I could quickly talk to Mrs. Hansen."

"Why did you want to talk to her right then? Couldn't you have waited until later on during your free time?"

"I guess so, but I wanted to fill her in, just in case something like this happened." Aurora sighed. "The thing is, I know Mara."

"What do you mean?" Mr. Sanchez continued.

"I met her before coming to the center. She's the biological kid of one of my old foster parents. We've never really gotten along."

"Okay, what was going on in the hall? What did Mara want?"

"She threatened me, Mr. Sanchez. She said I had to agree to do whatever she wanted. If I didn't, she said that I'd regret it," Aurora explained. "Mr. Sanchez, she knows." Aurora looked away from the warden and closed her eyes. She felt so stupid.

"I know," Mr. Sanchez replied.

"How?" Aurora questioned.

"Mara told me. She was screaming about it in solitary confinement. How does she know?"

"She overheard me and Mrs. Hansen talking," Aurora cried, feeling tears run down her cheeks. "She said that she's going to tell the entire center."

"Well, she can't do anything right now, so don't start worrying just yet," Mr. Sanchez assured her.

"Why?"

"Well, as I said, she's been put in solitary confinement; she'll be there for at least twenty-four hours. Hopefully, that will give her some time to think about her actions," Mr. Sanchez explained.

"What about me?"

"What about you, Aurora?"

"Am I in trouble?"

"Yes, you are—for fighting back when you should have tried to walk away and get help. Even though I do understand why you did what you did, it doesn't let you off the hook. Do you understand?" he asked her.

"Yes, sir, I understand."

"Good. Once you get out of here, you will both be put on kitchen cleanup duty for after dinner. It will just be until your release date, since that is only a couple of weeks away," Mr. Sanchez explained.

"But I'm not in the work program."

"You are now, unless you'd rather be thrown in solitary confinement. It's your choice," the warden said.

"No, sir, I'd rather clean dishes." Aurora sighed.

"I thought so. Seeing that Mara knows your secret, I felt I should let Mr. Marino know right away."

"So you told him already?" Aurora asked.

"I did," Mr. Sanchez confirmed.

"What did he say?"

"He's very concerned about you. I'm sure he'll want to talk to you about it as soon as you are well enough to call him," Mr. Sanchez said to her.

"He's not going to be happy with me." Aurora sighed.

"He's not upset with you. It's not your fault; it was an accident. Now, I have some things to do, so I'll check in on you later. Now try to get some rest."

"Yes, Mr. Sanchez," Aurora responded.

"Alright," Mr. Sanchez said as he stood up from where he was sitting and started to leave the infirmary. As he was leaving, he could hear Aurora crying, which made his heart ache for her. *She has been through so much, and now this had to happen*, he thought as he walked down the hall to his office. *If anyone can get through this, she can. She's a tough kid.*

Chapter 16
Friday, April 5th

Aurora slowly walked into the busy classroom, filled with teenage girls chatting and arguing, and slid into her assigned desk chair. She laid her head down on the old, wooden surface, wishing she could go back to bed. Her head was throbbing, and she hurt all over.

"Aurora! Aurora! Are you okay?" Sandra and Lexi asked in unison, as they entered the classroom and ran to her side.

"I'm fine. Everything hurts, but I'm okay," Aurora assured them as she sat up at her desk.

"Are you sure?" Lexi questioned, frowning suspiciously.

"Yeah, I'm fine. Don't worry about me," Aurora said, trying to sound braver than she felt.

"We're allowed to worry about you, and you don't sound fine. Are you sick?" Lexi continued.

"No, I'm not sick. I already said I'm fine!" Aurora snapped.

"'Ora?" Sandra put her hand on Aurora's shoulder. "What's going on? You know you can tell us, right?"

"Yeah, I know. I'm sorry I snapped at you two. It's just—I cried all night," Aurora admitted. "I'm so scared."

"We figured that from looking at your red eyes, girl," Sandra said. "What's wrong, 'Ora?"

Aurora glanced at Sandra and sighed. "It's Mara. When she was pummeling me, she seemed to want to do more than hurt me. I really thought she was going to kill me. Something isn't right about this."

"Oh wow! Did you tell anyone, maybe like the warden?" Sandra asked.

"No. What's the point? I mean, who would believe me? It's not like anyone has ever listened, and if they did and then Mara found out, I would be labeled a snitch and things would get even worse for me," Aurora said in a frightened tone.

"What about your dad? He would believe you, right?" Lexi asked.

"Yeah, he would, but I would still be labeled a snitch, and my release date isn't until a few weeks from now," Aurora said, looking away from them. She couldn't stop thinking about Mara's attack. Something was really wrong, but she didn't know what. As she thought about it, she felt herself starting to space out. *Please, God, don't let me black out here in front of all the girls.*

"Aurora, I think we are past that point," Sandra replied. "Hey! Are you listening?"

"Uh, yeah, sorry, I'm just thinking," Aurora said, forcing herself to keep her heavy eyes open. "Something with Mara just feels off."

"Like what?" Sandra asked.

"I don't know. I just don't get it," Aurora said tiredly. She stifled a yawn with her elbow.

"Get what? Why Mara hates you so much? We don't understand that either, especially since you're one of the nicest girls in here," Lexi said.

"It's not just that. She has always hated me for no reason, but why would she want me dead now especially when we are both stuck in juvie? She knows bad behavior will land her in solitary or worse?" Aurora questioned. "Any ideas?"

"Nope," Sandra answered.

"I'm stumped too," Lexi agreed.

"Maybe she's just nuts and is thinking that if she does end up killing you, she could just use an insanity plea," Sandra proposed.

"That's just great," Aurora grumbled sarcastically, as she rested her chin on her propped-up hand.

"Hey, I'm just throwing out ideas about Miss Whacko," Sandra said defensively.

"I know," Aurora mumbled. "You're probably right. I just can't stop thinking about it."

"Well, you can't worry about it too much. It's just gonna make you paranoid," Lexi said.

"I suppose; what do you think will happen if I don't get out of here soon?" Aurora questioned. Sandra and Lexi just looked at each other, trying to avoid Aurora's gaze. "Well?"

"Hopefully nothing," Sandra said quickly.

"Hopefully nothing? Sandra, can't you be a little more supportive?" Lexi scolded her.

"I'm just being realistic. Look, Mara knows about Aurora's dad, and from what we know, she's gonna continue to try to make 'Ora's life miserable as long as she's in here," Sandra explained.

Glancing at Lexi and then at Sandra, Aurora groaned softly, "She's right. We really can't be hopeful right now. I have to be realistic—Mara hates me, and she's out to get me. She knows about my dad, and she's most definitely going to use it against me. To top it off, she wants me dead for some reason. Those are the facts, so what do we do now?"

"Can't we just ignore her, and just let her get in trouble if she starts a fight?" Lexi asked.

"Or we can get her in trouble first! We could get her thrown in solitary and not have to deal with her drama for a couple of days," Sandra laughed.

"That's a terrible plan. We just need to keep our heads down," Lexi said.

"We? Who said anything about 'we'?" Aurora asked.

"Did you really think we were gonna let you go through this alone?" Sandra questioned, crossing her arms and glaring at Aurora.

"Well, think again, 'cause I'm not gonna let either of you get hurt or in trouble because of me," Aurora voiced boldly.

"Too bad, girl! You can't stop us. We've got your back," Sandra said, giving Aurora a side hug.

"We'll get through this together," Lexi added.

"Fine, but if anything happens, you both have my permission to be a snitch," Aurora told them.

"I will have *no* problem with talking! And this whole situation has gotten waaay too crazy," Sandra pointed out.

"It really has. Anyway, let's get through this class, and then I will go see the counselor for my session," Aurora said, sighing.

"That's annoying—" Lexi started, but was cut off by Mrs. Sterling.

"Hey! Ladies! If you three are done chatting, can I start my class? Or is there something you would like to share about the lesson?" They looked to the front of the room and saw their teacher Mrs. Sterling glaring at them, as she crossed her arms and tapped her right foot impatiently.

"Sorry, Mrs. Sterling," they mumbled in unison. The other girls in the classroom snickered at the three girls getting caught chatting.

"Good. Now that we have that settled. Let's continue with our lesson on the War for Independence," Mrs. Sterling continued, going through slides on the overhead projector.

"Hey, Aurora, is it true?" Aurora heard someone behind her ask in a soft tone. She glanced back and saw Myra smirking at her.

"I have nothing to say to you," Aurora whispered.

"Well, I heard you have a rich daddy. I wonder how you accomplished that," Myra snickered.

Aurora turned back to face the front, ignoring Myra's taunts. She closed her eyes, praying everything would be fine. She struggled to keep herself from shaking, trying to pay attention to the teacher, but she couldn't focus on what she was saying. She felt like everyone in the room was watching her. Did everyone know now, or was it just Myra? Her head spun, and she couldn't see straight.

"Hey, loser! The teacher is talking to you," Myra said gruffly, as she kicked her chair from behind.

"What?" Aurora asked. She was sure her cheeks had turned bright red from embarrassment, as she heard the entire class laugh, except for Sandra and Lexi, who were looking at her sympathetically.

"I asked if you are alright, Miss Bennett," Mrs. Sterling replied, turning toward the girls who were laughing, shutting them up.

"Yes, Mrs. Sterling," Aurora said quietly, hoping the teacher would listen to her words and not see how she really felt.

"Good, now let's continue," she heard the teacher say. She looked down, trying to avoid the curious stares of her classmates.

As soon as class ended, Aurora packed up her stuff, jumped up from her seat, and dashed out of the classroom.

"Hey, Aurora! Where are you going?" she heard Sandra yell.

"Counseling, remember? I'll fill you in later!" Aurora called back.

"You better!" she heard Sandra say, as she made her way down the hall.

"Yeah, yeah," Aurora mumbled, as she headed to the counselor's office. She was walking so fast that she stopped short in front of the open door. "Hey, Mrs. Hansen... I'm here," she said breathlessly.

"Miss Bennett, what's your rush?" she heard Mrs. Hansen ask as she tried to catch her breath.

"What was that?" Aurora asked.

"I asked, what's your rush? Are you that excited for our counseling session?" Mrs. Hansen teased.

"Umm, sure," Aurora mumbled.

"First of all, how are you feeling?" Mrs. Hansen asked, looking concerned after seeing the dark circles under Aurora's eyes.

"I'm okay," Aurora said, as she walked over to the chair across from the counselor and plopped herself down.

"Are you sure you're okay?" Mrs. Hansen wondered, evaluating the bruises from Mara's recent assault.

"What do you want me to say?" Aurora asked, crossing her arms.

"How about how you really feel?" Miss Hansen continued.

"What if I don't know how I feel?" Aurora questioned.

"Well, that's why I'm here, to help you decipher what you are feeling. So, what was going through your head when you woke up in the infirmary yesterday?" Mrs. Hansen asked.

"I was in a lot of pain. I felt like I got hit by a truck," Aurora stated.

"I'm sure you did, but how did you feel emotionally?" Mrs. Hansen asked again.

"I don't know," Aurora answered, looking down at her hands.

"I'm sure that's not true," Mrs. Hansen replied. "What would you tell Mr. Marino?" She paused for a second and cleared her throat. "I'm sorry. I meant to say your father—what would you tell your father if he asked?"

"It's different when I talk to him," Aurora replied, as she looked back up at the counselor.

"What do you mean? How is it different?" Mrs. Hansen leaned back in her office chair.

"I trust him. I don't really trust anyone else."

"I know you don't, and I don't expect you to. It's very hard to put trust in others when you have been let down by so many people. Have you told your father anything from your past?"

"Yeah, I have."

"Good. Why do you feel you can trust him and not others?" Mrs. Hansen probed.

"Because he hasn't messed up—yet, that is," Aurora said.

"Do you think he will?"

"I don't know. But if he did, I don't think it would be on purpose," Aurora commented.

"Are you afraid of that?" Mrs. Hansen asked.

"No, not really. I'm more afraid of Mara right now," Aurora admitted.

"You have every reason to be scared of Mara; you went through quite an ordeal."

"What do I do?" Aurora asked, shaking slightly.

"What do you usually do?"

"Keep my head down. Maybe avoid the person. Pray nothing bad happens."

"That's one way to handle it. Have you ever talked to an adult about Mara's bullying?"

"No, this is the first time," Aurora mumbled.

"Well, normally, who would you tell first?"

"My friends, but now, I have my dad that I can talk to. Actually, I didn't get to tell him the details of my attack yet. Honestly, I wasn't going to tell him, but my friends convinced me that I should."

"Why wouldn't you tell him?"

"Because I didn't want him to worry."

"I see. Were you afraid he'd think that you were starting trouble?" Mrs. Hansen asked compassionately.

"No, I wasn't worried about that. I just didn't want him to worry, but I did promise him that I would tell him stuff that was happening with me," Aurora explained.

"Good."

"Yeah, he said that it would help him worry less."

"Does he seem to worry a lot about you?"

"I think so...and before you ask, it makes me feel—thought about," Aurora answered.

"What does that mean?" Mrs. Hansen asked.

"I mean, I feel like he really cares about me. Maybe he even loves me in some way." Aurora smiled.

"Well, you are going to be his daughter, so that makes a lot of sense," Mrs. Hansen said, smiling back at Aurora.

"So...since I told you how I feel, can I call him now?" Aurora asked, scooting forward so she was sitting on the edge of the chair.

"You may." Mrs. Hansen grinned, grabbing her desk phone and handing it to Aurora.

"Yay!" Aurora shouted in glee. "Thanks, Mrs. Hansen." Aurora quickly dialed Mr. Marino's number and waited for him to answer.

"Hello?" she heard him ask.

"*Papà*. Hey, it's me," Aurora answered.

"Aurora, I'm so glad to hear your voice! How are you feeling today?" She could tell by his tone that he was really concerned.

"I'm fine," Aurora replied.

"Aurora, are you really fine?"

"Yeah, I am. I'm nervous about Mara, but I'm okay."

"Good, are you still in pain?"

"I'm still pretty sore, but it's nothing I can't handle," Aurora assured him.

"Are you sure, *bella*?"

"Yeah, I've had a lot worse," Aurora said. "One of my foster dads once beat me so bad he broke my arm, so this is nothing."

"Oh, I'm so sorry, Aurora," she heard him say.

"It's fine. You know, *papà*, you really need to stop apologizing for things that are not your fault. Save the apologies for after you yell at me for doing something stupid." Aurora smirked.

"I'll remember that, and I'm glad you still have a sense of humor." Sirius laughed. "Darling, as much as I'd love to chat with you, I can't right now. I have somewhere I need to be."

"Oh, sorry," Aurora mumbled.

"Hey, don't apologize for something that's not your fault. Save it for when you actually do something," Sirius teased.

"You're using my words against me," Aurora taunted.

"Funny." Sirius laughed. "Anyway, I need to get going."

"Oh, okay, so where are you going?" Aurora asked.

"I'll tell you about it later."

"Promise?"

"Absolutely!" he promised.

"And you won't forget?" Aurora questioned.

"Aurora, I don't think that's possible, but I promise I will tell you all of the details the next time we talk," Sirius assured her.

"Thanks, *papà*," Aurora responded. "Bye."

"*Ciao, bella*," Sirius replied.

Aurora put down the phone and pushed it towards Mrs. Hansen. "Thanks, Mrs. Hansen."

"Is everything okay?" Mrs. Hansen asked.

"Yeah, he had something to do, but he said that he would tell me about it later," Aurora explained. "Are we done?"

"Yes, we can be done. Enjoy your time with your friends," Mrs. Hansen answered.

"Thanks!" Aurora exclaimed. As she jumped up from the chair and pulled open the door, she accidently slammed it against the wall with a bang. "Oh, sorry," Aurora called out to the counselor.

"It's fine. Now, go enjoy your day." Mrs. Hansen laughed.

"Great, bye!" Aurora yelled, as she sprinted down the hall to where her friends were waiting for her. She knew they would want to know the details of her chat with the counselor and with her dad. She couldn't wait until she could go home with him and start living her new life.

(Friday, April 5th)

Sirius stared out of the car window, thinking about his conversation with Aurora earlier. *I'm so glad that she is fine—well, fine as she can be considering what happened.*

"Are you excited for the movie premiere, Sirius?" he heard his friend ask, interrupting his thoughts.

"What?" he asked, looking at her from across the limo. "Did you say something, Giuliana?"

"Yes, stop daydreaming. I asked if you're excited for my movie premiere," Giuliana answered.

"Oh, of course! I can't wait to see Director Peterson's take on the story. You know I love anything that has to do with the Roman Empire. And you should be ecstatic, Giuliana. You and the rest of the crew have been working on this project for over a year," Sirius explained.

"True, and thanks for being my date," Giuliana said.

"You're welcome, *carissima*. It will be fun."

"You know, I'm surprised you didn't come out with Sierra," Giuliana commented.

"Giuliana, Sierra and I aren't together; we never were."

"Are you sure about that? 'Cause she thinks you two are soulmates by her social media posts." Giuliana chuckled.

"Oh my, you know how she is." Sirius tried to make light of the irksome influencer.

"Yes, I do. Remember, she and I did work together for the past year, and I'm aware she can be eccentric."

"Eccentric?" Sirius questioned. "Don't you mean manipulative or narcissistic?"

"Sirius, be nice. I'm sure there's probably a better adjective for her than that," Giuliana commented.

"How about using the term *pazzo*?" Sirius laughed.

"You're terrible."

"I'm just being truthful. Would you rather me be nice or honest?" Sirius questioned.

"I suppose I'd rather you be honest," Giuliana admitted. "Anyway, what about this new girl the media is talking about?"

"There's no new girl in my life; it's just a rumor made up by the media. You know how they are; they probably made it up so they can get more views on their websites and sales for their gossip magazines. There's no truth to it whatsoever."

"Are you sure about that?"

"I'm absolutely positive," Sirius confirmed. "Why?"

"Because guess who has been talking about it and claiming she has all the details?"

"Sierra," Sirius mumbled.

"You got it."

"Well, don't listen to her. I'm one hundred percent single—in fact, I'm still the ultimate bachelor," Sirius stated confidently.

"Oh Sirius, you are going to cause someone some serious trouble in the future. You're such a heartbreaker," Giuliana teased.

"Who? Me?" Sirius asked, pretending to be offended. "I'm absolutely ideal."

"Says you, *rubacuori*," Giuliana teased.

"Hey, I'm anything but a heartbreaker," Sirius laughed.

"It's good to hear you laugh like that—it's been a while." Giuliana giggled.

"I know, it's been a crazy few months."

"Is everything alright?" Giuliana asked.

"Everything's fine," Sirius confirmed.

"All right, are you ready to make an appearance?"

"Dai, andiamo," Sirius declared, stepping out of the limousine and proceeding to assist Giuliana by offering his hand.

"Such a gentleman," Giuliana commented, as she took Sirius' hand and walked onto the red carpet with Sirius.

"That I am," Sirius teased, glancing at his date as she graced her way down the red carpet in a stunning princess pink gown that showed off her silhouette. Her long, brown hair flowed down her shoulders in loose curls, framing her captivating features.

Sirius looked away from her and glanced at the crowd. There were people everywhere—celebrities walked down the red carpet, while the media and fans swarmed all around them. It was all so intense. Cameras flashed in his face as he and Giuliana continued down the red carpet. He could hear people screaming his name, wanting him to either sign an autograph or pose for a photo. He looked over to

Giuliana as she seemed to say something to him, but all he could hear were the shouts from the crowd. He watched as she walked over to a group of fans to take some photos and sign some autographs, and after a couple of moments, he joined her and talked to some very excited fans.

After signing a bunch of autographs and taking photos with fans, Sirius continued his walk down the red carpet. He loved interacting with the fans at events, but tonight was Giuliana's night; he didn't want to take any attention away from her. As he waited for Giuliana, he heard fans continue to scream compliments at him. "Thank you," he replied, throwing them a smile.

"Sirius," he heard someone yell his name and saw Giuliana walking towards him. She took his arm in her hand and leaned close to him, kissing his cheek. "Are you enjoying yourself, superstar?" she whispered in his ear.

"I am. Are you?" he asked her.

"Absolutely," she said ecstatically. "But I think they like you more than me."

"Not at all, darling. Look around—all these fans are here for you. Seeing me here as your escort is just a bonus for them, but you are the reason they came out in the first place. You are the star," Sirius explained.

"You know, I'm glad you're here with me and not Sierra. She definitely doesn't deserve your attention," Giuliana flirted.

"Is that so?" Sirius felt his heart skip a beat, looking down into her brown eyes. *Why have I never noticed how beautiful Giuliana is before?*

"Absolutely." She grinned.

"Shall we go inside?" Sirius smiled back at her.

"Lead the way," she replied. He placed his hand under her elbow as they made their way into the theater.

As they walked, Sirius heard someone yell out, "We love you, Sirius! You are amazing!"

He turned toward the fan and yelled back, "No, my friend. You're amazing!" He smiled as he heard the fans' ecstatic reaction to his response. Dealing with fans was the simple part of his job; sadly, managing his private life and trying to shield it from the public eye was not as easy. His thoughts turned to Aurora, and a cloud of worry came over him. *Pull yourself together, man. This night is about Giuliana.*

Sirius cleared his throat softly and bent down to whisper in Giuliana's ear, "Hey, *bella*, maybe sometime we can talk more about how thrilled you are to be here with me, as well as how amazing you think I am," Sirius teased as they walked into the dark theater away from all of the noise.

"Heartbreaker," she scolded him.

"Guess I am," he said, snickering. "Hey, how about we meet for some *caffè* sometime soon?" he asked sweetly.

"How does tomorrow morning sound?"

"Ahhh...wish I could. Unfortunately, I have somewhere I need to be," Sirius replied.

"I understand; we all have crazy, busy lives, but lucky for you, I'm also available tomorrow night."

"That does sound tempting, but I'm unavailable for the next few days." Sirius escorted Giuliana to her reserved seat in the theater and waited until she had seated herself, before he took the seat to the right of her.

"Aww, why's that?" she wondered.

"Umm," he cleared his throat. "I have some personal things to deal with."

"I'm guessing you are referring to Sierra," she said quietly.

"Not at all," he said quickly, not wanting her to think he was ditching her for someone else. "It's an important family matter. I actually have to fly to New York."

"Oh, wow! I didn't realize you had family out there," Giuliana said in a surprised tone.

"Yeah, I try to keep my personal life out of the media as much as possible. Hopefully, everything will go well, and I can get back here sooner than later."

"You don't sound too happy about your trip. Is it really worth it if it's going to stress you out?" Giuliana questioned.

"Worth it? Absolutely, someone over there needs me, and I'm not going to let this person down. She—um—has been through a lot and hasn't been able to depend on anyone but herself. That is, until now." Sirius felt himself opening up to Giuliana. *Why do I feel like I can trust her with this sensitive information? I have never felt this way before.* Giuliana's soft voice pulled Sirius out of his musings.

"Who is she?" Giuliana asked, giving him a curious look.

"She's a family member who just needs a little extra love," he responded cryptically.

"Come on! You have to give me more than that."

"How about when I get back, I can tell you more—as well as talk about other topics?" Sirius flirted.

"You are a true mystery," Giuliana said, gazing at him.

"Am I really?"

"You very much are, my dear Sirius. And fortunately for you, I love solving a good mystery," Giuliana flirted back.

"Oh boy, it sounds like I'm going to be in trouble then, especially if you find out any of my secrets." Sirius laughed.

"I'll take that as a challenge, *signore* Heartbreaker."

"You may take it any way you like, *signorina investigatrice*," Sirius responded, picking up and kissing her hand.

"Perhaps you are a gentleman after all," Giuliana said slyly.

Sirius couldn't help but laugh at her antics—she was an amazing woman. *Ridicolo!* What was he thinking? He shook his head, scolding himself for thinking of even attempting a relationship at this moment. The next few months were going to be interesting enough without trying to keep up a romantic life. That was still something he had to figure out—how to be a father. *Oh, God, help me*, Sirius thought to himself, glancing over at Giuliana, who was smiling at him sweetly.

(Friday, April 5th)

"Mara!" Ms. Davis barged through the door of the solitary cell, making Mara jump. "You stupid girl, what happened?"

"What do you mean?" Mara asked innocently. She pretended not to know what Ms. Davis was screaming about. "And how were you allowed in solitary?"

"You know exactly what I mean, and to answer your second question, a guard owed me a big favor. Now back to my question—why is Bennett in the common room laughing with her friends?" Davis questioned, her eyes narrowed at Mara.

"Of course you bribed someone, that's all you do." Mara sighed.

"Don't get smart with me. Answer the question!" Ms. Davis yelled.

"Uh, what was that again?" Mara asked sarcastically.

"Are you deaf as well as stupid? Why is Bennett in the common room with her friends and not elsewhere!?"

"Um, because that's where she's supposed to be."

"Did you not hear or remember my instructions?" Ms. Davis asked.

"I heard you loud and clear," Mara proclaimed with a smirk.

"Glad to hear, I was thinking I'd have to find someone else willing to help me," Ms. Davis stated.

"Willing? You're blackmailing me! I'm not doing this out of my own free will!" Mara yelled, clenching her fists.

"Keep your voice down, you brat," Ms. Davis seethed. "So here's the thing: if you can't accomplish what I say, you can rot here."

"You know, I wonder what would happen if someone knew about what you were up to? How you set me up and what you want me to do," Mara threatened.

"Who would believe you?" Ms. Davis smirked confidently.

"My parents would. My mother is a lawyer; she would take you to court and put your business into the ground. She has the resources to uncover all of your dirt," Mara threatened.

"You really think they would believe you after everything you've done? You've sold drugs, pimped yourself, stolen, and that's only a few of the many illegal activities that put you here. Your parents know all about your previous schemes; so of course they would believe it if you happened to resort to murder, especially if Aurora threatened to rat you out."

"She wouldn't do that! She may be a goody-two-shoes, but she's no snitch!"

"She would talk if she had to save her own hide. She already told the warden and probably her new daddy all about your threats."

"Well, I wasn't exactly quiet about it. I bragged so much the whole center should know," Mara announced proudly. "I'm not afraid of you."

"You did that on purpose, you little brat, and you should be afraid! I can do a lot worse than just let you rot in here," Ms. Davis seethed.

"Are you going to try to kill me too?"

"I'll do whatever it takes to keep my affairs off of the radar. It won't be good if I get caught, and I won't have either one of you messing up my plans."

"What? Are you afraid of prison?" Mara laughed.

"No, of course not, but no matter—if anything does happen to Aurora, you will be blamed and end up rotting in prison for a long, long time," Ms. Davis bragged. "Unless I am here to fix it for you."

"Not if someone connects the dots first. The warden isn't exactly stupid, and neither is Aurora," Mara continued.

"No, but why would he believe you? And why would Aurora believe you, especially after everything you've done to her? You're all alone here, girl. You will only get out of here if I let you out. All I would have to do is make that planted evidence just disappear. No evidence means no case, but only if you are able to do what I ask."

"I will get out of this, and you will be sorry," Mara threatened.

"Threatening me?" Ms. Davis asked, pretending to be surprised. "If you don't do as you're told, it won't be just your head on a platter."

"What's that supposed to mean?"

"Don't worry about it!" Ms. Davis snapped. "Now, as long as you do as I say, we won't have a problem. Do I make myself clear?"

"Crystal," Mara responded.

"Good, because you won't like what happens next if you don't." Ms. Davis stomped out of the solitary room and slammed the door behind her, leaving Mara alone with her thoughts. *What is going on with Ms. Davis? I have never seen her this desperate. What's got her so panicked?*

Chapter 17

Monday, April 8th

"HEY, LOSER!" AURORA CRINGED as she heard someone yell. Ignoring whoever it was, she continued to finish her math work in her notebook and hoped whoever it was would go away. Aurora sat cross-legged outside in the grassy area of the recreation yard, enjoying the small amount of fresh-air that she was allowed to have each day.

"Hey! Loser! I'm talking to you!"

Aurora sighed; she recognized that voice. She looked up to see Mara hovering over her.

"Ugh...what do you want, Mara?" Aurora asked reluctantly.

"Thank goodness you haven't gone mute, or I wouldn't have anyone to talk to."

"Go away, Mara. I'm busy." Aurora cringed inwardly, knowing that she had just poked the bear. *Mara is sure to be an even bigger problem now*, she sighed.

"What's the matter, Aurora? I thought you'd want to be friends."

"Friends? With you?" Aurora scoffed. "No, thank you, I try to avoid wolves in sheep's clothing."

"You and your stupid Scripture, do you really think your God cares about you?" Mara's eyes narrowed spitefully.

"It's none of your business what my beliefs are," Aurora mumbled. "So go away."

"Awww, did I hurt your little feelings? Well, too bad for you," Mara said.

Aurora ignored her, rolling her eyes. She looked back at her notebook, glancing over her work.

"Hey! I'm talking to you!" Mara yelled, ripping Aurora's notebook right out of her hands.

"Mara! Hey, give that back," Aurora shouted, jumping up from where she was sitting.

"What are you doing? Writing in your journal?" Mara asked.

"You know what I'm working on. That's the math assignment we had to do. You know, the one that's due tomorrow morning," Aurora explained.

"Crud, I didn't do that," Mara whined.

"Then I suggest you give me my notebook back, leave me alone, and get to work on your own stuff."

"Nah, I don't feel like it."

"Then you can fail the assignment," Aurora commented.

"I don't want to, so you are going to give me your work," Mara said with a devious smile.

"What!?" Aurora clenched her fists, getting ready for a fight. There was no way she was going to let Mara steal her homework and pass it off as her own.

"You heard me. You can finish this for me, and then redo it again for yourself," Mara said. She waved the notebook in front of Aurora's face, taunting her.

"Come on, Mara. Give it back, or else…" Aurora threatened. She reached out to grab the notebook but missed as Mara moved it away from her.

"Or else what? Are you going to snitch on me? Oooh, I'm so scared," Mara teased her.

"With how loud you're being, I won't have to," Aurora warned. "One of the guards will hear you."

"You know you should be nicer to me. How about this? If you give me your work, I won't pound you into a wall the next chance I get. Or…I could just tell everyone about your famous daddy. Sound fair?"

"No, but go ahead. I don't care."

"You should! I can make life really hard for you," Mara bullied.

"Whatever, leave me alone, or I'll go get one of the guards," Aurora threatened. "That is, if someone hasn't already heard us."

"Look around, no one else is out here. It's just you and me." Mara sneered. "I'll give you another chance; just say yes."

"No, do your own assignment! Give me back mine!" Aurora yelled, reaching for her notebook again.

"Fine, go get it then," Mara taunted as she tossed it behind her. Aurora watched as her notebook landed in a puddle with a splash.

"Mara!" Aurora shrieked in frustration. Sighing, she went to pick it up. As soon as she crouched down, she was kicked in the back and landed face forward into the same puddle. "Ugh! Mara! You have got to be kidding me!" She quickly got up and tried to shake the water off her soaked body.

"Oops! My bad. Looks like you'll have to redo it anyway. You should have just done it for me. Have fun!" Mara laughed loudly and walked away from a soaked Aurora.

"You'll regret that, Mara! Just wait 'til I get my hands on you!" Aurora threatened, not caring who heard her. "Drat!" Grabbing her notebook, she went to the guard on duty to get permission to go to her cell; once there, she went straight to the sink and peered into the metal mirror hanging above it. "Ewww." She cringed as she saw the dirt smeared all over her face from the grimy puddle. She threw her notebook to the floor before washing her hands at the sink. Grabbing a wash cloth, she started to wipe the grime off her face. "I guess that's as good as it's going to get," she muttered to herself, as she dried her hands on a towel and went to her desk. She quickly looked among her things, trying to find a spare notebook. "What am I going to do?"

"Hey, Aurora, why are you talking to yourself?" she heard Lexi say outside her cell door.

"Hi, Lexi," Aurora replied.

"Umm, did you hear what I said?" Lexi asked.

"Huh? Sorry, what did you say?" Aurora looked up from her frantic search.

"Never mind. What's got you panicked?" Lexi questioned.

"Do you have a spare notebook I can borrow?"

"No, I don't think so. Why?" Lexi asked, walking into her cell.

"Drat! It's Mara. She—umm—messed with me earlier. First, she tried to steal my math work and when I demanded she give it back, she threw it in a puddle. Now it's all wet, and I have to redo it!" Aurora explained.

"Wow! Please tell me you got her back, like pounded her into the ground or something," Lexi said.

"Nope, I didn't."

"You're an idiot. Now she's going to think she can use you as a doormat."

"Thanks for the encouragement," Aurora said sarcastically.

"Sorry, just telling you how it is. Come on, let's go to the common room and chill. Grab your notebook, and we can talk while you redo your math assignment. There has to be a spare notebook or paper you can use somewhere." Lexi grabbed Aurora's arm and started to pull her down the hall.

"Here's hoping," Aurora sighed. "And don't pull too hard."

"Sorry, just move it! We have lockup soon," Lexi said. She let go of Aurora's arm and started to push her along instead.

"I'm moving. I'm moving," Aurora protested as she rubbed her arm, trying to make it less sore.

"Ladies! Where do you think you are going?" Officer Walters' voice could be clearly heard from around the corner, causing the two girls to halt abruptly.

"Hi Officer Walters! We're just going to the common room," Lexi replied. "Is that a problem?"

"Yes, it is actually. It's time for lockup. Go back to your cells," Officer Walters ordered.

"Already!?" Aurora asked, panicked.

"Yes! Now get going!" Officer Walters barked at them.

"Alright, alright, we're going! You don't need to yell!" Lexi yelled back at the guard, who was glaring at them.

"Drat!" Aurora said. "Guess I'm not going to be able to redo my assignment, not unless I find a spare notebook in my cell."

"Sorry, girly," Lexi replied, as Aurora and Lexi turned to head back to their cells.

"Hold on," they heard someone yell. They looked down the hall and saw Mrs. Hansen was walking towards them rapidly, with a frantic expression on her face.

"Good evening, Mrs. Hansen. What's wrong?" Officer Walters questioned.

"I need Miss Bennett immediately," Mrs. Hansen answered. "Don't worry, Warden Sanchez knows about this."

"Very well," Officer Walters answered. "Aurora, go ahead."

Lexi waved goodbye at Aurora, and gave her a thumbs-up symbol for good luck, while mouthing the words, *Ask Mrs. Hansen for homework paper!*

As Aurora mouthed back *okay*, she followed Mrs. Hansen out the cell area. "Umm, Mrs. Hansen? Am I in trouble?" she asked nervously.

"Oh goodness, no—not at all," Mrs. Hansen replied, giving Aurora a reassuring smile.

"Uhh, okay...so then, where are we going? I mean, we just passed your office."

"To the common room," Mrs. Hansen simply answered.

"Why?" Aurora asked nervously. She looked around the hall, trying to figure out what was happening.

"There's someone here to see you."

"Who?" Aurora questioned. She was not sure if she should be scared or excited, depending on who it was.

"Well, why don't you go in and find out?" Mrs. Hansen replied, pushing open one of the doors to the common room.

Mrs. Hansen gently guided Aurora through the doors. Aurora glanced at Mrs. Hansen before turning toward the person standing in the common room. "*Papà?*" Aurora said, slightly stunned.

"Go on, Aurora. Enjoy your time," Mrs. Hansen replied, a huge grin spread across her face.

"Thank you, Mrs. Hansen," Aurora replied. "*Papà*!" Aurora yelled, running up to him.

"There she is!" Sirius greeted her with a gentle hug. "How are you, *principessa*?"

"I'm good. I didn't know you were coming," Aurora replied, hugging him back. *Wow, this day is getting better; maybe God has been hearing my prayers after all. Just when I thought I couldn't take another day of Mara bullying me, my papà came to visit.*

Mr. Sanchez's voice cut into Aurora's thoughts. "Well, we thought this would be a nice surprise."

"True, but to be completely honest, seeing you is not the only reason I'm here," Sirius added.

"Why? Is something wrong?" Aurora questioned.

"No, I just have some minor court details to deal with," Sirius replied.

"So something is wrong?" Aurora asked again.

"It's nothing you need to worry about," Mr. Sanchez answered.

"Mr. Sanchez is right. Don't worry, I have everything well-handled," Sirius assured her.

"Well, you two enjoy your time together. You have about thirty minutes for the visit. I don't want anyone getting suspicious about why you are not in your cell, Aurora." Mr. Sanchez quickly turned and left the room, leaving Sirius and Aurora alone.

"Aurora, I know we talked on the phone not long ago, but how is everything?" Sirius asked.

"It's fine," Aurora replied, sitting down on the floor.

"Just fine?" Sirius asked. He sat down across from her.

"I think fine is as good as it's going to get for me as long as I'm stuck in here." Aurora sighed heavily.

"Alright, how is everything with that girl, Mara? Has she given you any more trouble?" Sirius looked intently at Aurora, waiting for an honest response.

"She's been bullying me a little each day, but it's nothing I can't handle. I mean, I've dealt with worse."

"So you've said. What do you have there?" Sirius pointed to Aurora's notebook.

"Oh, it's just my notebook for school stuff," Aurora answered casually, as she tried to hide the notebook behind her back.

"Hmm, what happened to it? Why is it wet?"

"Um—well, it kind of fell in a puddle when I was outside," Aurora responded.

"And how did that happen?"

"It was Mara," Aurora admitted. "She took it from me; she said that she wanted to use my homework and pass it off as her own. I told her to get lost, so she threw it in a puddle when we were outside."

"That only explains why your notebook is wet, but why are you?" Sirius questioned with concern.

"When I went to pick up my notebook, she kicked me in the back, and I kinda landed in the puddle too." Aurora sighed. "Of course, this is due tomorrow morning, and I have no time to redo it."

"Hmm, let me see that," Sirius said, and motioned for the notebook.

"Why?" Aurora reluctantly grabbed her notebook from behind her back and handed it to him.

"You know, this is salvageable," Sirius said, looking over the notebook. "The pages are wet, but if you carefully rip them out of the notebook and lay them out to dry, it should be dry for tomorrow. Then you can hand it in."

"Really?"

"Yeah, don't worry. It should be fine," Sirius assured her.

"That's great. Thanks!" Aurora exclaimed happily.

"No problem. Did you tell anyone about this?" Sirius asked.

"Umm, not really. I just told my friend Lexi, 'cause she was trying to help me find another notebook. I didn't have the chance to tell anyone else yet," Aurora explained.

"Have you talked to anyone about the physical violence incident with Mara?"

"Yeah, I talked to the warden, the counselor, and my two friends."

"Did talking about it help at all? I know she really scared you," Sirius said compassionately.

"I guess. My friends have been sticking up for me whenever she gets in my face, so I know I'm not alone. It's still hard though," Aurora answered.

"I know it is. I'm glad you're talking about it, and you have good support," Sirius said.

"Me too," Aurora agreed. "How's life on the outside?"

"It's fine. Normal, I guess."

"So how was that thing you went to? What did you do? Did you do something, like, really exciting?" Aurora rambled, leaning forward in anticipation.

"Umm, let's see. It was good. I went to a movie premiere with an old friend, and it was fun. I'm not sure if it was exciting though." Sirius laughed.

"What's the movie? Are you in it?" Aurora asked.

"It's called *Livia Augusta*. It's based on the history of the first Roman Empress, and no, I'm not in it. I went to support my friend, Giuliana," Sirius explained.

"That's cool you supported your friend like that, even though it wasn't your movie. Are you going to be in any movies this year?"

"That's something I need to figure out, but I'm planning on taking a small break," Sirius reminded her. "Currently, I'm getting your room ready for your homecoming."

"Home. That sounds nice."

"I'm sure it does, especially after everything you've been through." Sirius paused and continued, "Has Ms. Davis given you any trouble lately?"

"No. Has she given you any trouble?"

"Nothing too serious," he replied.

"I don't believe that," Aurora rolled her eyes at his comment, not believing him for a moment. "What did she do? I mean, she's always up to something."

"Aurora, you don't need to worry about anything that's going on," Sirius assured her.

"Is that why you need to go to court again?"

"Why do you think that?" Sirius looked surprised at her guess.

"Because that's something Ms. Davis would do—drag you into some twisted court case. I don't think you would come to visit without telling me first. Either you or Mr. Sanchez would let me know. So, you would have to be here for another reason, and you already mentioned you were here for court."

"*Ragazza brillante.*" Sirius laughed, shaking his head in admiration.

"What does that mean?" Aurora asked.

"It means smart girl, which you are. You're right—I'm here for court because of Ms. Davis," Sirius admitted with a sigh. "I was in court on Monday, and we have to go back this Friday."

"Why? What did she do?" Aurora looked worried.

"I'm going to be one hundred percent honest with you, Aurora. She's trying to portray me as an unfit parent, so I can't adopt you. She's bringing up some things from my past, but it's nothing you need to worry about. The judge was actually pretty upset with her."

"What's going to happen?"

"No clue, but Ms. Davis was really rude to the judge. She was very disrespectful."

"Is that bad?" Aurora asked.

"Oh yeah, you never disrespect the judge—ever! You don't talk out of turn, and you don't question or yell at the judge. I'm surprised she wasn't held in contempt."

"What's that mean?"

"What?" Sirius asked.

"Being held in contempt," Aurora clarified.

"Ahh, yes. Contempt is a crime within the court. It's when someone is being disrespectful or defies the authority of the judge."

"Oh, okay. What's going to happen? Like, after I get out of here?"

"Well, hopefully you'll come home." Sirius smiled at Aurora reassuringly.

"Then what?"

"What do you mean?" Sirius asked.

"It's just, I've never been in a normal home since my parents died, and I was really young. I guess I don't know what to expect." Aurora looked down at the ground, shifting uncomfortably.

"Well, don't worry about it," Sirius said. "To be honest, I don't really know what to expect either. Remember, I grew up mostly with my grandparents, and then my aunt and uncle. I didn't exactly have a normal childhood."

"That's right. I forgot about that."

"Well, it's not something we discuss often," Sirius responded. "Anyway, it's going to be a learning experience for both of us. Neither one of us was raised in what's considered a normal home. Also, I've never been a parent. This is something we'll figure out together. Sound good?"

"Yeah, it sounds great," Aurora answered, smiling.

"Good, so what do you want to do after you get out of here?" Sirius asked. "I know I asked you before. Have you thought about it?"

"Yeah, kinda. I want to do things I've never done, like—never mind, it's silly."

"What is? Come on, tell me," Sirius said. He sat back and leaned against the palms of his hands.

"I want to do ballet," Aurora responded shyly.

"Ballet?" Sirius asked. His eyebrows raised slightly.

"Yeah, my mother did ballet. I remember when she took me to New York City—I think I was five or six years old. She took me to see *The Nutcracker*. It was so magical. That's something I wanna do; experience something my mother loved," Aurora explained. Sirius noticed how her eyes lit up just talking about it.

"Done," Sirius said.

"Wait, really!?"

"Aurora, you can do whatever you want, within reasonable means at least." Sirius grinned.

"Can I learn equestrian?"

"You want to learn how to ride horses?"

"Yeah, my father loved horses. Before he died, he was going to teach me, but he never got the chance."

"Alright then, I guess I'm going to sign you up for equestrian lessons and ballet classes," Sirius said.

"Are you serious!?"

"Absolutely," Sirius confirmed, grinning at Aurora's growing excitement.

"Wow! I can't wait. I wish I could go with you tonight," Aurora said with excitement. "I don't think anyone has ever been this nice to me since my parents."

"I know the feeling," Sirius said empathetically.

"You do?" Aurora asked, curious to what he meant.

"Aurora, you know I went to live with my grandparents after my parents were killed, right?" Sirius asked. He watched Aurora as she nodded her head in response. "But what you don't know is that living with them wasn't great. My grandfather was an alcoholic, and the only time he was nice was when he was sober. That was almost never. He was in and out of my life. My grandmother was fine. She was a wonderful woman, but she had no clue how to deal with a crazy, troubled, and dramatic teenager like me."

"Seriously?"

"Yeah, seriously, and after a while, my grandmother couldn't deal with me anymore. She said I was too much to handle. That was when I was sent to live with my aunt and uncle in Sienna."

"Where's that?" Aurora asked.

"Sienna is a province in Tuscany. Here." Sirius took out his phone and pulled up the maps app. "It's right here in the central part of Tuscany."

"That's so cool. What's it like?"

"Well, we lived in the countryside, and we had an amazing view of the hills that encased the area. The house that we lived in was actually an old *agriturismo*, or farmhouse."

"Where did your grandparents live?"

"They lived in Rome, which is the capital city of Italy, which is here," Sirius answered, pointing to the map.

"Umm, are your grandparents still around?"

"No, they died when I was fifteen years old."

"Oh," Aurora mumbled. "I'm sorry."

"It's alright. I wasn't with them long, and to be honest, it wasn't the best situation."

"Why?"

"Well, that's a story for another day," Sirius replied, hoping she would drop the subject. She didn't need to know all the stress and grief he caused his grandparents—at least, not at this moment.

"Alright. Umm, can I ask you something?" Aurora asked nervously.

"Sure, of course. And you know, you don't need to ask every time."

"Umm, right, well—when I get out of here, can we do something else? Like go somewhere?" Aurora questioned.

"That depends on where you want to go."

"Can we go to my hometown in New Jersey? I want to visit my parents' graves," Aurora said reluctantly, not knowing how he was going to react to that.

"Yeah, yeah, we can definitely do that."

"Thanks, *papà*," Aurora answered quietly. She looked slightly down, not wanting to meet his gaze.

"Why are you still so nervous around me?" Sirius asked.

"I don't know," Aurora said. Sirius reached out to her and hooked his fingers under her chin. He gently pushed her chin up so she would have to look at him. She still seemed so scared, and he didn't completely understand why.

"Aurora, you don't have to be. Have I ever given you a reason to be afraid?" Sirius questioned, letting his hand fall to his side.

"No," Aurora answered him, shaking her head. "Well, maybe, when we first met, you did a little."

"Mmm, did I scare you that much?"

"Not that much, I was more worried about what was going to happen to me if you called the cops. I think I was more afraid of Ms. Davis and my foster parents," Aurora admitted, glancing to the side before looking at him again. "I'm really sorry about that."

"I know you are, but that's in the past. *È acqua passata*," Sirius replied.

"What does that mean?" Aurora asked.

"Umm, it means it's past water. It's another way of saying it's water under the bridge," Sirius explained.

"Oh, okay, that makes sense, and I promise I'll never do anything like that again!"

"I'm going to hold you to that, because if you do anything like that ever again, you're going to be in serious trouble. I'll probably ground you until you're twenty," Sirius said, giving her a stern look.

"*Papà*, I don't think you can do that!" Aurora said in shock, watching Sirius closely. His façade quickly faded and they both started to laugh.

"Well, I promise when you get out of here, you will have no reason to be afraid—not of anyone."

"You can't promise that," Aurora giggled, thinking it was funny that he believed she would never be afraid again. "I do trust you, and I believe you will try your best to help me face whatever obstacles come my way."

"You're right about that," Sirius confirmed.

"Thanks, *papà*."

"You're welcome, and it looks like our visit has sadly come to an end," Sirius said, as he saw Mr. Sanchez walking toward them.

"Too soon!" Aurora grumbled.

"Yeah, that's for sure."

"Hey, you two! Mrs. Hansen needs to take Aurora to lockup," Mr. Sanchez said, pointing toward Mrs. Hansen, who was waiting near the doorway.

"Alright, looks like you need to go," Sirius said to Aurora. He stood up and then helped Aurora up.

"Fine," Aurora mumbled.

"Hey, be nice," Sirius scolded her teasingly.

"Whatever you say, *papà*." Aurora laughed.

"Oh boy, she's not even living with you yet, and you're already acting like father and daughter," Mr. Sanchez teased.

"Yeah, well, the way I see it, she is my daughter," Sirius said earnestly.

"I'm glad to hear that," Mr. Sanchez stated. "Alright, Aurora, get going!" he ordered.

"Yes, Warden Sanchez," Aurora said as she grabbed her notebook and started to head over to where Mrs. Hansen was standing. Pausing, she turned back to face Sirius and Mr. Sanchez. "Bye, *papa*." She ran back to Sirius and gave him a big hug.

"*Buonanotte, principessa*," Sirius spoke softly, hugging her back.

"*Buonanotte, papà*," Aurora said, smiling as she walked towards Mrs. Hansen.

"Did you enjoy yourself?" Mrs. Hansen asked.

"Yes, Mrs. Hansen, thank you," Aurora said.

"You're welcome, but it's Warden Sanchez you will want to thank. He's the one who set this up," Mrs. Hansen responded.

"I will," Aurora said. As she walked with Mrs. Hansen, she thought about what she said. She couldn't believe Warden Sanchez set up that visit with *papà* for her.

"Aurora, how do you feel about being the daughter of Sirius Marino? You know who he is, right?" Mrs. Hansen asked.

"Yeah, he's an actor."

"Aurora, Mr. Marino is not just an actor. He is one of Hollywood's biggest stars. He is what is considered an A-list star."

"What's that mean?"

"An A-list celebrity is a person who has made it in Hollywood. They are one of the best that everyone wants in their movies. Those who have A-list status are Hollywood's biggest names," Mrs. Hansen explained. "And Mr. Marino is on that list."

"So everyone loves him just because he's Hollywood's biggest star?" Aurora asked.

"Yes, that's part of it. Hollywood loves him because of his status. Everyone else loves him, because he is just a great guy."

"So is he just great because of the fame?"

"No, not at all. He is actually a great guy, and that's because of his character. He is one of the few stars in the industry who has remained human."

"What does that mean?" Aurora questioned.

"When it comes to most actors, they have a tendency to sell their soul to Hollywood—that's how people put it. They get mixed up in the fame; they become rude and arrogant." Mrs. Hansen paused a second, thinking of how to say what she wanted to say. "Sirius Marino is one of the biggest stars in Hollywood, but he hasn't let it go to his head. He has remained the same throughout his career. He is one of the purest celebs out there, and people see that. That is why he is so well-loved."

"I didn't know that," Aurora responded.

"According to the media, he is a great guy," Mrs. Hansen said, taking out her phone. "I want to show you something."

"What?"

"This is a video of Sirius at some event he was at recently," Mrs. Hansen said, pulling up the video.

In the video, Aurora saw a limo pull up to a red carpet, and a couple moments later, she saw Sirius step out of that same limo. "Wow," she thought out loud. The commotion she saw was crazy. People were shouting his name and cameras were flashing in his face, as he walked down the red carpet with a gorgeous woman hanging on his arm.

That must be the friend that he told me about, Aurora thought. After a couple of steps, he stopped and smiled for the cameras, and then he continued walking down the carpet. All she could hear were the fans and paparazzi screaming, but she could tell he was saying 'thank you' after hearing a compliment. After a bit, she heard a fan scream, "We love you, Sirius! You are amazing!" Then he did something that made her smile. He turned toward the fan and yelled back, "No, you're amazing!" She continued to watch as he walked down the rest of the red carpet, until he walked into the building with Giuliana on his arm and was out of sight.

"What did you think of that?" Mrs. Hansen asked.

"That was crazy! I can't believe he deals with that all the time," Aurora commented.

"It is, but I don't think he deals with that level of craziness every day—probably just at events."

"What event did he got to?"

"I'm not sure. I think it was a movie festival or something like that. The video was taken on Friday though."

"That must be the movie premiere he went to for his friend. He told me about it today," Aurora said.

"Alright, let's get you back to your cell. It's not going to be long until lights out."

"Yes, Mrs. Hansen," Aurora responded as they continued to her cell. Once they got there, Aurora walked in, and the door closed and locked behind her. She plopped down on her bed and smiled, thinking about how a day that started out so terrible could turn around and become so wonderful.

"Aurora, Aurora," she heard someone say urgently. She walked to the door of her cell.

"Hey, Sandra," she said through the metal door. "What is it?"

"Are you okay?" Sandra asked.

"Yeah, why?"

"What happened?"

"I'll tell you tomorrow," Aurora answered her friend.

"Come on, spill it," Sandra said, talking a little louder.

"No, not now. I don't want to get in trouble. I'll tell you tomorrow."

"Fine, good night," Sandra mumbled.

"Good night, Sandra," Aurora said, quietly. She looked at the digital clock in her room, thinking, *Good, I have some time.* She quickly grabbed her notebook and carefully ripped out the papers that had the assignment on it, just as *papà* told her. She set them out on her desk, hoping they would be fine for tomorrow. She took a deep breath as she lay on her bed and waited for the lights to turn off. *Ballet classes and equestrian lessons. I can't wait to get out of here and start my new life with Sirius Marino—my papà.*

Chapter 18
Wednesday, April 10th

AURORA MEANDERED DOWN THE detention center hall, silently dreading kitchen cleanup duty. This was her fourth day working with Mara, and it was torture the entire time. Mara would either insult her or glare at her. It was not something Aurora wanted to do, especially at the end of the long day. She was figuring out how to ignore Mara when she bumped into someone walking the opposite direction.

"Ms. Davis!" Aurora exclaimed. *Why is Ms. Davis here? Oh God, please don't let her cause trouble for me.* Aurora breathed the prayer silently, before looking up into those eyes that despised her. She cringed, realizing that this day was going to be a whole lot worse than she had expected.

"Miss Bennett," Ms. Davis proclaimed, acting rather coy. "What a surprise to see you up and about."

"Hello, Ms. Davis," Aurora said quietly. "Umm, what do you mean?"

"Well, I heard about your little unfortunate incident, and from what I've heard, it was serious. I'm just surprised to see you out of the infirmary this quickly. I'm also surprised you don't have any noticeable injuries." Ms. Davis looked Aurora up and down menacingly, making her shiver.

"I guess I was lucky enough to have some guardian angels," Aurora boldly declared.

"Oh, I doubt that." Ms. Davis laughed in disbelief.

"What's that supposed to mean?"

"Miss Bennett, if you really want someone to believe you were seriously attacked, at least pretend you were injured. Who's going to believe you if you make up stories like this?"

"But I didn't make it up!" Aurora protested, her anger rising slowly.

"Oh, please. Of course you made up the attack," Ms. Davis retorted.

"No, I didn't!" Aurora argued. "There is evidence—video surveillance that shows that I didn't. I was the victim."

"Then you must have antagonized whoever attacked you or found a way to convince her to do it without causing too much damage. What else could explain your lack of injuries?" Ms. Davis smirked.

"I can think of something," Aurora snapped.

"Aurora, don't tell me you are still using that line as an excuse?"

"It's not an excuse!" Aurora yelled. Ms. Davis knew how to rub her the wrong way. *I wish Mr. Marino was here beside me now, because I know she wouldn't act this way towards me.*

"Watch your tone, young lady! I can't believe you still believe in fairy tales. You're in the real world; fairy tales won't help you here," Ms. Davis sneered.

"Angels aren't fairy tales!"

"Even if they are true, who would believe such a story?" Ms. Davis asked condescendingly.

"Warden Sanchez believes me," Aurora snapped at her.

"You think that he believes you, but all he is really doing is tolerating your delusions to keep you obedient."

"My *papà* believes me," Aurora said, using the Italian accent her *papà* had used in the past.

"Your Papa? Aurora, speak English," Ms. Davis scolded.

"Sorry, Ms. Davis. I mean—my dad."

"Do you mean Mr. Marino?" Ms. Davis asked, eyebrows raised slightly.

"Yeah, he's going to be my *papà*—I mean dad, so I might as well start calling him that," Aurora proudly said.

"Well, I see he has been filling your head with more fairy tales. You really do live in your own little make-believe world, don't you?" Ms. Davis asked in one of her most patronizing tones.

"What's that supposed to mean?" Aurora countered.

"That man is so sure he's going to get custody of you that he's having you call him something he's not and never will be," Ms. Davis scoffed.

"What? Why?" Aurora asked frantically.

"Because it's not going to happen. The judge will never let him adopt you."

"Why not?" Aurora could feel her breathing getting heavier. *Please don't let me have a panic attack in front of Ms. Davis, God.* Aurora willed herself to take a deep breath in and slowly release it. *Where are the guards when I need one of them!?* Ms. Davis's response jerked her back to the reality she wanted to escape.

"...because of his lifestyle. He's an actor and not just any actor. He's an A-list celebrity—not that you would know what that is. He would never have time for you. Mr. Marino probably would leave you with a nanny and tutors all day and forget about you. Also, it's not like he'd be a fit parent with his past. His past is actually quite sketchy—I mean how he attempted murder and all," Ms. Davis explained. She smirked as she saw the shocked expression on Aurora's face. "I doubt he's told you about that. Or has he?"

"No, Ms. Davis," Aurora answered, looking nervously down the hall for any sign of a guard or another inmate. She desperately wanted this conversation to be over.

"Of course, Mr. Marino wouldn't bring up his darker side to his prospective adoptive daughter. Anyway, I suggest you get used to life here for now, and prepare to be sent to a group home. Lucky for you, a spot just opened up, that is actually why I am here today. I'm planning to chat with Warden Sanchez about the possibilities when the adoption falls through. You'll probably end up there, if they even want someone like you," Ms. Davis said disdainfully.

"A-a group home?" Aurora stuttered, trembling.

"Yes. A group home for orphans is exactly where you belong. You should count yourself lucky that you're not on the street right now thanks to me," Ms. Davis said bluntly.

"I don't belong in a group home! I'm more than just a foster kid!" Aurora fumed. She glared at Ms. Davis with a courage she didn't know she possessed.

"Who told you that? Was it Mr. Marino? He really is filling your head with fairy tales," Ms. Davis scoffed. "You are nothing more than a foster brat. Nobody cares about you, and no one ever will. You're lucky I don't commit you in a psych ward with all your delusions."

"They aren't delusions! I know the adoption is really happening! You're the one who's delusional, Ms. Davis!"

"Tell yourself whatever you need to. You will be going to a group home, and you will most likely stay there until you are eighteen and out of the system. Until then, be good. Don't give me a reason to let you rot in here," Davis threatened. "I'll be sure to keep you updated on your next placement. Goodbye, Miss Bennett." She abruptly turned and walked away in her black pumps and dress suit.

"Bye," Aurora whispered, tears spilling from her eyes. Her dad—Mr. Marino said that Ms. Davis was all talk, but Ms. Davis seemed awfully sure of herself. She didn't know whom to believe. Aurora quickly turned around and ran down the hall in the opposite direction until she came to the warden's office, and she banged on the door. She waited impatiently, hoping she could get some answers.

"Aurora, what are you doing here? You should be in the kitchen. Don't forget you're on kitchen duty," Warden Sanchez scolded her.

"I'm sorry, Mr. Sanchez!" Aurora started crying and shaking uncontrollably.

"Aurora, what's wrong?" Mr. Sanchez asked sympathetically.

"I need help. I don't know who to believe!" Aurora sobbed, tears streaking her face.

"Aurora, that doesn't explain what's wrong. What happened?" Mr. Sanchez grabbed a tissue from a box on his desk and handed it to Aurora.

"Ms. Davis happened," Aurora choked out hysterically. "She said some things to me today. Are they true?" She blew her nose and wiped her tears.

"Calm down, Aurora. Come in and tell me what happened today from the beginning," Mr. Sanchez said, ushering her to the chair across from his desk. "Take a seat, and we'll get this figured out."

"Yes, Warden Sanchez," Aurora answered, as she sat down and tried to calm herself with some more deep breaths. *God, please give me peace. Help me.*

"Now, what exactly did Ms. Davis say to you?" Mr. Sanchez asked.

"She said that my dad—I mean, Mr. Marino—won't be able to adopt me because he's an actor and because he has a shady past," Aurora replied.

"She said that to you?" Mr. Sanchez questioned.

"Yes, sir," Aurora confirmed.

"Aurora, when was Ms. Davis here? Where exactly did you see her?" Mr. Sanchez asked, getting out his pen and notepad to scribble something on it.

"I just passed her in the hallway outside the kitchen right before I ran over here," Aurora cried, as she tried to wipe away her tears with her sleeves.

"Well, I was not informed she was here. I wonder why," Mr. Sanchez thought out loud. "Anyway, none of what she said was true. There is no reason for the judge to not give Mr. Marino custody. The judge is actually quite fed up with Ms. Davis."

"That's what my dad said—I mean, Mr. Marino," Aurora commented as she shuddered.

"Aurora, what else is bothering you?" Mr. Sanchez questioned, noticing her discomfort.

"Ms. Davis got upset that I was calling Mr. Marino my dad." Aurora sighed.

"Ugh, that woman," Mr. Sanchez grumbled under his breath; he was clearly upset that Ms. Davis was interfering again. "Aurora, what do you want to call him?"

"I wanted to call him what he'll be—my dad," Aurora answered.

"Then do that," Mr. Sanchez said, writing again on his legal notepad.

"It's okay if I do?" Aurora asked.

"If I remember correctly, he himself said it was alright. If you want to call him Dad, call him Dad. If you want to call him Mr. Marino, then you can call him that. It's all up to you," Mr. Sanchez replied.

"Are you sure?" Aurora questioned.

"I'm positive. I don't know if I should be telling you this, but I don't think the judge is going to have you stay here much longer."

"Am I going to be put in a group home?" Aurora asked.

"Now why on earth would you think that?" Mr. Sanchez countered.

"Because Ms. Davis said that's where I'll be going." Aurora sobbed.

"No, you won't. You will be placed with Mr. Marino," Mr. Sanchez said firmly.

"You're just saying that," Aurora accused; her body shook with each sob.

"I'm not. In fact, let's clear this up right now." Mr. Sanchez grabbed his phone and dialed Mr. Marino's number, waiting for him to answer. "Hey, Sirius, it's me."

"Hello, Warden! Is everything alright?" Sirius questioned. Warden Sanchez could tell he was concerned.

"No, not really. I have Aurora here with me. Do you mind if I put you on speaker, so we can all have a chat?" Mr. Sanchez asked.

"That's fine," Sirius answered. "What happened?" Aurora flinched, hearing his tone. Both she and the Warden could tell he was not happy.

"Well, Aurora is quite upset. Apparently, not more than a few minutes ago, Ms. Davis approached her in the hallway without my knowledge and told her some things that are one hundred percent untrue. I feel we should set things straight," Mr. Sanchez said.

"Yes, I agree. Aurora, are you alright?" Sirius asked, his tone softened.

"No," Aurora choked out.

"What did Ms. Davis say to you?" Sirius questioned.

Aurora quickly looked to Mr. Sanchez, not knowing what to do. "It's alright, Aurora. Tell him what you told me," Mr. Sanchez assured her.

"She told me that you wouldn't get custody of me because of your lifestyle and your past, and I have no reason to call you my dad," Aurora mumbled just loudly enough for Sirius to hear her.

"That woman is *una piantagrane!* Aurora, none of what she said is true. She's just being mean and petty. Don't listen to anything she tells you," Sirius said.

"But—" Aurora started to say, but was interrupted by Sirius before she could say anything else.

"No buts, Aurora," Sirius said loudly. "Aurora, have I ever lied to you?"

"No, but that doesn't mean you won't," Aurora murmured.

"Let me ask you this: has Ms. Davis ever lied to you?" Sirius continued.

"Yes, she always lies," Aurora answered.

"Alright, so who should you believe—Ms. Davis or me?" Sirius asked.

"I believe you, *papà*," Aurora said.

"Good," Sirius responded.

"Hey, *papà*? Can I ask you something?" Aurora asked quietly, unsure if she wanted to know the answer.

"Of course," Sirius replied.

"I know Ms. Davis is a liar, but she said that you attempted to murder someone once. I'm guessing that's not true," Aurora wondered.

"I'm sorry, Sirius. She's twisting the truth again," Mr. Sanchez said to him.

"I'm not surprised she's doing this," Sirius grumbled over the line.

"So...something did happen?" Aurora asked.

"In a way. When I was sixteen, I was in a car accident, and the person who was involved unfortunately died. The person who died was drunk and driving, and my friends and I were lucky. It could have been a lot worse for us," Sirius explained.

"So, you didn't do anything wrong?" Aurora wondered.

"No, nothing illegal whatsoever," Sirius said. "She's twisting the truth to fit her narrative, Aurora."

"That's right," Mr. Sanchez agreed.

"That's good to know. I mean, I didn't think you did anything wrong, but Ms. Davis sounded so official," Aurora said.

"Well, Ms. Davis has a way of doing that," Sirius said to her. "Now, do you have any other questions for me? You know you can ask me anything."

"Are you really gonna get custody of me?" Aurora asked.

"That's the plan. According to the judge, it may happen sooner than later," Sirius told her.

"Really!?" Aurora asked ecstatically.

"That's what it seems like," Sirius responded.

"That's great!" Aurora exclaimed, trying not to jump for joy.

"It absolutely is, especially since you've had a pretty rough time here," Mr. Sanchez agreed. "Now, Aurora, I believe you are on kitchen duty."

"Yes, Mr. Sanchez," Aurora said, slightly disappointed she wasn't off the hook for the dreaded duty.

"Would you like me to go with you, Aurora?" Mr. Sanchez asked.

"No, thank you, Mr. Sanchez. I'll be fine," Aurora answered. Aurora knew if Warden Sanchez came, she would probably get bullied more than ever next time. "Goodbye, *papà*."

"*Ciao, bella*," Sirius replied. Aurora left the room, just as Mr. Marino and Warden Sanchez started talking again. She quickly walked to the kitchen, thinking about what Ms. Davis had said. Why would she say such things if they weren't true? *I know she is a devious liar, but does she really hate me and papà so much that she has a personal vendetta against us? I'm not sure what to think.*

"Now that we're alone, Warden Sanchez, what is going on?" Sirius asked.

"Hold on," Mr. Sanchez responded, walking over to his office door. He opened the door slightly and saw Aurora walking quickly down the hallway to the kitchen. Mr. Sanchez quickly closed the door and picked up his office phone, taking it off speaker mode. "Sorry, I just wanted to make sure Aurora wasn't listening to our conversation. She doesn't need to know about all this; she has enough to worry about."

"I agree. So what's going on over there?"

"I honestly don't know anymore. I'm apparently not informed about everything that happens in this building. First, Aurora gets attacked by Mara. Then Ms. Davis is stirring up trouble and coming in and out of this center without my knowledge. This is getting out of hand," Mr. Sanchez complained, as he rubbed his forehead in dismay.

"I can tell. At this point, can't you just ban Ms. Davis from the center for coming in unauthorized?" Sirius asked.

"I don't know. I need to figure that out. In the meantime, I'm going to report her to her superiors. She is way out of line."

"Can I do anything?"

"Nothing I can think of right now. Maybe just check in with your guy, and please make sure Aurora is fine. I know she told us that she was, but I don't believe it. Perhaps touch base with her again and make sure she knows that we are both on her side," Mr. Sanchez suggested.

"Of course, I'll do that. Hopefully, this court thing will be over soon, and then the adoption process can be finalized."

"Have you heard anything else from your guy?"

"Yeah, but he hasn't found out much. I already told you that he found out Ms. Davis is involved in some kind of trafficking ring. It looks like she's running it, but he's not completely sure; he's still looking into things."

"You did mention the kid trafficking before. I just can't believe she has been doing these things under my roof without me knowing. I'm supposed to know everything that happens in this place—who comes in and who goes out," Mr. Sanchez stated.

"You can't be everywhere or have eyes on everyone. Someone is bound to slip through the cracks, especially someone as shady as Ms. Davis. It seems that she's been playing the system for a very long time now, and no one has been brave enough to take her to court."

"True. Hopefully she won't get away with this for much longer. Lately, Ms. Davis hasn't been very subtle in her approach, which is also very strange."

"This is true. But she is probably getting too comfortable in her trafficking. With me adopting Aurora and threatening to bring her whole operation down, she's probably freaking out and trying to figure out how to keep things going. Who knows?"

"Let's hope for the kids' sake, she won't be able to keep things going for much longer." Mr. Sanchez sighed.

"None of this makes sense. How can someone who is supposed to be taking care of kids do the things Ms. Davis is doing? What alarms me is that Ms. Davis is sabotaging everything good that we are trying to do for Aurora. It's absolutely *ridicolo*."

"I agree. The only motive I can think of—if your guy was right—is that Ms. Davis is making a huge amount of money from exploiting foster kids."

"As I said before, it's *ridicolo*! And it's very, very wrong!" Sirius exclaimed.

"Don't worry, Sirius. Ms. Davis won't get away with any of this."

"No, she won't. This is one fight she won't win," Sirius agreed before continuing. "Have you figured out what's going on with that girl, Mara? I don't think it's a coincidence that she is here at the same time as Aurora, especially with her release date right around the corner."

"After the attack, I looked into Mara's case file; she's here on some interesting charges. Her situation is concerning, but it's all legit of why she would be taken out of her home environment and detained here."

"Interesting, well, it sounds like Mara also needs a change if her parents are letting her get away with illegal activities."

"I agree, and I have a feeling Ms. Davis messed with the wrong person." Mr. Sanchez laughed.

"That she did! I'm not going to let her get away with what she has done to Aurora," Sirius stated. "Has she said anything to anyone in the center about the things Ms. Davis has done prior to her admission to the center?"

"No, not really. Hopefully, we'll find out more without Aurora having to tell us. She has been through so much already."

"Agreed. Okay then, thank you for keeping me updated."

"Not a problem. in the meantime, I'm going to talk to someone about Ms. Davis and have an emergency meeting with my staff. I'm getting control of who comes in and out of this center if it's the last thing I do!" Mr. Sanchez affirmed.

"Good luck with that," Sirius said sincerely.

"Thanks, I'll see you on Monday."

"Monday?" Sirius asked, confused.

"Oh, yeah. I forgot to tell you I'm going to watch everything that's going down in court, and I want to be a big nuisance to Ms. Davis when they call on voluntary witnesses."

"It's going to be an interesting day."

"That it is. See you on Monday," Mr. Sanchez said, hanging up the phone.

"Finally! What took you so long?" Aurora heard Mara ask irritably as she walked into the kitchen.

"I got held up, Mara. Chill out!" Aurora remarked, not really wanting to deal with Mara and her antics.

"I just didn't really want to do all of this by myself," Mara explained, gesturing to the pots, pans, and trays they needed to clean.

"Whatever. Just stay out of my way, and let's get this over with," Aurora said as she walked over to the big metal sink and started to wash a crusty pan. "I'll wash, and you can dry."

"Fine," Mara agreed. They worked in silence for a good while, trying to get the work done as fast as possible while trying to avoid each other as much as possible. "Hey…Aurora," Mara said awkwardly, breaking the silence. "We need to talk."

"Leave me alone, Mara! If it's not about washing pots and pans, leave me be!" Aurora stated.

"This is really important, Aurora. I really need to talk to you," Mara insisted, sounding desperate.

"I have nothing to say to you. How many times do I have to say this?" Aurora asked, scrubbing the pan furiously.

"Aurora, you listen to me right now! We need to talk!" Mara shouted frantically, and banged a pot on the counter.

"What? What insult do you have to say to me that I haven't heard before? What are you up to now?!" Aurora questioned.

"I'm not going to insult you or ridicule you or anything like that. I want to warn you, Aurora." Mara's voice lowered, and she glanced out the kitchen door to make sure the guard on duty in the hallway couldn't overhear what she was going to reveal.

"Warn me? About what?" Aurora asked, still not believing Mara could all of a sudden have a change of heart. *Be on your guard, girl. Innocent as a dove and wise as a serpent.* The Bible verse popped into her head out of nowhere.

"It's about Ms. Davis," Mara whispered hoarsely.

"You've got to be kidding me." Aurora rolled her eyes.

"Aurora, you have to trust me!" Mara pleaded.

"Trust you? No way, no how. Leave me alone, or I'm calling the guard over here!" Aurora threatened.

"You have to listen! Do you have a death wish!?" Mara asked, grabbing Aurora's arm and making her face her. Mara's eyes were wide with fright.

"What? Are you going to try to kill me, like you tried the other day?" Aurora wondered, jerking her arm away from her nemesis.

"No! I already told you; I'm trying to warn you. As much as I don't like you, I don't actually want you dead," Mara said.

"That's funny, coming from you." Aurora backed away from Mara slowly and clenched her fists, ready for a fight.

"I know, but you have to trust me this time. Please!" Mara pleaded.

"Okay, what is it?" Aurora went back to finish rinsing the pan and handed it to Mara to dry.

"It's that snake Ms. Davis. She's done something really bad," Mara revealed, still whispering, and glanced around nervously as if Ms. Davis was going to pop into the grubby kitchen any second.

"What? What could she possibly do to me now that she already hasn't done?"

"She said she's going to pay someone to try to—you know—kill you."

"How do you know this?"

"Because I didn't go through with it," Mara explained, looking ashamed.

"Wait a second—the other day, when you were pummeling me, you were really trying to kill me?!"

"No, I was only trying to make it look like that. That's why I'm in juvie, because of Ms. Davis," Mara admitted.

"And I thought your illegal fun had finally caught up with you," Aurora said sarcastically, leaning her back against the counter. *Maybe I can trust Mara. If she could have killed me and didn't, and she is risking the wrath of Ms. Davis to warn me, then maybe she's on my side after all.*

"Just so you know, I'm in this particular situation because Ms. Davis set me up and is now threatening me," Mara said.

"That doesn't surprise me at all. What does she have on you?" Aurora asked.

"A lot, and she's been using it to blackmail me. She said that if I don't do what she says, she's going to make sure I rot in prison or worse," Mara answered.

"How is that possible? How is she able to even do that?"

"She's been paying people, both adults and kids, to help her. How do you think she's able to get in here?"

"Why are you telling me this?" Aurora questioned.

"Because I can't do this anymore," Mara admitted. "I may have hated you, but I don't want to torture you. It's really exhausting."

"Wow. Really?" Aurora said sarcastically.

"I guess that's not my best apology."

"That's an apology?"

"No, I guess not, but this is—Aurora, I'm really sorry I treated you like trash. If it wasn't for Ms. Davis, I probably would have left you alone," Mara apologized in a sincere tone.

"Seriously? I feel like you're mocking me or something," Aurora answered, still wary of the troubled girl across from her.

"I'm being serious!" Mara's eyes looked genuinely apologetic.

"Okay. I accept the apology. But I can't say that I forgive you now, or if I ever will."

"I totally understand. I don't care if you ever forgive me. You can hate me forever, but I'm going to try to make up for all of that," Mara explained. She dropped her voice to a whisper again, and leaned closer to Aurora. "We're in danger."

"We?"

"Yeah, *we*—as in you and me. Ms. Davis just threatened me before you got here, and it's not the usual stuff. She's going to use someone else to get rid of both of us. I think."

"Who? How?"

"Some girl named Darcy. You know her?"

"I think I've heard of her. She's in a different unit though, right?" Aurora asked.

"Yeah, the girls in that unit are the real criminals. Anyway, I think Ms. Davis is going to get her some kind of deal to get her out of here if she does her dirty work," Mara said, shivering.

"So what is Ms. Davis waiting for? Why hasn't she already had Darcy released to try to kill us both?" Aurora probed.

"I don't know, maybe she's waiting for us to get mad at each other and do something stupid to use it to her advantage. Ms. Davis is pulling a lot of strings, but I don't think it's just her behind all of this."

"What do you mean?"

"I think she's working for somebody. Why do you think she's so desperate? She seems like she is losing her marbles. I have never seen her like this; have you?"

"No, she's usually more discreet."

"Exactly, I think she's being threatened. Last time I saw her, she said something like it won't just be my head on a platter if I fail," Mara said.

"That's scary. And here I thought this place couldn't get any worse," Aurora complained, washing some nasty-looking trays.

"I know what you mean, but what I figure, a murder by Darcy is Ms. Davis' backup plan. She still wants me to terrorize you—enough that you'll hurt yourself," Mara explained, drying the metal trays. "Ms. Davis said that if you commit suicide, it would get you out of her hair."

"Why? Why does she want me out of her way?" Aurora wondered.

"I don't know. She didn't say why. All she said is that you're a thorn in her side and that your adoption is going to cause problems," Mara explained. "What do you have on her?"

"Seriously? I could write a novel with all of the stuff I know about her dirty work."

"Same here," Mara muttered. "I think we both know too much."

"What are you going to do?" Aurora asked nervously.

"I was going to ignore her, but then I was approached by Darcy yesterday and Ms. Davis today—" Mara started.

"Wait," Aurora interrupted. "Back up, Darcy talked to you!? In person!? How did she get out of her unit?"

"Knowing Ms. Davis, she probably bribed someone or cashed in a favor—you've seen how she plots to get what she wants. I was gonna ignore her, but now I need to do something to save my hide. I need to keep up the act, because I really think Darcy will do something bad if we don't get in each other's faces again."

"What do you think she'll do, exactly?"

"You mean Darcy? I don't know," Mara mumbled. "Maybe cut in and finish you off and make it look like I did something? Or she could make it look like you hurt me and then committed suicide because of the guilt?"

"Do you really think she'd do that?"

"I really think I need to keep my distance. Maybe I can do something really stupid and get moved to another section. This way I can't get to you."

"No, I don't think that's a good idea. You're going to get more stuff on your record. That's your permanent record. It'll mess you up for life," Aurora warned. "Also, if you do something minor, you'll just get thrown in solitary again. Then Warden Sanchez will have us work together again; you know how he is about us working out our differences."

"Then what do you suggest, genius?" Mara asked.

"As you said, keep up the act. Just do it from a distance," Aurora suggested.

"I guess, but will it be enough for Ms. Davis to back off?" Mara wondered.

"Maybe. It will only be a few weeks until I get out of here, and then she can't do anything to hurt me after that," Aurora said.

"But you or I could be dead in a few weeks 'cause of Darcy!" Mara exclaimed.

"Hey!" they heard someone yell, as they saw a guard walk into the kitchen, scowling. "Why do I hear shouting and not you two working?" he demanded.

"Sorry, I just splashed some water on us, and we just reacted," Aurora replied.

"Our bad," Mara added, looking apologetic.

"Fine. Just get back to work and hurry up. I have better things to do than watch you two delinquents," the guard said, as he walked out of the kitchen and stood right next to the open door. They figured he was listening to them, making sure they were doing what they were supposed to do.

"Use my dad," Aurora whispered, as she went back to washing.

"What do you mean?" Mara asked quietly.

"Do what you threatened to do before. Tell everyone about how he's going to adopt me and that he's a big celebrity. We already expected you to do it so do that," Aurora suggested, as she handed a pot to Mara. "Also, according to the warden and my future dad, I may be getting out of here sooner than later."

"That's good—for you at least," Mara muttered. "You know, maybe that's why Ms. Davis is bugging me so much about this, because time is running out."

"Mara, Ms. Davis actually approached me today—by accident, in the hallway when I was on the way here," Aurora admitted. Aurora watched Mara as she took the pot and dried it. It looked like she was deep in thought.

"What did she say?" Mara asked.

"She said some stuff about my dad, how he won't be able to adopt me because he's unfit to be a parent."

"She's probably trying to get you to say that you don't want to be adopted by him, because there's no way he wouldn't be able to adopt you otherwise."

"Why do you say that?"

"You know who he is, right? He's Sirius Marino, the superstar," Mara said.

"I've heard," Aurora replied, rolling her eyes.

"He's also the cleanest celebrity out there. No drama, no scandals, nothing crazy—he's just an all-around good guy. If it wasn't for his good looks and his talent in movies, he'd actually be very boring." Mara chuckled.

"I'll take boring over what I've been dealing with any day." Aurora laughed.

"I'm sure," Mara agreed. "Anyway, back to your plan. That might work for a bit; but if I don't do anything, Ms. Davis will get suspicious."

"If Ms. Davis approaches you again, tell her that Warden Sanchez wants you to be nice, so you're keeping a semi-low profile," Aurora suggested.

"That could work, but then she could send Darcy after us immediately," Mara warned.

"That's true," Aurora agreed. "For now, just stick with the plan. I'll pretend to be devastated about the adoption reveal. It will be my acting debut."

"What about your friends and your dad? What are you going to tell them?" Mara asked, sounding worried.

"Nothing for now, they don't need to know about this. We need to be careful, or we are so dead."

"Yeah, so we agree this stays between us. It's the only way this can work," Mara confirmed, turning to Aurora. Mara held out her hand cautiously, waiting for Aurora to shake it in agreement.

"Absolutely," Aurora agreed, shaking her hand before returning to their work. "And Mara? Thanks for warning me."

"No problem, and thanks," Mara replied.

"For what?"

"For trusting me on this one," Mara said, grinning.

"Of course. Whether we like it or not, we're in this together," Aurora responded. She watched Mara as she nodded in agreement. Aurora took a deep breath, trying to settle her nerves. Finishing the last few dishes, Aurora ran over the facts internally. *Mara doesn't really want me dead; Ms. Davis is actually threatening her too. Ms. Davis doesn't want me to be adopted for some unknown reason. What is Ms. Davis so worried about? Is someone threatening her? Why is Sirius Marino's adoption of me going to cause Ms. Davis problems? Would Ms. Davis really go so far as to bribe Darcy to kill me?* Aurora didn't understand, but she knew all she could do was pray. *God, please have get me out of here as soon as possible. Please have everything be alright.*

Chapter 19
Friday, April 12th

"Hey! Look who it is—it's the movie star's new brat!" Aurora heard Mara snicker to her friends, as she walked into the common room. Aurora clenched her fists and kept walking to where her friends sat, pretending to ignore the insult.

"Hey, Sandra! Hey, Lexi!" Aurora greeted them with false enthusiasm, as she sat on the floor with them.

"Hey, are you alright?" Sandra questioned.

"I guess. Just trying to ignore the vultures," Aurora muttered.

"Are you sure? I mean, the whole center is talking about you and how you're being adopted by a celebrity," Lexi commented.

"Yeah, I've been preparing for this; I'm kinda surprised she didn't say anything earlier. I guess she was trying to make me panic." Aurora bunched up her knees and hugged them tight to herself. *I hope Lexi and Sandra don't catch on to our plan.*

"If you say so," Lexi answered, looking skeptically at Aurora.

"But don't you find it weird Mara didn't straight up say who your dad is? All she said was that you're being adopted out of the system by a *celebrity*! Aren't you curious about what else she's got up her evil sleeve?" Sandra asked, suspiciously.

"Well... knowing Mara, it's probably the same reason she waited so long to tell everyone. She just wants to make me anxious," Aurora explained.

"Wait a sec...why are you so calm about this?" Sandra asked.

"As I said, my *papà* and I have been prepared, and he will be happy that she's keeping his name out of it," Aurora said convincingly.

"That's true," Lexi agreed.

"But aren't you worried about Mara?" Sandra questioned.

"Of course, I am! I'm just staying out of her way for now and trying not to get too annoyed. Trust me, I have my reasons," Aurora explained.

"Like what?" Lexi wondered.

"I-I don't know if I'm supposed to say," Aurora stuttered, nervous that her friends thought she was hiding something.

"Why not?" Sandra asked.

"According to my sources, I might be getting out of here sooner than later, and I-I really want to stay out of trouble," Aurora said quietly.

"Sources?! Like your dad?" Sandra questioned in a bold voice.

"Maybe—as I said, I can't say," Aurora hushed her.

"Getting out of here soon still doesn't solve your Mara problem. What do you plan to do until you get released?" Lexi asked.

"Keep my head down, which is exactly what I've been doing. It's worked so far," Aurora said calmly.

"Really, 'Ora? Until she pummels you again? And what happened to 'something's not right?'" Sandra probed.

"Sandra has a point—you were convinced she was trying to kill you. What changed?" Lexi added.

"Nothing! I'm just going to ignore her as much as I can," Aurora explained, hoping they would buy into her story.

"Whatever you say, girl. Anyway, we all have to go to dinner," Lexi said.

"Oh, joy to us! Another day of inedible food," Sandra complained sarcastically.

"At least we get to eat. Even if the food tastes awful, they won't let us starve in here," Aurora replied as they walked to where the rest of the girls were forming a line.

"That's true. But the food is still terrible," Sandra whined.

"Never said it wasn't." Aurora laughed.

"Girls! Time for dinner! Line up!" They heard a guard yell.

"Let's go, before we get yelled at again," Aurora mumbled.

"No problem," Lexi agreed.

As they entered the line up, Aurora stood behind Sandra and Lexi until someone cut in front of her. She got pushed to the back of the line, as well as getting separated from her friends. "Hey, loser." She looked behind her to locate the taunting voice and saw she was standing in front of Mara.

"What do you want?" Aurora whispered.

"Just wanna talk," Mara whispered back.

"Is that why your friends butted in between me and my friends?" Aurora asked, rolling her eyes.

"Yeah. I told them I wanted to bug you," Mara replied.

"Girls! Get moving!" the petite guard called to them.

"We're moving, Little Miss Drill Sergeant," Aurora heard Mara mutter under her breath. "So... my friends are bugging me about not bugging you enough," Mara said casually, starting up their conversation again as they marched in single file to the cafeteria.

"Seriously? Your friends think that spreading word about my *papà* isn't bugging me?" Aurora wondered.

"They were just curious why I toned it down," Mara said.

"That makes sense. What did you tell them?" Aurora asked.

"I told them Warden Sanchez is keeping a close eye on us and wants us to be buddies as much as possible, so I've been playing along to stay out of any serious trouble and out of solitary," Mara explained.

"Did they actually buy that?" Aurora asked, as they walked into the cafeteria and picked up their trays.

"Not really, but I got them to shut up for now," Mara said.

"So...what's the problem?"

"I'm just worried," Mara answered, looking around nervously.

"About what? Darcy? Well, don't freak out too much. She can't be watching you every minute of every day," Aurora said.

"Darcy is the type that would catch me when I'm *not* keeping an eye out. That's why I'm worried. Also, Ms. Davis could have someone else watching me, like a bribed guard. I wouldn't put it past her," Mara stated bitterly.

"That we can totally agree on. Ms. Davis is our biggest problem. So what do you wanna do? Make it look like you're harassing me more?" Aurora questioned, as she received her food from one of the kitchen employees.

"No comment. I can't have you know about everything I'm planning—it will give up the surprise. Just know that I need to be more of a problem," Mara warned, "and sorry in advance."

"Thanks for the warning and the apology." Aurora chuckled quietly.

"No problem. Heads up—all our friends are watching us," Mara pointed out.

"You might as well give them a show," Aurora suggested.

"Just what I was thinking," Mara agreed with a smirk, as Mara put her leg out and used her foot to trip Aurora. Aurora fell to the ground hard, with her face landing in her food, splattering everywhere. "You're such a klutz, loser! Why don't you pay better attention?" Mara laughed.

"Mara!" Aurora seethed, trying to wipe the food off her face.

"Oops! My bad! Aww, what a shame about your dinner being all over you. Too bad you can't shower yet," Mara sneered. "Here—I'll help!" She laughed, as she poured her cup of water over Aurora's head.

Aurora could hear the gasps around her. Mara did have a knack for causing drama, so she wasn't surprised that she had the room's attention. She clenched her fists, making it look like she was angrier than she was. "Wait till I get you back!" Aurora exclaimed, as she quickly stood up and got in Mara's face with her fists clenched.

"Hey! Break it up!" They heard Officer Edwards, as he came over and got between the girls. "That's enough! You two," he yelled, pointing to both Aurora and Mara. "Go to Warden Sanchez's office! Now!"

"Whatever," Mara grumbled.

"Yes, sir," Aurora replied quietly.

"Move it!" Officer Edwards yelled loudly, making both girls jump.

"Now what?" Aurora whispered, as they made their way down the hall.

"We face the music," Mara responded, glancing behind her and seeing the guard walking behind them. "Just act normal, and we'll be fine."

"If you say so," Aurora mumbled.

They continued in silence until they made it to the warden's office. Officer Edwards came to the open door and announced, "Warden Sanchez, we have a problem."

"I heard already—Officer Walters filled me in. Aurora and Mara, come in and have a seat." Mr. Sanchez sighed disappointedly, pointing to the two chairs in front of his desk. He looked at Mara and then at Aurora, trying to see which girl looked guiltier. "Alright, girls. Let's make this as painless and as fast as possible. What happened?"

"Don't be a snitch," Mara whispered loudly enough for Mr. Sanchez to hear.

"What was that, Mara? Do you have something to say?" Mr. Sanchez asked her.

"No," Mara grumbled.

"What about you, Aurora?" Mr. Sanchez asked, looking right at her.

"No, sir," Aurora gulped. *Please fall for our plan, Warden Sanchez. Please.*

"Well, I heard from Officer Walters that Mara either pushed you or kicked you to the ground. Is this true, Mara?" Mr. Sanchez questioned, giving Mara a knowing look.

"I just gave her a little push, because she wasn't paying attention. I didn't mean for that to happen," Mara replied, pointing her thumb towards Aurora.

"Really? Then why did you feel the need to dump your dinner on her as well?" Mr. Sanchez interrogated.

"I didn't!" Mara argued, as she banged her fists on the desk.

"That's enough, Mara!" Mr. Sanchez scolded. "Anyway, that's not what I heard."

"She didn't dump her dinner on me. She just pushed me," Aurora interrupted.

"Aurora, you don't need to lie for her," Mr. Sanchez said in a softer tone.

"I'm not lying! She didn't dump her food on me. That was all mine. When she pushed me, I kinda landed in my food," Aurora explained.

"Are you sure about that, Aurora?" Mr. Sanchez looked at her skeptically.

"It's true," Aurora protested.

"Mara, if I look at the cameras, is that what they're going to show?" Mr. Sanchez questioned, leaning forward and placing his hands together on the desk.

"Maybe," Mara mumbled.

"To summarize your story so far—you pushed Aurora, and Aurora got covered in her own food?" Mr. Sanchez asked.

"She may have tripped." Mara smirked.

"I'm going to guess that your foot is what tripped her," Mr. Sanchez said crossly.

"It was just an accident," Mara whined, as she lightly kicked Aurora under the desk.

"Yeah, right," Aurora piped up, getting the message. "The trip was definitely on purpose!"

"You can't prove that," Mara sneered.

"I don't need to prove anything. You've mocked me, beat me, and now you're talking trash about me. I'm your favorite punching bag, so of course you did it," Aurora accused.

"Don't be such a baby," Mara mocked.

"Just wait 'til I—" Aurora started to threaten, but was interrupted by Warden Sanchez, who sounded completely exasperated.

"Girls! That's enough! Mara, you need to fix your terrible behavior! Aurora, you need to fix your attitude problem. You two of all people should know better than to be acting like this, especially when you've specifically been instructed to work things out."

"Yes, Warden Sanchez," Aurora and Mara said together.

"Good. Now, there better not be any more incidents, or I will have you both thrown in solitary together. Then I'll keep you there until you learn to get along," Mr. Sanchez threatened. "Do I make myself clear? Aurora?"

"Yes, sir," Aurora answered, sounding apologetic.

"Mara?" Mr. Sanchez asked, glaring at the defiant teen.

"Sure. Whatever you say," Mara muttered.

"I'm glad we all have an understanding," Mr. Sanchez said. "Now, it's time to go back to the cafeteria before dinner time is over." The warden walked around his desk and opened the door and addressed the guard who was waiting patiently for the meeting to be completed. "Officer Edwards, please escort these two girls back to the cafeteria. If cleanup has already started, make sure they get something to eat before they start their cleanup duties."

"Come on! We don't need a babysitter!" Mara whined.

"It looks like you do based on your previous behavior. Now, hurry up before the food is all gone," Warden Sanchez ordered.

"Yes, Warden Sanchez," Aurora said, stepping out of Mr. Sanchez's office with Mara at her side. "Now what?" Aurora whispered, as they walked to the cafeteria with Officer Edwards keeping a close eye on them from behind.

"Nothing for now," Mara replied in her quietest voice possible, without looking over at Aurora. "Let's just eat dinner, and get this day over with."

"That's what you said before, but I still think we need a better plan," Aurora whispered back without glancing at Mara. "You know, we should tell someone about you know who and what is going on."

"Are you nuts? That's the last thing we should do. I mean, who would believe us?" Mara asked in a hoarse whisper.

"My *papà* would," Aurora said.

"*Papà?*"

"Yeah, that's what I call him. Remember?"

"Fine, so you tell your dad. Is he really going to believe you when he finds out I'm the one who gave you the details?"

"I don't know—maybe?" Aurora said.

"Well, just think about it. Do you really think he'll believe anything that I have to say after what I've done?" Mara questioned.

"I guess not." Aurora sighed.

"Well, duh—I did almost kill you," Mara said.

"I thought you were trying to make it look like that."

"I was, but I still put you in the infirmary." Mara glanced backwards to make sure Officer Edwards wasn't listening in on their muffled conversation.

"That's true."

"I mean, I could have easily killed you that day. I'm surprised you weren't hurt worse," Mara whispered. "Must be some kind of miracle."

"I thought you didn't believe in that stuff," Aurora said, sounding surprised.

"Well, it wasn't luck."

"Why do you say that?" Aurora asked.

"Because no one is that lucky." Mara laughed.

"Thanks for that," Aurora scoffed.

"Hey, I don't mean it like it's a bad thing."

"Then what do you mean?" Aurora asked.

"Nothing," Mara answered. "Maybe you're onto something."

"What was that?" Aurora wondered, picking up half of what Mara said.

"I didn't say anything. Must be your angels," Mara teased.

"Umm, okay," Aurora replied.

"Forget I said anything. Let's just get through the rest of this day."

"Alright," Aurora replied. They walked in silence until they came to the cafeteria, where Officer Edwards shut the double doors behind the two girls. "See you at cleanup duty."

"Whatever," Mara said.

Aurora watched Mara as she walked to her friends. She sighed, knowing this weekend was not going to be easy.

(Saturday, April 13ᵗʰ)

"Frank, I don't know about this," Sirius said into his phone.

"Come on, Sirius! You owe me one," Frank said, clearly frustrated.

"I know I do. I just have a lot on my plate right now. I don't know if I can take that much time out of my schedule," Sirius explained.

"I understand, but filming doesn't start until July, and it's here in L.A. It's not like you have to leave America, or even California for that matter," Frank said convincingly.

"That's true. Let me think about it. I'll get back to you in a couple of days," Sirius said.

"Okay, the sooner the better," Frank replied. "I'll talk to you soon. Bye."

"*Ciao*," Sirius said, as he hung up the phone. "This is going to be a headache," he thought out loud, as he made his way to the sports bar to meet Warden Sanchez. He had so much on his mind, with Ms. Davis causing trouble and another court date around the corner; Sirius felt overwhelmed. And of course, his director friend Frank decided to remind him again that he promised to be in a movie that Frank was producing. *When it rains, it pours*, he thought.

"Hey, man!" he heard Mr. Sanchez's voice, calling out from a corner table at the dimly-lit sports bar. Not wanting to draw attention to himself, he pulled his baseball cap down, so it would cover his face. Sirius quickly walked over to Mr. Sanchez hoping no one would recognize him.

"Hi David, I really appreciate you not yelling out my name for everyone to hear," Sirius joked. "How's your day been?" Sirius greeted the warden with a firm handshake.

"It's been fine, but the last few days have been crazy," Mr. Sanchez complained, returning Sirius' handshake with a firm grip.

"Anything I should be concerned about?" Sirius asked, taking a seat across from Sanchez and looking at the menu to make sure that anyone glancing over just saw two guys out for food and a chat.

"No, everything should be fine now."

"That's good."

"Thanks for coming out here," Mr. Sanchez said. "I'm sure you have an insanely busy schedule."

"It's no problem. I was still here in NYC for the court case. I didn't see the sense to go all the way back to California, seeing as court is on Monday morning."

"By the way, you are doing a great job with Aurora." Mr. Sanchez grinned. "I think you're going to be a great dad. Take it from me. I was awarded 'best father of the year' by my girls ten years running." Mr. Sanchez laughed.

"Love the honesty." Sirius laughed with him. Sirius turned to look up at the waitress who had come over to their table to take his order, pen and pad in hand. "Hi, there."

"Hey there yourself, handsome. What can I get ya?" the waitress asked.

"Can I get an Irish coffee?" Sirius asked her.

"No problem! Be right back," she said, smiling sweetly at him as she walked back towards the bar counter to prepare Sirius' coffee.

"Thank you," Sirius called out.

"Wow," Mr. Sanchez commented. "Does she know who you are? Or is she just flirting?"

"She's probably just flirting. If she had recognized me, she would have made a big commotion about it already. Then everyone in this bar would be staring over here. That's why I wore the hat," Sirius explained, pointing to his hat.

"Good to know. Does it help?"

"Usually, but unfortunately, the paparazzi and fans are still able to get shots of me," Sirius admitted.

"Thankfully, she didn't recognize you," Mr. Sanchez commented, taking a sip of his drink and swirling around the ice in the bottom of the glass.

"Agreed. We don't need anyone knowing our business or overhearing our conversation today."

"That's the truth. So, tell me: what have you heard from your private investigator?" Mr. Sanchez asked, leaning forward in anticipation.

"Nothing good," Sirius responded, glancing around to make sure no one was looking over in their direction.

"It can't be worse than his last update, can it?"

"Oh, but it can." Sirius sighed.

"Hello, luv. Here's your drink," the waitress interrupted with a smile as she placed the Irish coffee on the table, along with check.

"Thank you," Sirius replied with a grin.

"Hey, do I know you from somewhere?" she asked, looking Sirius up and down. "Your smile and eyes look familiar for some reason."

"Don't think so," Sirius said nonchalantly, keeping his head down.

"Are you sure? You look really familiar," she persisted.

"You know my friend here must have one of those faces, since this happens to him all the time," Mr. Sanchez interjected.

"Oh, that's too funny. Well, is there anything else I can get you or your friend?" she flirted with Sirius.

"We're good, thanks," Mr. Sanchez replied, sensing that Sirius didn't want to keep talking and giving her any more ideas about his identity.

"Alright, then, if you need anything, just let me know," she called out over her shoulder, as she quickly walked away.

"Well, she didn't seem happy about that answer," Mr. Sanchez commented.

"No, she didn't," Sirius agreed as he took the first sip of his drink.

"Back to the important stuff, what did your PI say?" Mr. Sanchez questioned.

"Right now, he's in D.C. reporting the information to the Federal Bureau of Investigations," Sirius said, pausing to take another sip of his drink.

"Jack is in D.C. right now?" Mr. Sanchez asked, eyebrows raised.

"He is. What he found out is concerning; that woman is one hundred percent making money off of trafficking kids," Sirius answered in a low tone.

"We figured that one out already," Mr. Sanchez replied.

"True, but what we didn't know is that she's not working alone; she is apparently working for someone," Sirius explained, clearing his throat. "I don't want to say too much, since I'm assuming it's going to be an ongoing investigation."

"Alright, do you know if Ms. Davis did the same thing to Aurora?" Mr. Sanchez asked.

"I'm not sure, but I wouldn't be surprised," Sirius stated.

"That poor girl. It's no wonder she doesn't trust anyone," Mr. Sanchez agreed.

"Mm-hmm. How has Aurora been since the Ms. Davis incident?"

"She seems fine. There was a small incident last night between her and Mara, but nothing too concerning."

"I have a bad feeling about that girl."

"I agree." Mr. Sanchez paused. "It's crazy how Aurora isn't even fourteen years old yet, and she's already been through so much. My oldest daughter is turning ten next month, and in comparison, has had such an easy and innocent life. I wish I could protect all the girls at the center from this crazy world."

"Be happy your daughters are innocent. It's truly a gift in this world we live in. Hopefully, Aurora won't be traumatized by anything else." Sirius looked at Warden Sanchez intensely.

"Let's hope for the best. That would be a blessing for Aurora if the last few weeks in the center were calm and peaceful."

"It would," Sirius replied, finishing off his coffee with one big swig. "Well, sorry to run after just arriving, but I need to head out. I have some things to figure out."

"Nothing bad, I hope," Mr. Sanchez commented.

"No, not at all," Sirius confirmed, getting up from his chair and throwing down a generous tip on the table for the waitress. "Anyway, I need to get out of here before one of the girls over there recognizes me. They keep glancing over in this direction." He nodded to some twenty-somethings giggling a few tables over.

"Do you think they do?" Mr. Sanchez questioned.

"Not sure, but I don't really want to take that chance. I don't want the world to know I'm in the Big Apple," Sirius explained.

"That makes sense. Well, see you in court on Monday," Mr. Sanchez replied.

"Alright, *ciao*," Sirius said, as he made his way out of the bar and onto the busy city sidewalk. He hadn't even made it all the way to the first crosswalk from the sports bar when he heard his phone buzzing. "Oh boy." Sirius sighed, taking his phone out of his pocket. "*Zia* Liv" flashed across the screen as the caller ID. "*Buonasera, zia* Liv."

"*Buonasera*, dear," Aunt Liv answered cheerily. "How are things going over there?"

"Fine. I just finished talking with the warden, and now I have to figure some things out," Sirius replied. "How's everything at home?"

"Everything is great. Aurora's room is painted and furnished and ready for her to come home—whenever that is. All it needs is minor décor, but I'm going to wait to do that with Aurora," Aunt Liv explained.

"Great! I'm sure she'll be happy," Sirius said, as he walked down the busy street.

"I hope she likes the comforter set I picked out for her—I hope this watercolor rose design is her style," Aunt Liv said, sounding slightly worried.

"Aunt Liv, don't worry. I'm sure she'll love everything you've done for her."

"I hope so. I must say I can't wait for her to come home; I'm so excited just thinking about all the fun we'll have together!"

"Are you planning on moving to America? Because if you are, I feel I should be informed about any definite plans."

"No, silly! We're not moving to America. We're happy right where we are, *ti ringrazio*. However, I am planning on being here at your house with your Uncle Dario when Aurora comes home."

"I wouldn't have it any other way," Sirius laughed. "She'll be like the daughter you never had."

"This is true. However, I can't complain about the child I did raise; I have to say he turned out pretty great." Aunt Liv complimented her nephew and herself in one fell swoop.

"Thanks, Aunt Liv," Sirius chuckled. "You know, you're going to overwhelm that girl, as well as spoil her."

"That's my job as her *zia* and honorary *nonna*."

"Wonderful. I know you'll enjoy every second of it!"

"I will. Anyway, how are *you* doing?"

"I'm fine—of course I'm a little stressed about this court hearing on Monday. Ms. Davis has been causing a lot of trouble." Sirius sighed.

"So you've said. Anything new happen?" Aunt Liv wondered.

"No, thankfully not. I'll keep you updated."

"You'd better," Liv said. "Oh, one more thing—how is everything going with that movie role?"

"I'm figuring that out. Thankfully, it's here in America, so I'm planning on doing it."

"Oh, *mama mia*!" Aunt Liv mumbled.

"You can say that again. Hopefully, it won't take too much time." Sirius sighed.

"If it does take you away frequently, I can make sure I'm here at the house to be with Aurora," Aunt Liv suggested. "It's not a problem."

"I know it's not. I just don't want to leave her alone too much, especially so soon after she gets home," Sirius replied.

"I understand, darling. Just don't worry too much about it. You'll figure it out," Aunt Liv said reassuringly.

"I'll try not to. I'll talk to you later, Aunt Liv."

"*Buona serata*," he heard her say.

"*Buona serata*," Sirius said, as he pressed the 'end call' button. *Let go of all worry and conflict and trust the path I am on,* he thought to himself, as he continued walking in the direction of his hotel along the crowded sidewalk. *I just hope this weekend will be peaceful; court will go well on Monday; and things won't get any worse for Aurora.*

Chapter 20

Monday, April 15th

"HEY, AURORA!" SANDRA CALLED out, walking up to Aurora as she and the other girls walked in line to their classrooms.

"Hey, Sandra. How was your breakfast?" Aurora quietly replied.

"It was good. Where were you? Lexi and I didn't see you in there." Worry was written all over Sandra's face.

"I was there; I was just keeping a low profile."

"That makes sense. So...how did everything go last night?"

"Fine. Why?"

"Weren't you working with Mara?"

"Yeah, and it went okay. It was our typical cleanup duty, ignoring each other while glaring at each other until we had to talk. It was an absolute blast," Aurora said, trying to sound as sarcastic and annoyed as possible. She breathed a prayer silently. *Dear God, please don't let Sandra suspect anything. I don't want her to be in danger because of me.* Sandra's voice pulled Aurora out of her prayer.

"You're something else, 'Ora. It would take everything I have not to throw something at Mara's head the first chance I got."

"Sandra, remember I'm trying to get outta here?" Aurora asked. "I thought you wanted that too." Aurora picked up her walking pace to keep up with the girl in front of her in the line. They were almost at the classroom, which meant they didn't have much time to talk, but Sandra would make the most of whatever minutes they had left.

"I do wanna get out of here, but I'd still throw something at her—maybe just not at her head. I would hose her down with the sprayer if she got on my nerves. That wouldn't get me in too much trouble." Sandra laughed deviously.

"I'm sooooo glad I'm on cleanup duty with her and not you." Aurora joked. "I'm trying to be as civil as I can be to her."

"Why? What has she ever done for you—not counting giving you a major headache?" Sandra replied.

"Umm…"

"Exactly—nothing!" Sandra insisted. "That's what."

"Haven't you heard the golden rule, do to others what you would have them do to you?" Aurora asked quietly.

"Is that one of your Bible verses?"

"If you mean, is it in the Holy Scriptures, otherwise known as the Bible? Then yes, it is. I think it's in the book of Matthew. You should read it sometime."

"Nah, not my style—you know that," Sandra said uncomfortably.

"True, you're not a big reader. But you can still agree with me that if I'm kind to Mara, then maybe she'll be nice to me for a change," Aurora declared boldly.

"Did you tell your dad about that strategy of killing Mara with kindness?" Sandra asked.

"What do you mean?"

"Well…you tell him everything, so I figured you might have mentioned it."

"Umm, no—I actually didn't tell him about my latest and greatest idea of how to deal with Mara; but he does know of Warden Sanchez's order of me doing the dishes with her, so we can learn to get along."

"Okay, girl. Whatever works for you," Sandra said, rolling her eyes as they walked into their classroom for the day.

"Hey Aurora!" A petite girl with curly red hair and freckles called out from the back of the classroom. "How is your new daddy?"

"He's great. Thanks for asking." Aurora rolled her eyes. The other inmates had been bugging her about her adoptive dad every day since Mara spread the news. Thankfully, they didn't know who her dad was—not yet, anyway.

"Aurora, I'm curious—how did you get your dad's attention?" one girl asked, grinning maliciously.

"Who knows? She probably weaseled her way into his life somehow. How did you do it?" she heard another girl ask.

Aurora ignored their questions. She quickly sat at her assigned desk next to Sandra and Lexi and waited for Miss Thompson's class to begin. As she was trying to block out their voices, she was whacked in the back of the head with a slap.

"Owww!" Aurora yelped.

"Oops! My bad." Mara smiled at her.

"What do you want, Mara?" Aurora asked, rubbing the back of her head.

"Just wanted to say hi," Mara replied, as she leaned on Aurora's desk. She dropped her voice to a whisper. "Oh, and watch your back."

"Knock it off, Mara!" Lexi yelled at her.

"Um, she wasn't talking to you, so butt out," Myra threatened as she joined Mara.

"Wonderful, if it isn't the wicked twins," Lexi mumbled sarcastically.

"Think again, Mara. If you mess with Aurora, you mess with us!" Sandra said defensively.

"If you know what's best for you losers, you'll stay out of my way!" Mara threatened.

"Mara! Go away!" Aurora warned.

"If you insist. Come on, Myra," Mara said, as she stalked away from their table, pulling Myra along with her.

"What a creep!" Lexi shuddered.

"Yeah, she really is," Aurora mumbled. She looked down at the table and saw a small folded up piece of paper where Mara's hand just was. She quickly hid it under her notebook. When no one was looking, she took a peek at it.

"S.O.S. NEED TO TALK. NOW!"

Aurora looked over at Mara. "Miss Thompson!"

"What is it, Aurora?" Miss Thompson asked.

"May I use the restroom?"

"Now?" Miss Thompson questioned.

"Yes, please, I'll be quick."

"Okay, but hurry up. I trust you won't get lost coming back," Miss Thompson said.

"Thank you, Miss Thompson," Aurora called out before rushing out of the classroom. She dashed down the hallway to the bathroom, where she waited for Mara to show up.

"Glad I got you alone," she heard Mara say as she walked into the bathroom a few minutes later. "I was worried Sandra or Lexi might do something to prevent me from meeting you."

"Glad they didn't. What's up?" Aurora asked.

"Darcy is on my case," Mara admitted.

"That's not good!"

"It's really not. Apparently, Ms. Davis is getting impatient. She wants me to do something, and she wanted it done yesterday," Mara said with fear in her voice, as she paced around the bathroom frantically.

"When did Darcy bug you?" Aurora asked.

"Saturday night. I tried to make an excuse, but I don't think she bought it. Darcy said that Ms. Davis gave me 'til the end of the weekend. Now, I'll be lucky if she gives me until the end of today," Mara explained. "I just don't understand what the big deal is and why she's freaking out now."

"I don't know either," Aurora said, slightly confused. "Wait a second...it's Monday!"

"So what?"

"Court!" Aurora exclaimed.

"Court? What do you mean?" Mara questioned.

"They have court today—Ms. Davis and my dad!"

"You're going to have to explain it again in simpler words," Mara said as she stopped pacing and leaned against one of the metal sinks.

"The court date is why Ms. Davis is so desperate all of a sudden. I think this might be the last day of court. Today's the day the judge will either grant my dad custody or deny it. If he does, I might be going home with my dad—maybe even today!"

"That makes so much more sense," Mara concluded.

"So, what do we do now?" Aurora asked.

"I don't know. I'm really scared, Aurora," Mara admitted. "Maybe we should go to Warden Sanchez."

"Are you serious? You're the one who didn't want to say anything the last time we talked. It was your idea to deal with it ourselves!" Aurora declared.

"I know, but I was wrong. I'm sorry. We should have gone to him a long time ago—my bad. We need to talk to him now, though," Mara suggested.

"Is he even here?" Aurora wondered. "Wouldn't Warden Sanchez be in court already?"

"I'm not sure, but I'll go check," Mara thought out loud.

"What about class?" Aurora asked.

"I'll be quick; I'll just sneak to his office. If he's there, I'll tell him what's going on, and hopefully he'll believe me. No one will even notice I'm gone," Mara explained.

"I don't know, Mara..." Aurora replied with concern.

"Why not?" Mara questioned.

"It's too risky. We should wait till after class. Maybe Officer Walters or Officer Anderson can escort us, and then we can both talk to him."

"Then let's go now. You and me, let's go," Mara said, sounding slightly panicked.

"We can't—we need to wait. We have to be in class now. We are going to get into trouble!" Aurora argued.

"Then I'll just go to Warden Sanchez by myself to tell him what's going on. It will all be fine," Mara assured her.

"Are you sure?"

"Yeah, I can handle myself. Don't worry so much."

"Alright, alright, if you say so," Aurora said reluctantly.

"Stop worrying," Mara stated with false bravado as she left the bathroom. Aurora immediately followed Mara out into the hall, but instead of going with her to the warden's office, she walked in the opposite direction to Miss Thompson's classroom. Aurora slipped into her seat and tried to listen to the lesson. Unfortunately, she could hardly pay attention because of her fear for Mara. Her heart was racing, and her hands were trembling. She felt tears rolling down her face as she struggled to control her breathing. She didn't know what to do, and her mind was plagued with concern. What would happen if Warden Sanchez didn't believe Mara? What if the judge denied her *papà* custody? So many 'what-ifs' were racing through her mind. With everything going on, Aurora felt as though the world was crashing down around her.

She shook her head, trying to rid her mind of all the doubts. She knew what she needed to do. She needed to pray, and ask God to make everything right. *God, please help us. We need You.*

Throughout the class, Aurora kept glancing at the clock. First, only about five minutes went by, so she wasn't too worried. Then five minutes turned into ten minutes, then fifteen minutes, and finally thirty minutes. Before she knew it, class ended, and Aurora started to panic again.

"Aurora, Aurora," Sandra's voice interrupted.

"What?" Aurora questioned.

"What's up with you? Are you feeling okay?" Sandra asked with concern.

"Yeah, I'm fine. Did Mara come back to class?" Aurora wondered, looking around frantically for Mara.

"No. Why do you care?" Sandra asked suspiciously.

"Sandra's right. Mara would just cause more problems," Lexi agreed.

"Oh no!" Aurora said in a panicked tone.

"What?" Lexi questioned.

"No, no, no! Something's wrong! Something must have happened to her!" Aurora shouted.

"Aurora! Seriously, just chill," Sandra said, grabbing her arm.

"I need to find her," Aurora insisted, pulling away from Sandra. "I'll be right back," Aurora said, running out of the classroom. She could hear her friends yelling after her, but she ignored them. She sprinted down the hall towards Warden Sanchez's office. Aurora visualized Mara sitting in the office, explaining everything to Warden Sanchez. She kept praying as she turned the corner, but stopped short when she saw a figure lying on the floor. She paused. "Mara!" Aurora yelled frantically, hoping she was just unconscious and not dead.

Aurora quickly knelt at Mara's side, and slightly shook her. "Mara! Wake up, please!" Aurora carefully looked over Mara's body and saw the she was bleeding; it looked like she was stabbed with something. Aurora quickly pulled off the sweater she was wearing and pushed it against Mara's open wound. "No, no, no! I should have gone with you. I'm so sorry! This is all my fault," Aurora rambled on as she put more weight on Mara's wound.

"Darcy…" Mara faintly whispered.

"What!?" Aurora asked. "Mara! What did you say?"

"Hi, Aurora," she heard a voice say. Aurora shivered from the evil tone in her voice. She quickly turned around and saw a stocky girl with brown eyes and pixie-length black hair walking up to her. Aurora rushed to get up but slipped on the bloody floor. Quickly trying again, she got up on her feet and jumped out of the puddle to the dry floor.

"You were so dumb to let Mara go alone," the girl sneered, hands on her hips.

"Darcy, I presume?" Aurora asked, trying not to sound terrified. *Jesus, please help me! Please send a guardian angel my way.*

"I'm guessing Mara warned you about me and told you what Ms. Davis wants?" Darcy asked maliciously.

"You could say that," Aurora answered cautiously.

"Looks like you and Mara don't hate each other as much as Ms. Davis thought. Who knew?" Darcy asked rhetorically.

"You know nothing. Now, get lost!" Aurora warned.

"Not happening! Now, I suggest you do what Ms. Davis wants and end it," Darcy demanded.

"Do what?" Aurora asked.

"You know what." Darcy knelt to the ground and slid a sharp pocket knife across the floor to Aurora. "Ms. Davis wants you to make it look like you killed Mara, and then killed yourself."

"No!" Aurora shook her head in horror and backed away from the open pocket knife.

"Do it!" Darcy ordered.

"Forget it! You can tell Ms. Davis that you both need to back off," Aurora said with a courage she didn't know she possessed. Aurora clenched her fists and kicked the knife behind her so neither of them could reach it easily.

"How stupid can you be?" Darcy mocked.

"Darcy! Just turn around and walk away. Mara needs help! Let me get her the help she needs before it's too late," Aurora begged.

"No way! She can die, and it will be all your fault," Darcy said maliciously.

"You'll regret this," Aurora warned.

"How? I'm not afraid of puny little you or your new rich daddy."

"Darcy, it's not worth it! Ms. Davis is not your friend. Trust me on this—she's not going to help you. She's going to toss you away like trash once she's done using you," Aurora explained.

"Don't pretend you care about me!" Darcy shouted, taking a step towards Aurora.

"I do care. Ms. Davis has hurt enough people, and she needs to be stopped! Help us bring her down, please," Aurora begged, hoping to get through to her.

"Like you care about Mara? She's going to die because you made her go alone," Darcy said in a mocking tone.

"That's not true! Now, let me through and leave me alone."

"I have a better idea. I'll just get rid of you myself, and Ms. Davis will reward me big time," Darcy said, taking a swing at Aurora. Aurora quickly dodged the punch.

"You've got to snap out of this delusion. Ms. Davis is not going to help you! And the security cameras will show what you've done!" Aurora yelled as she backed away from Darcy slowly.

"Shut up!" Darcy screamed, as she tried to get into Aurora's space and throw another punch. In the blink of an eye, Darcy was right in front of her. Aurora gasped and dodged Darcy's fist, which was aimed right at her face. She tried to go around her to get help, but Darcy was too fast. She kept hoping someone would hear their yelling and come to the rescue, but no one was coming. *Where is everyone?* She thought.

"It was stupid for you to come alone. Where are your friends? I mean, you must have a death wish," Darcy seethed. "You're just too much of a coward to do it yourself."

"I'm no coward! That title should be reserved for someone like Ms. Davis—someone who blackmails kids to do her dirty work."

In a rage, Darcy continued to throw punches at Aurora, backing her up against the hallway wall. As Aurora tried to get around Darcy again, she saw Darcy pull something from underneath her sweater. Looking closely, she saw it was a shank. Darcy swiped the shank at Aurora. With that swipe, the blade tore right through her long sleeve shirt and sliced her arm. Aurora let out a scream as she stumbled backwards, clutching where Darcy had cut her. Darcy pulled back her fist and pounded it into the side of Aurora's face. Before she could get away, Darcy slammed her foot into Aurora's chest, shoving Aurora back towards the cold concrete floor. Gasping for air, Aurora tried to stand up and regain her composure, but it was then that she felt a sharp pain in her side. Black dots darkened her vision, and she dropped to her knees. Blood dripped from her arm onto Mara, who was lying unconscious on the floor.

"No wonder you came alone. You're so incredibly pathetic and weak. Who would want to help you?" Darcy laughed wickedly. "Looks like you're the one going to hell! Tell Mara I said hi when you get there." Darcy swung her arm back for one last punch to Aurora's ribs.

Exhausted and weak from the blood loss, Aurora fell on her side. She faded into a heap of numbness as darkness consumed her vision. The last thing she saw before closing her eyes was Darcy's wicked smirk. *Please, God, help me,* Aurora whispered, letting the darkness wash over her.

Chapter 21

Monday, April 15th

"ALRIGHT, LET'S GET BACK to where we left off on Friday. Mr. Hamilton, does your client have anything else to share that is of relevance to this case?" Judge Hawkins asked, looking down from his elevated court seat.

"No, Your Honor," Mr. Hamilton, Ms. Davis's lawyer, responded.

"To summarize your case, the only real evidence you have against Mr. Marino being an unfit parent is that he was involved in a car accident while intoxicated?" Judge Hawkins questioned. His eyes narrowed, clearly not in a good mood. "Is that right, Mr. Hamilton?"

"Yes, Your Honor. However, if you give us more time, we would be able to bring you more evidence that Mr. Marino is unfit to be Aurora Bennett's legal guardian. I'm sure of it," Mr. Hamilton rambled nervously.

"Mr. Jameson," the judge said, looking towards Sirius' lawyer. "Your client, at the time of the aforesaid crash involvement, was sixteen years old. That would make him a minor, correct?"

"Yes, Your Honor," Mr. Jameson replied.

"And Mr. Jameson, you also said he was not the driver of the vehicle, and the driver was in fact sober during the accident," Judge Hawkins continued.

"That is correct, your honor," Mr. Jameson replied.

"Let me get this straight—Mr. Marino was involved in a car accident when he was a minor while intoxicated, but he was not the driver. The driver was one hundred percent sober, so this accident wasn't even the result of Mr. Marino being intoxicated. Mr. Hamilton, with this information, why would you or your client think this would be credible evidence of Mr. Marino being an unfit parent?" Judge Hawkins asked directly.

"Well, Your Honor, you see..." Mr. Hamilton mumbled, glancing at Ms. Davis nervously. Ms. Davis looked furious, like she was about to explode.

"Never mind, there's no need to answer that," Judge Hawkins interrupted. "What I really want to know is how you got this information."

"I don't know exactly...um...what you are referring to, Your Honor," Mr. Hamilton said, clearing his throat. His face paled as he looked at Ms. Davis, who glared menacingly at him.

"Well, I think you do. This incident happened when Mr. Marino was sixteen years old, so he was a minor. That being the case, his record would have been sealed. Second, this man did not break any laws," Judge Hawkins explained. His voice rose a notch as he continued. "During this time, according to Mr. Marino and the documents he provided, he was in the British Virgin Islands for a movie role. There, the legal drinking age is sixteen. Is that correct, Mr. Marino?"

"Yes, Your Honor, that is correct," Sirius responded.

"With that being said, Mr. Hamilton, how on earth did you even get this information? Obviously, it wasn't through any office in this courthouse!" Judge Hawkins hollered, his face turning red. His voice echoed throughout the courtroom.

"Y-Your Honor, I did not f-find this information. It was b-brought to my attention by my c-client, Ms. Davis," Mr. Hamilton stuttered, wiping his sweaty brow with his handkerchief.

"Is that so? Ms. Davis, I ask you then—how did you receive this information?" Judge Hawkins asked.

Ms. Davis stood up and cleared her throat nervously before speaking. "I would like to exercise my Fifth Amendment rights to remain silent!" She quickly sat back down.

"Oh, I'm sure you would," Judge Hawkins said, staring down at her. "Well, with that being said, I see no reason to continue with this circus, and I will not allow it to go on any longer…"

"Your Honor, if I may be so bold as to—" Ms. Davis interrupted, standing up again swiftly.

"No! You may not! Sit down, Ms. Davis!" Judge Hawkins ordered. He waited until Ms. Davis took her seat before continuing with his verdict. "Mr. Marino, effective immediately, you have full parental custody of Miss Aurora Bennett, with all the rights, privileges, and responsibilities thereof pertaining. By the power vested in me from the State of New York, I declare this court case to be settled in favor of Mr. Marino, represented by Attorney Jameson."

"Thank you, Your Honor," Sirius said.

"Your honor? May I remind you that Aurora Bennett is being held at the detention center and cannot be released at this time!" Ms. Davis intervened.

"Excuse me, Ms. Davis, but Miss Bennett was only being detained because the group homes were full. Miss Bennett has committed no crimes, and she has been on her best behavior at the center, according to Warden Sanchez. I see no reason for her not to be released into Mr. Marino's custody immediately."

"But—" Ms. Davis started, standing up again.

"Ms. Davis! One more word out of you, and I will hold you in contempt!" Judge Hawkins stated loudly. "Mr. Hamilton, would you please keep your client under control before you are both held in contempt!"

"Yes, Your Honor! Whatever you say, Your Honor," Mr. Hamilton said, grabbing Ms. Davis's arm and pulling her back to her seat. "Will you knock it off?" he whispered in her ear, clearly agitated. He saw her nod her head in response, and he looked back at the fuming Judge Hawkins, silently hoping she would keep her mouth shut.

"Case is closed!" Judge Hawkins grabbed his wooden gavel and banged it heavily on his desk.

"I object," Ms. Davis said confidently, her red lips narrowing into a thin line. Everyone in the room gasped and looked at the judge, curious to how he was going to respond.

"Objection denied!" Judge Hawkins authorized.

"But, Your Honor!" Ms. Davis spoke out again.

"That's enough, Ms. Davis! You will be held in county jail for contempt of court for thirty days. One more word out of you, and I will make it sixty days!" Judge Hawkins proclaimed. He turned to face Sirius. "Mr. Marino, as I said, Miss Aurora Bennett will be released from the detention center to your custody immediately."

"Thank you, Your Honor," Sirius replied respectfully.

"Good luck," Judge Hawkins said, giving him a nod. "And Ms. Davis, if I ever see you in my courtroom over something as ridiculous as this case again, we are going to have a serious problem. Is that understood?"

"Y-yes, Your Honor," Ms. Davis stuttered.

"Good. Officer," Judge Hawkins motioned to a broad-shouldered officer standing at the back of the room. "Please take Ms. Mildred Davis into custody."

"Yes, Your Honor," the officer responded, walking over to Ms. Davis and putting her in handcuffs before leading her out of the room. She glared furiously at her attorney and Sirius as she left the courtroom.

"Mr. Marino! Congratulations on becoming an adoptive parent, and again, good luck," Judge Hawkins said to Sirius, offering a congratulatory handshake.

"Thank you, Judge Hawkins," Sirius said, smiling from ear to ear. He watched the judge exit the courtroom.

"Sirius! Sirius!" Sirius looked behind him and saw Warden Sanchez walking swiftly towards him.

"Mr. Sanchez, I'm surprised you made it! I thought you would be too busy at the center," Sirius said.

"I decided it would be a good idea to be present, just in case Ms. Davis tried something."

"*Sei un grande*," Sirius replied. "I guess I'll be heading over to the center now."

"Hold on Sirius—something happened," Mr. Sanchez said, concerned. "I just got a call from the detention center. It's Aurora."

"Is she okay?" Sirius felt his heart start to race.

"Sirius, Aurora has been attacked by another inmate."

"What!? Is Aurora okay?" Sirius asked.

"I don't know. When the guards found her, she was unconscious. They called an ambulance, and she is being transported to the hospital right now. They just left ten minutes ago," Sanchez explained.

"Where was she taken? Which hospital?" Sirius questioned, already moving towards the courthouse entrance. *I have to get to my daughter!*

"Manhattan Hill Presbyterian Hospital. It should only be about thirty minutes from here by car—maybe less," Mr. Sanchez replied. "I'll meet you there later; I'll bring Aurora's possessions, so there's no need for you to come back to the detention center."

"Thank you, Mr. Sanchez. I appreciate it," Sirius said, practically running out of the courtroom. "I'll see you there. *Ciao a dopo!*" Sirius didn't slow down until he made it to his car parked at the parking garage. He hopped into his Maserati rental and raced to the hospital. Before he went too far, he pulled out his phone and pushed the icon to call his aunt. "Hi, Aunt Liv," Sirius said into the phone, slightly out of breath.

"Hello, darling! How was court? Did you get custody?" Aunt Liv's voice crackled over the speaker phone.

"I did, but something terrible happened," Sirius answered quickly.

"Oh no! What happened? What did that woman do?"

"I don't know if Ms. Davis had anything to do with this, but Aurora was attacked at the center! She's been taken to a hospital nearby, and I'm on my way there now."

"What!? What happened!?" Aunt Liv shrieked.

"I don't know the details! I just wanted to call to give you a heads up."

"Thank you, darling, for letting me know. I'm sure she's going to be okay; I'll be praying for you both. Let me know when you find out what happened, as well as how Aurora is doing," Aunt Liv said.

"I will. I've got to go. I need to concentrate on driving without getting into an accident," Sirius replied.

"Alright. *Ciao!*"

"*Ciao*," Sirius said, pressing the red 'end call' button. He continued driving as fast as he could, without breaking any traffic laws. As he drove, Sirius found himself praying. *I haven't prayed since I was a teenager, but I guess this is a good time to start again. Please God—if you're out there, look out for my daughter. Help Aurora to be okay and keep her safe.*

Sirius finally pulled into the hospital parking lot. Taking a deep breath, he tried to calm his racing heart; he felt like the drive had taken an eternity, even though it took less than thirty minutes. Stepping rapidly out of the car, Sirius all but ran into the main entrance of the hospital.

Sirius barged through the automatic doors leading into the hospital lobby, as the doors slid shut behind him with a hiss. He took a second to catch his breath and regain his composure. Approaching the reception desk with as much self-control as he could muster, he calmly said, "Excuse me, ma'am?"

"Hello, sir. How can I help you?" the middle-aged receptionist asked.

"Someone was brought in a little while ago—a young girl; her name is Aurora Bennett," Sirius answered.

"Okay. What is your relationship to this girl?" the receptionist asked, glancing up at Sirius and then back at her computer screen.

"I'm her father."

"I see. Let me check to see where she is," the receptionist answered, typing in her name. "Umm, I'm so sorry, sir. There is no record of any Aurora Bennett."

"That's impossible!" Sirius replied, starting to lose whatever composure he had mustered a minute before.

"I'm so sorry, sir, but let me try searching one more time," the receptionist mumbled nervously.

"Excuse me." A young man in a white doctor's coat walked up to the receptionist desk. He looked Sirius up and down, noting the designer suit and wristwatch he was wearing. "Sir, are you Sirius Marino?"

"I am," Sirius responded.

"I'm Dr. Williams. I just wanted to let you know I got a call from your friend, David Sanchez. He called a few minutes ago to give us some vital information about your daughter," Dr. Williams said.

"Umm, Dr. Williams, I'm sorry to interrupt, but his daughter isn't in the database," the receptionist interrupted.

"Are you sure? Did you spell her name correctly?" Dr. Williams questioned, looking at the computer. "Oh, I see the problem—you put in Aurora Bennett. Try Aurora Marino."

"Okay, well in that case, she's in Room 117," the receptionist replied; her eyes widened as she realized that a world-famous celebrity was standing in front of her. "I'm so sorry about that, Mr. Marino."

"Don't worry about it, Jane. You're just doing your job," Dr. Williams said to her kindly. "Sirius, I'll take you to Aurora directly."

"Thank you for your help," Sirius said to the receptionist, before following the doctor down the pale green hallway, decorated with floral and landscape artwork.

As they continued to walk further into the hospital, Dr. Williams gave Sirius a briefing. "I didn't want to say anything too confidential in front of Jane or anyone else. Warden Sanchez called to let us know that Aurora is no longer a ward of the state and has officially been released into your custody," Dr. Williams explained.

"Thank you, I greatly appreciate that."

"Of course! I'm sure you don't want the media to get wind of all this," Dr. Williams commented.

"This is true. How is Aurora doing?" Sirius asked with concern.

"To put it bluntly, Aurora is lucky to be alive; she is currently in a coma. The worst is a stab wound on her right side. She was lucky that whatever she was stabbed with didn't puncture any major organs. Warden Sanchez said from the video surveillance it looks like she was stabbed with a shank. She also has a deep gash in her forearm, and she has some bruised ribs. We made sure to stabilize her in the ambulance on the way to the hospital, and as soon as she arrived, I stitched up anything that needed stitches. The pain meds that we are giving her will make sure that she doesn't feel too much of the assault once she wakes up."

"Thankfully, she's in good hands now. Thanks for patching her up, Dr. Williams," Sirius said.

"Well, it's not going to be a fun recovery, and she's going to have some nasty scars that might not completely fade with time," Dr. Williams pointed out matter-of-factly, glancing down at his clipboard.

"Something tells me those scars are not going to bother her too much once she finds out she's officially adopted," Sirius commented.

"I'm glad to hear that." Dr. Williams and Sirius continued walking to Aurora's room.

Sirius braced himself before walking into the room after the doctor, anticipating the worst-case scenario. His eyes immediately went to Aurora. He shuddered, glancing over her small body. Her eyes were closed, and her face was badly bruised. Sirius quickly grabbed a chair that was in the corner of the room and brought it to the side of Aurora's hospital bed. He sat down and gently grabbed her hand into his. Trying to block out the sound of the machine beeping softly beside her, he said a silent prayer for her to wake up and for everything to be okay. "Tell me the truth, Doctor—is she going to be alright?" Sirius questioned, his voice breaking slightly.

"She should be in time. She's been through quite an ordeal for someone her age, and trauma can affect even the strongest adult. We'll know more when she wakes up. After that, she's going to need a lot of rest and recovery time," Dr. Williams answered. "I'll be back to check on Aurora later. If she wakes up, just press the red button on the side of her bed for the nurse, so we can check on her right away."

"Thank you, Dr. Williams. I really appreciate everything you are doing for her," Sirius replied, watching Dr. Williams slip quietly out of the room. Sirius held Aurora's hand, and watched her slight breathing. He jumped slightly as he heard his phone ring. "*Non ora,*" he muttered. He grabbed his phone from out of his back pocket and saw that it was Felix. "Hey man, it's not really a good time."

"I know. Your aunt called me. I figured I'd give her details so you don't have to," Felix replied.

"Thanks man, I know I can count on you," Sirius responded.

"So, what happened?"

"Aurora was attacked at the center. She was stabbed."

"Whoa...that's insane! Is she going to be okay?"

"I don't know. The doctor said she should be, but she is unconscious right now and has some pretty serious injuries. She has some bruised ribs, and two stab wounds that have been stitched up," Sirius explained.

"Sheesh, I'm sure you have your hands full, so I'll leave you be. Just let me know if you need anything," Felix offered.

"Thanks for the offer. I think I'm good for now, but...where are you?"

"Bridgette and I are in Manhattan. Why?"

"Is there any way you two could get some decent clothes for Aurora? She has nothing here, except for what she was wearing at the center, and she's not going to be wearing that again."

"Of course! Just send me—actually, send Bridgette her approximate clothing sizes. Bridgette and I will get whatever she needs," Felix said reassuringly.

"You guys are the best! Hey, can you get her a pair of shoes too?" Sirius looked around the hospital room for sneakers, but saw nothing. "Not sure of her shoe size though."

"Shoes. Got it. Good luck over there—we are apparently going shopping right away, according to Bridgette's facial expression. Bye—gotta run," Felix said.

"Thanks, Felix. *Ciao a dopo,*" Sirius replied as he hung up his phone. Everything rushed over him at once, causing tears to run down his cheeks. Sirius continued to hold Aurora's hand, hoping she could sense his presence. "Oh, my *bellissimo angioletto*, what happened? Who did this to you?" Sirius asked out loud, hoping she would wake up and answer him. He cringed, looking down at her swollen face and bruised body that was covered in a thin blue hospital gown.

Sirius felt so helpless. He thought about chanting a mantra. Sirius had chanted the same mantras every day, hoping for a better outcome, but it never worked. At this point, it felt pointless. Then he thought about how Aurora prayed to God every day while she was in the detention center. Stroking Aurora's hair, he thought—*if the prayer thing worked for her, maybe it will work for me too*. Sirius remembered the frantic prayer he had prayed on his way to the hospital, but it wouldn't hurt to pray again. He prayed out loud so Aurora could hear that he was praying to the God she has trusted all this time. "God, please help my daughter wake up. Help her be okay. I love her, like she's always been my daughter. P-please give us time," Sirius cried, rambling. "God, I want to see Aurora succeed—to graduate high school, go to college, and get her dream job. I want to see her get engaged, and I want to walk her down the aisle to her future husband. I want to see her have her own family someday. Please, have her be alright," Sirius begged, tears still welling up in his eyes and falling onto the hospital bedsheet where his daughter lay unconscious.

Chapter 22

Monday, April 15th

Sᴜʀɪᴜꜱ ꜱᴀᴛ ɪɴ ᴛʜᴇ hospital room with Aurora for what seemed like forever. He couldn't stand the waiting—it was agony. After a few hours, Sirius needed to stretch his legs, so he decided to walk around the hospital, hoping to clear his head. Since arriving at the hospital, he had received multiple texts from both his Aunt Liv and Felix. David Sanchez also called to let him know that he'd be over soon; he wanted to drop off whatever meager possessions Aurora had with her when she was admitted to the center. David didn't give him many details, but he did say that the police were now involved in a formal investigation. After returning to Aurora's room, Sirius sat in the beige lounge chair in the corner of the room; he sighed as he put his elbows on the wooden armrests and rested his head in his hands. Sirius thought about how relieved he was that Aurora was no longer at the detention center, and she was here with him—safe and loved.

"Sirius!" He heard David Sanchez's familiar voice from the door-way.

"David," Sirius said, looking up at the warden.

"How is she?" David asked as he approached Aurora's bed and looked down at her.

"The same as earlier; nothing has changed, which is driving me *pazzo*! I can't stand the waiting," Sirius grumbled. "The doctor said that the longer she is unconscious, the more serious her head injury could be; so we are hoping she wakes up really soon."

"I'm sorry to hear that. I brought her possessions from the center," David said, handing Sirius a plastic container.

"Thanks," Sirius replied, opening the small container and looking at the small number of items. "Her t-shirt, jeans, sweater, her bag, and her journal. Is this all she had?"

"Yep, that's it."

"Good to know," Sirius replied. "So, how did this happen? Who did this to her?"

"I can't say much, but what I can say—a girl from the restrictive unit attacked both Mara and Aurora."

"Mara was attacked too? I would have thought that Mara did this to her."

"From what the cameras showed, Mara was coming towards my office when she was attacked. Then not long after, Aurora walked up. She ran to Mara to see if Mara was alright. That's when Aurora was attacked by another inmate; Aurora put up quite a fight," David explained.

"This is *assurdo*," Sirius grumbled. "What doesn't make sense to me is this inmate attacked both Mara and Aurora, even though she knew she was being filmed."

"Actually, I don't think she realized the cameras were still on. From my knowledge, someone went into the security office early this morning and tried to turn off the cameras in the hallway where the attack occurred. What this person didn't realize was if they didn't put in a code, the cameras would automatically turn back on after two minutes. I'm assuming it was another inmate or guard who might have been blackmailed by Ms. Davis. Now, the police are handling the investigation. I gave them everything I had that was suspicious—the issues with Aurora's intake physical; records of Ms. Davis entering and leaving; and who was possibly helping her. Some of the footage has been deleted, so that's going to be analyzed."

"Wow, that sounds like it's going to be a hassle."

"It will be. But at least I'll know what's happening in my own facility."

"That's good," Sirius agreed. "I just have one more question. What happened to the girl who was bullying Aurora—Mara?"

"She's here in the same hospital. Can't say much, but it doesn't look good. She was hurt much worse than Aurora." Mr. Sanchez sighed. "However, Dr. Williams is hopeful that she will make a full recovery."

"That's good to hear; I hope everything works out for her."

"Yes, me too. Well, I need to get back to the center. Sirius, if I don't see you again before you two leave New York, I hope everything goes well."

"Thank you, I really appreciate everything you've done for both of us." Sirius stood and offered David a firm handshake.

"No problem, Sirius. It made me happy to see Aurora placed in a good home. Have a safe trip home," David said, returning Sirius' handshake.

Sirius walked David to the hospital room door. "Thanks again—for everything," Sirius said.

David smiled slightly in response. "It's the least I could do. *Ciao.*"

"*Ciao.*" Sirius watched Mr. Sanchez as he turned the corner at the end of the hallway. He turned back to look at Aurora lying in bed and couldn't help but stare at her. All he could think about was how thankful he was that she made it out of there alive. *"Finché c'è vita, c'è speranza,"* he whispered out loud. *As long as there's hope, there's life.* Feeling a sudden urge, Sirius grabbed his phone from the side table and clicked on the icon for his app store. He entered the search term "Bible" and downloaded the first free Bible app he saw. As soon as it was downloaded, he pressed 'open' and started to read. "Might as well start from the beginning," he said out loud, going to Genesis. As he read how God created the world and how God had a master plan for all of life, Sirius felt a calmness wash over him. He felt his heartbeat return to a regular rhythm, and his anxiety fade away.

Aurora slowly opened her eyes. Her head was pounding, and her body ached. Everything was blurry, and the room seemed to spin. For a second, she wasn't sure where she was, and she started to panic. She closed her eyes for a moment and took a deep breath. As her vision cleared, she slowly looked around the room; she saw that she was in a hospital room. *How did I get here? How long have I been asleep?* Realizing she was safe, she prayed in relief. "Thank you, God."

"Aurora, my *bellissimo angioletto*," she heard someone say. She looked towards the left of the room. She saw her *papà* sitting in an armchair in the corner of the room.

"*Papà*," Aurora whispered.

"Thank God!" Sirius declared as he rushed over to Aurora and gave her a hug. Holding her tight, he started to cry. "You're finally awake."

"*Papà*, you're crushing me," Aurora said breathlessly.

"I'm sorry, darling. I'm just so happy you're awake," Sirius cried as he sat back in his chair.

"How long have I been asleep?" Aurora glanced around the room for a clock.

"It's been quite a few hours. How are you feeling?" Sirius asked.

"Everything hurts," Aurora complained. "My head hurts the worst."

"I'm sure; after what happened, you must feel awful," Sirius said. "Let me call the nurse to let her know you're awake. I'm sure she can give you something for the pain."

"So, what now?" Aurora asked.

"What do you mean?"

"Do I have to go back? Like what's going to happen now?"

"Aurora, just relax, darling. Everything is fine," Sirius assured her. "It's great, actually. The judge gave me custody."

"Really?" Aurora asked.

"Yes, he did; and not only did the judge give me custody, he also had you released from the detention center."

"That's great!" Aurora replied. "So, this nightmare is over?"

"Absolutely," Sirius confirmed. "Once you're discharged from the hospital, we can go home—after we make a few important stops along the way."

"You mean like visiting my parents' graves?" Aurora wondered.

"Yes, as well as a couple of others, before we make it home." Sirius smiled kindly.

"Aren't we taking a plane home?" Aurora asked.

"No, I think we're going to either drive or take a train," Sirius stated. "It will take us about three to six days, depending on how we do it."

"Why?"

"I thought it would give us the opportunity to stop where we want and see what we want to see. It will be fun," Sirius explained.

"That makes sense. Hey, what's that?" Aurora looked over at the box near the side table.

"That's your stuff from the detention center. Warden Sanchez brought it over earlier," Sirius replied.

"Wow, it feels like a lifetime since I handed these over to the guard. So much has changed since then."

"Yeah, it has," Sirius commented.

"*Papà*, when Warden Sanchez was here, did he say anything about Mara?"

"Umm...yeah, he did," Sirius replied.

"Do you know if she's going to be okay? She was in really bad shape the last time I saw her."

"I heard she's badly hurt and unconscious, but hopefully she will be fine," Sirius explained. "Well, that's what the doctor told Warden Sanchez."

"I'm glad she'll be alright."

"Aurora, why do you all of a sudden care about Mara?" Sirius wondered, holding her hand comfortingly.

"Um, I should have told you earlier, but we're kind of friends now, or allies at least," Aurora answered.

"How did this happen? When did this happen?" Sirius asked.

"Well, she confided in me after she beat me up that one time. She told me she needed to tell me something that was really important. I didn't want to deal with her at first, but she was annoyingly persistent," Aurora continued to explain. "She told me Ms. Davis set her up and had her thrown in juvie to get to me. Ms. Davis told her she had to kill me or suffer the consequences. Mara told me that she was afraid and didn't want to do it. So, we made a truce and came up with a plan; the plan was to carry on with the act that we hated each other. We hoped we could keep it up until I was released. Did Warden Sanchez tell you about that incident in the mess hall?"

"*Sí.*"

"That was an act. Mara only did that because her friends were nagging at her about not messing with me enough. I guess she figured if her friends noticed, then Ms. Davis would too, especially if she had someone watching us," Aurora explained.

"That makes sense."

"Anyway, Mara told me not long after that there was a girl who approached her. Her name was Darcy, and she was in the restrictive unit. Darcy told Mara that if Mara didn't do what she was sent to do, then Darcy would do it herself, and Mara would pay. Then we found out that Ms. Davis had given her a time limit, and she had 'til the end of this past weekend. Mara said she would be lucky if she survived until the end of the day on Monday," Aurora expounded. "So, Mara went to the warden's office. She wanted to tell him what was happening, like I suggested days ago. I guess Darcy was waiting for her in the hallway and attacked her. I went looking for Mara when she didn't come back to class, and that's when I was attacked by Darcy."

"That's a tough situation for someone your age to deal with." Sirius sighed. "Aurora, you know you should have told me, Warden Sanchez, or even the counselor."

"I know," Aurora mumbled.

"Both you and Mara are fortunate. You could have died. Dr. Williams is surprised you're not worse off."

"I'm sorry, *papà*."

"Don't be sorry; it's fine. I'm just glad you are okay, and the important thing is we are now together as a family," Sirius reassured her.

"So when can we go home?" Aurora asked.

"Hopefully soon," Sirius said. They both turned toward the doorway as they heard a knock on the door.

"Excuse me. I'm sorry to interrupt, but I thought I would come in to check on Aurora myself," Dr. Williams interrupted, coming into the room.

"It's fine. Come on in," Sirius said.

"I see that Miss Marino is finally awake. How are you feeling, Aurora?" Doctor Williams asked, smiling kindly in her direction.

"In pain," Aurora answered.

"I'm sure. I'll have a nurse give you something for the pain. Hopefully, that should give you some relief," Dr. Williams responded.

"Thank you," Aurora said quietly.

"I need to check your vital signs and stitches to make sure everything looks good, okay?" Doctor Williams approached the bed and put on his stethoscope to take her heart rate and pulse.

"Alright," Aurora responded, as she shifted position to let the doctor check the stab wounds on her arm and side.

"How do they look?" Sirius questioned.

"Fine...Hopefully, they won't bother you too much," Dr. Williams commented. "Well, I'll have a nurse come and bring you something for the pain. In the meantime, if you need anything, just call the nurse."

"We will. Thank you," Sirius said.

"Good. If no problems arise, we should be able to discharge you in a few days or so," Dr. Williams said as he left the room.

"That's good, right, *papà*?" Aurora asked.

"It is," Sirius commented. Just then, he heard his phone buzz. *I wonder who that could be*, as he quickly grabbed his phone from the side table. "Everyone's worried about you and wants updates on how you're doing."

"Like who?" Aurora wondered, sipping a cup of water from her hospital table. "I thought no one knew about me or the adoption."

"I only told a couple of people I knew I could trust, like my Aunt Liv and my Uncle Dario," Sirius answered.

"Isn't that the lady I talked to on the phone?" Aurora asked.

"Yes, that's her. I also told my friend Felix and his fiancée, Bridgette."

"Really? What did they say?"

"Something along the lines of me being crazy for adopting a teenager." Sirius laughed. "They were mostly teasing though."

"*Papà*, will they like me?" Aurora wondered.

"Darling, they are going to love you—just not as much as I do." Sirius couldn't help but smile at her.

"So who texted you?" Aurora asked.

"That was Bridgette."

"Oh, so what are they like?"

"Well, Felix is and has been my best friend since forever. He can drive me nuts, but I don't think I've ever had a more loyal friend. And Bridgette is the one who tries to keep us out of trouble—mostly him, though," Sirius explained.

"What kind of trouble did you guys get into?" Aurora asked, adjusting the hospital bed to a more upright position.

"No comment."

"Why not?"

"Because I don't need to give you any ideas. Also, I don't need the hospital staff knowing about our shenanigans," Sirius said with a chuckle. "Besides, I don't need you to aggravate your stitches with the hilariousness of it all. So, we'll just save those stories for another day, and you need your rest so you can heal fast," Sirius stated.

"Okay, *papà*, I am kinda tired," Aurora said with a yawn.

"I know you are," Sirius said softly. He looked at his daughter, feeling so relieved and glad that she was safe. Things could have been so much worse. Thankfully, everything was alright. Sirius came to the conclusion that Someone must have been looking out for them this whole time. It was a good thing too, because he didn't think Aurora would have made it out of juvie alive if Someone wasn't.

(Wednesday, April 17th)

"What happens when we get home?" Aurora asked, turning to her *papà*, who sat across from her hospital bed, watching her eat her breakfast.

"Well, we will start living out life in L.A. You'll have your activities as well as preparing for school in the fall. I will be figuring out some things for work," Sirius explained. He looked exhausted from having barely slept the last couple nights.

"What kind of work? Are you still going to act?"

"That's the plan. I was hoping to take a break from it, but I promised a friend a while ago that I'd be in his movie," Sirius answered, yawning.

"What kind of movie?"

"It's a mystery movie. From my knowledge, I'll have a small part. I'll probably only be in a few scenes, so it shouldn't take up too much time."

"Cool, what's the part?" Aurora took another bite of fruit from her hospital breakfast tray.

"I think I'm playing a detective. I don't really know much else. To be honest, I barely looked at the script," Sirius explained. "The thing is—it was supposed to be filmed in L.A., but I just found out it's going to be filmed in Tennessee."

"So?" Aurora wondered.

"Depending on the filming schedule, you will either be coming with me or staying home with *zia* Liv. I'd rather you come with me, but I don't want it to interfere with your schooling. I hope filming will happen in the summer, but I'm not sure. My friend isn't the most organized person, unfortunately."

"Ugh, do I have to go to school?" Aurora whined.

"Not until the fall. Until then, I want you to work on catching up. From my knowledge, you're a little behind."

"Okay." Aurora sighed.

"You will be fine," Sirius assured her, shaking his head.

"When can we go home?"

"When the doctor discharges you, probably tomorrow or the next day," Sirius explained. "You're so lucky. Your injuries could have been so much worse."

"I know. Mara said after the first attack that I had angels watching over me."

"It sure seems that way, and I'm thankful for that. If you didn't, you might not be here right now," Sirius said, grabbing her hand and giving it a squeeze.

"I'm glad for that too," Aurora agreed, smiling up at him.

"Anyway, I need to give Bridgette a call and let her know some things."

"Like what?"

"Bridgette offered to pick up a few things for you, since you'll need some stuff for our trip home. I'm just letting her know to text me when she gets here, so I can meet her outside."

"How is she able to do that if she's in L.A.?" Aurora asked.

"She and Felix actually live here in New York. Well, in New York State, not the city. They came to the city for moral support."

"That makes sense," Aurora said around a bite of scrambled eggs.

"Hey, do you mind if I run to the café downstairs and grab us some more food? I'm sure you're still hungry." Sirius glanced at Aurora's almost empty breakfast tray.

"Yes, please, that would be great," Aurora responded.

"Any requests?"

"I don't care, anything is better than prison food," Aurora mumbled around her last bite of toast. She handed him the empty tray to bring out to the nurse's station.

"All right, so why don't you find a movie to watch?" Sirius suggested, handing her the television remote. "As soon as I'm done talking with Bridgette and getting food for us, I'll watch it with you."

"You'll watch whatever I want?" Aurora asked, eyebrows raised.

"Sure," Sirius smiled.

"Awesome! I don't think I've picked out a movie in like forever," Aurora said, sounding overly excited.

"Sounds good, and Aurora, please keep it PG," Sirius replied.

"What!? I'm thirteen," Aurora argued.

"I'm aware of that fact, and I also recall I'm now legally your father." Sirius smirked at Aurora, as she rolled her eyes. "For now, please just stick with stuff that's PG."

"Fine," Aurora grumbled, already flipping through movie titles to see if there anything that looked interesting.

"Thank you, darling daughter," Sirius said as he headed out of her room with the breakfast tray.

"Alright, *papà*! Whatever you say," she called out, assuming Sirius could still hear her. As she looked through the movie selections, she took a deep breath. She finally had a home with a father who cared about her, and there was no way she was going to mess that up. *Thank you, God, for everything—for my papa; for keeping me alive; and for letting me finally get adopted into a good family.*

Aurora couldn't wait to start heading home. She thought about the road trip, her new life, and the adventures that awaited her; she felt dizzy with excitement. She finally had a home. It was the home that she has been praying for since she was put in foster care. Even though it might not be perfect, it would be perfect for her. She would be safe and loved for whom she was and for whom she would become. *Aurora Marino.* She smiled to herself, imagining her future as Sirius Marino's daughter. *Let the adventure of being a celebrity's daughter begin...*

About the author

Emily Jean is an indie author who grew up in Lancaster County, Pennsylvania. As a writer, she is passionate about writing stories that inspire hope and lead readers to a deeper understanding of God's love and redemption.

www.ingramcontent.com/pod-product-compliance
Lightning Source LLC
Chambersburg PA
CBHW020545120726
47903CB00001B/130